PARIS DREAMS

DENISE COVEY

Published by Pichets in Paris Publishing
Cover art by Kimberly Killion at the Killion Group
ISBN: 978-1-922486-16-5

Denise Covey @ Pichets in Paris Publishing
Author can be contacted at her blog:
https://dencovey.blogspot.com/
Sign up for Denise Covey's readers' group here

Silver Tree
Pichets in Paris Publishing

Boldness rewards those who know how to seize their opportunities.

— MARCEL PROUST

"Sometimes the worst day of your life is the best time to start a new life. Goodbye New York. Paris Here I come."

— SASKIA BELL

CHAPTER ONE

THE HAMPTONS - MAY

In the pre-dawn darkness, I stretch on the house steps, inhale lungsful of salty air. Unlatching the gate at the end of the garden, I cross the boardwalk between the beach house and the water. The sand warm beneath my feet, I slow jog along the public path to the inky-black Atlantic Ocean.

Skirting the water's edge, I run, fast, faster, faster, ignoring the throb in my leg from my old shrapnel wound. A sob bursts from my throat. Crying? In the chic and stylish Hamptons? Home to celebrities and billionaires? The Hamptons have always been my happy place where I've spent the best of times—lazing on beautiful beaches, leisurely walking to nearby Bridgehampton village, the fun of backyard barbecues on Memorial Day weekend —just Mom and me in the quaint, gray-shingled house she inherited from her parents.

How could anything go wrong in such a fairytale setting?

I sink to my knees and sob.

I don't know how long I crouch in the sand, but when I stand, the first glimmer of light shimmers at the edge of silver clouds.

I knuckle my tears, brush my knees. Sucking in a deep breath, I sprint back the way I came. I'm pouring sweat by the time I take the house steps two at a time and land flat-footed on the wide timber deck we repainted in gray and white only a month ago.

Rubbing my hands over the back of Mom's favorite brown leather wing-back chair in the corner of the deck, I imagine sitting with her, sipping coffees, watching the sunrise over the ocean. Pushing open the French doors, I glance at the coffee machine on the kitchen counter, silver and silent. When I was down from the city, Mom would have my first coffee of the day prepared at the end of my run. We'd sip our brew together while I cooled down.

No more.

My throat catches. I clasp my chest, hurry through the pale jade sitting room decorated in seaside shabby chic and original seascapes painted by my French grandmother. The gentle morning light spills onto the artworks, creates patches of color on the timber floor and whitewashed pine walls. I love how the light changes throughout the day as the sun moves overhead and the patterns shift.

Before I left for my morning run, I'd opened the windows so now the white curtains billow like sails. Taking a deep breath, I stand at the bottom of the staircase, tracing the leadlight seams of Mom's favorite rose-patterned art deco lamp. Before the tears start again, I run up the stairs, avert my eyes as I pass Mom's bedroom where we spent so many happy hours on rainy days. Perfectly in sync, we'd read in front of the blazing fire, snuggly and warm.

In my bathroom, I throw handfuls of water over my face and neck, clutch the sink, breathe in and out, struggle for equilibrium. I kneel at my open bedroom window, chin resting on my hands. The ocean has changed to steely blue, silent except for the gentle push and pull of the tide whispering: *time's passing, time's passing, time's passing.*

Shivering, cold despite the warm breeze pressing my damp skin, I cannot stop the thoughts wisping through my mind.

This is not happening.

It *is* happening.

It *has* happened.

Accept it.

Mom's dead.

The person I loved most in the world is dead.

Mom, my rock, died two weeks ago. Just when I was making progress with my PTSD which started after the Boston Marathon bombing. Therapy winding down. Suicide or accident? I question that every day.

Rising from my knees, I toss back mouthfuls of water from the glass on my nightstand.

Guilt squeezes like a skin-tight dress. I clasp my hand to my neck like I'm tugging a leather choker. I pour more water down my throat. It trickles from the sides of my mouth. I brush it away with my palms.

How did I miss the signs?

Mom stopped accepting travel assignments. She rarely slept. Scarcely ate. I thought it was because she had worried about me and my mental state for too long, but was there another explanation? Had the depression that plagued her for years reached the point where she could not carry on?

The dawning light silhouettes the strip of beach where I saw her the morning I rode out of New York on my motorcycle. I had not seen her for weeks, having been buried under an avalanche of work at Romance is Born, the fashion house in Manhattan, pulling all-nighters for my bosses', Roberto's and Isabella's, next show. I rode down to spoil Mom on her special day. I had cleared my schedule, planned to take her for coffee, a picnic by the beach before hitting the shops together. I never expected to find her wading in the ocean, her floaty orange skirt swirling around her waist, her hair soaked and straggled instead of fashioned into her sleek bob.

"*Mom*?" Heart in mouth, I'd propped my Harley near the house fence, tossing my helmet into the rose garden. Sprinting the short distance to the shore on legs that felt weighed down by steel bands was the hardest run I had ever done. "What are you doing? Come back," I cried.

Meeting me at the water's edge, she took my hand, shrugged. "Take me for a ride on your motorbike, Saskia. I need to have some fun. It's my birthday after all." This was not the mother I knew. This mother talked like she was shedding the cares of the world, instead of holding the cares of the world in her generous heart.

"No, Mom, we need to get you inside, dry you off, talk about what just happened." Was this the first time she had waded into the ocean, toyed with the idea of drowning herself? I hate that I have not been here for her when she so obviously needs me. Trouble is that my bosses demand my attention 24/7. That must change.

As we walked the crushed shell path toward the house, her sopping skirt twisted around her legs, tripping her so she lurched like a drunk. I stopped for a moment, just stared at her. Lost for words. Mom was never disheveled or disorientated. I thought, *what's going on?* Pa's the drunk, not Mom.

She threw her arms around me, hugged me tight. I held her shaking body or she would have collapsed onto the sidewalk. Rubbing a hand up and down her back, I felt the sharp knobs of her spine. *When did you lose so much weight?* "Mom. What's wrong? What's happened?"

She had sobbed on my shoulder, "Saskia, my whole life is wrong. I want to feel happy again, to feel free. If you won't take me for a ride, I'll go myself. I'm ready."

I had only given her a couple of lessons over the past year. She was so not ready to ride my powerful bike. But before I had a chance to react, she pushed me hard. I lost my footing. She jumped onto the seat, pressed the start button, wrenched my rearing bike into submission, shot around the corner out of sight.

I scream and groan, thumping my head onto the windowsill, hearing again the godawful crunch. I'd raced to the scene. She lay in the middle of the road, blood oozing from a head wound, beside where my motorcycle's wheels still spun. The truck driver who had hit her stumbled around in shock, looked over my shoulder, yelled into his cell phone, "... she came out of nowhere. It's not my fault. I swear it's not my fault ... She's hurt ... bad ..."

"*Mom*." One hand under her head, I'd dialed 911, screamed into my phone. I ripped the bandana from my throat to staunch the bleeding. Soon it was a sopping red mess.

"Saskia," she'd whispered, her voice hoarse and hollow. The trickle of blood at the side of her mouth terrified me. "Come ... closer, darling."

I put my ear to her lips. They were turning blue. She needed oxygen. Making her as comfortable as I could, I began CPR. She blinked, shook her head. Blood gushed from her mouth, ran down her throat.

"Pick your battles, darling," she whispered, her voice slurred. "You're a survivor ... embrace it. Stop feeling guilty ... for surviving ..."

I dabbed at the blood on her head and mouth. Her eyes were closing. My heart shattered into millions of tiny pieces. "*Mom*? Don't leave me." *Nooooooo*.

From lips whiter than the shells we collected on our beach walks, she mouthed, "Don't do what I did ... my darling." Tears sprung from the corner of her eyes and into her ears.

"What do you mean, Mom?" I pressed the bandana harder, my one thought to stop the bleeding.

"Saskia ... you ... are young ... strong ... be who ... you want ... not ... who .... someone else wants ... you to be. Your Pa ... Xavier ... don't ... marry him —" Sirens drowned her final words ...

"*Mom*! Come back to me!"

It's my fault Mom's dead, I think for the thousandth time.

But it's too late.

I might be a survivor, but Mom was not.

On her forty-fifth birthday, my mother died in my arms.

Slapping my palm against the windowsill, I tell myself to accept what has happened. Move forward. Survive. Alone. Without my rock.

The tissue box is empty by the time I puzzle again over Mom's last words. *Pa. Xavier. Marry.* Why were her last words about those two? And marriage? She knows I don't plan to marry until I reach the top in my chosen career. But Pa? Xavier? Why? They don't figure in my life except for an occasional real estate social event in New York when Pa forces me to attend as Xavier's plus-one. But Mom was trying to warn me about something.

A giant orange ball, bright and wonderful, bounces above the horizon. *I wish you could see this, Mom. Perhaps you do ...* The Atlantic turns silver, then smudges to dark blue as if a giant hand waved a paintbrush over the scene. My eyes ache with the beauty of water rippling like lush fabric swirling around the legs of a catwalk model. I reach for my pencils and sketch book. In my meeting at Romance is Born tomorrow I'll show them my sketches for the new collection. Perhaps they will forgive my two-week absence.

I shower, throw on my brightest sundress in one of my favorite designs, its patterns mirroring a brilliant Hamptons' sunrise. I'm determined to make the most of my last day at the beach before I return to New York.

Walking through the kitchen, I throw open the French doors, walk to the top of the deck stairs and watch windsurfers pop up and down on the water like corks from champagne bottles. Life does not stop for grief. Life goes on. I'll make Mom proud. She always said one day she'd have a front row seat at Fashion Week and applaud loudest for my designs. She's going to miss the show, but I'll make it happen. However long it takes.

The deck was our favorite place to hang out when she returned from her latest overseas assignment for *Conde Nast,* or I came down for my college break. I would make cappuccinos and we'd sit and pull apart my therapy sessions. I was eighteen going on nineteen when I was injured. Rocked to my core. For the past six years, Mom has helped me work through my pain. Without her support I would never have the career I love so much. She told me I could do it, and with her help, I did.

But she's gone. Tears roll down my cheeks ... *breathe ... breathe ...*

breathe. I practise the side-to-side eye movements my therapist recommended when memories overwhelm me. I grow calmer.

A runner stops on the boardwalk outside our fence. He leans over, smells one of my mother's pink roses which has bloomed overnight. Mom's gone, but she has left a legacy for others to enjoy.

Through my tears, I see a wobbly image of Mom, garden shears in hand, calling, *Come help, Saskia. These roses won't deadhead themselves.*

I gaze at the sweet briar roses until my tears dry and my lips unclench. I pray that whatever decisions I make moving forward, wherever life takes me, I'll treasure the memory of perfumed roses, to me, the essence of love.

CHAPTER TWO

"Saskia."

I jump. Clasp my heart.

God no. Pa. Not him. Anyone but him.

I clutch the stair post with one hand, brush tears away with the other. My last day in the Hamptons, ruined.

"Saaskiaaa."

What's he doing here? Please God, make him go away.

Just the thought of him here in Mom's and my favorite place angers me. As far as I know, he's never visited in all the time Mom's lived here. Why now? I ache all over with grief. Pa has mostly ignored me since I was eight years old. He was married to New York life – the wheeling and dealing I read daily on my Google feed, the latest woman on his arm splashed over the social pages, his meteoric rise up the Forbes 400 List. Once Mom and I moved out of the Fifth Avenue apartment to live in the Hamptons, he promptly forgot he had a wife and daughter except when he wanted something.

"Saaskiaaa."

"Go away." I mumble through clenched teeth, eye the ebb and flow of the tide. "You can't just waltz in here now Mom's dead."

"Saaskiaaa! Don't talk to your father like that. Turn around."

I want to run along the beach and never stop, but I take a deep breath, turn and face him. My cheeks burn at the sight of him sitting in our snug little room off the kitchen in Mom's cream leather armchair. As bad as that is, it's even worse to see beside him in the matching chair where I usually sit, my faux boyfriend Xavier who bestows on me a limp wave. Why would Pa bring Xavier to my house? Mom's last words have me on high alert.

I clear my throat, step into the sitting room, hold onto the door. "Pa. What a surprise." I hate how my voice is breathless, but the lump in my throat strangles me. After all these years, he still terrifies me. One look at him takes me back to my eight-year-old self, flinching each time he hit me.

He crosses his legs, plays with the crease on his trousers, smirks the way he always does when he has me cornered. He knows I'm afraid of him and uses the advantage. "We're here to talk."

I need to get some perspective on the situation. I'm not faced with a terrorist pointing a Kalashnikov at me. Yet Pa knows how to terrorize me using words as a weapon. Even though the sight of him makes me sick to my stomach, I tilt my chin, pretend nonchalance. I will no longer let him intimidate me. "What have we got to talk about?" Behind my back, I clutch and unclutch the doorknob.

"Plenty." Tapping his fingers on the chair arm, he tilts his head, eyes me like I'm a specimen under a microscope. He is dressed in a boring charcoal suit, white shirt and sickly pale-yellow tie. When I was a little girl, he would ask my advice on which color tie to wear with which color suit and his signature white shirt. *My little fashion guru*, he'd called me. That's another lifetime. Another Pa.

Xavier rises to his feet, smiles his plastic smile. "Hello Saskia. You look well. Tan and fit. Very Hamptons' summer." Speech over, he sits again and continues working on his broody hotness in *his* boring charcoal suit, unperturbed by my stony stare.

Mopping his face with a large handkerchief, Pa lurches to his feet, strides over to me. He slams the French doors, switches on the air conditioner. He cannot abide sea air, or any air except what comes out of an air conditioner. "Hear us out." He grabs my shoulders, walks me backward, pushes me into my red tub chair near the door, tisking at the chair's peeling leather. He sits again, crosses his legs, leans back, studies me through half-closed eyes. There's no alcohol on his breath, but his pasty face, puffy eyes and shaky hands give him away. Vodka? This early in the day? His alcohol abuse began when his real-estate business took a massive hit during a run of property downturns. His finances are now flourishing, but so is his love affair with the bottle.

He addresses me in a voice laced with impatience, irritation and exasperation. "Saskia. What's wrong with you? We've been sitting here," he glances at his Rolex, "for three minutes while you've been staring at nothing. I know your emotions are shaky, but really, three minutes. Get a grip."

I cringe. Three minutes. Any time he has summonsed me to his office, he has stressed the importance of three minutes. In three minutes, he could make a tidy million on the futures market, procure some lucrative real estate deal or appear as a talking head on CNN in his role as money analyst.

"Staring at nothing?" I place my hand onto my chest, still my crazy beating heart. "This view reminds me of Mom. We sat here every day in this very ro—"

"Stop it." He bangs his fists together. "She's gone. Move on, why can't you?"

I shiver, shocked. "Moving on is my plan." I dab a tear with a corner of the woolen blanket Mom knitted for my thirteenth birthday. It usually hides the broken leather in my tub chair which I must get reupholstered. I clutch the wool tight around my body. It's not warm enough to shield me from Pa's coldness. Where is the father I once knew? Before he became a violent drunk? He would not have dismissed Mom's death like it was just a bad business deal.

"I'm here to help guide you." His eyes flit to Xavier who smiles his All-American smile. Since Xavier began working in my father's firm a couple years ago, he has become Pa's devoted slave. He worships the ground Pa's hand-tooled leather shoes walk on, whereas I am nothing to Xavier except to ingratiate himself with his idol.

Reaching up a hand, I cover my trembling chin. Even when Pa turned up for Mom's funeral in his flashy Town Car with Xavier in tow, it was to make a huge display of grief for the media who had come to cover the story of *Conde Nast's* famous travel writer's demise. Pa and Xavier are fakes who care about nothing except themselves.

"Time to get serious." Pa picks up the *Wall Street Journal*, smacks it onto the arm of his chair, *wop, wop, wop*. "Down to business."

Seeing that paper triggers bad memories. I sit on my shaking hands, relive the times he walloped me with that paper, but I refuse to give in to the tears building behind my eyes. Overnight, he became a remote, withholding father, putting me down at every opportunity. He would inspect the tiny hand-stitched dolls' clothes I had created with meticulous care, laugh, toss them into the bin. He stopped bringing home glossy magazines so I could copy the latest designs. He stopped taking me to New York Fashion Week where I'd loved seeing the latest fashions and meeting my idols over cocktails, or in my case, pop.

He shouts like I'm five, not twenty-five. "Saskia. Stop dreaming. Listen up. I said ... time to talk."

"Hmmh?" I scrunch handfuls of wool blanket, wanting only one thing now – to be alone. When Pa talks, he issues orders. Stuff that. He will not see me cry. I've got this. I open my mouth to tell him to get out of my house and take his lap dog with him, but a car backfires on the road in front of the house. I lurch forward in my seat, clutch my heart, breathe shallow breaths.

Xavier slides a glance at my father who draws his lips into a scowl. Xavier hates my anxiety. *Control yourself, Saskia,* he sneers when under Pa's orders I hang on his arm at yet another meaningless New York society event. When the flashbulbs pop, it is *Chin up. Smile. Put your arm around me. Closer. Kiss me. Don't spoil the shot.* Putting up with my baggage has been the price of playing the role of Pa's pawn amongst the social elite.

I settle in my chair, inhale a jerky breath, Mom's warning front of mind. Giant goosebumps creep up my arms. "Why are you and Xavier here, Pa? What's so urgent?"

Pa taps his chin with a finger. He uncrosses his legs, spreads them apart on the floor. Folding his arms, he holds my eye. His power pose.

Uh-oh. I'm faced with a grizzly bear and can't remember whether to stand still or run. I look longingly at the French doors. I want to run. But that will only delay the inevitable. I zone out, their voices become buzzing bees, *zzzz, zzzz, zzzz.* A sudden, swelling ache burns in my chest. My heart beats crazy fast like it did when I reached the finish line in Boston as the first bomb exploded and pellets and nails cut my forehead and shot through my limbs. I couldn't see for the blood. I thought I was dying. Thought I was blind.

I survived.

My heart lurches. My throat closes. My ears ring with the screams of the injured, the screams of the sirens, the screams of the crowd. My therapist, Sheila, told me how to get through these flashbacks ... *breathe ... picture a happy place where you feel safe. Where no one can hurt you ...*

My happy place. Running along the beach. Pushing myself to beat the clock. My heart no longer hammers with fear; it hammers with the excitement of a personal best. *Go, Saskia,* Mom calls from the sidelines. When she died, I'd been in training for the New York Marathon. Without Mom, can I still run? Can I overcome my fears?

Xavier's lips are moving; he smiles at me, but his smile doesn't reach his eyes. His words roll over me. "Saskia." His honeyed tone coaxes, like he's training his mischievous chihuahua, Foxy Lady. "Blah, blah, blah ..."

I try to focus on his words rather than my marathon training. "Hmmmm? You were saying?"

Xavier tisks. "The least you could do is listen. We want to help."

"How could *you* possibly help?"

Elbows on knees, hands clasped, Pa leans forward, glares. "Saskiaaa." *Wop* goes *The Journal.*

Xavier holds up his hand, smiles at my father, lightbulbs glowing under his cheekbones. "I've got this, Edward." He rubs his hands together like it's an icy cold morning. "Saskia, I have your father's blessing. I'd be honored if you'd marry me."

He ignores the *ouf* when I picture my heart splattering onto the floor.

Since my father has called me worthless most of my life, yelling drunken insults down the phone if I failed to get straight As at school or failed to get accepted into the college of his choice, he has tainted my relationships with men. I never intend to let a man get close enough to hurt me. Xavier already treats me the way my father does, giving orders, pushing me around, demanding I fall into line. He probably plans on hitting me too once he gets a ring on my finger. Marriage to him would kill me where the bombs failed. No. No man is going to rule me. Ever.

Xavier leans across the table. "We've set a date. "July 14th."

I grab my throat, try to stuff my heart back into my chest, but he's in the middle of one of Pa's multi-million-dollar takeovers. "That's like only two months away."

"No problem. Seeing you're a basket case now, Mother will take over the arrangements. All you must do is buy the dress and show up. The good news," he waltzes his fingers along the chair arm, "is that Brackness Hall is available."

Pa does not miss his cue. "True, Xavier. Everyone will be down for the summer." His eyes drill into mine, dare me to object. "Saskia, you've had a rough two weeks since your mom died. Hell, you've had a rough six years since your brush with death. Marriage will help you move on. Your mom always wanted you to have a Hamptons' wedding."

My face burns. "How could you possibly know what Mom wanted for me?" I grind my words from between clenched teeth. "You hardly ever spoke to her after she left you years ago." So Mom knew that Pa would pressure me to do his bidding after she passed. No way. She didn't help me through years of PTSD therapy, ketamine infusions and drug monitoring to have me marry into the New York social set. She wanted me to follow my own dreams, no one else's. I keep my voice civil. "Not possible. You have to book Brackness Hall years in advance."

Pa and Xavier exchange sly looks. Pa waves his hand dismissively. "Possible. Money talks."

"Well, you would know, wouldn't you?" Even his voice sounds like the rustle of dollar bills. Mom's idea would have been a beach wedding, me barefoot, sand between my toes. Pa loathed Mom's hippie ways which is the only reason he financially supported my tilt at becoming a high-end fashion designer and pays for my apartment in NoHo. It is designer all the way for him while Mom hounded charity shops so she could help save the planet one dress at a time.

Xavier's narrative rolls along like a relentless tide. "It'll be the wedding of the season," he gushes with more animation than I've ever seen him display. "The media will be falling over themselves to feature us in the papers, the glossies, social media. Instagram's still buzzing with that dress you made for the Realtor's Ball. Truly a stunner. Set off my tux. Have you checked the 'likes' on that lately? Stupendous. We're superstars. It'll be a rush, darling." He bares his teeth in a semblance of a smile which looks more like a rabid animal about to bite.

I cringe, tug the shawl tighter. Stop short of choking myself. Did he just call me *darling*? I would like to vomit on his fancy shoes. This man craves a media event, not a wife.

Xavier drones on, oblivious to my revulsion and the tic that has developed in my right eye every time I look at him. "Saskia Marguerite Willard has a nice ring to it." He reaches into his pocket and flashes a blue Tiffany box. "Ta da." Flipping it open like he is a magician performing to a crowded Madison Square Garden, he reveals a rock the size of Alcatraz. "Imagine the images of this fantastic jewel on Instagram. My God." He turns it this way and that to catch the light. He seems truly mesmerized. "Only a video will do it justice. I'll hire a professional. The most expensive engagement ring in New York, I kid you not." He slides his eyes to my father who nods sagely. *Aha.* Pa bought it, probably called in some favor at Tiffany's, got it for a pittance, the schmoozer.

"*Whaaat?*" I shake my head, rest my ankle onto my knee, massage my aching calf which throbs when I'm stressed.

Xavier stares at me with his dark blue eyes, the exact shade of a shark's, which is fitting. I don't try to hold back the snigger that bursts from my throat. He frowns, waits for me to pay attention to him rather than my leg. He holds the Tiffany box in one hand while with the other polishes his fingernails on his suit trousers like he's practicing his pose for the cover of *GQ* magazine.

Marry? Him?

No. Freaking. Way.

CHAPTER THREE

"Pa. Xavier. You're kidding, right?" Even to my own ears, I sound unhinged. I honestly do not know which of them is more intimidating – Pa with his furious red face as he reads in mine my increasing resistance to Xavier's ridiculous proposal or Xavier with his smug don't-even-think-of-turning-me-down look.

I will never marry Xavier. He's Pa through and through. If I married Xavier, I'd go from being a dutiful daughter to a dutiful wife. I'd sooner die and rot in hell.

Pa leans forward, wags his finger in my face. "Saskia, think about your future."

I stop massaging my leg and carefully place my foot onto the floor. Adjust my skirt. Toss my head. I'm getting into this nonchalant act. "Honestly, Pa, I've thought about little else since Mom died." Most of my school mates are married. Some operate mompreneur businesses from their fancy renovated homes in Maplewood or Montclair, creating sustainable, ethical baby clothes, brain-enhancing toys, and vegan baby food. I have my sketch pads and pencils, embroidery threads, sewing machines and dreams. It's been enough. It's still enough. I don't need a man. Especially one like Xavier. *Urk.*

Xavier drops to his knees before my chair, gazes at me with puppy-dog eyes. I push myself backward; he leans closer. "Saskia. Do I look like I'm kidding? See this wonderful ring. The blue captures your eyes, and the pink diamonds are as unique as you." He wiggles his eyebrows at his clever line, shoves the Tiffany box under my nose with absolutely no finesse. "Marry me, darling," he says, sounding like the robot he is. "We'll make a great team."

I give him the death stare.

"Saskiaaa?" Pa's voice is clipped. He taps the toe of his boot on the floor. "Take it. Now. I order you."

I fold my arms. No one's putting that ring on me. "No." My anger is a pot simmering on the back of the stove. "Never."

Pa flinches, sits ramrod straight. "How dare you, you ungrateful—"

"Ungrateful what?" He orchestrated the whole farce, down to the ring and bended knee. The Willards are property moguls from way back. If he can swing this merger, the two families are in with a chance of clawing to the top of the Forbes list. The Forbes list is Pa's life. Not me.

How dare he treat me like property, traded to increase his stock? "Forget it, Pa." I slap the chair arms. "Xavier, I'm not your *darling,* never will be." I refuse to look at his conceited face every day for the rest of my life. "Get up. Go back to the city where you belong. Take that gaudy bauble with you." *Pa's fool.* I turn away, clutch my roiling stomach.

"Saskiaaa?" Pa's voice grates while Xavier remains on his knees, eyes flicking between Pa and me. "Marrying Xavier is your plan for moving forward. The ring clinches the deal. It's just the start of riches untold for you, for us."

"*What?*" It's like Pa pulled Xavier out of a hat and wonders why I'm not delighted at his magic trick. Acid burns my throat. "Your plan, Pa. Not mine. We buried Mom a week ago. Even you should understand it would be unseemly to have a wedding so soon after a funeral."

Xavier wobbles to his feet, falls back into his chair like a puppet without strings. He clutches the box to his chest, resumes his position mimicking his idol.

Pa's face has two red spots on his jowly cheeks. He yells, slaps his thighs, but I tune out. Blah. Blah. Blah.

I turn up the heat under the pot on my metaphorical stove. It's no longer simmering. It boils like the blood surging through my veins. *How dare they?* Why should I settle for a loveless marriage like Mom did? She was only nineteen when she married, blinded by Pa's brilliance and power. That power turned into drunken rages, he hit her in places where it wouldn't show, then demanded she smile for the cameras. No man will ever hit me like Pa hit Mom and me. I want love, adventure, happiness. I'll never have those things with Xavier.

If I could turn back time, I would have defied Pa two years ago when he ordered me onto the social circuit as Xavier's plus-one. I should have called his bluff when he threatened to withdraw his financial support if I did not fall into line. Terrified of losing my apartment, my ability to support my fashion career, I caved. Now he has taken my complicity to the next level. Pa and Xavier no doubt imagine the frenzy if we two media darlings have a society wedding in the Hamptons, then a society baby ... *Oh My God. Gross.* My days of falling into line end here.

Mom's dying words inspire me. *Pick your battles, Saskia.*

Here is a battle I must win.

"Saskia?" Pa's steely voice threatens, but I refuse to be intimidated.

I lean forward, swing my bare foot, eye the two men sitting, faces tense. Marriage to Xavier would mean wearing the right hair, the right clothes, joining the right committees, being the total society wife. No. No. No. I'd become my mother—miserable, depressed, suicidal—locked into a toxic marriage, unable to break free. No doubt they have already compiled a water-tight pre-nup to lock me in. I grit my teeth. Take a deep breath.

I'm ready.

Pa claps his hands loudly in my face. "Saskiaaa? You're drifting again."

I have not had much practise in contradicting Pa, but I'm learning fast. "Drifting? Hell no. I've never been so in charge of my faculties." I take a deep breath, gather my thoughts, say the very thing which will change the direction of my life. "I'm ... not ... getting ... married. Not to Xavier. Not now. Not ever. It's one thing to pretend for the cameras, and by the way, that's no longer happening, but marriage? That's a step too far. Both of you, please leave my home."

Pa chokes, jolts forward, stabs a finger in my face. "What did you just say? How dare you throw me out of my house."

"*Your* house? It's never been remotely yours. This is *my* house now, Pa. Get out." I stare at Xavier until he breaks eye contact. "My plan for moving forward involves neither of you. Have either of you thought to ask what I want?" I doodle daggers on the chair arm with the finger I nearly lost from the nail bomb.

Xavier fists his hands on his thighs, mirroring Pa's body language. "You can't do this to me." He whimpers like a wheedling child; he's so pitiful.

"I just did."

He frowns. "Saskia, you're grieving. Stop grieving. Life is for the living, not the dead. You're marrying me in two months. July 14th." He stands, adjusts his pocket handkerchief, passes his hand over his oiled hair, runs his snake-like tongue over his thick lips. "Isn't she, Edward?"

Pa stands shoulder to shoulder with his darling boy, the male heir my mom failed to produce. No doubt he expects me to be overwhelmed by two towering men in charcoal suits, but I won't give them the satisfaction of knowing how terrified I am.

"Yes. Don't worry about Saskia. It's all arranged, Xavier." Pa's eyes singe me with the force of his fury. "You'll fall into line, Saskia." He releases his inner lion. He has the roar; he just lacks the fur. "Or else."

I release my inner lioness, proud to be standing up to him for the first time. "Don't threaten me. Those days are over. Mom never reported you to the police. I may not be so kind."

"You wouldn't dare." He picks up his paper, slaps it onto his open palm, steps closer, his eyes daring me to back down. "You will do as I say."

I stand, ready to face him, even though my stomach clenches at the hatred in his eyes he doesn't try to hide. Inhaling a deep breath, I look away. "Just you try. I'm done with your abuse, Pa. It's the 21st century. How did I manage to be born to a father who treats his daughter like it's the 19th?"

"You watch that mouth of yours, my girl."

"You mind yours. When and if I marry, it won't be a business contract like you've proposed here today. It'll be for love. Only for love. What would either of you know about that human emotion?" I place a hand over my heart. "Shut the door on your way out."

Leaving them open mouthed, I flick off the air conditioner, push open the French doors, step outside onto the deck. Once out of their sight, I bend over, gasp for breath. Clasp my knees with my hands. Shake all over. The breeze cools my burning skin; my heartbeat slows. Turning Pa and Xavier down took so much mental energy, but I'm proud of me. I should have done it years ago.

I head for the sanctuary of the sunlit garden. Here my heart feels stilled, peaceful, rested. Fingers of silence smooth the edges of my anxiety. Picking up Mom's garden shears, I set to work. I refuse to let her years of hard work turn into a jungle. When I've worked off the adrenaline, I'll have a cappuccino and croissant at our favorite café down the road, gaze over the endless sea, make plans for a future without her, without Pa, without Xavier.

I hear the scrape of leather soles on the floor inside the house, the rumble of muffled voices, the chime of cell phone notifications. They have finished planning their next strategy. I wonder who will hunt me down and continue to harangue me? *Pfft*. Do I even need to ask?

Pa finds me amongst the roses. His face is ugly with fury. "Xavier's gone to the car. What I say is between you and me. My office. Early tomorrow."

A hot flash of anger scorches my cheeks. I stab the garden shears in his direction. "Is that another order?"

His phone pings. He taps it, looks at me with hooded eyes. "You know damn well it is, my girl."

I deadhead the nearest rose, toss it onto his shiny shoes.

He glares, kicks it back. "I'm waiting."

A thorn pricks my bare foot, draws blood. "Waiting for what?"

"For you to be an obedient daughter. Otherwise, there'll be consequences, mark my words."

My hands shake so much I hack a fresh bloom in half. "What can you do? Disinherit me? Why should I care? I don't want or need your money. I own this summerhouse. I have a great job. I'm in line for promotion. I'll cope without your help from now on. I want you out of my life."

"You? Cope?" He laughs, I cringe. "There's no cure for PTSD. You're looking at a lifetime of mental instability and exorbitant treatment fees. I won't be paying them any longer. You can end up a nutcase for all I care; spend the rest of your days in an institution, hmmm, maybe the Meyer Center will take you. That's what you deserve for treating me with such disrespect."

I had not thought the pain of these past two weeks could get any worse. But Pa has succeeded in lacerating me yet again. Here outside in Mom's rose garden, the noise and chaos of the world recedes. I could pretend the same was happening on the inside, but no, the reality is he has shaken me up again, made me feel inadequate. *Breathe.* I will not let him see how shattered I am. "I have strategies to take care of my mental health. Mom believed I could overcome. Why can't you?"

"Listen to me, Saskia." He steps closer, softens his tone. "I know what's best. You need a man to look after you. I'm getting on in years. Xavier will take over from me. Do this for your old man. Your future will be assured with scarcely any effort on your part. Just become a Willard, for Christ's sake." By the time he finishes his speech, he's yelling.

He's using every weapon in his arsenal. My heart rams against my ribcage. "You don't know what's best for me or you'd never suggest I marry Xavier. That's what's best for you and your plans for world dominion of the property market. Why don't *you* marry him? He prefers men." I don't miss the explosion of rage behind his eyes.

My badass attitude surprises me. But Pa's a douche bag. "I'd like us to get along, but that can't happen while you bully me. Why can't you be a normal father?"

"Pah. Normal is average. Nothing average about me." His phone pings again, he taps the screen. "Gotta go." He kicks another dead rose my way. "Eight o'clock tomorrow. Before beginning of business." He spins on his heel and joins the path around the side of the house. "I'm not done," he slings over his shoulder. "We have a lot to discuss."

I don't breathe until the car doors slam; the engine revs and the black Town Car glides up the street like a slow-moving hearse. I cannot see through the blackened windows, but I imagine the two of them, heads together, planning the method of attack tomorrow, feeling sure I won't be able to withstand their arguments.

Sighing, I snip deadheads, caress velvety petals, fill my lungs with delicate perfume and salty air to calm myself. Mom's death taught me life is short. I refuse to spend the rest of my life living in fear or living my father's dreams.

From now on, I'll follow my own dreams.

It's time to take control.

Pa just issued his final order to me.

I imagine Mom just smiled.

She's given me the means.

I've found the will.

The will to live my life. On my own. For me.

CHAPTER FOUR

MANHATTAN, NEW YORK CITY

Next morning, I'm a no show at Pa's 55th floor penthouse office of Bell Properties in midtown Manhattan. Instead, I paste a cheerful expression on my face and walk into the meeting with my bosses, Roberto and Isabella. I'm wearing my own designs – wide-legged yellow satin trousers, hand-embroidered (by me) red T-shirt, and cobalt blue topcoat. Despite dressing for success, there is that niggling feeling of inferiority despite how hard I've studied and worked toward my goal of becoming Head Designer. I'm so over being one of many design assistants, although Isabella always chooses to use me to direct all facets of her collections. Overseeing my own collections is what I want. Today my foot is poised to climb another rung on the ladder to my eventual success in the industry.

"Sit." Roberto doesn't stand or offer his hand. He drags his eyes from his iPad long enough to check out what I'm wearing. He's dapper as always in his red bow tie and his favorite fashion accessory, a red Montblanc pen stuck over his ear.

Isabella hurries in, waves, sits next to her husband. "Hello Saskia."

She's flustered, her eyes look everywhere but at me. Uh-oh. *What's going on?* "Won't be a moment." She shuffles papers.

I take the chair opposite their huge black desk. I'm not concerned by Roberto's underwhelming welcome. Isabella told me when she hired me that he has Asperger's Syndrome. Despite his abruptness and the strange way Isabella is acting, it's good to be back. To have less time to think about how empty I feel without Mom and the pressure from Pa to marry Xavier. I don't want to think about Pa's fury when I stood him up this morning. I've turned off my phone. I'll deal with him later. I need to focus on this meeting.

While I wait on Roberto and Isabella, I pump myself with positive self-talk. *Yes.* They have hinted at promoting me often enough. Today is the day. Perfect timing. I'm moving up. I'm ready. This promotion will set me up to live without Pa's allowance or interference. He's the first obstacle to my plan to be independent. I'm confident I can beat Pa at his game. Now that I've shown him I won't fall into line with his wishes, from here on, my path should be much easier.

While Roberto works his iPad and Isabella sorts her papers, I gaze around and smile, thinking of all the good things that have happened in this office – drinking champagne after a successful launch, drinking more champagne when Roberto and Isabella made the *New York Times'* Top 10 New York fashion houses, cracking open a bottle of Bollinger when my embroidered silk frock coats caused a sensation on the catwalk last season, the first time my name was broadcast at a show and in the media. I study the framed awards on the white walls, the dozens of trophies on the specially crafted shelves. One day I'll have an office like this displaying my awards and trophies.

Tapping his iPad with both thumbs, Roberto clears his throat, breaks the silence. "You're looking good, Saskia. That azure shade is *fab*ulous with your blonde hair and blue eyes. Your own designs? Of course. *Fab*ulous. Haven't seen you around lately." He looks up from his screen. "What-ya-been-up-ta?" He flinches, his iPad jerks. I guess Isabella kicked him under the table again.

I brush my fingers over my face to cool my flushed cheeks. I swallow, mumble, "Er, Roberto, my mom died."

He draws his brows together, leans back, scrutinizes me with his big black eyes. "Wasn't that, erm, two weeks ago?"

"Yes, but I needed time ..." Uh-oh. I should have listened to Mira, my best friend at the fashion house. *Sia, get yourself back to work no matter what it costs you,* she'd nagged when she stayed overnight with me in the Hamptons after the funeral. *It's New York, sweetie. Your mom's accident shattered you, but in this city, competition is the word.*

Isabella pours soothing oil over Roberto's *faux pas*. Smiling her bright-red lipsticked smile, she says, "So sorry about the accident, and so sorry we were too busy to attend the funeral what with the Braganza account keeping us busy with you away. I hear it was beautiful, the funeral I mean. The papers said you arranged the whole service yourself and it was beyond words. Oh, did you get our card and flowers?"

I nod. "I did." It took two men to carry it in and out of the chapel. "Sorry. I haven't finished sending out acknowledgements."

She tosses her shoulder-length black curls. "You're doing that yourself? You're an absolute marvel."

We don't all have servants. "I like the personal touch."

Roberto drags his eyes from what's hot and what's not in the fashion world, opens his eyes wide, trying and failing to look compassionate. "How-ya-doin'-now, kiddo? All better?"

I suck a sharp breath. *How ya think I'm doin'?* "I'm good." I press my hand against my heart, try to slow the beats. "I missed you guys. I'm sorry I took so much time if it was a problem." *Such a freaking liar.* With the tip of my finger, I dab moisture from my top lip then ruffle around in my bag. "But I've been sketching most days, capturing those Long Island sunrises and sunsets you love to see on your fabrics. Isabella, you'll love my ideas for your 'Essence of a Hamptons' Summer' collection. Some of my best work if I say so myself."

Roberto drops his iPad onto the desk, temples his fingers. Flicking a glance Isabella's way, he holds my eye. "There's no need, Saskia." He flicks his wrist, showing off his gold rings. "It's New York, darling. You were our special protégé, fast tracked for promotion, but even protégés can be replaced. You're done." He folds his arms, frowns at me. Do I see a flash of regret in his eyes? No, it must be my imagination. Roberto regrets nothing.

"*Whaaa—?*" Goosebumps creep along my arms. "Sorry? *Whaaa—?* For a minute, I thought you said—" I try not to choke on the bile that rises to the back of my throat. "I'm done? Because I took leave? Surely not. I've worked around the clock for you guys for years, always at your beck and call. I was owed a little time. You can't—" Emotion thickens my tongue.

Roberto shakes his head. "We can. It's not about your taking leave, not directly. But we lost the Prixmark account when we couldn't supply your shadow embroidery. That got us thinking that it's not the first time we've lost accounts because of you. We understand why you're up and down. I'd probably be a basket case myself if I came that close to having my body parts sprayed over Boston. But it's not our problem." He shrugs. "It's yours. And you don't seem able to fix it."

I deflate like a pricked balloon. There go my dreams. The second time in two days I've been called a basket case.

Isabella takes over. "I don't see why you didn't come back to work straight after the funeral ... you have so much talent ... we had plans—"

Roberto pulls his Montblanc pen from above his ear, jabs it at my face. "You shoulda come back sooner. Any time before today." He exchanges a strange glance with Isabella which leaves me wondering what happened today. Before I can follow the thought, he twirls his pen between his fingers, leans forward, eyeballs me. "You were never ambitious enough, that's the thing. Nothing trumps this." He waves his hand around the office. "I didn't fly to Italy when my padre died. Too busy. What could I do with him dead? All the same, we'll miss your design ideas, your expertise in the workroom, your embroidery and appliqué. It's rare to find someone with such talent for intricate work. Really, we hate to lose you, but needs must. The demand for expensive specialties won't always be there."

Isabella chimes in, a fake smile on her face. "In this uncertain economic climate, we need reliability as much as talent in our staff. Our new girl, Vittoria, is a quick study. She brought similar skills as yours from Botticelli in Milan. Her stitching is not as exquisite but give her time and our clients will be happy with her work. She scarcely leaves her desk."

"Really?" Another me. My heart slams so hard against my ribs it's a wonder they don't crack. This can't be happening. *Breathe. Don't let them hurt you. Breathe. Don't let them cause a meltdown. Breathe.* "Roberto. Isabella. This fashion house is my life." Since I talked my way into an internship nearly four years ago, I've worked my way up from pattern cutter to the sewing machine, then design assistant, loving every aspect of the job, especially since they called on me for my embroidery in the last year or so. "Fashion helps me focus. It hasn't been easy when anxiety overwhelmed me, but I thought I'd managed to work through it. I've always given this house my all." Obviously, my all wasn't enough.

"Don't beat yourself up." Isabella reaches across the desk and would have patted my hand if I wasn't sitting on it. "You've been through a lot, but after losing your mom, you'll be even more distracted. I know how close you were. You were like sisters. Finances shouldn't be a problem with that father of yours. Perhaps consider giving up work for a while. Regroup. Take a holiday. You've often visited Paris with your mom. Why not take this opportunity to travel? Take in the fashion scene over there. You never know where it might lead."

I don't need travel. I belong at my desk, researching fashion trends and interpreting them for Roberto and Isabella. Many wealthy clients buy Romance is Born designs because of my embroidery and appliqué. How many all-nighters have I pulled because a favored client wanted embroidered lapels at the last minute? *Not ambitious enough? If only you knew.* "I hadn't factored relocation into my plans." I brush away a rogue tear.

"There's a generous severance." Isabella taps a yellow business envelope. "We're paying for your current designs which we're using in the upcoming collection. And a generous bonus for your fabric patterns and the exquisite fine stitching you've already completed. I agree with Roberto. You're sooooo talented, but ... well ... it's a shame ... We always had you in mind for Head Designer as you were aware, but we can no longer afford you."

Hurt washes over me, wave after bitter wave. I cover my face with shaky hands. For all their fabulous talk, I mean nothing to them. Two weeks I wasn't available 24/7, so they fire me. I've spent years working my fingers till they bled. For nothing. Nada. "So that's it then." I keep the shake out of my voice but can't keep the shake out of my legs when I stand. My knees knock together, my stomach has a lead ball rolling around inside knocking me off balance.

"Sit." Isabella holds up her hands and I drop like a lead ball. "Times are tough in the fashion trade at the minute. Copycats are stealing our designs before they hit the catwalk. We need to trim overheads, downsize. You understand, don't you, Saskia?"

"Sure." I clench and unclench my fists, the anger surges through my blood like I'm being burned alive in hot oil. *Hiring people in my place is downsizing?*

Isabella shuffles her paperwork, then acts surprised when she picks up a card. "This must be fate." She taps the card on her desk. "If you do go to Paris, we have a contact at L'Amour dans sa Vie on Champs-Elysées. I just got off the phone to Catherine, a close friend of mine. She could use your fine stitching. I showed her some samples online." She holds out the card. "No pressure."

"Thanks." I accept the card, tap in on my palm, consider how bizarre are these two. Sack me one minute, shunt me off to Paris with a calling card the next. They're probably sweetening me up, so I don't sue for breach of contract. No way I could put myself through a court case now, and they know it. I'd like to tell them where to stick Paris, but Mom often suggested I move there. Maybe this is fate dressed in strange clothes. I must have nodded because Roberto jabs his pen at me again like he's a kid ready to throw a paper dart in my eye.

"Don't think you'll walk into a Head Designer's position over there, mind you. You'll have extra study before a Paris fashion house will look at you. They won't care that you've worked in a top New York fashion house. *Pfft.* To them Paris is everything. It'll take years—"

I grit my teeth, interrupt. "I know how Paris works." *Do I really?* Anything to shut him up before I say something I'll regret.

Isabella walks around her desk, hands me the fat yellow package. She startles me by putting a hand onto my shoulder and squeezing it. I can't remember her touching me except when she had a fitting for one of the gowns I'd sewn for her. "We're sooooo sorry, Saskia. You're very young. But you'll learn that life hands out challenges or threats. Look on this as a challenge. We each have to do what's best for us, and who knows, it won't seem like it now, but this may be what's best for you."

"We'll see." Why does everyone think they know what's best for me? First Pa and Xavier. Now my bosses.

"I'll miss you." Isabella brushes imaginary fluff from her sea blue silk Romance is Born suit with my intricate shadow embroidered roses on the lapels. She'll miss my handiwork is all until Vittoria is up to speed. Smoothing her baby bump, she smiles her dreamy mother-to-be smile. "We'll courier your things to your apartment. You still live in that cute little number in NoHo?"

"Yes. At the minute." *Until Pa sells it from under me.*

I pack up my desk and my dreams, ignoring the shifty glances from those in the room, hard at work on the upcoming collection. It kills me not to be part of the buzz seeing most of the fabrics and many of the ideas are mine.

Wrapping my arms around myself, I walk to the window, look down to buzzy Wooster Street. Fingers of hazy sunlight dance through a rainy mist, bathing pedestrians in soft golden light. For the last time from this posse, I take in my favorite view of Manhattan.

My cell phone goes *buzz-buzz-ping*. I turn from the window. Check the screen. *Mira.*

`Just heard. U ok, sweetie?`

`Gutted. Lunch?`

`Got mtg. Call u.` Followed by a dozen emoji smiley faces.

A new girl—must be Vittoria—eyes my prime window workstation with lust in her eyes.

"It's all yours, *amici*," I say, walking over, swiping the remaining threads of embroidery silks onto the floor to join the carpet of threads that coat every workroom surface. "Knock yourself out."

Vittoria's already packing up her desk before I throw my jam-packed tote over my shoulder and head for reception. No one says a word, but they stop what they're doing and stare at me, confusion on their faces. Maybe they have no idea what's happening. Which is how I feel. I'm light-headed. The walls close around me. I've got to get out before I have a full-fledged panic attack and am carted out in an ambulance. Not my preferred exit plan.

Rookie, the office gossip and receptionist, waves black fingernails and a blood-red fake you-poor-thing smile in my face before stabbing a thumb at my ex-bosses' door. "Mira's in there. What d'you think of that, hey?"

Ants crawl over my body. I stare at Roberto's and Isabella's shiny black door with its wonderful silver sketches of catwalk models in silhouette. I have a Wonder Woman moment where I kick it open and scream, "What's going on here?" I wipe my forehead with the back of my wrist, ignore Rookie's sly look. She's seen a couple of my meltdowns. Expecting me to break, she watches me closely, but I won't give her the satisfaction. I suck a breath. Hang on tight. "Bye." I flip the keys onto her desk, walk out real slow. I know what she wants me to think. *Your bosses screwed you. Did your best friend screw you too?*

I can't think that way.

Mira would never betray me.

I'm choosing positivity.

I'll turn this thing on its head.

Accept the challenge.

Make it work.

Mom's not here to help, but she's given me the coping skills I need.

In the elevator, I take my phone, turn on my MindShift app. which gives me tools to take charge of my anxiety. I pull up a coping card.

I can get through this, it says.

I totally can.

CHAPTER FIVE

"Double espresso, Tara, Candice, Clarke! Piccolo Coconut, Georgia!"

The familiar voice and smells greet me as I push open the door into Dominique's, the street-level café under the Romance is Born building. The coffee machine clunks and hisses, shoots steam into the air. I join the line, but instead of the aroma of coffee, the smell of fabric dressing, steam from the machines, the odor of pattern paper clog my nostrils.

I've been wandering the streets in the drizzly rain for hours, trying to make sense of why I was fired. I'd gone into the meeting with Roberto and Isabella filled with dreams of promotion and left with my dreams shattered.

My wanderings have led me back to Dominique's to slake my fearsome thirst for caffeine. In the past, whenever I needed a breather from the *go-go-go* upstairs, I'd come here for his silky almond milk cappuccino. I've nowhere to be. No clients to meet. No appliqué to stitch. No ideas to discuss with the design team. I flick my fingers. Shake the tension from my body.

Dominique greets me. "Saskia. Don't usually see ya at this time of day. How the hell are ya mate? What's ya poison?"

I avoid his eyes. Even Dom's brash Australian swagger fails to cheer me. "My usual, thanks."

Dom frowns. "Your coffee's on the house. So's your favorite raspberry crumble muffin. You're my thousandth customer today."

"You're so sweet, Dom." I'm touched by his kindness, but I'm sure he made it all up because I'm sad. It'll take more than a free coffee to cheer me.

Squeezing into a chair at a cramped corner table, I sip my cappuccino and watch the New York lunch crowd hunt down their bagels. Emptiness sits in my gut where pride in my job used to be. I'm a boxer who has taken a knockout blow and lies spread-eagled on the floor for the count. *Mom? Is this karma for what I did to you?* I offer the guy next to me my muffin; he shrinks away, probably on the Keto diet and terrified of carbs or maybe I look as weird as I feel.

I reach for my coffee cup. It rattles in the saucer. I'm feeling rattled myself. What just happened with Roberto and Isabella? They've shattered my Plan A, to become Head Designer. My raise would have allowed me complete financial independence from Pa. What about Plan B? I gulp a mouthful of coffee, wince. There is no Plan B.

I open the yellow envelope and peek at the check. It's more generous than I expected, but even so, my severance won't support the cost of living in New York for long. Most of the money Mom left me is tied up in a trust until I'm thirty. She left me some cash, but I've no savings. I've got to find another job. *Tout de suite.* Pa has probably already put my apartment on the market. I could move to the Hamptons and commute, but the realtor told me I'll collect at least a tidy quarter of a million in rental over the season. If Pa sells from under me, maybe Mira will take me in until I find some shabby little hole-in-the-wall apartment while I sort myself out.

I check my phone. Mira hasn't called. Losing my job's bad enough, but what if I've lost Mira? No, there's no way. We're besties.

My cell phone vibrates. A grin splits my face. *Mira.* She'll explain the *tête-à-tête* with the bosses.

Crap. Not Mira. Pa.

I mean to stab *Decline*, but my shaking finger hits *Accept*.

"What's wrong with you, girl?" Disappointment weaves through his voice. "Why didn't you turn up this morning? Xavier's father had already told the media about the engagement, and they were in a bidding war for the story. Any girl should be happy to marry into his family."

"I'm not any girl then. I don't care about money." As soon as I say the words, shame washes over me. Mom's money will make all the difference now that Pa has withdrawn his financial support. And even though Pa has been physically absent most of my life, he's made sure I wanted for nothing materially. I've enjoyed a life of wealth and privilege which I did nothing to deserve.

Pa's retort is exactly as expected. "You don't care about money because I've always filled your pockets. Now it's time to give back. Won't you do this one little thing for me?" I hear him unscrew the stopper on his decanter and the drink gurgles onto ice. His tone slips easily from mean to helpful. "Listen, how about a sweetener? I'll buy you an apartment in my building. One's coming up. Xavier said he'd love to live on Fifth Avenue."

I kick the table legs so hard my coffee cup jiggles. "I don't care where he lives. I'm happy in NoHo."

"NoHo's not for someone in your position. It's for bohemians. Like SoHo."

I hold my phone with my raised shoulder, rip a napkin from the dispenser, mop up spilled coffee. "I just got fired. That's my position." I cringe as I say the words. Flick my eyes over the coffee drinkers. It's like someone dropped a bomb. They stop talking, hold their cell phones away from their ears, brazenly eavesdrop. Getting fired in New York is a biggie, a potential precursor to homelessness. "I've got to convince another fashion house to take me on." The eavesdroppers lose interest. Fashion? *Pfft.* Nothing for them to worry about. By the look of their black suits, they're from the financial district.

Pa's glass thumps onto his desk. "No need. Give up that dead-end career. Look, they promise you a promotion, then fire you. How's that for gratitude? Move away from rags to a life of riches. Take what's yours."

"It's not mine, that's the kicker." A fleeting thought has niggled at the back of my mind all morning. Did my father arrange for my bosses to fire me? His way of cutting off my tilt at independence. Tears form at the traitorous thought, but it persists. Roberto and Isabella acted weird, like they were following a script. *A script written by my father.* Just his style. "Fashion means to me what real estate means to you, Pa. This setback won't change that."

"Forget fashion. I have much bigger plans for you. You can stay in your apartment for now although I could rent it out in a heartbeat."

I'm tempted for a nanosecond. "Thanks, but no. I'll find my own solutions."

"You?" He spits the word over the phone like a viper spitting venom. "You've been reliant on Mom for every decision you've ever made."

I won't let him know how much that hurts, even though there's some truth in it. "How's this for my own decision, hmmh? I'll leave New York, take myself to ... um ... Paris." *Paris.* I say it to annoy him, but it flies out of my mouth as natural as a breath. Ever since Isabella mentioned it, images of walking in *les jardins*, drinking *les cafés*, eating *les croissants* keep popping into my head. There would be a seven-hour flight between Pa and me, and, bonus, he hates flying. "It's time to spread my wings. Paris is it. I'm going home."

"New York is your home," he splutters, probably choking on an ice cube. "It's your mother's fault. You were born in France, so your mom wanted you to keep your dual citizenship. Once I talked her into coming back to me when you were two," he clears his throat, "after our little ... disagreement and an almighty row with those parents of hers, that should have been it."

"But it wasn't, was it?"

"No. Instead, she gave you a taste for French champagne and French food, so you turn your nose up at good Napa Valley wine and American burgers. She kept you in touch with your French heritage because she never forgave me for bringing you back to New York and forcing her to follow. No way I was never seeing my only child, and my lawyers made sure of it. Why do you think we argued?"

"Argued is a tame word for your abuse. Rant all you like to me, but Mom's not here to defend herself. She never took a dollar from you after she left you. Why didn't she report you for domestic violence? You had some hold over her, didn't you?"

"Yes. You. You were my insurance. You were her weakness. She'd never risk losing you, so she had to put up with me."

"Why shouldn't she take me to France every chance she got? We were safer away from you. And now I still am. That's what Mom wanted."

"Saskia, I won't have you dredging up the past and throwing it in my face. At the time I was under pressure from the markets. I regret hitting you both, but if you persist with your ridiculous idea of going to live in Paris, I'll ... I'll ... I'll ... sell your apartment, toss you and your sewing things onto the street. You'll never see another cent. And when I die a broken-hearted man, I'll leave it all to Xavier."

Suddenly, the day makes sense. "That was always your plan, wasn't it? It's all about you and Xavier, not about me." *Why did I expect anything different?* "Do it. I wish you'd be happy for me. I'd rather starve than stay in New York and take orders from you."

I press *End* and ignore his constant calls. My flash of confidence dissipates like steam from Dom's espresso machine. Ignoring my father, I concentrate on the knives stabbing my insides. Leave the States? What have I done? I let Pa force me into a hasty decision. My heartbeat triples in speed. I'll be all alone. The small annuity from Mom won't be enough to live on. Screw that ... I'm going to make it in the fashion world and Paris is the next logical step. Until rent starts coming from the Hamptons', I'll do anything short of selling my body to make ends meet. The world will fall in love with me and my fashion designs. I won't let a setback orchestrated by my father stymie me.

I drum my fingers on the table, watching day segue into afternoon and afternoon segue into early evening. Dom's refills keep me wired. The evening light looks incredible after the earlier rain. The buildings are washed sparkling clean. Towers of light shimmer up the windows of high rises in a dusky glow. Cars meander in rows like giant caterpillars, their eyes moving rivers of headlights. My heart aches at how New York has chewed me up and spat me out, but despite that, I love this city.

My mind keeps flicking to Paris. I imagine the opportunities for endurance training, running up the 600-odd Eiffel Tower steps, jogging down Champs-Elysées, trying out different tracks each day. I'll be entering the Paris Marathon, not the New York Marathon.

I text Mira at 7.30 pm:

`Mtg ova? Wassup GF?`

I order more coffee. Check my messages a gazillion times.

Finally, she rings.

She's sobbing loud, rasping sobs.

"Mira? Spill. What did they do to you?"

"What could I do, Sia?" She hiccoups into the phone. "They made me Head Designer. I've been rooting for you all this time. I never saw it coming, I swear. I did nothing—"

Someone just kicked me. I clutch my stomach. Manage to croak, "Congratulations, Mira. It couldn't go to a sweeter person." Then a thought pops into my head. "Did they say why they guzzumped me?"

"You wanted to go work for your father, they said."

So, I do have my father to thank. "That's total crap. I've never wanted anything to do with my father's business."

"I told them it didn't sound right, but they just shrugged and looked shifty."

I slap the table. "Mira, I'm thinking maybe for reasons of their own, Roberto and Isabella took the chance to fire me when my father asked them to. They claimed I wasn't ambitious enough. Me? Wasn't my ambition in everything I did?"

"You've got every right to feel betrayed, Sia."

"I so do." Pa has hit me again, not with the *New York Times*, but he still packs a wallop.

"I hope you're okay. Don't let this set you back."

Mira's seen my full-blown anxiety when too much stress triggers a panic attack. "I admit these past two days have tempted me to crawl into bed until it all goes away, but no. I won't give up. I'll be strong for Mom."

Mira blows out a breath. "That's awesome. I was so worried about your reaction to all this shit on top of losing your mom, I dreaded calling you."

"What's done's done. Good luck, girlfriend. Head Designer, wow." I try to swallow, but my throat is dry. "But, hey, I'm seriously thinking of saying fuck it all and moving to Paris."

Mira's squeal is the boost I needed. "That's so frigging glamorous. When? We gotta catch up before you go." Then she pauses. "Who am I going to binge watch Netflix with? We're only halfway through *Game of Thrones*."

"I hadn't thought of that. But I don't think I'll even get a television in Paris. I'm going to put all my energy into cracking the Paris fashion world. You'll have to tell me how it ends. But I'll call. Soon."

"Please. Now I've gotta get back. The terrible twins aren't finished with me yet. No doubt they've got an all-nighter planned for me. You're at Dom's, right? I hear the clatter. I'd come down, but who knows what time I'll get outta here."

"Chill, Mira. I understand. Later. I'm heading home. Gotta pack my apartment. Pa's throwing me out." I press *End*. Pa is right about one thing. I'm a New Yorker. I'll flip this thing on its head. Maybe the worst day is the best time to start a new life. I'm going to take life by the scruff and shake it. *But how?*

By leaving this town. With a new attitude. I'll never rely on a man—not my father, not Xavier, not any man—to fill my pockets again.

What's stopping me?

Nothing.

Paris. The home of haute couture. I'll be right inside fashion's beating heart. I could be picked up by Dior. Or Gaultier. Maybe, just maybe ... okay, I'm dreaming. Why should a top Paris fashion house hire me when Romance is Born fired me?

But Paris has something New York doesn't. Distance from my father.

Goddamn, I'm doing it.

Shaking off my doubts, I know my power lies in my determination to start a new life. One day I'll look back, laugh at my fears, think how silly I was to worry.

I know it's cheesy, but I make eye contact with the coffee drinkers, hold up my cup in a toast and say:

"Goodbye, New York.

Paris, here I come."

CHAPTER SIX
TWO MONTHS LATER – JULY - SUMMER IN GAY PAREE

I wake from a river of grief, the recurring nightmare of Mom's death. I quickly shower and dress. Slam the tiny window of my minuscule hotel room with its view of graffitied walls, black-clad pedestrians, and tiny cars bumping up and down the hilly street. In my skinny black jeans, loose white linen shirt and light floral scarf, I'm effortlessly put together for a Parisian summer's day. I have neither job nor apartment, so as I spritz my L'Occitane fragrance, I focus on my first *café au lait* of the day. Hmmm. I'll dunk a buttery croissant studded with melted chocolate chips into the frothy, milky goodness. *Ooh là là.*

I straighten the old chenille bedspread and tug at a silken thread that's unraveled after a gazillion washes. Taking a deep breath, I ask myself, am I unraveling too? Being positive is my goal, but self-doubt creeps in. My Paris dream isn't going according to my playbook. Instead of living on prime real estate belonging to my gazillionaire father in New York, I'm living in one of the shabbiest quartiers in Paris. Spread along the north-eastern hills, Belleville is my home until I find a cheap apartment, if such a thing exists in Paris.

I toss my tote over my shoulder, stand still, worry a hole in the brown carpet with the toe of my black ballet flat. I try not to miss Mom; try not to miss Mira back in the States; try not to miss New York where my life was so regimented, so predictable, so hopeful.

Until it ... wasn't.

It was my decision to come to Paris. Well, that's not exactly true. Mom had always urged me to come and live here. Sure, I'd holidayed with her each year in her parents' Paris apartment, but to have me find my roots in the city of her birth was one of her dearest wishes. "Just go, Saskia," she'd say when I was overwhelmed with work, feeling shaky from lack of sleep or Pa's demands. "Paris is much more relaxed than New York."

"You're wasting your breath, Mom," I'd say, terrified of such a radical move. I hate change. I was happy in New York. I loved my job. I loved my apartment. But I didn't love the way my father insisted I marry Xavier and join the firm.

When my New York life unraveled, it felt like some evil marionette was pulling my strings.

That was another life.

With no job prospects at any New York fashion house, I turned my back on my old, safe life. I turned my back on my domineering Pa. I turned my back on New York.

I will survive.

My knees shake. I flop back onto the bed. Clutch my arms around my waist. I love New York, but I'm in Paris now. A new life. I push myself off the bed. Grit my teeth. *Get on with it.*

I clutch the ancient doorknob. The bronze is worn down to metal. I've never seen such a thing in all the houses I've lived in. Here even shabby manages to look chic. How lucky am I to be in Paris? Hold that thought.

I slam my door before my courage flies out the window. I run downward circles around the eighty-nine spiral staircase steps, hoping and praying today is the day my new life falls into place.

I trip on the ripped carpet on the landing of the second floor, grip the banister until my knuckles hurt. Thinking about Pa's attempt to control me, I want to bang my head on the smooth polished wood.

An elderly French gent touches my elbow, asks, "*Est-ce que ça va?*" I look at him blankly; he repeats his question in English – "Are you okay?" When I nod, he smiles and continues his journey to the first floor.

I drum my fingers on the banister, wonder again what else could I do when faced with what Pa thought was a fait accompli? Run. I needed to put distance between us. I will live life my way. Follow my own dreams. Mom's words ring in my head: *... be who you want, not who someone else wants you to be.* Right.

As I reach the tiny foyer, Madame Page, the front-desk manager, holds up her hand, looks over the top of her bright green glasses. "*Bonjour* Mademoiselle Bell." She flicks her flaming red hair over one shoulder. "You asked about cheap apartments. 'Ere." She hands me a hot pink sticky note with a name, address and phone number scribbled in curly French script in purple ink. "Eet ees tiny, but verra eenexpensive."

Magic words. "Montmartre. Wow." Every trip Mom and I took to Paris began and ended in Montmartre, the arrondissement where her parents lived after retiring from their vineyard in the Loire Valley. Sadly, they died in a plane crash near Kathmandu when I was fourteen. What I know about them I learned through the stunning landscapes Grand-mère painted to decorate the Hamptons' beach house. Landscapes she painted from every country she and Grand-père visited.

Madame Page raises her impeccably plucked eyebrows and drums a little tune on her desk with flawlessly manicured fingernails. "You know Montmartre?"

"*Oui.* I know it well." It was love at first sight for me and the artsy 18th arrondissement. Mom and I would sit on the steps of Sacré-Cœur Basilica, elbows linked, gazing over the panoramic view of Paris's terracotta rooftops, chimney pots and creamy Haussmann buildings, serenaded by harpists and opera singers, and winked at by silver-painted mime artists. Montmartre would be a step up from the cheapest room in the cheapest hotel in one of the cheapest streets in Paris. "I'll take a look. *Merci* Madame."

Madame Page picks up a newspaper and with a manicured green fingernail, points to an advertisement circled in purple ink. "You also seek a job, *non*? Marcel's Bar een Pigalle ees hiring. Eet ees just down the road from zee apartment."

"A bar?" I regret my tone. She expertly knots her handkerchief-sized paisley scarf around her elegant neck and presses her lips together until I stumble out an answer. "I've no experience." *Unless drinking champagne at Marjorie's on Long Island counts.* Pa would have a fit. But he has no control over me now. That gives me a sense of satisfaction. And makes Marcel's Bar just the thing until the rent from the Hamptons' summerhouse starts trickling in.

"You can try anything once," Madame says. "Marcel ees *gentil*."

"*Merci*. I'll check it out." At least it's better than scrubbing someone's toilet. I take a screen shot and Madame shoots an eyebrow under her bangs. Flicking open my pocket metro map, I trace my finger along blue Line 2. "I'll have to change to green Line 12 at Pigalle and ride one more stop to Abbesses. "*Merci*, Madame. I've got it." I wave, head for the door.

I'm halfway across the foyer when she calls out, "*Un instant, s'il vous plaît.*"

I puff out a breath. Turn. "*Oui*, Madame?"

She picks up her cell phone. "I will call Madame Lavelle, concierge of zee apartment, and tell 'er you are coming, *non*? I will text you zee meeting spot. *Bonne journee.*"

"*Bonne journee. Merci beaucoup.*" I push open the heavy timber door, step onto the uneven cobblestones of rue de Belleville. I'm sucked into the life of the colorful main street. Scooting down the hill in the direction of the metro, I pass Asian grocers and Turkish smoke rooms and side alleys awash in street art. Men in jellabas and groups of women in burkas join me in the rush to the train. Tears prick my eyes. Loneliness is a pain roiling in my stomach.

It has rained earlier and here comes the sun. I scrub away my pitiful tears. Taking a deep breath, I inhale the peculiar wet limestone smell which is, to me, distinctly Parisian. This day could produce a perfect job to meet the rent on this perfect apartment I'm about to find. Happiness rises in my gut. Maybe this day could offer up a perfect Frenchman. That would totally put the icing on the cake. I give myself a mental slap. My priority is finding a place in Paris's fashion world. But I've spent two fruitless weeks scuffing my designer heels on the sidewalks, practically begging a fashion house to hire me. But Paris doesn't work that way. Roberto was right.

Near the metro steps, workmen smash concrete with jackhammers, reminding me of the pain stabbing inside my head when I flashed my resum*é* and references under the noses of Paris's Head Designers.

"*Désolé, Mademoiselle,* but a Paris Institut fashion course is a must to gain entrée into Parisian fashion houses." Each Head Designer sniffed, shoved my papers back into my trembling hands. "Call again when you graduate."

As I clatter down the steps to the train, I sigh. I'd finally approached L'Amour dans sa Vie and asked for Isabella's friend, Catherine. In a ritzy back street, a short walk from Champs-Elysées, I found one of those sleek black chrome and glass buildings. I'd not wanted to owe my old bosses anything after the way they'd handed me a severance package instead of a promotion. But the overwhelming desire to eat and sleep with a roof over my head was the clincher.

Hurrying along the platform, I remember how Catherine greeted me quite warmly. Her warmth increased when she inspected my appliqué samples with a magnifying glass.

"*Bien. Bien.* Isabella is correct." As she moved from one sample to the next, she'd rubbed her thumb over my fine stitching, looking over her black glasses to inspect me. "This is exquisite, Mademoiselle Bell. Hmmm." Her black-lipsticked lips smiled, her long black eyelashes fluttered. She was wonderfully put together if you like the all-black vampire look. "This type of work is fast disappearing. It is rare to find such attention to detail." Handing back my samples, she said, "I can offer you freelance work for our current evening wear range. But we cannot, how you say? match your New York salary, *bien sûr.*"

"*Bien.*" Her offer will keep me in coffee and macarons. That's something.

The electronic sign shows a train arriving. I tap my foot and wonder if freelancing for Catherine is just the beginning. Yesterday, I gave up my ideas of a fast track to a fashion career in Paris and enrolled in a four-month refresher course at the Paris Institut of Fashion, beginning September, a couple of months away. I'm impatient to be lectured by famous designers from top houses in Paris, but the cost gave me heart palpitations. But with the rent from the Hamptons', it's doable. I'm sure Mom meant it as a place for me to live, but I've no doubt she'd be equally pleased to know it's going to make my Paris dream affordable. For a moment I tear up, visualizing the beautiful house and its memories of times spent with Mom, the lapping waves relaxing me, the weekends entertaining friends, the cute coffee shops. No. I'm in Paris. Living a new, exciting life. *Get on with it.*

Stepping onto the train, I sink into a vacant seat. Staring into the black tunnels as the train whooshes along, I thread my fingers through the tassels of my tote. I'm nervous but hopeful I'm heading in the right direction. Will Paris's hilltop village, the Butte de Montmartre, be my new home, the starting point for my new life? I rub Mom's black opal ring on my middle finger. She told me it symbolized a good future, so I send up a prayer which ends up being *please, please, please.*

I have no illusions regarding how expensive forging a fashion career will be in this city. But Paris might fall in love with me like they did with my fashion idols like the late greats Lagerfeld, Chanel and St Laurent. At the end of the day, I'm on a journey of self-discovery. I've been messed-up, coping with survivor guilt. I need to get over it and move on.

For the first time in my life, I'm paying my way. I'll never let anyone pay my way again. Paris is forcing me to grow up. Rather late in life at twenty-five, but better than not growing up at all.

I'm hungry. Thinking about food has me drooling over the rose-jasmine macarons from Pierre Hermé near the Jardin des Tuileries. Every day I stroll in the gardens from the direction of the Louvre to Place de la Concorde, anticipating that delicious pop when I bite into that decadent combination of crisp, sweet outer layer and silky center. Eating macarons every day delights me, but it's not a wise long-term plan. Paris is a long-term plan. It must work.

And I must work. Even if it's in a bar.

I clamber up the two hundred stairs from the bowels of the earth that is the Place des Abbesses's metro station in Montmartre, studying the stunning murals, imagining what spectacular fabric designs I'll create using this art as inspiration. I snap pictures on my cell phone, capturing lush orange and red poppies, the outline of the city, the white winged Pegasi flying on the blue background. I hate closing my eyes for a second in Paris. It's a never-ending feast for the eyes.

When I exit into the glaring daylight of a brilliant blue sky, my phone pings. Madame Page has texted the meeting place and time:

`Saskia, rue des Martyrs in a half hour.`

I zip along the narrow cobblestones to the Place du Tertre at the top of the hill. Restaurants have set up in the center of the Place and I salivate over the delicious menus. It's full of life – bearded artists in smocks, hopeful tourists posing on rickety wooden stools while artists tilt their heads, flourish brushes and chew on pencils, trying to capture their image with as much drama as they can summon. I browse the paintings displayed around the perimeter. Artwork selling here today for a few euros could one day be worth thousands, even millions. I recently read that a van Gogh gathering dust in someone's attic sold for $7 million. Now that they have passed, Grand-mère's Hamptons' seascapes sell at the quarter million mark and are deposited into my trust account. I have much to thank art for.

"*Désolé,*" I say to the artists in berets who clutch their clipboards with blank art paper and charcoal at the ready, begging to paint my picture. Soulful cries of 'Pretty Woman' don't break me. Until I earn some decent money, if I can't eat or drink it, I'm not interested. I check my watch. No breakfast or lunch for me today.

Rounding the corner, I look down the rue de Cardinal Guibert to the terracotta rooftop of my grandparents' Montmartre apartment, a short downhill walk from Sacré-Cœur. The church is directly ahead. I have time to slip inside and light a candle for Mom. Inside, standing before the flickering candles, I cross myself, whisper, "Please forgive me, Mom". My eyes fill with tears. Am I to blame for her death? Should I have been faster, grabbed her before she revved off on my motorcycle? I find no answers in the flickering candles.

"*Et vous,* Madame Lavelle?" I ask the tall African woman standing at the top of the street beside a painted red wheelbarrow overflowing with potted plants. She's more colorful than any exotic plant in her flowery green maxi dress, matching turban, and gold earrings with metallic tassels that brush her long, slender neck the color of my favorite *café au lait.*

"*Oui,* Mademoiselle." Her dazzling smile is enhanced by a slash of shiny red-orange lipstick which matches the poppies in her dress.

I trot out my best French which I have rehearsed during the metro ride. "*Je m'appelle* Saskia Bell. I'm about the apartment."

She leans forward and air kisses me, *bisou, bisou, bisou,* smelling faintly of garlic and citrus. One of us has had lunch. "Speak English, Mademoiselle. I am from Burkina Faso. I need to practise." She smiles to take the sting from her words. Obviously, my American-accented French hurts her ears. "Welcome to rue des Martyrs, to me, the best street in Paris." Her

English words have a sing-song French lilt. Adjusting her huge shoulder bag, she gestures down the street with wide-open arms. "Whatever you need, you will find here. Bookstores, baguettes, and bistrots selling creamy Mont d'Or cheese you eat with a spoon."

I lick my lips, imagine the runny cheese on my tongue, washed down with a glass of bubbly. The street delights me with its narrow cobbles weaving down the hill. So exotic, so cute, so medieval. What a contrast to Fifth Avenue with its clamor, its stylish tall buildings, and wall-to-wall yellow cabs. Here, people sit a short distance apart drinking wine or espressos, enjoying a cigarette on the sidewalk outside cafés under red awnings with gold script and fringes. I spy quaint antique shops I can't wait to explore. "It's amazing." I breathe it in.

We've only walked a few steps down the street when Madame Lavelle holds up her hand. "*Arretêz.*" She points to a creamy art deco styled building opposite, the regulation five Haussmann stories high with black lacework balconies rising, slightly crooked, above a fancy pâtisserie called Pain. I've missed my morning *café au lait* and croissant. I'll visit the pâtisserie after I inspect the apartment. Hopefully the lines will not be so long then.

"It's beautiful, Madame Lavelle." The building fulfils my fantasies of where I want to live in Paris. I'm in love, imagining the aroma of coffee and cake on my doorstep every day. I wonder if they will make an almond cappuccino like Dom in New York. Ah, look at that woman on the second floor. Her long blonde hair is blowing in the breeze, her elbows rest on the balcony rails while she puffs smoke from a cigarette in an elegant holder. In her shiny black fitted dress, does she think she's Audrey Hepburn in *Breakfast at Tiffany's*, a film I watched over and over with Mom?

Madame Lavelle follows my eyes. "We call her the Grande Dame because that is who she is. No one knows her real name."

When the Grande Dame raises a palm and blows smoke in my direction, I wave back. She looks so glamorous. I'm dying to meet her.

"Come." Madame Lavelle keys in the door code. "You will like the apartment very much."

"I'm sure I will." I swallow the lump in my throat. Take breaths to calm my crazy heartbeats. I have the best feeling.

We clamber up flights of rickety stairs, the stairwell dim except for sensor lights added sometime in the modern age. I stifle a giggle. How fit will I become running up and down these stairs every day. Great incidental training for the Paris Marathon. Even after the disaster in Boston, I have decided to enter, lay my demons to rest, prove to myself fear will no longer be the controlling factor in my life.

"There are two apartments on each floor." Madame Lavelle's breath wheezes and she leans against the wall clasping her chest.

I'm very concerned when I see the pallor on her face. "Are you okay, Madame? Do you need to rest?"

"*Non*, Mademoiselle. I find stairs very difficult. Thank you for asking." She takes my elbow, and we begin to walk to the next floor. "Because it is very old and very inexpensive for Paris, there are several tenants like you, recent arrivals, who move on when they find employment."

"Suits me." I love the 'inexpensive' part. As we near the top floor, Madame Lavelle's wheezing grows louder. She clutches my elbow harder. I help her climb the narrow steps, surprised when we don't stop at the fifth floor. The last few stairs are so tiny I walk sideways to fit my shoes to the treads.

Madame Lavelle stops in front of an old arched door studded with huge copper nails. "We are here," she says, her chest heaving. "The attic."

I shiver, clutch the doorframe. Even before I walk inside, I know.

My Parisian adventure just took an upward turn.

Here on the sixth floor of an old apartment in Montmartre.

CHAPTER SEVEN

The door is heavy hinged, its navy-blue paint peeled and weathered. I doubt anyone has taken a brush to it in centuries. It's the anthesis of every door I've entered in my life, but that makes it more appealing. My heart hammers, but in a good way. I'm convinced this is it, the place for me to live, to work, to launch my fashion career. I can't wait to get inside.

Madame Lavelle ruffles about in her tote. "I do not often rent it, but Madame Page tells me you are desperate." She shoves a huge ornate metal key into the hole, turns it, then it screeches open inwards. "Be careful." Bending her head, holding her skirts above her knees, she squeezes her generous figure inside.

I crouch and jump down the three small steps. Into the quaintest, dreamiest doll's house. A *très* elegant furnished space.

Madam Lavelle falls into a dining chair and clasps her chest, taking shallow breaths. "Please make yourself at home, Mademoiselle. I will sit awhile and recover."

I watch her closely and ask, "Are you unwell? Shall I call an ambulance?"

She flaps her hand in front of her face. "*Non, non, non.* I am short of breath after that climb, that is all." She rummages in her pocketbook, slips a pill under her tongue. "You are very young and fit. I need to walk more." She reaches into her shoulder bag and produces two small water bottles. "Here, one for you. Now look around. Take your time."

"*Merci.*" Sipping the welcome water, I walk around, glancing at her often to make sure she really is okay. She appears content, so I give my attention to the tiny apartment. The attic smells of time, of layers of life, of people who've lived here in the past. My eyes prick with tears at the simplicity of the light-filled space, loving its original scuffed uneven herringbone parquet floors which will probably give me splinters if I walk barefoot, shabby rose-tinted walls and distressed cream trims. There are two ancient die cast radiators to keep me from freezing in winter. Above me are two small ceiling roses with utterly beautiful miniature chandeliers hanging from them. I have grown up in luxurious homes decorated with bespoke furniture, antiques, and gold-leaf trim, but they never excited me like this little attic with its sloping roof and two cute boxy shuttered windows either side of one full length shuttered grilled door. The skylight bathes the room in sunshine. The light will be perfect for sketching my fabric designs.

I go to the French doors; golden shafts of sunlight warm my face. Waves of Parisian zinc rooftops and terracotta chimney pots shimmer in the summer heat, and ooh là là, there's the Eiffel Tower. I struggle with the door catch. I jiggle it and finally it loosens enough to pull both doors toward me. There's a faux balcony with black lacework and three dead pot plants hanging dejectedly from the ironwork. I can't go outside, but that doesn't stop the delicious bakery smells wafting up from the street.

Reluctantly turning my back on my view of Paris, I imagine how the space will work for me. I'll push a long desk against the wall beside the tall window, creating a workstation. It will be a tight squeeze to fit the industrial sewing machine and mannequin I have yet to buy, but I can work around that. I visualize sketch books, jars of pencils, swatches of embroidery fabric, boxes of beads, sequins, silk threads, mood board, corkboard. Ideal.

"The salon." Madame Lavelle waves her arms to indicate the combined sitting/dining room, which is not much larger than the entrance hall in my New York apartment. "Your bed." She points to a tiny alcove with a full-length gilt-edged antique mirror adorning the wall. Beside the single bed, (I haven't slept in one since I was a tiny child), there's a nightstand with curved legs where I will arrange photos of Mom and my travels, especially the small dot painting from Australia. The bed is directly below the skylight. I'll have a twenty-four-hour view of the Parisian sky as it changes with the times and seasons. My sketch book and colors will be within easy reach.

The leather two-seater sofa facing the doors is the same pale rose as the walls. The metal and glass coffee table with scrolled legs in front of it is very Parisian chic. "I couldn't have chosen better, Madame Lavelle." Some throw rugs, large cushions, Mom's handknitted blanket, jugs of flowers from an enchanting boutique I often pass in Le Marais, where fragrant blooms tumble onto the sidewalk. I will find art for the walls at secondhand markets, maybe from a yet-to-be-discovered artist, and I'll be set.

Her breathing much easier, Madame Lavelle pushes herself upright and walks to a battered carved cupboard fitted into an alcove in the wall close to the bed. Wrenching open two ornate doors, she says, "It is nigh impossible to move furniture up here with the tiny stairs. It is also a little high for the cranes to reach, which is how most people furnish their apartments. So, everything, including this armoire, stays, along with the linens inside left behind by the previous tenant."

She walks me into a tiny, white-tiled bathroom with a little shower, spotlessly clean, then shows me the minuscule kitchen under the sloping roof at the far wall. "It is very basic, but Parisians do not often cook at home. Will this be a problem?"

"I don't expect so Madame Lavelle. I never learned to cook." A flash of regret passes through me. Why didn't I learn? Mom cooked such wonderful

French dishes. I'm so glad I brought along her book of handwritten recipes. With YouTube's help, I'll try some simple dishes after I settle in.

I inspect the kitchen with more interest. On a laminated bench sits a battered cafetière; there is an ancient stove, but no pots and pans; a plastic, yellowed sink, and a rather rusty bar refrigerator make up the rest. If the refrigerator works, it will keep my cheese and champagne chilled. In a drawer there is some old cutlery, enough for two people. Some vintage white china totters haphazardly on the shelf above the sink. There is a small, scrolled steel dining table and two matching chairs pushed into the opposite corner. That's it.

Madame Lavelle watches me spin around, measuring with my hands. "It is very small, I know this, but for you, it is enough?"

"Oh yes." I'm stiff with anticipation. I don't know how Paris real estate works. Will I have to fill in an application and compete with others as desperate as I am? I've heard finding a rental in Paris is every bit as difficult as in New York. That's a depressing thought.

"Once you find a job you may wish to move to something bigger. Apartment 5A, just below the attic, is being remodeled. It will be soon complete, and you could have it if you so desire."

Madame Lavelle talks as if my moving in is a *fait accompli*. "The attic is enough for now, but I'll keep 5A in mind." I smile at her hopeful face. Inside, I'm doing cartwheels. "Can I have it?"

She smiles and her whole face lights up. "Pay me a month's rent and it is yours today."

I can't bear not to have it. Crap. Can I afford it before I start receiving rent from the Hamptons'? A bit late to think of that. My savings have disappeared at an alarming rate since I left New York. But where in Paris could I find something that suits me so well? Even when I have an income, I won't want to leave. The remains of the cash I brought with me is in my purse. I'll spend every dollar, er, euro, if I must. I rub my opal ring, send up a little prayer. *Please God. Please God. Please God.* I clear my throat. "How much?"

Madame Lavelle smiles, quotes a ridiculously low figure which will make scarcely a dent in my cashflow.

Are you kidding? I suck a deep breath then blow it out. I look her in the eye; she winks. Maybe the owner of the building doesn't care about the attic. Maybe it's hers to rent out as she pleases. "A deal," I say before she changes her mind. Unzipping the secret compartment in my tote, I count out a wad of cash and push it into her hands.

She flicks through the notes; holds out her arms like we are secret conspirators. After we hug, she digs around in her pocket and produces a ginormous key.

"Mademoiselle Saskia, welcome to rue des Martyrs," she says formally. "You may move in this evening if that is convenient. I will have the apartment cleaned and the linens aired. If you need anything more, just ring the bell at Apartment 1A." She hands me her card, scribbles the door code at the bottom.

"*Merci*, Madame Lavelle." Inside, I'm screaming and clapping. I have an apartment. In Paris. I've done it. All by myself. I've traded my father's 3,000 square-foot NoHo apartment for what is probably a 400 square-foot garret in Montmartre. But it's mine. All mine. I'm paying for it. I'm decorating it. I'm never sharing it with anyone.

As I follow Madame Lavelle down the stairs, I shiver. Feel my mom close. "Mom," I whisper. I know she's watching over me, cheering me on. "I'm home."

I have found the first step on my new path.

It's my lucky day.

Will my luck stretch to a job?

I feel as if drumsticks are beating on my chest. Two miracles in one day? That's a bit too much to ask.

Just before twilight, I push open the door to my attic, bump two large suitcases inside. Jogging downstairs, I pick up the other two, which the cabbie left propped inside the street door. So much of my life has been spent in taxicabs and chauffeur-driven Town Cars, but today it felt completely decadent to hand over €25 for a ride.

As I haul my last two suitcases up the stairs into my apartment, I think what a great workout it is. By the time I finish hauling luggage, it's that magical time of day Parisians call *l'heure bleue*. The evening sky shimmers through my skylight, and I bathe in dusky purplish-blue hues which remind me of van Gogh's painting, *Starry Night*. I scuttle to the balcony door for a better view. Propped on the window ledge a jug of yellow and white roses greet me.

Roses. The essence of love. The fragrance takes me back to Mom's rose garden in the Hamptons. I smell again the delicate perfume wafting on the evening breeze. There we are sitting on the bench in the garden sharing a glass of wine at day's end.

Under the jug I find my rent receipt and a sheet of white notepaper. In flowery French script, I read:

> *Welcome to Paris, Mademoiselle Saskia. May your time in The Attic be a time you remember with joy, wherever your Paris dream takes you. I wish you great happiness.* Signed, *Madame Lavelle.*

Beside Madame Lavelle's note, there's another. This one is written in shaky black calligraphy on parchment that would be at home in an Ancient Egyptian palace. I'm delighted to see it's from the Grande Dame.

> *Mademoiselle Saskia. Welcome to Les Martyr's Residences. Please accept my invitation for drinks at Café de Flore at your earliest convenience. Slip a note under my door at Apartment 2A.* Signed, *The Grande Dame.*

I hug both notes to my chest. Something cracks open in me. It feels like happiness. I clench my fists, try to block out my father's words. *Saskia, there's no cure for PTSD. You're looking at a lifetime of mental instability and exorbitant treatment fees. I won't be paying a cent if you leave New York.*

Will I end up in a mental facility like he suggested? No. I shrug my shoulder. Anything and everything is possible, despite what he said. I re-read the notes. Yes. *I'm going to stay calm. I won't let anything rattle me. I'll defeat this thing one step at a time.*

I rise on tiptoe and look through the door down into the street in the direction of Pigalle but can't quite see the red and black bar where I'll start work tomorrow. The manager, Marcel Petit, was very gung-ho about my zero-bar experience and my tentative French. He cemented his new best friend status when he gave me a bottle of Duperrey champagne. I'll pop it this evening, toasting my new apartment and job.

While the champagne cools, I set about making the attic home. I dress my bed with my favorite set of dusky blue linens from the States and shake an old quilt I find in the armoire. Coughing, I cover it with the Monet waterlily print set I bought at the Hammer Galleries in New York. I don't care that my linens fit a king-size bed and the covers pool onto the floor. It's charming. After firing up my diffuser with lavender and rose oil, I kick off my shoes, throw myself onto the bed, prop myself against the pillows. Shivering with excitement, hands linked behind my neck, I watch the darkening pink-purple sky dance above my head.

I'm in paradise.

I reach for my cell phone. My reflex is to ring Mom and share my fabulous news. I chew my lip, toss the phone onto the nightstand. *Breathe. Breathe. Breathe. Think of your happy place.* Through the skylight I focus on a bird. Flying. Free. I sip from my water bottle, taking deep breaths until the anxiety leaves me and my heartbeat slows. My pillows are super comfortable. I relax and drift into pleasant dreams on a soft white fluffy cloud ...

Buzz. Buzz. Buzz.

Shooting one eye open, I grope around, grab my bouncing phone.

Uh-oh. *Pa. Paradise Lost.* How long will he keep calling me? Sighing, I press *Accept.*

"Saskia, come home," he says, no preamble. "Now. Get on a plane. Stop this nonsense. I won't have it."

I groan, roll off the bed, walk barefoot to the French doors, loving the feel of the wonky old parquet flooring underfoot. *Ouch.* I hobble to the sofa, inspect my foot. A splinter. Not too deep. Gritting my teeth, I carefully extract it between finger and thumb.

Pa huffs a breath. "Answer me. You can't be in Paris alone. I hear those idiotic sirens that sound like donkeys braying. Shut the windows. Turn on the air conditioner. Paris is a dangerous place."

"Compared to? New York?" I laugh, a slightly deranged sound. I have just woken up after all. "And there's no air-conditioning."

"No air-conditioning?" His voice rises until he's shouting. "Are you mad? My little girl should want for nothing."

I tear up when I remember when I *was* his little girl many years ago, when he was a decent human being not given to violence against his wife and child.

Now there's distance between us, I decide this is the right time to set him straight. "I'm hardly your little girl, Pa. How long since you cared about what I want or need? Trying to blackmail me into marrying Xavier was a low blow. Just so you know, I'm doing a good job of living on nothing."

He smacks his hand onto some hard surface. "I hope you're just jerking my chain. If you're destitute, your mother will haunt me. What was I thinking all those years? I missed so much."

"You did. You missed being my Pa. Your choice. You can't just rock back into my life now that Mom's dead. We no longer have a relationship which is why I don't get why you're calling me every day."

"I was wrong. Let me make it up to you." He puts on his best wheedling voice. "I just put ten grand into your account to tide you over until you start receiving rent from the Hamptons. From now on, I'll deposit a monthly sum so I can rest easy."

"Uh, thanks, no need. I have enough to get by. I don't want your money."

"Saskia, I didn't realize you were saying goodbye when you asked me to dinner that night at Per Se. If I had, I would have helped you out."

Yes. Thrown me into your Town Car and locked me in my room until I promised to marry Xavier.

"Dinner was my farewell gift, Pa."

"I didn't think you had it in you to walk away. Even though I hate your decision, you make me proud. You got grit like your old man. But you gotta come home." He makes a clicking sound with his tongue. "I'll get you your old job back."

A fist closes around my heart. My breaths are ragged gasps. "You say that so casually. Do you have any idea of the pain you put me through when you got me fired? It's too late now. My best friend got the promotion. No way I'd make Mira unhappy."

He makes a *pfft* sound. "One lesson you gotta learn in life girly is to put yourself first. And New York's the best place to learn this. Come home. Put that ten grand to good use. First class all the way for my girl."

"Economy feels good." I lean with my elbows propped on the windowsill listening to the thump *thump thump* of tires on the old cobbles, the honking of cab and bus horns from the main thoroughfare further down the street, French musical voices drifting into my apartment. I check my watch to see how long before the Eiffel Tower lights up, when the sunset changes to purple-gold and the rooftops shimmer fiery red. I want to capture these colors for my new fabric designs. Not for Isabella and Roberto. For me. No handing them over to someone else like I did at Romance is Born. My fingers twitch. I look longingly at my brand-new sketch pad and pencils calling me from the dining table.

Pa breaks my reverie. "Why make it hard on yourself? Your mother was

French, but New York's your home. Come back. I want to make up for those lost years. Anything you want, anything."

"I have all I need. I love my new life. I want to live in Mom's city. I feel close to her here." If things cost more than I expect, I'll sell the Bvlgari Serpenti watch with the wraparound rose-gold straps he gave me for my twentieth birthday. I checked at a jeweler in my street today and it's worth about $20,000 because of the diamonds on the teardrop face. Pa liked me to wear it to those New York soirees I attended with Xavier. No more of that.

"Don't be silly, Saskia. You've staged your little rebellion. Listen, I'll give you your old apartment back. I'm sorry I kicked you out. That was low of me."

"Hmmm. It was. Even for you." The Eiffel Tower lights turn on. *Wow.* I strain my eyes for the best view of the twinkling lights scooting up and down the lacy frame. "I'm not leaving Paris, Pa. It's my dream. I've found an apartment and a job."

He sucks in a loud breath. I practically hear his synapses zapping. I'm not surprised when he changes his tone. "Listen, my girl," he shouts, "if you refuse to come home, I'm ... er ... flying to Paris to fetch you. Or I'll send Xavier."

"Don't ... you ... dare." I lean as far as I can out of the door for a better view, clutching the iron railing, stabbing my finger on a dead plant. My excitement bubbles like good champagne. I can't wait to pop my Duperrey to wash down that decent-sized chunk of Mont d'Or cheese I bought at the fromagerie on my way up the hill this afternoon.

"Baby girl." He returns to wheedling. "You're not thinking straight. You need your therapist. I'll pay despite what I said. I don't want you to go crazy. It's crazy enough for you to be in Paris alone. Doctor Sheila will help you find your way back to reality."

"Paris is my new reality, Pa." Down in the street, people fill the well-lit cafés and bars, laugh, hug, stroll arm in arm, dressed in elegant clothes, disappear through black doors into mysterious dens. Why would I go back to New York? There's so much to discover on my doorstep. "Forget it, Pa. I'll find a therapist here eventually. And I'll pay myself. If you try to find me, I'll never come back."

"Saskia, I need you." His voice breaks. He's such an excellent manipulator.

I summon up the right amount of steel in my voice. "As if you've ever needed anyone, except to do your bidding. You need me to marry Xavier, is all. You can't stand losing."

"Don't discount Xavier. He's handsome, rich, on his way up. What more could you want?"

I clench my teeth, spit out the words. "What more could I want? To make my own choices."

While he continues his fake sweet talk, I pull my cell phone away from my ear. I've had my fill of his daily calls. Lifting my phone high, I drop it into the jug of roses, then smile at the plonk it makes as it spirals to the bottom. "Goodbye, Pa." The few numbers I need are seared into my brain.

I have drowned my New York life.

Now to toast my freedom.

Bottle under my arm, I settle on the sofa for what's going to be the nightly light show. The champagne could be more chilled, but it will do. I pour golden bubbles into a wide-mouthed tooth glass. Note to self: *buy champagne flutes.* I salute the sunset. "To me and my dream of world dominion in the fashion industry." I wink at the twinkling Eiffel Tower. I swear she winked back.

I love this city.

I raise my tooth glass into the air. "*Salut!*"

I'm on my way.

Paris means trying new things.

I'm going to try everything Paris throws at me.

CHAPTER EIGHT

Pinch me. I'm working in a bar in Pigalle, Paris's naughty end of town. The new me is excited to be trying something different, but the old me still imagines Pa perched on my shoulder, screaming, *Get your ungrateful ass back to New York.* Sorry, Pa, I'm living my dreams, not yours. I'm paying my dues. Working in a bar. Keeping my Paris dream alive.

I stand at the counter taking deep calming breaths, blanking Pa from my mind. I don't know what to expect on my first day in my new job, but I certainly don't expect a tall stranger dressed in black motorcycle leathers to push his way through the side entrance while I'm struggling to tie my apron. I'm used to seeing men in charcoal suits and short hair, so this guy gets my tick of approval for looking nothing like Xavier or any of the New York men I've dated.

He strides into the room like he owns the place. Stopping in the middle of the floor to light a cigarette, he hunches his hands around the flame, giving me time to check him out. He draws heavily, eyes closed. When he opens his eyes, he catches me staring at him.

Whoops.

Our gazes collide. I'm captivated; he just looks curious.

He loops a thumb through his jacket pocket. Raising one eyebrow, he gives me a what-are-you-doing-here? kind of look, adjusts his satchel across his shoulder, rocks on his heels. Puffing on his cigarette, he stares at me while he blows smoke rings above his head.

I'm more than a little taken aback by his direct stare. My heart goes *thumpedy-thumpedy-thump*. It's different in a good way from my heart palpitations when I'm anxious. Surely, it's first day nerves, not this hunk of gorgeousness swaggering my way.

He raises an arm in greeting, then drops into a funky leather bar stool in front of me. He's even more handsome at close range. His long chocolate-colored thick and glossy curls bounce on his shoulders, while his dark stubble adds to his mystery. It's like he's been sculptured by a loving hand. Every plane and angle of his face is flawless. He's the epitome of cool with incredible bone structure, smoky black eyes, lips that curl upward at the edges, eminently kissable.

My face burns. What am I? Some goon, staring like this? I smooth my hair. Rub my sweaty palms on my skinny jeans.

He smirks like he's read my mind. Blowing smoke from his foul cigarette into the black glass chandelier, one of three that decorate the ceiling, he finally speaks. "Hello, *ma petite*. Where did Marcel find *you*?"

His sexy French accent with British inflections surprises me. I hang the wine glass I've been polishing over and over into the rack above my head. "Actually, Monsieur, *I* found Marcel."

"Hmmm." He nods, concentrates on the serious business of smoking. Leaning back on the stool, he tilts his head and watches me through half-closed eyes.

What's he doing here, randomly walking in off the street? A small frisson of fear makes me shiver. "Monsieur, we aren't open yet." I try for an officious tone, hoping it will send him running back into the street. *Am I kidding?*

He raises his eyebrows. "I'm a friend of Marcel's." There's an undercurrent of affection in his voice. "We live together in the apartment above the bar."

"Oh." Marcel had pointed out the apartment from the street – massive glass windows, black paintwork and red Renaissance carvings around the eaves and above the windows. My cheeks tingle. I try to shut my gaping mouth. From the vibe I was getting from him, I could have sworn—

"Aha." He smiles, wags his finger, then laughs a deep, husky, teasing laugh. No doubt the cigarettes are slowly scorching his throat. "Marcel's and my relationship is friendly, but not that friendly. We're long-term friends and business partners." He checks his Rolex. Drums his non-smoking fingers on the counter. "We have a meeting."

"Oh?" *Oh My God.* I clap my hands on my burning cheeks. Fabulous start. "Uh, Marcel stepped out for a minute. Something about white wine. He didn't tell me to expect you." I clear my throat. Grasp for a change of subject. "I must say, your accent is interesting."

His amusement vanishes. He flicks ash into the tray I pushed in front of him. He grins, but his eyes are cold. His face darkens. "Long story." His bitterness surprises me. "I spent years in England receiving a 'superior education.'" He makes quote marks in the air. "Turns out, only the accent stuck." He blows smoke out the side of his mouth.

I cough into my elbow. I've heard French cigarettes are wiffy, and the stranger's fumes certainly prove it. Judging by the blue tinge in the air picked up by shafts of sunlight, it looks like Marcel's Bar is the last bastion of smoker tolerance in Paris. According to *Trip Advisor*, smoking in bars in Paris is banned like in the rest of the civilized world, but also according to *Trip Advisor*, Parisians aren't averse to flouting no-smoking laws.

"Sorry." He stubs out what's left of his cigarette, then holds out a hand which is oddly paint splattered.

I'd tagged him as a louche who hasn't done a stroke of work in his life, but his hands tell a different story.

"I'm Raphael Valentine." He flashes me a brilliant smile. "You are—?"

I lean across the counter to take his hand, get a whiff of Eau de Chimney. "Pleased to meet you, Monsieur Valentine. I'm Saskia Bell."

"*Enchanté*, Saskia Bell. That has a nice ring to it." He quirks his lip at his little joke like most people do when they first meet me. "Call me Raphael. You hail from the States, *non*?"

"*Oui*."

"You took Luiz's job?"

"*Oui*."

Raphael sucks his lips inside his mouth. "Marcel's upset about how that turned out. Luiz flew home to his ex in Argentina and broke up with Marcel via text."

"That's too bad. Marcel said they had a fight. Something about drugs." I assume Luiz was the one on drugs as Marcel doesn't seem the type. How could he run a bar if he were shooting up or popping pills?

"Who knows? Marcel didn't give details." Raphael leans back in his chair. "But look at you. Sun-kissed skin, sand in your hair, sea in those shiny blue eyes. You a California girl?" He hums the opening bars of the Beach Boys' song.

"You're very poetic. Like the song."

"I like that song."

"Me too. Well, to answer your question, I'm a New Yorker, but I spent most of my last weeks in the Hamptons soaking up the sun."

"Lucky you. I've been to New York City several times to check out the art galleries, but I've not been to the Hamptons."

"There are plenty of galleries in Bridgehampton near where I live. Fabulous beaches too."

"Maybe one day. How about I take you to Paris's beach at the Hotel de Ville? It pops up every summer to prove Paris does supply your every need. In winter it's a skating rink." He checks his watch again. "Where's Marcel?"

"'ere." Marcel walks through the back door into the kitchen. Sunlight streaks into the bar giving him a halo effect. "*Bonjour* Raph. *Pardon*, I'm running late. You 'av met our new bartender." He heaves a cardboard box onto a plastic chair. "Come and 'elp. Not you, Saskie, Raph." He rips open the carton with a knife, and there's the happy clink of bottles.

I polish the already-shiny dark timber counter and watch them chat and stack. They make a startling contrast – Marcel, so light, so carefree, Raphael, so dark, definitely not carefree.

"So, you two are friends," I say when Raphael returns to his bar stool and lights up another cigarette. "Marcel's one of the good guys, isn't he? I really need this job. He took a chance on me when I parlez Français the American way."

"We French can be picky about our language." He laughs which is more of a grimace. "Do you know the play *My Fair Lady*?"

"Of course. I'm Eliza since I arrived in Paris."

"Is it that bad? Well, I had to learn some lines for a school production in England, the part where Henry Higgins says, 'The French people don't care what they do, as long as they pronounce it properly.'"

"Ha. That leaves me out in the cold."

He folds his arms, leans forward. "I could be your Henry Higgins. We could practise French conversation together. There are some occasions where French is the only language that will do."

My mouth drops open. *Wow*. This guy. I turn away, looking for an ice bucket to plunge my face into, but make do with a bottle of water from the chiller. Rubbing the coolness over my cheeks, I return to the counter.

"I'm sorry." He rubs his hand over his mouth. "That was a bit—"

My heart hammers against my rib cage. "Not at all. Just feeling the heat." *Liar*. I take a gulp of icy water, swishing it around in my mouth, buying time while he watches me, one lip curled in a smile.

He hums a few more bars of *California Girls*. "Back to language. Can I help?"

"Yes. Could I run a phrase by you? '*Qu'est-ce que vous desirez?*'" I say slowly, taking care with the pronunciation.

"Not bad. You need to say it much faster." Raphael raises his eyebrows, so they disappear under his hair. "You have a phrase book in your apron pocket?"

"*Au contraire.* I stay connected." I flash the home screen of my new cell phone. "Language emergency? I've got translate.com."

"Show me. I rarely use my mobile phone, but we could swop numbers in case you have a language emergency." He grinds his half-smoked cigarette, leans across the counter. "Pardon. I forgot. Like everyone in Paris, I've been meaning to give up, but we cling to our bad habits."

"It's okay." I try not to sound prim. "I'm not used to people smoking inside buildings is all."

We put our heads together over our phones and one of his black curls whispers against my cheek, so close I smell his shampoo. My heart pounds an erratic rhythm. I never connected with Xavier, no matter how many times my father threw us together, but here I am, swapping phone numbers with Monsieur Suave French Guy. But I'd be crazy to think a gorgeous guy like Raphael would be interested in me when he has his pick of sophisticated French girls. I imagine them swooning, *ooh là là,* throwing themselves at his feet.

He scrolls through some words and phrases on my app., highlighting some for me. "These should help while you work." He hands me my cell. "Add them to your *Favorites.*"

I do, then drop my cell into my pocket.

He cups his chin in one hand and our eyes lock. His eyes are deep, dark and mysterious with a hint of danger. He's way too sexy. Way too attractive. Way too out-of-my-league.

I feel like a frumpy American in the face of his smooth sophistication. I've gone to a lot of trouble for my first day at work – full make up which has probably already sweated off in the heat, false eyelashes, hot red lipstick. I even curled my long blonde hair which I only do on special occasions, but the humidity is fast ironing them out. Those girls I pass on the street never have a hair out of place. Their clothes are classic, draped over bodies finely honed by working out, semi-starvation and a careful relationship with alcohol. I've got a slim runner's body but prefer my long hair in a ponytail and my face scrubbed clean. And I'm never careful with champagne unless I'm in intensive training.

Raphael breaks the silence. "When I got out of bed this morning, I never expected to meet a beautiful American girl behind the bar before evening."

If I were a Regency heroine, I'd swoon and reach for my fan. Instead, I ignore my trembling knees and tug at my T-shirt, smooth my sweaty palms on my jeans. "You think? Flatterer. I'd better get on." I decide he's one of those too-handsome guys who hit on every girl they meet. "Things to do before the hoards arrive." I look for something that needs my attention. "Er, the cash register."

"So, to answer your earlier question." He watches my fingers key in my code and today's date. "I desire a lot of things ... but ... I'll be happy with a Kronenbourg. I could get it myself, but I'll let you practise on me."

"Hmmm, France's favorite beer."

He tilts his head. "*Quoi?* How do you—?"

"Google. Where else?" I slam the register, look at Marcel polishing the refrigerator. He set us up for sure.

Marcel catches my eye, walks over to us, his blond quiff drooping. The French have no relationship with air conditioning that I can see and with the doors closed, the place is sweltering. Marcel's not your average bar manager in his tight designer jeans, button-down striped shirt, dotty pink bowtie, and pointy leather shoes. He'd be right at home mincing down the catwalk during Paris Fashion Week.

"Raph," he says, joining me behind the counter. "Let's have this meeting. Saskie, would you open while I talk with Raph for a few minutes?"

I clasp a hand over my mouth. *Oh My God! Noooooo.*

Raphael quirks an eyebrow. "I'm good, Marcel. Catch you tomorrow. I'm doing on-the-job training."

Marcel smiles. "I knew you two would get along." He strokes his goatee, watches us. "It will be great to 'ave 'elp from both of you today. It ees going to be craazzeee."

Uh-oh. "Why's that, Marcel?" My voice quivers.

Marcel massages his temples. "There ees a new art ex'abition up on Montmartre 'ill."

"No chance of a quiet first shift then." I try to quell the panic that feels like a thousand butterflies pounding against my stomach wall.

Raphael buckles his bag. "It's never a quiet night here, Saskia. So, Marcel, you're talking about the surrealist exhibition at the Centaquatre?"

Marcel nods, his quiff flops to the side. "*Oui*. Dali. I was sure you'd be going which is why I asked Saskia to start tonight."

"I'd planned to take a look." His gaze slides to me. "But I'll see it another night."

My heart does a little dance. Then I stop myself. What the hell am I doing? I've been in Paris five minutes and I'm already goofy over a guy. My career comes first. Men can wait, even one as hot as Raphael. "Please don't miss it on my account, Raphael."

"Don't worry, Saskia. I've been to my fair share of opening nights."

"Okay. I'll appreciate your help." The clock strikes two. I take several deep breaths. Crunch time. *Am I nervous?* I chew my knuckles. *Hell, yeah.* I reach under the counter for my tote. Flipping open my compact, I fix my jungle red lipstick, then remember I haven't served Raphael his beer. *Crap.*

"Ready?" Raphael looks over his shoulder as he strides across the room to push open the folding glass and timber doors. Half a dozen men in suits surge into the room, shake Raphael's hand, give Marcel first orders before I've stored my bag.

"Here I go," I say to Raphael who's returned, giving me a worried look. "Sorry, I forgot your beer." I grab the can from the refrigerator, rip the tab and plonk it on a coaster in front of him. Even though my legs feel close to collapse, I hurry to where three businessmen raise their hands in my direction.

"*Qu'est-ce que vous desirez?*" I speak fast, slide a glance at Raphael.

He winks, gives me the thumbs up, takes a mouthful of beer, then removes what looks like a sketch pad from his bag, flips it open.

The bar is go, go, go. The drinkers call to each other, call to Marcel for their wine and beer, call greetings to Raphael while he sketches. Occasionally he stands, shakes hands, grasps shoulders, and chats like each customer is an old friend.

The men slide secretive looks at me. Wink at me. Stare at me. Flirt with me.

Marcel's told me the afternoon clientele is mainly suits grabbing a quick bevvie between shady deals, street walkers coming in from the cold, the homeless needing a jolt of alcohol to see them through the long night, and dancers from the Moulin Rouge, thirsty from kicking their legs in the air and swimming naked with snakes. And the odd tourist who stumbles in, mistaking Marcel's Bar for the risqué den of iniquity next door.

My first customers, the three red-wine-drinking businessmen, empty two large bottles of Bordeaux in record time, raise their hands for another while they work their phones and each other. No different to a New York bar.

Serving Raphael his second beer, I notice he covers his drawing each time I pass. I wonder what he's sketching. I also wonder how it would feel to run my fingers through his thick black hair, how it would feel to kiss those lips, how it would feel to have those strong hands on me.

Stop it. Stop it. Stop it.

But I can't stop it. I keep seeing things I like about him. He's a mighty fine dresser. From head to toe he's in black – a black T-shirt hugs every gym-toned muscle, and that black leather-fringed vest is so Peter Fonda out of *Easy Rider*, one of Mom's favorite films. Then I see his belt buckle and my breath hitches in my throat. 'Harley-Davidson' stamped in gold plate. My mind flashes to my Harley, wheels spinning as Mom lay dying beside it. My legs shake. I cover my mouth, push back a scream. The image of Mom dying on the road, blood oozing from her head wound, flashes through my mind.

It's my fault Mom's dead.

"What's wrong, Saskia?" Raphael frowns, looks concerned. "Did a ghost walk over your grave?" He taps a nub of charcoal on the counter. When I don't answer, he says, "If it's the job, no need to panic. You're doing great. The customers love you." He rips open a packet of nut bread from the basket on the counter and takes a large bite. "No lunch." He winks at me. "Did you miss lunch too? Is that why you're so pale?"

There's a lull in orders. I force my breathing to slow. No panic attack on my first day, please God. I regret boasting to my father that I had my anxiety under control. I shake my head to clear it. "Strange for a Frenchman to miss lunch. I thought you had three-hour lunches. I took mine on the run as always."

He covers my hand with his. "You're welcome to grab a snack when you arrive. You need energy for this job. It's long and hard."

"Thanks. Listen, Raphael." I make a quick recovery, remove my hand from his, step back, jut out a hip. "You seem too comfortable here. Do you own the place?"

He stares at me as if deciding whether answering my question is a good idea. "Hmmm. Temporarily. Marcel's my good friend. I had some spare cash, so I helped him when his bottom line took a hit." He munches his bread with his beer chaser. "I prefer this side of the counter, although I step in and help when it's crazy. My real work is becoming the most famous living artist in France."

"An artist. Of course." *Wow.* Makes sense. Now I'm really interested. Seeing my customers are momentarily satiated, I lean over the counter, trying to see what's in his sketch book, but he slams it closed. "Are you famous? Should I know you?"

"Not yet, but you will." He winks, and I don't miss the double meaning. He tosses his piece of charcoal from hand to hand. "I'm paying my dues.

Working toward my big break. Spend most days sketching tourists on the Pont des Arts. A pretty good gig, you Americans would say. I'm working on name recognition."

"Awesome." I picture him flourishing his brushes for the tourists, flirting with the girls. I'm dying to know more, but a sea of thirsty customers surges into the bar waving money and credit cards, calling, "*Ici. S'il vous plaît.*"

A classy couple walk up behind Raphael, tap him on the shoulder. The guy's drop-dead handsome in his tux, his scarf loosely knotted in a faux casual way and his dark hair flops endearingly over his eyes like a young Hugh Grant's. She wears her light summer coat slipping slightly off her shoulder as though she can't make up her mind whether she's arriving or leaving. She's typical of the French women I've seen – stunning and sophisticated with her glossy, straight long black hair, kohl-ringed eyes and red-stained lips pursed in that decidedly French pout.

Raphael stands, shakes the man's hand, holds the woman's shoulders, kisses her on both cheeks. "*Bonjour,* Lamar, *bonjour* Bernelle." He turns to me. "Saskia Bell, meet Lamar Babin and Bernelle Barre. You'll see a lot of them. They come in most nights and share a bottle of Bordeaux on their way to the Centaquatre. Set them up, please."

"*Enchanté.*" I reach across the counter and shake hands.

"*Enchanté.*" Lamar's smile is friendly and curious, but Bernelle frowns, puffs out a breath, rolls her eyes, treats me to a what-rock-did-you-crawl-from-under? stare.

Despite Bernelle's silent insult, I load a tray as Raphael directs – Bordeaux, two small bottles of Evian, glasses, packets of nuts. "Here you go." I use my friendliest voice, carrying the tray from behind the counter. "Would you like the table near the door?"

"I've got it." Raphael takes the tray from me, beckons his friends, "Come."

While I pour beers with ever-improving heads, I watch them out of the corner of my eye. Raphael holds out the chair for Bernelle, whose coat has slipped farther down her shoulder, revealing a silky black low-cut dress. A small diamond winks from a gold chain at her throat. Raphael leans over the table to chat. Bernelle rubs the tip of a finger over her red bottom lip, edges her body closer to Raphael like he's a magnetic force. So, that's how it is. Why would I ever think someone as gorgeous as Raphael is single?

"Super glam couple," I say when he returns and helps me arrange more baskets of snacks down the counter.

"They're not a couple." He sits down after helping me serve the next wave. "She's the gallery hostess at the Centaquatre; Lamar's an artist's agent. They hang out professionally."

"Oh?" My heart plummets to my toes. "Is Bernelle *your* girlfriend?"

"Bernelle?" He laughs, slaps the counter, gives me a puzzled smile. "Never."

I wasn't expecting that. "She'd like to be."

He raises his eyebrows, glances across the room to where Bernelle chats with Lamar, her blood-red nail polish catching the light as she stabs a finger at him. Raphael leans closer to me, his lip curled, his expression hard to read. "Really?"

"Really." Sometimes, men don't have a clue. Bernelle would fall at his feet in a heartbeat.

But I'm pleased that Bernelle isn't his.

I pour. I serve. I smile.

I love this town.

Paris.

My happy place.

The place where I'm a different person from the one I was in New York. Out from under my father's influence. No Xanax in two weeks. Living life on my own terms. Who would have thought Paris would have this positive effect on me?

Marcel's Bar might be a hazy hole-in-the-wall drinkery, but it's in the chic-est city in the world. And there's a dreamy Frenchman whose dark and mysterious eyes watch me when he doesn't think I'm watching him. But I'm not interested, not one bit. I'm in Paris for my fashion career, not for men.

Not even one as gorgeous as up-and-coming-artist Monsieur Raphael Valentine.

CHAPTER NINE

As I exit the street door at the end of my shift, I'm surprised how much I've enjoyed the buzz in the bar. Even though the crowd was hectic, I stayed grounded, didn't panic too much and my rusty French improved with use. Tomorrow morning, I'll visit Madame Page at the Belleville hotel and take her a bunch of hot pink roses to say thank you for arranging the attic apartment and the job at Marcel's.

I stand just outside the bar door, rummaging through the fistful of notes and coins Marcel pushed into my hand as I left. The tips will cover the next two weeks' rent. *Woo hoo.* Along with my contract for freelance embroidery with L'Amour dans sa Vie, I'm on my way to financial independence. I'll keep my Hamptons' rent money for those expensive PTSD treatments and to launch my fashion career.

Raphael disappeared hours ago. No goodbye. Not so much as a wave. We were bantering like we'd known each other all our lives. He helped at the bar when we were slammed, then melted into the night when things dropped off. Perhaps he went to the Centaquatre to catch that art exhibition after all.

I jump back in fright when a shadowy figure steps from the dark passage between Marcel's and the barred-up shop next door.

I shriek, clutch my heart, back into the lit bar door behind me. Then ... "Raphael?"

"*Bonsoir*, Saskia." He saunters over, stands in front of me where I'm clutching the doorframe. The ubiquitous lit cigarette dangles from his fingers. Huddled in front of the next-door entrance is a homeless man. The man gathers his blankets around himself, leans back and watches us.

"Sorry for scaring you, Saskia." Raphael looks up and down the street where buses, cabs, and cars zip by. The sidewalk is crowded with revelers talking and singing at the top of their voices. "I came by to see you home

Uh-oh. We've enjoyed a flirtation tonight, but it's time to call a halt before I get sucked into Raphael's slipstream. "No, I'm good, thanks. I live just a short walk up the hill."

It starts to rain. I shrug into my light summer coat. I'm sweaty after the heat inside the bar, so I'm grateful for the cool. Or I would be if Raphael wasn't looking so damned hot with his black leather jacket slung over his shoulder à la James Dean.

He grinds his cigarette stub on the footpath with his boot heel, a habit I hate. I want to pick it up and throw it into the bin, but there's no bin in sight. "I'd rather see you home just in case," he says. "It's been a long night."

I tug the tie of my coat belt, leave the buckle dangling. "For you or me?"

"Both of us. I had a lot to do while you were working." He shoots up an eyebrow. "Are you saying you missed me?"

"Too busy." I blow out a breath. Well, not exactly a lie.

I shuffle from foot to foot, tempted by his offer, but I have no intention of starting something. "I didn't notice you leave." That much is the truth. "You've been great tonight, Raphael, and I appreciate it, but I've got this."

"No, I won't allow you on the streets this time of night. We're in the red-light district. No place for a woman to walk alone." Raphael steps closer, and I feel intimidated just like when I'm in a standoff with my father.

I grit my teeth. "You won't *allow* it? *Pfft*, I'm from New York. I can take care of myself, thanks all the same."

Raphael frowns at the homeless man who has just burped, then gestures toward the street where people dodge the rain and each other. Some meander down the sidewalk in a drunken dance. "Look at this crowd." A drunk throws his arm around Raphael's shoulder before wobbling inside Marcel's Bar. "You're new to Paris. Drunks, druggies and dealers are all over this place after dark. They don't tell you that in *Lonely Planet*."

The homeless man bangs his water bottle onto the pavement. "Hey, watch it," he says in French. "That's not nice."

"Give me a break, Enzo," Raphael says. "Go to sleep already."

I recognize the man. He came into the bar earlier for his free snacks and Evian which Raphael supplies to the local homeless. He keeps a supply under the bar and tonight, he handed them out himself, along with words of encouragement. Raphael is obviously a kind person, and he might be overprotective, but I loathe his bossy tone. Reminds me too much of Pa.

He reaches out, puts a hand on my shoulder. "I feel responsible for you. Marcel shouldn't have kept you so late."

"Don't blame Marcel. I'm responsible for myself. Please let go of my shoulder."

He drops his hand like he's been burned. "Pardon."

"Come on, girlie. Give him a break," Enzo says between noisy slurps of Evian. "He's quite a catch, you know." He rubs his thumb and middle fingers together.

Having this three-way conversation is bizarre. I turn on my heel, walk along the street in the direction of my new home. Raphael keeps pace, his heavy boots pound the sidewalk behind me. I keep walking, ignoring the light rain, but hyperaware of Raphael's closeness. "Raphael, I came to Paris with a list of rules." I sling the words over my shoulder. "Top of my list is taking care of myself."

"But Saskia." He lightly touches my elbow. "Don't live by rules. You're in France, not New York. Be wild and free."

That does sound tempting, but I'm far too stitched up to live wild and free. What would that be like? I stop. Spin on my heel, hands on hips, face him. "Without rules, Raphael, we're just animals."

He flinches. "I'm an animal then." He bares his teeth, growls. "But I'd love you to tame me."

"I'd love to see that." Enzo totters behind us, his blanket wrapped about his shoulders like an Egyptian mummy.

Enzo's too funny, but I'm exhausted. I'm used to different workdays, sitting at my workstation, creating fashion. Being on my feet for close to nine hours has sapped my energy. I crave my attic where I'll sip champagne, soak up Paris by night while I process all that's happened today. Raphael is keeping me from what I crave. "Raphael Valentine, go tame yourself. I'm walking home. Alone." Tossing my head, nose in the air, mouth in that French *pouf*, I hurry along the street putting distance between us.

"Goodnight, little bartender," Enzo calls. "You're a sassy one. I'll dream of you tonight."

Behind me, I hear the dull rumble of Raphael and Enzo in conversation. My thoughts keep time with the clack of my combat boots on the sidewalk. Raphael's definitely the most intriguing guy I've ever met, but I'm reaching for the stars. Men aren't in my orbit.

I brush raindrops from my face. Tugging up the hood of my coat, I push my way through the misty rain, passing flashing neon signs and late-night, edgy crowds and pimps slouching in doorways and risqué sex shops. I cringe when I see a group of men in shiny jackets and baggy trousers standing beside a garish pink sign of naked women, smoking, watching me through hooded eyes. I told Raphael I wasn't scared, but I am, just a little. I puff out rapid breaths, round the corner into rue des Martyrs, keep looking over my shoulder in case anyone's following me.

I'm making headway up the hilly street when a motorcycle purrs close to the sidewalk beside me. Its engine makes popping sounds as it idles. I stop breathing. *A Harley*. My hands fist. My fingernails cut into my palms. Stealing a peek, I press my heart with a closed fist. The Harley's black and red like mine, but a later model. I grab hold of a lamp post to stop falling like a drunkard.

The rider brakes beside me, props his bike against the curb, swings his leg over. "Saskia?" Leaning against the bike, legs crossed, he is smokin' hot. "Come for a ride."

I stare at him, saying nothing. A woman skids in her high heels, bumps into me, drops her umbrella, nearly knocks me over.

"Pardon." My boots dance over the slippery cobblestones.

Madame throws me a filthy look. "*Faites attention*, Mademoiselle." She picks up her umbrella, snaps it open and shut, sprays me with water, then huffs down the street.

Raphael laughs, takes off his helmet, tosses his hair loose, then watches me with those deep black eyes.

I focus on his helmet. A helmet would have given Mom a chance of surviving the head injury she sustained in the accident. No. No. No. I can't keep thinking of all the 'what if's'."

I'm not sure how long I've been crying when Raphael clears his throat. When I look up, he walks toward me. "Saskia? Can I help?"

"No. No one can help." I scrabble through my tote. Mop my face with a bunch of damp tissues. Face Raphael full on. I'm bewitched by both him and the bike. But ... if I cave, I'll hate myself. I swore on my dead Mom's grave I'd never ride a motorcycle again, even though my friends said that was the worst idea. *Face your fears head on, Sia*, Mira had said. *If you don't, you'll be afraid for the rest of your life.*

But – Oh My God, it's hard.

Raphael holds out another helmet. "This is for you, *ma belle* Saskia." He narrows his eyes at my sharp intake of breath. "Marcel keeps a spare. I'm better than an animal, *n'est-ce pas*? I wouldn't see a hair on your pretty head harmed." He turns and places both helmets onto the bike saddle and is at my side in one long stride.

I step through the misty rain to meet him.

"Saskia." His voice is husky. "It's been a long night waiting to get you alone."

I watch him watching me, his eyes deep in the shadows of his face. "Raphael. No. We can't do this," I mumble to my boots. "You're my boss."

"So?" He cradles my fingers in his, brushes his lips over the back of my hand. "What does being your boss have to do with anything?" He tightens his grip, a slight smile on his face which crinkles the fine lines around his eyes. He cups my chin, lifts my face until we're eye to eye. "Maybe it's different in New York, but we don't worry about such things in France."

Of course not.

"Come here." He wraps an arm around my waist until we're standing body to body. I smell Kronenbourg and Gauloises and that cologne he wears. He cups my chin in his rough artist's hands, tilts my head, then his lips press mine.

Holy crap. So many sensations – his smell, his warmth, his hands firm and strong on my back. But it's the movement of his mouth and his tongue that stands me on tip toe.

He trails a line of kisses down my neck like he's branding me. "You're captivating."

When he kisses my lips again, a whole new world opens. Even in the chilly rain, I feel hot. My eyes press tight, shutting out the world, not caring when passers-by applaud. The French do love lovers. *Lonely Planet* got that right.

Raphael rubs his hands up and down my back, drawing me closer to his body. Our lips touch again in the lightest of caresses, a fire flames in my belly.

"Now," he pushes back my damp hair, kisses my forehead, runs his hands down my arms, "let's get you onto my bike."

"No. Raphael, I can't. I'm almost home. I'm—" How can I admit I'm afraid of something I've loved since I bought my first bike at seventeen? Mom was against it but came to see it was a good way to travel fast between Manhattan and the Hamptons. If she knew exactly how fast she may not have been so enthusiastic.

Raphael places his hands onto my shoulders, I tremble all over. He looks at me and something in his eyes tells me he knows I am not just being coy. "You're upset about something. Are you afraid of motorcycles?" he asks quietly. "All you have to do is hang on. Leave the rest to me."

I fist my hands into balls, wondering if his words are prophetic. If it proves to be, our relationship will be short lived. But my legs are so weak after that kiss, I'd have trouble walking up the hill. I clear my throat, decision made. "All right." Before I chicken out, I slide onto the back saddle, sink into the soft damp leather, thinking how odd not to be in the driver's seat. *Okay, Mira, I'm facing my fears. I'm in Paris. Tonight, I'm wild and free. Happy?*

"Here." Raphael clips the spare helmet under my chin, snaps the face guard closed. "I'll show you central Paris. It could get chilly if the rain gets heavier. Got any gloves?"

"No. I hardly thought I'd need gloves in summer."

"True." He tugs on his long leather red and black gloves. "Lean forward and put your hands into my pockets if you want. Ready?"

I nod. Smile to myself. I'm having a crazy moment. I'm not giving into my fears. *Who would have thought I'd kiss a Frenchman tonight then take a bike ride in Paris?* This new life is *très* exciting.

He swings his leg over, revs the engine. Loud and throaty. The way I like it.

I lean against the backrest, clutch the bars.

"Here we go, Saskia. Hang on."

He merges into the traffic, cutting off a black Mercedes. He maneuvers his bike close to the big black car. The driver scowls. Thumps his horn – *aaht-aahht-bloooot, aaht-aahht-bloooot,* then winds down his window and flips us the bird.

Raphael laughs. "Okay back there?"

"Sure." I totally get the Mercedes driver's anger, but this is fun. How could I ever have thought I would never ride a bike again?

Raphael weaves between buses, taxis, motorbikes and scooters like he's on a racetrack, but so does everyone else. They drive like maniacs in this town.

We *vroom* through traffic faster than laser lights across the night sky. My face guard is saturated. Streets blur. Car lights bounce off the surface of the water. The Seine glitters from graceful arcs of bridges and walkways. Boats on night tours shimmer, their lights twinkling. The City of Lights. Lights everywhere. Enough to power whole countries. I've seen the Eiffel Tower many times, but tonight she sparkles in the distance like frothy champagne, lights zipping up and down her lacy steel frame like a runner on steroids.

We bounce along the cobbles in Place de la Concorde, past the monumental green and gold fountains that flank the Egyptian obelisk, onto the Champs-Elysées and the prettiest boulevard in the world sparkles with streams of light, bathing cars, double-decker buses and late-night strollers in a misty golden glow. We zip up the avenue, the Arc de Triomphe in our sights. I tighten my hold on Raphael's waist, hold up a finger and thumb, as if I'm taking pictures of every inch of Paris. I want this night burned forever in my memory.

Raphael plays dodgem with the traffic navigating the Arc. He zips between cars, bicycles, buses and cabs, hand working his horn. This is Raphael's city, and he owns it.

The rain pummels down, falling like a waterfall, a silver flowing veil in the streetlights. I lean forward, put my hands into Raphael's pockets, press my body against his damp leather jacket.

"Let's get you home," he says, after we idle on the sidewalk near the Arc to admire the twinkling lights on the Eiffel Tower and the laser beacons shooting through the heavens in rainbow colors. "What's your address?"

"An old building at the top of rue des Martyrs. Can't remember the name or the number."

"I'll find it. I know the street well."

We thunder through the backstreets behind the Champs in the direction of Montmartre. My adrenaline zooms into overdrive when he accelerates full throttle up the hill from Pigalle, past crowds spilling out the doors of Moulin Rouge, past old windmills, closed cafés, bouncing along slick cobbled streets.

"A little detour." He keeps going right to the top, brakes on the curb beside Sacré-Cœur. Crowds sit on the wide steps under umbrellas. Some strum guitars, others eat, drink, and laugh together.

The rain stops just for us. Through a halo of fog, Paris's rooftops are visible all the way to the horizon. A shimmery moon hangs over the city, cascading surreal light across my shivering shoulders. "This is magical," I whisper.

"It is that." Raphael helps me off the bike, removes my helmet.

I wring water from my dripping hair. "I've seen this view in daylight, but night and rain takes it to a whole other level."

"You can never move for the crowds," he looks around, "but tonight it's jam packed."

I don't like crowds pressing around me, but I wouldn't miss this experience for the world. "I'm glad you brought me. The view ... wow."

"Come with me." Taking my hand, he walks me to a little arcade to the side of the funicular. "This view is even better." Pushing his way through the crowd, ignoring the occasional protest, he leads me to an iron fence.

There's the Eiffel Tower in all her glory. I could reach out and touch her. I'm taken unawares when she explodes with lasers, twinkling lights and fireworks shooting into the air. The crowd behind us surges forward, we're pushed hard against the fence. I clutch Raphael's hand, imagining toppling to the ground below. Around us there are whistles and cheers and cries of, '*Vive la France!*'

A surge of adrenaline shoots through my veins at the sights and sounds surrounding me. "What's going on, Raphael?"

He holds up my hand, kisses the back of my palm, a smile lighting his face. "It's our *La quatorze juillet*. The Fourteenth of July. Today we celebrate Liberty, Equality, Fraternity. Those three concepts are never far from the French collective mind."

I knew the French were fiercely patriotic and loved their country and culture with passion, but now I see it for myself. The crowd lurches into the French national anthem. People wave little tricolor flags, join arms with their neighbors, sway, belt out 'La Marseillaise'. Raphael joins them, singing in a pleasant baritone. It hardly seems fair that he has looks, artistic talent *and* a voice. People link hands with us, I try to follow the words while we all swing to the rhythm of the rousing anthem while the night sky explodes in front of us. I love the 'Star-Spangled Banner', but I love the French anthem too. I'm going to learn every word and its history at my French language class next week.

'*Vive la France*!' is still ringing in my ears when Raphael revs his Harley for the ride down the hill to my seventeenth-century building.

It's been an exhilarating night, nothing like the quiet after-work meditations I'd planned for myself. "That was amazing, Raphael." I remove the helmet, lay my face against his back for the briefest moment. I'm sorry the night has to end.

He leans to the side, rubs my soaked thigh with his gloved hand. "There'll be many more nights like this," he says, then dismounts.

"You think?" This man doesn't suffer from lack of confidence.

"Of course." He holds me around the waist, steadies me while I swing my leg over. Removing his helmet, he takes mine and we stand hand in hand under the awning, bathed in garish red neon lights like we're waiting to see what's going to happen next.

He turns, puts a hand onto my shoulder, kisses the top of my head. "Okay?"

Despite my hammering heart, full of anticipation of his next move, I whisper, "Okay."

He places the helmets into the bike trunk, then locks the bike around a fire hydrant. Taking my hand, he walks me to the entrance. "I'll see you upstairs."

"Uh. No need. Uh. All right." My head is so scrambled, I'm surprised I remember the door code. I have left Madame Lavelle's card in the attic.

He places his hand around my shoulders, helps me inside.

Crossing the old black and white tiled foyer, I say, "I take no responsibility for your safety on the stairs, they're pretty crap."

He throws an arm over my shoulder. "I'll take my chances. I'm a Frenchman. I won't sue."

Laughing and falling over each other like a couple of drunks, we hang onto the banister, groping our way around and around and around the spiral staircase, laughing each time the lights activate just long enough to show us to the next landing.

My wet jeans chafe my thighs, my coat twists between my legs. I trip on a ripped piece of carpet and land knee first onto the stair. "Ouch."

Raphael hauls me to my feet. "Are you hurt? No? Why do you live in this place?"

"It's an adventure." I see a black shape. Hope it's not Mario, the drunk Italian from 5B. Turns out it's a big bag of rubbish someone's tossed on the step.

I giggle. "Fun, isn't it?

"Fun?" He holds my hand tight as we head ever upward. "It's like some broken-down medieval inn. Reminds me of my parent's country pile to be honest. There should be fires burning in sconces on the walls." He stabs a finger at the small round electric light that flicks off and on, threatening to plunge us into darkness. "I want to whisk you away from here."

"What? You're my knight in shining armor? That's taking medieval a bit far."

"Wait." He spins me around, points to the door of 5A, the apartment directly below the attic. "Why's that door boarded up? Is this building condemned? Are you squatting?"

"You're too funny, Raphael. The owner is remodeling. He's been working up from the ground floor. Apartment 5A is the last one to be finished. Hopefully he'll fix these rickety old stairs before someone breaks their neck. Come on." I tug his hand. "We're nearly there." I stumble up the last two steps, flop in front of my attic door, breathing hard. "*Phew*. First order of business tomorrow, find a gym."

He sits beside me, takes my head in his hands, turns me to face him. "Let's not worry about gym tonight." He kisses the tip of my nose, pulling me so close I feel his heart thumping against mine. "The night can't end here." He removes my hood, runs his fingers through my wet hair, lifts it from my face. "Invite me in and we can continue the adventure. You could make me coffee, or I could help you out of your wet clothes or we could practise French conversation. Or all three."

Oh My God! What do I do now?

CHAPTER TEN

"Hmmm." Raphael and I sit close together on the attic stairs under the light of one flickering overhead beam. "I'm not sure whether I should let you come in or not, Raphael. I've no coffee. There's hardly room enough for one person. And I've spent all night working on my French conversation. I need to chill." I hesitate while my thoughts crash around my head. "And you're a big guy. I'm not sure you'd fit inside the door. I'd hate you to get hurt."

His warm fingers rub the nape of my neck. He draws me close, kisses me. Nothing tentative about it. His mouth, so hot. A kiss that demands only one ending. "Don't worry about coffee," he murmurs. "Let's move straight to Plan B. You'll need help with those wet jeans and I'm willing to risk being hurt. I'm adventurous too."

I'm sure you are.

He's mastered the power of persuasion. Then he kisses me again, *very* persuasively.

I love the feel of his soft lips on mine, how his fingers skim my back under my wet coat, under my shirt. I shiver. "My door is so low you could be decapitated and your dreams of becoming the next Dali will be toast."

"Now who's being too funny? Are you going to let me in?" His voice is deep, alluring. "If you don't tonight, you'll let me in another night, so why not tonight?"

"Is that a trick question?" I wring water from my hair while I struggle with my conscience. Mom would shake her head if I had a one-night stand. Or would she? She'd prefer me to have a wild adventure with a hot Frenchman than marry Xavier and have not one, but two, men controlling me. Pa would be furious if I slept with a Frenchman. Thinking about the way he tried to foist Xavier onto me, Raphael suddenly becomes even more appealing.

"You know what, Raphael." I fling my rattails over my shoulder. "I'm not someone who rushes into things. I like to give things a lot of thought."

He holds my shoulders; we look into each other's eyes. He whispers, "Tonight, be a different you. Take a chance."

Yes. I could. Definitely. Tonight, I could be daring and shocking. Just once in my life. How would that feel?

"You're in France," he whispers, draws me close, goes for the jugular. "Live like the French."

I'm shivering from my wet clothes and the pressure to sleep with him on a first date, if that's what it was. But tonight, I'm a new person. I'm in this city to try new things. Raphael is a gorgeous new thing. But it's going to be on my terms. Once we're done, he can go back to being my boss. I take a deep breath. "When I came to France, I promised myself I'd try everything once, but this is a little more complicated than choosing espresso over a milky latte. But hmmm ... I'll try it. Once only. I'm not into casual sex."

"Okay. If you only want it to be once, I'll live with that." I feel the tension in his body as he takes my hands, lifts me to my feet. Without letting go, he lowers his head, kisses me, tasting, exploring, until my head swims and I stumble. Holding me tight around the waist, he bends low at the door, "I'll be careful not to lose my head."

I'll bet you will, handsome.

And so will I. I would have been happy sitting next to him all night, listening to his velvety smooth voice, but all at once I'm desperate to do more than listen. Heart pounding, I suck a deep breath. Where is the harm? We can sleep together tonight, just this once. But even while I think that, I know it's not going to be as simple as I'd like. My misgivings slide away one by one until I'm aware of only one thing – Raphael holding me close. Who better to tick 'having sex with a Frenchman' off my list?

Raphael holds my head while we crouch and enter my apartment. We laugh at the ridiculousness of a four-foot Hobbit door, especially when he's about six foot something, then our laughter stops. He scoops me into his arms. I wrap mine around his neck, lay my head against his shoulder. "Hard to see in here," he says, voice hoarse. "Don't you use sconces?"

"Ha." I reach over his shoulder, flick the switch.

"That's better, but not much." He staggers across the room.

"Put me down, Raphael. You'll hurt yourself."

"Fuck." He bumps into the coffee table. "I swore I saw a bed when you turned on the light." He hits the steel bed end with his knee and nearly topples forward.

He lays me none too gently on top of my Monet print bedcover, then manages to find a little space to wedge beside me. "Nice cover," he gasps. "You like Impressionism?"

"I do. My favorite style." I reach over him, flick the art deco Tiffany lamp I picked up at L'Objet qui Parle, a great little antique shop in my street. The rose-colored light bathes our bodies.

"You haven't seen my style yet. Come here." Under the glow of the lamplight, we wrestle wet clothes, laughing, kissing, fumbling with clinging T-shirts, tight trousers and squishy boots. I'm down to my black lace underwear; he's down to his Calvin Kleins.

I reach up and slide my hands down the length of his torso, feeling the well-honed muscles, silky-smooth skin, the dense bristle of dark chest hair. I've slept with my fair share of men and mostly enjoyed the experience, like trying different tastes from a smorgasbord. Something tells me that making love with this man is going to be a taste not easily forgotten.

Raphael jumps out of bed, then after a few bangs and curses, returns from the bathroom with one of my soft white towels. "I'm going to dry you," he says. "You're shivering."

Sure, I'm shivering, but not from rain. "Okay."

He unclips my bra, flicks off my undies, holds the towel above me, looks at me. "*Vous êtes si belle, Saskia.*" Then he busies himself drying my hair.

"Hey there, Monsieur Frenchman." My voice shakes. "Shouldn't you use '*tu*' not '*vous*' to someone you've seen naked?"

He chuckles, dabs my face with the towel. "You're taking our French conversation seriously. *Tu as raison,* uh, you're right. *Tu es si belle.*"

My heart goes *ka-boomb, ka-boomb, ka-boomb*. I'm loving this French conversation. Happiness bubbles up inside me.

He pays careful attention to my breasts, dries them, kisses them, works his way south, massages my stomach, my hips, my thighs. By the time he flips me over and massages my back, my heart is ready to jump out of my mouth.

"How does that feel?" His whisper is sexy as he dries my legs, feet and toes with great care.

"Divine," I gasp.

He rolls me onto my back and leans over me, his elbows on either side of my head, his face so close I imagine we see into each other's souls. "I love your body," he says, running his hands over my shoulders, my breasts and down the sides of my waist.

I've always been self-conscious about my body, seeing myself as too thin from all the running I do, so his words give me confidence. I take the towel from him, dry his damp curls, rub it across his shoulders, tug behind his neck, draw his face to mine. I love how his muscles ripple and flex at my touch. "I love yours, too."

"Enough," he says, his voice shaky. He takes the towel and gives himself a quick rubdown, then throws it onto the floor on top of our discarded clothes. Then he dives headfirst into my breasts.

The rain pummeling on the skylight increases the intimacy as we discover the secrets of each other's body. Everything vanishes into a veiled world where only the two of us exist. Whimpers of pleasure moan from my mouth. Everywhere he touches me, he scorches my skin. New sounds erupt from my throat. New whispers. New sighs. New moans. My heart contorts as Raphael's caresses breathe new life into me.

He parts my thighs, his mouth curved into a devastating grin.

"Raphael, do you have—?"

He rips a foil. "I've been thinking about sleeping with you all night. I came prepared."

My hands hold his head, rumple his long damp curls while my toes tangle in the sheets.

Oh My God!

If only this feeling could last forever. The nerves of my skin, the blood in my veins, the thoughts in my head swirl with Raphael. I squeeze my eyes tight, feeling the burn of his skin against mine. The silken stroke of his tongue. The skilled slide of his fingers. Every movement feeds my hunger. My desperation matches his. I urge him on, driven by a need I don't recognize. As he sinks into me, he groans, a raw primal sound. My body explodes with sensations. I call out, "Raphael! Raphael!" I lose sight of everything but him and the way he makes me feel.

Afterward, I lay in his arms listening to the rain drumming on the roof. We're wrapped in my damp bedcover, whispering French love words in each other's ears as we kiss, not wanting it to be over. So, it's not.

Pulling me close, he wraps me in front of his body, his arm encircles me. He murmurs soft French words, words I don't recognize, but they make me shiver in a protected cocoon where I feel dreamy, languid, loved. He brushes strands of damp hair from my face and just as I'm about to drift off, he startles me with a question. "What brings you to Paris, Sassy?"

Sassy. Tonight, I have been sassy. Being with him has brought out the dormant Sassy I didn't know existed. "What brought me to Paris? Hmmm," I mumble. "I came to Paris to live my own life, not the life someone else chose for me." A giggle erupts from my throat, my body shakes.

He leans on one elbow, puts his chin on my shoulder. "What's so funny?"

"I just got the joke. July 14th. Your Bastille Day or *La quatorze juillet*. It's the day of my liberation and revolution against my father's absolute rule. He'd planned to marry me off today. I feel like I've just been unfaithful to my new husband on our wedding night."

We laugh together at Xavier's and Pa's expense, then Raphael rolls onto his back, lights a cigarette, takes a few drags. "That's ironic. We're all trying to escape something. Some people escape by moving to another country or another city. To Paris, in your case. Mine too. I'm from down country, *la France profond*." I don't miss the sarcasm in his voice. He reaches for my hand, squeezes it. "But I'm glad you escaped and chose to be unfaithful with me." He blows smoke into the air. "Did you plan it or was it spur-of-the-moment?"

Outside my door, down the street, neon signs flicker in a rainy haze. Car tires go *thar-unk-thar-unk-thar-unk* on the wet cobbles below. That repetitive *NEE-eu-NEE-eu-NEE-eu* of police sirens seeps into my cozy little room. I suck a deep breath. "Spur-of-the-moment. My whole life in New York crashed and burned in one day. I had to escape or every dream I ever dreamed would have been crushed."

He brushes light fingers down my face. "I'm glad you chose Paris for your solo adventure."

I lift his free hand and kiss it. "Me too."

"*Ma petite*. I'm sorry." He drops his cigarette into the water glass on the nightstand. It sizzles in the dregs; a choking smell catches my throat. He picks up my tiny dot painting propped against the lamp, glancing at me when I cry out. Sitting up, tucking a pillow behind his back, he studies it under the lamplight. "What's this? Why are you upset?"

I grab my stomach; tears prick my eyes. "So many memories. It's my favorite memento of when Mom and I traveled together to Australia before I began my fashion internship."

He doesn't take his eyes off the painting. "So where in Australia was it painted?"

"In the northwest, in the Great Sandy Desert of the Kimberley." I scoot up in bed, gather the cover around me, wrap my arms around my knees.

"Why were you so far away?"

"Mom flew over to research an indigenous community of women for a *Conde Nast* article. It was surreal. We sat cross legged in a circle in the dirt in the ferocious sun beside artists in colorful print dresses and rag turbans. I tasted red dust on my tongue. We watched them paint against a backdrop of deep red escarpment and a freshwater soak. These women were amazing. Mom and I gazed, fascinated, as the different colored dots merged into figures that told a story, a weaving of sacred myth and legend."

He holds the picture closer to the light. "This is extraordinary. Every dot. Every color. I'd like to paint this style, but it's a sacred form." He carefully puts it back onto the table, takes my hand in his, rubs his thumb over my palm. "Dot paintings always hold secrets. Do you know the secrets behind this one?"

"I do, but it's a long story. Not for tonight." The whole desert experience was like being in a fortune teller's booth. If only I knew what I now know.

"We've got time." He slings an arm over my shoulder, pulls me close so my head lies in the crook of his arm. "Tell me the story." Raphael's voice is scarcely above a whisper.

I wipe my sweaty face with the sheet. He's so intense. Must he delve the depths of everything? My throat burns. My tongue goes numb. I want to burrow under the covers. A panic attack threatens. I've been doing so well. Until now. No. I won't give in. I'm in control. Taking several deep breaths, I hold my throat and launch into my tale. "Kumpaya Bidu Ngalangka was her name. She didn't sign her work. Her rendition, her style, is signature enough. She painted Mom's life." *And death.*

"Kumpaya has other paintings in this style?"

"Yes. Her paintings are very spiritual. She's a diviner who reads the spirit world." My throat clogs and I struggle for words. "It was like every other element in Mom's and my life was stripped away that day, only the aboriginal symbols of air and fire, representing some aspect of the heavens, remained."

"Ah, you're coming to the part where she paints this." He holds my treasured painting again.

"Yes," I whisper. "Kumpaya wielded her tiny stick with pigments sourced from the earth, watching Mom as the dots chased across the canvas like her hand was propelled by a spiritual force." I am mute. The memories pour over me, overwhelming in their ferocity.

"Come, Sassy." Raphael squeezes my shoulder. "Don't stop."

Blowing out a long breath, I begin again. "Under a scraggly river red gum, Kumpaya held Mom's hands. Her prophecy flowed over us, each syllable an arrow to my heart."

"Why?" Raphael runs his fingers through my hair. "What did she say to get such a strong reaction?"

"She prophesied Mom's death less than five years from our visit." My tears run freely but I don't bother to dab them away. "Mom was all calm acceptance, while I froze like a petrified tree. I adored Mom. I leaned on her. Life without her was beyond imagining. I rejected Kumpaya's words, told myself she was rubbish."

"It must have been stressful hearing something like that to say the least." He kisses my wet cheek.

"It has been. But there's more. After she warned us of Mom's death, it was my turn. "My child," she said, "what you dream will come true, but not the way you expect. Raphael, how could she know of my dreams of success in the fashion world? My reaction was pure anger. How could she possibly know when Mom was going to die? At the time I thought, oh, for God's sake. What a charlatan."

"Sassy. Don't tell me—"

I nod my head. "Kumpaya spoke the truth. About Mom."

I press my face into his chest, my mind filled with the image of Mom roaring away on my Harley. "Mom died in an accident exactly four years after our trip to Australia. I killed her."

"I'm sure you didn't kill her, *ma petite*." He brushes hair from my eyes, kisses my forehead. "Whatever happened, it wasn't your fault."

"You don't understand. That's why I was so upset seeing your Harley tonight. Mom died riding *my* Harley. I should have watched her more carefully. I had the knowledge, but I dismissed it because I rejected Kumpaya's words."

"I saw something in your eyes tonight when I pulled my bike to the curb, something beyond fear."

I nod. "Guilt. Regret. Remorse." I take the painting, tilt it his way. I need to finish this conversation. It's too much. Emotions rage through me. Loss. Oh, the loss. "Raphael, the dots and figures show a person's spirit entering the Land of the Dead. Kumpaya believes the human spirit is indestructible. From the ashes of fire come regeneration, she assured us." Tears form behind my eyes like a dam about to break. "This painting means Mom's spirit lives eternally."

Raphael's deep dark eyes bore into mine. "That is a comfort."

"I'd rather have her with me." My voice breaks.

"Of course. But maybe Kumpaya spoke truth about you, too, Sassy. You were focused on success in New York. But your success will happen in Paris. I feel it in my bones."

"I'm pleased to have your vote of confidence."

He wraps his arms around me. "You have more than my vote of confidence," he murmurs.

I turn away from him, sobs wrack my body, my pillow soaks with tears.

Raphael pulls the quilt around me, whispers my name over and over, strokes my back. "Sassy. I'm sorry I pushed you. Forgive me."

"Mom. Mom. Mom," I sob. Eventually I drift off to sleep in his arms while his voice whispering soft French words soothes me.

Like every other night since the accident, I dream of Mom in the Land of the Dead. She calls to me. I scream her name, my heart shatters. She turns her back on me and runs away so fast I can't catch her. *Guilty. Guilty. Guilty,* the voices shriek. *You killed your mom.* I wake, screaming, sweat dripping down my temples, my body trembling.

Raphael holds me close, cradles me in his arms. "Ssh, *ma petite.* It's a nightmare. You're safe. I've got you. Ssh. Ssh. Ssh." He rearranges the quilt around me, and the warmth helps lull me back to sleep.

We wake, bathed in the colors of sunrise pouring in through the skylight, windows and door. Raphael is ecstatic, not because there's a naked girl in his arms. He jumps out of bed and strides the five steps to the floor-to-ceiling windows, frightening the doves sleeping under the eaves. They flutter off, making grumpy noises.

"The light." He waves his arms. "It burns the zinc rooftops, pours through your windows and skylight, setting your whole room alight. I see why you love it here in the attic." He slaps the windowsill, then turns to me, grinning like he's found the holy grail.

I like sunrise too, but this morning I like Raphael more. Warmth washes over me when I remember his tenderness through the night when he understood my nightmares. Maybe he suffers nightmares too.

While he bathes in the marvelous light, I visit the bathroom, pick off my false eyelashes and splash my face. I clutch the sink rim, lean close to the speckled mirror, sigh at my pitiful reflection – puffy eyes, creased cheeks, swollen lips, ratty hair. Hmmm. I don't do so well on a couple hours sleep. I clean my face, brush my hair, jump back into bed. Propping myself onto one elbow, I whisper, "Come back to bed, Frenchman." Raphael has turned on some switch and I want to enjoy having sex with him again before he leaves. I want my flesh to melt into his. I want to forget that lost look in Mom's eyes as she turned away from me in my dream.

I smile at my Frenchman standing naked at the window, mesmerized by my view. The doves flutter in the distance, waiting for him to return to bed so they can go back to sleep. Finally, over his fascination with the sunrise, he turns to me, smiles, crawls back into bed, pulls the covers over our heads so we're lost in our own magical world.

I'm in Paris. I'm living a little. I'm wild. I'm free.

"I want to spend every night in your bed, Sassy," he murmurs, driving me crazy with his caresses, his kisses, his French love words.

Oh My God!

What have I done?

I came here to escape men.

I've broken my no-man rule.

And loving every moment.

CHAPTER ELEVEN

If I wrote a book a month about Raphael's and my relationship, this is how it would read:

July. *Summer Love is Sweet.*

August. *Summer Love Hots Up.*

When I'm not struggling with French language classes; sweating over my translations of *Le Monde*; stitching embroidery for Catherine; working at the bar; running in the hills behind Montmartre, I spend every moment with Raphael. When he's not painting or selling his creations, he knocks at my door, smiles his devastating smile, and we embark on another of our moveable feasts of Parisian delights. I put on my bikini; he puts on his board shorts. We swim and play volleyball at the man-made beach at the Hotel de Ville; we picnic on baguettes and champagne on the banks of the Seine opposite fire-blackened Notre Dame, dangling our feet above the water, tossing breadcrumbs to the ducks, taking selfies to send Mira, with the Gothic church behind us bursting into shimmering gold, scorched by the setting sun. We push our way through enchanting doorways hidden from tourists behind vine-covered walls, sip drinks in tiny, intimate bars in dark alleys in Montmartre, but best of all, Raphael often joins me in lighting a candle to Mom in Sacré-Cœur. Standing arm in arm before the flickering lights, I say a little prayer of thanks to God for sending me Raphael. Raphael buys a candle and says his own prayer and I wonder what he prays for that makes his face so dark.

We share romantic dinners at Lasserre near the Tuileries with its open roof, gold chandeliers and tasting menus, which is like eating the food of angels. Every day he brings me a bouquet of perfect red roses to fill my attic with a to-die fragrance.

Raphael's my angel. How did I exist before he came into my life?

But our sizzling summer crashes to an end. With the approach of autumn, everything changes and not just the foliage on the trees. I question everything that has happened between us these past months.

September's title: *The Chill of Autumn.*

A bump. A curse. My bed shakes. A voice rumbles. "It's time you moved out of this ridiculous little doll's house."

Huh? What? How did Pa find me? I squint one eye open. *Not Pa. Raphael.* He's plonked himself on the edge of my bed and holds out a takeout of my favorite brew. I slowly sit up, wrap the coverlet tight around my shoulders against the chill, reach a shaky hand for the coffee. I'm mad tight right now. "Thanks." I say through clenched teeth. "What brings you here so early? Er ... what did you just say? For a minute I thought I heard you talking about my moving out, but I must have been mistaken."

He lowers his cup. "I came early because I need to talk to you. I know you love your attic, Sassy, and I get its charm, but you deserve something much, much better. What would your father think of your living here?"

My whole body stiffens with outrage. What a dirty trick. "*What.* How dare you bring my father into it. He's a total douche bag. Where I live in Paris is my concern. Not Pa's. Not yours." I swallow my fury with another gulp of coffee, scalding my throat. Just when I was thinking Raphael was pretty close to a god, he channels Pa.

He takes my cup, carefully places it on the nightstand. Holding my head between his hands, he forces me to look at him. He's the epitome of hotness in his low-slung jeans, black T-shirt, boots and messy curls. He always looks photo-shoot ready 24/7. It's hardly fair when I'm half asleep, naked, my hair messy and no doubt I have creases in my forehead from frowning. "*Mon ange*. Don't overreact. Madame Lavelle tells me Apartment 5A's remodel is nearly complete. I think you should move in. That way you'll have your own workroom, so much more space than you have here." He draws me close and kisses me long and hard. "I'm sorry to bring your father into it. I was out of line. But we could even move in together," he whispers. "Wouldn't you like that?"

I clutch my throat. "No. *What?* We're having a great time together. Why complicate things? If we move in together, we'll have to compromise to keep each other happy. We both have so much work to do to get our careers on track. It's far better to keep our work lives separate."

His face tightens. He looks vulnerable. It's good to see him not in complete control for a change. Then he cocks his eyebrow with the power of a Harley at full throttle. "We're doing far more than having a great time. And you know it." I don't miss the bite of ice in his voice.

Seriously? I do, but I thought that was just me. "Ummm." I scramble for a retort.

Raphael, unlike me, isn't short of words. "I love this building. It's got loads of character." He tilts his head to the side. "Apartment 5A is ours if we want it. I've already chosen the color scheme which Madame Lavelle was happy to accept. How does sharing a bottle of wine and watching the sunset over the rooftops from our balcony every evening sound?" He hands me my coffee, quirks an eyebrow.

I upend the cup, burn my throat again. "Just like that? Madame Lavelle knows more about your plans than I do."

He knits his eyebrows into a frown. Taking the cup from me, putting it out of reach, his hands band my wrists in that authoritative way he has when he wants to drive home his point. "You know more than you'll admit," he says in his sexiest voice. "I love being with you. You love being with me. It's time to take it to the next level." He squeezes my hands, kisses my knuckles, gazes into my eyes. "Lovers do it all the time."

I snatch my hands from his. "Raphael, this is not how it's done. We've only known each other, what," I count on my fingers, "eight weeks? Far too soon to move in together." Uh-oh. I never saw this coming any more than Pa's pick for my husband or Romance is Born giving me the bullet. Why do people push me around? Okay. The old me was an easy target. The new me doesn't take kindly to cavalier treatment.

"Sassy. It's great timing. You're two weeks into your fashion course. Look at this place." He points to my work area. "Every surface, littered with paper, fabric and sketches. Those IKEA shelves could collapse. Your sewing machines takes up so much room. And your mannequin?" He points to it standing in a corner half dressed, giving him the eye. His gaze searches mine like there could not possibly be any argument.

I remember the day he helped me move furniture into the attic. He heaved everything up those rickety six flights of stairs, including my industrial sewing machine. Then he built the worktable and bookshelves. Together, we assembled my life-sized mannequin, before we crashed onto the bed in an uproar of laughter, staring at the strange creature we created together.

He's right, of course he's right. But I hate being told what's best for me. My fingers flex. "I don't mind how small it is. I'm enjoying living with less." And I am. It's not like I don't feel grateful for the luxurious life Pa provided for me even when we weren't on speaking terms, but now with all the trimmings gone that I'd taken for granted, I feel happier, in control, my own person, beholden to no one. And I'm not about to give up that freedom.

Raphael's not finished sweet talking. "You do great work. Do something about the lack of space so you can expand your repertoire. This is an opportunity, not a threat."

My heart thumps wildly. Trigger words. I've heard enough about opportunities and threats during years of therapy. I lift my knees, hug them close to my chest. My walls go up. Raphael's arguments sound mighty close to how my father always pulled his snake charmer act, how he offered me things to get something in return. "So sweet of you, Raphael. And I *am* going to do something about moving. The day I moved in here, Madame Lavelle said I could have 5A when the remodel was complete. Maybe when you got involved, she thought I knew it was ready."

He rubs the back of his head. "I guess."

I raise my head, look him in the eye. "This Paris gig is on my own terms. I'll move into 5A, but not with you. It's far too early in our relationship. I need my independence."

"I'll never take away your independence. I've never held back any woman I've been with."

"That's good to know, Raphael, and that's as it should be. You've seen my frustration with lack of space to work in the attic, but I've just been so happy to have a place of my own for the first time ever. I love it in a way you wouldn't understand. I won't let it go. I'm keeping it when I move downstairs."

He leans over the bed. "Sharing with me won't be a huge change. I often stay over, or you sleep at my apartment. Is it such a big deal to move in together?"

I bang my head on my knees. "Yes. It *is* a big deal, Raphael. The attic is *my* place. I guess you think I'm selfish when you've been so thoughtful in so many ways, but 5A will be *my* place too. For now."

He kneels beside the bed, reaches up and brushes his fingers through my hair. "Tell me why you feel this way."

"Okay." I reach for his hands. "This may seem petty to you, but this is the first time in my life I've chosen where I live. Growing up, it was in Pa's luxurious Fifth Avenue apartment where I felt like a bird in a gilded cage. Holidays in France and the Hamptons saved me. The attic isn't much, but it feels like heaven because I found it and pay for it myself." I squeeze his hands. "I'll take the small step to a bigger apartment, but that's all the change I need for now."

He leans forward and kisses me full on the mouth. "Sassy, relationships aren't static. Think how amazing it will be living together." He teases his tongue along my bottom lip. "I want to have you beside me all night every night. I hate riding home alone, heartsick after leaving you, not waking up beside you every day."

That hot tongue of his messes with my head. I push him away. "Raphael, I slept with you on the first night we met for one reason only – to experience sleeping with a sexy Frenchman." There was a lot more to my decision to sleep with Raphael than the fact he was French and sexy. My first shift at the bar was made so much easier because he was by my side, considering my needs, supporting me in a new environment, flirting with me, taking me on the most exhilarating bike ride ever. He really is a keeper, but do I really believe I can keep him?

"So, you told me. Compared to sleeping with—?"

"A work-obsessed New Yorker checking his cell every five minutes and nearly having a coronary every time the stock exchange dipped." I joke. "I'll bet you don't even know where your phone is."

Raphael laughs, just a little, then stands and strides across the room, staring out the window. He turns around and faces me, leaning his elbows against the windowsill. He's a still-life, posed against blue sky and puffy white clouds. "Sassy," he says quietly, "I know I said I wouldn't lose my head when I came in here that first night," he points to the door, "but, I did. You're like no one else I've been with." He shuts his eyes, takes a deep breath. "I'm in love with you."

What? Is he kidding? "You *love* me? I thought it was just about great sex for you."

He picks my woolen throw off the floor where it fell last night when we started making out on the couch. He rearranges it over the sofa. Everything has to be a work of art with Raphael. "Maybe it seemed like it was just sex at first, but it never was for me." He props himself on the back of the sofa, folds his arms. "We're great friends. We get each other. We're in sync. Have been from that first night when you trusted me enough to tell me about your maman."

I tap my temples with my fingers. He's caught me completely off guard. So many people have manipulated me in the past it makes me paranoid. Does Raphael see some weakness in me he can exploit? That's not happening. I'm in control of my life. "You've never so much as hinted that you want commitment, so I've tried to dismiss the ways you hurt me."

He looks startled, pushes himself off the sofa, shoves his hands into his back jeans' pockets. Tilting his head, he strides toward me. "Hurt you? I had no idea. Tell me what I've done so I can fix it."

"You sure?"

"I'm sure." He frowns, rocks on his heels. "Let me have it." Hands on hips, he rolls his head between his shoulders then straightens, knits his brow.

"Okay." I reach for my coffee cup, but it's empty. *Crap*. I hold onto it anyway. "Women flirt with you and you flirt back. Would you like it if I did the same? You know, the old double standard." I squash the cup so hard the lid pops off.

Raphael swoops and catches it. He can't stand mess. How could he ever live with me? "Go on." He fiddles with the lid.

"We're never seated next to each other at your friends' dinner parties. That makes me uncomfortable, especially when the men I'm next to flirt outrageously right in front of you and you don't seem to care. Then I think, oh, well, it's not like we're committed."

He hits his forehead with his palm. "I can explain. Go on."

A pain shoots through my heart. "One word. Bernelle. She throws herself at you every night at the bar. She drapes her body against yours while she looks slyly over your shoulder at me." I toss my ruined cup onto the nightstand; wait to see how he's going to deal with this.

He rushes across the floor, props his butt on the side of the bed, takes my hand. "I'm sorry, *mon ange*. I was oblivious, *merde*. First, dinner parties.

There's an unwritten rule in France: if you sleep together, you don't sit together. It would look odd if I asked the hosts to change that custom for us. It's not personal, so I hope you can live with it. If not, I'll change it."

I flap my free hand over my face. "Oh, just another screwed-up French tradition. Everything is so regimented. Look at Charles at Café de Flore adjusting my beret last night because it sat wrong. Ridiculous. But it's Bernelle and your flirting I'm more concerned about."

A blush creeps up his neck. He looks guilty. *Aha.* "Bernelle's and my relationship is strictly business. She'll host my first exhibition at the Centaquatre, so I play along. I've no romantic feelings for her whatsoever. But I'll keep my distance if that's what you want."

I snort. "It has to be you who wants it. But you enjoy the flirt, don't you?"

He holds my hands, lifts them to his lips, kisses my fingers one by one. "I'm sorry. To the French, flirtation is a game. It's in our DNA. You're right. I'd be jealous if you did the same. From now on, you'll have all of me."

Having all of Raphael is a daunting proposition. "I'm flattered that you'd try to change for me, but I doubt you could if it's in your DNA. Which is why I don't think we'll make it long-term. I'd never trust you with other women." I run my hands through my hair. "You seem to know every woman in Paris and the way they look at you, I wonder if you've slept with most of them."

His lips turn up in a smile. I've pandered to his ego when I shouldn't have. "Paris is really just a big town," he says airily. "I know the movers and shakers, but that's because of the political events I've attended with my father when my mother refused to go. But no matter how many women I know, you're the only one for me. We *are* long-term. Trust me."

I shrug. He's told me about his father, the politician, a Minister of Something. How could I ever fit into that crowd of Parisian elites, the *demi-monde*? I never sat easily with New York elites even though I was one. "Maybe I'm just too American when it comes to relationships." Ignoring his shaking head, I continue. "We've shared some great times, but I'm constantly expecting you to move onto someone from your social set. God knows, you're spoiled for choice."

"Stop it, Sassy. You're just being silly. *You're* my choice." But his grin shows me he's pleased I'm jealous.

I reach for my coffee cup again, forgetting it's a ruined mess. Raphael hands me his untouched brew. It's cold, but it's coffee, so I pour it down my throat. "I'll never be accepted into Parisian society except as your plus-one. I've played that role in New York for the past two years and I hate it." I put the empty cup down. "I need time to think."

His words tumble over each other in his haste to firm the deal. '*D'accord.* Madame Lavelle needs an answer. I'll be disappointed at not moving in with you, but Sassy, take 5A for yourself. What about your attic? How will you use it?"

I shrug. "I'm not sure yet, but I'll find a use for it."

"How about we share it so we can both expand?" Before I try the idea out for size, he says, "I need space to try new techniques. I'm ready to take my art to a new level just like you're doing with your fashion."

My heart beats so fast, my words trip over themselves in my rush to get them out. "Sharing the attic is fine, but it won't work if we're there at the same time. But I like the idea of you painting, me creating fabric designs from the colors I see in here at sunrise and sunset."

"Of course." He throws himself on top of me, forcing my knees down so we lie face to face, body to body. He kisses me, his lips moist and delicious. "I admit I've been casual in past relationships, Sassy. But there was something special about you from the start." He looks into my eyes so I can see how serious he is. "I've not slept with anyone else since I met you."

I turn my head away, sucking my top lip with the bottom. "*Whoop-de-doo.* Raphael. Monogamous? You? I never thought that was a French thing." Why am I so ready to put him down? I know he's not cheated on me. When would he find the time seeing we've been together every day, whether working at the bar or getting around Paris?

His face turns bright red. "Bullshit. We French can be monogamous if we choose. And I choose." His eyes cloud over. I see a flicker of pain. "You've such a low opinion of me. I don't deserve it. I'm committed to you."

I drop my hands to my sides before I give in to my urge to stroke his curls like I do after we've made love. "Committed you say. That word sounds strange coming from someone who lives wild and free. Someone who doesn't believe in rules. Someone who admitted to being an animal."

He rises on his elbows, his face so close to mine I see red flush his cheeks and his eyes darken. "Don't insult me with my own words. Maybe it's unfair to expect you to know how much I've changed when you didn't know me before. But I have. Let me prove it." He brushes my cheeks gently with his fingers, sending heat flares down my belly. He places my hands behind my head and holds them in one of his while his other massages my bare shoulders, traces my face, my collarbone, stopping just above my breasts. "I love you, Sassy. I never want to let you go," he murmurs between hot kisses. Ending the kiss, he watches me, eyebrows raised, his face uncertain.

Hot breath tears in and out of my throat. I'd love to stay in his arms and make love with him. I know that's what he wants, but instead I say, "Raphael, I can't think while you're kissing me. I never expected you to fall in love with me."

He jerks his head back like I slapped him. "So why have you stayed with me?"

I can't help tears pooling behind my eyes and one or two running down my face into my ears. "You know I came to France prepared to embrace everything about French culture. In other words, I wanted to reclaim my Frenchness, if there's such a word. You were my first encounter here. The perfect partner." That is so true. He treats me wonderfully; he's a fabulous lover; he dispenses kindness along with drinks at the bar; he's thrilling to be with. He's opened up a whole new world I never knew existed.

Raphael screws up his face like he's tasted out-of-date yoghurt. "Do you want to try out more Frenchmen? Have more encounters? Is that what you mean?"

"Of course not. I hit the jackpot with you." I flash to Xavier and his endless conversations about his latest property development on Billionaire Row, Park Avenue, where his parents live on the ninety-second floor, then there's his dream of becoming mayor of New York. Heaven help us. Here's Raphael, honestly working on his art. "Just thinking about you does all sorts of naughty things to me."

He smooths my bed hair with gentle hands. "What naughty things? Tell me."

I'm not telling him how he brings to life parts of me that have been numb and cold and untouched for so long. I'm not telling him that I've loved him from the first night we met and have tried to deny it as I felt my independence threatened by his large personality. "Hey." I try for a flippant tone. "I never thought we'd last more than a night, a week, a month, let alone talk about moving in together. This is a whole lot of crazy." Typical me, drifting along, caught up in the slipstream of life. Raphael's a powerful slipstream. But it's time to wade to shore. Alone? Or together?

"Come here." He wraps his arms around me.

I feel safe and loved in his arms. His heart beats in rhythm with mine. *Boom-diddy-boom.* I rub my hands over his bare back under his T-shirt, loving the feel of his silky-smooth skin, my thoughts full of how he rocks my world.

"*Mon ange,*" he whispers. "I think about you, about us, all the time. It does naughty things to me, too. You're in my head when I'm painting. You're in my head when I'm sleeping. You're in my head. Constantly. You get me in a way no other woman has." He looks at me and a flicker of doubt crosses his face. There's another woman or two who got to him before I did.

I can't go any deeper into a relationship with someone, who despite his fabulousness, reminds me of my father. Falling for Raphael was dangerous. Chills shoot through me. I puff out shallow breaths and untangle from his arms. His eyes are gentle and soft, but I'm sure mine are panicked. "Raphael, Madame Lavelle will give me time." I wipe my forehead with the back of my hand, feeling the sweat. "And so must you. We can't rush things. You've given me a lot to think about."

Annoyance flashes across his face. "What's there to think about?" He jumps off the bed, grabs his coat, heads for the door. "Let me know when you make up your mind." He would have slammed the door I suppose, except it's hard to slam a creaky old timber door.

I shut my eyes, lie still, deep breathe, listen to his boots go *clumpety-clump* down the stairs. This is it. He's upset I won't do what he wants. He's walking away.

We've been having such a great time.

Now he's gone and spoiled it.

Bloody Frenchman.

CHAPTER TWELVE

I pound Montmartre's sidewalks in an effort to reclaim my equilibrium. Exercise is good for my PTSD, but it's not just that. Running has long been my exercise of choice. It became my focus when I entered my first marathon in my teens when Mom asked me to run with her. I was hooked. I'm entering the Paris Marathon which is only weeks away. Running the marathon will be a way of facing my fears, proving to myself I'm no longer afraid.

The conversation with Raphael has rattled me. When the sound of his boots faded, I'd dressed in my running gear, thrown on my puffa jacket, left the apartment. I'm determined to remain true to my vow to be independent. Which would be sorely threatened if we moved in together.

Running through the quaint back streets of Montmartre exhilarates me. I see history in every inch – the Renoir gardens, the tiny vineyard which produces really bad wine because it slopes the wrong way, the quaint half-timbered medieval buildings that evaded Baron Haussman's wrecking ball. But today exercise is not having its euphoric effect, even though sweat seeps from my body and my lungs burn. It's a chore to run to the top of the hill into the busy village center to the statue of the first bishop of Paris, Saint

Denis, who stands holding his decapitated head. According to legend, after being decapitated, he picked up his head and walked six kilometers. I've lost my head to Raphael; he claims he's lost his to me. But has he? Really?

Training over, I jump onto the metro at Lamarck Caulaincourt in the direction of Charles de Gaulle Etoile. While the train zips along, I wipe my sweaty forehead with the back of my hand, gulp from my water bottle, think about how love is like riding the metro with all its bumps and jolts. This morning I have been bumped and jolted out of my dream state.

The train screeches to a halt at the Arc de Triomphe end of Champs-Elysées. After I navigate the endless corridors, the escalator rises to ground level and the Parisian blue-gray sky bathes me in brilliance. The Champs always lifts my spirits. I keep my distance from the crowds as much as I can, close my eyes and hold my face to the sun. Opening my eyes, I turn around and look down the Champs at the thick alley of horse chestnut trees, so pretty with the first tinge of autumn gold brushing their leaf tips.

Finding a seat on the Champs side of the Arc where a dozen avenues meet, I gaze above sleek cars, red tourist buses, motorcycles, bicycles, and taxis, glimpse the steely gray lacework of the Eiffel Tower. This is the spot where Raphael idled his bike on the night of our exhilarating ride through Paris in the pouring rain.

The night I fell in love with him.

I can't deny it.

Resting my elbows on my knees, I cover my face with my hands. Today Mom's absence is overwhelming. Loneliness bites. It's tempting to call Mira, but she's still grappling to find her way as Head Designer under Roberto's and Isabella's judgmental eye. I won't worry her with my problems. I'm a grown up. It's time I sorted things out by myself.

I empty my mind, concentrate on finding a solution to the problem at hand. I've given Raphael precedence over my fashion dream. I've been sketching designs ever since I opened my first box of crayons, but now I'm in an intense relationship, I start a project, then toss it into the bin. I barely keep up with course requirements at the Institut. A panicked feeling roils in my gut. I need both Raphael and my fashion career, but how do I make them compatible?

I flash to my worktable which dominates the space near the attic windows. It overflows with my tools of trade and will get worse now I'm sketching and sewing for my assignments at the Institut. Moving out of the attic is the right thing. Raphael moving in is the wrong thing.

I need my own space. To grow. To become strong. To dream.

"Are you safe, Mademoiselle?" A tour bus driver stands in front of me, speaking in deeply accented English. Leaning down, he peers at me, his soft, wavy black hair falling to his shoulders like Raphael's. He offers me a pristine white handkerchief.

I shake my head, grab some tissues from my pocket, dab my eyes, touched by his concern. "Thank you, sir. I hope so." I stand and hurry back to do the metro trip in reverse.

I ride the train home in the direction of Pigalle and Raphael, listening to the whoosh of the fat rubber tires on the tracks, willing the driver, if there is one, to put his foot down. At ground level, I zip through the Montmartre streets, flash to the Wall of Love in the Jehan Rictus gardens on my left, where the word 'love' is written in over two hundred languages. What's Raphael's and my language of love? Is it evident in the way we work so well together? In the way we make love. In the way we encourage each other to reach for the stars. The elegant Saint-Jean de Montmartre church opposite the Wall rings its bells and I jump. Taking deep breaths, I run the rest of the way to rue des Martyrs. My heart flips when I see Raphael's motorbike near the curb. I take the stairs two at a time. When I practically fall inside the door, Raphael's there.

He looks up, hair tousled, stubble shadows his face. "Hello, Sassy."

My heart thrums to life. A surge of energy shoots through me. Only Raphael does this to me. "Hello," I whisper, so glad he's here. Then a thought crosses my mind - maybe he just came to say goodbye.

Raphael's sitting on the floor beside my bed, studying a scrap of fabric. Even from a distance, I see remorse in his gaze, and uncertainty. He holds up a half-finished embroidery, a commission from Catherine of an ancient Parisian scene of the French king of the time hunting in the Forest of Compiègne. "My girlfriend is so talented. Such tiny figures, so lifelike." When I say nothing, he puts it down and picks up a magazine from my nightstand and flips the pages. "But this? You never thought to show me?" He holds up the latest issue of *Condé Nast Traveler* with Mom's picture on the cover, flanked by Kumpaya and me with the Great Sandy Desert backdrop.

Every nerve in my body jumps and hums like an overload of caffeine surging through my veins. I flop onto the bottom step and drop my head between my knees, take ragged breaths. I came back prepared to talk about our relationship, not about Mom. Sudden tears spring to my eyes. How am I going to answer his questions? He'll be relentless until he knows everything. I grab my chest and force myself to breathe.

The magazine drops onto my bed. Raphael stands and strides across the tiny space, closes the door and sits beside me. I catch the flicker of fear that tightens his mouth and shadows his eyes. "*Mon ange.*" He wraps his arm over my shoulder. "How compassionately she wrote about oppressed women around the world."

I clench my fists, lean into him, needing his body against mine or I would have completely lost it.

He kisses my cheek so tenderly I start to sob. He knuckles away my tears. "Why are you so upset? Is it because of me? I'm sorry for pushing you this morning."

I suck in a deep breath; it rattles in my throat. "No. It's not that. It's about Mom. She was oppressed by my father, which is why she wrote about similarly oppressed women. Women trusted her with their stories of how they worked hard to provide for themselves and their children after escaping abusive relationships."

He turns me so we're looking into each other's eyes. "Have you been in an abusive relationship? Is that why this is so painful?"

I hold his gaze. "There's so much pain in me, Raphael."

He pulls me closer, gently caresses my shoulder. "Share the pain. I totally get pain."

Chewing my bottom lip, I say, "This pain is why I fight so hard for my independence."

"Okay. Tell me, *ma petite,* so I understand."

My tongue is heavy, but I press on. "My father is a controlling, abusive man. I fell into the habit of doing his bidding. It was easier ... but inside I was angry and repressed ... it made me anxious and weak." My heart is heavy with sorrow, remembering the blows. "Mom and I endured six years of physical and emotional abuse. He broke her arm once when he threw her down the stairs. We tried to escape him several times, but he had his goons stalking us. They'd bring us back and he'd be so furious, the beatings grew more intense. I was terrified he'd kill us, so slept with my sharpest scissors under my pillow. We finally made our break when I was fourteen, when we moved to the Hamptons and changed the locks. He left us alone after that. So yes, I've been in an abusive relationship. After Mom died recently, Pa forced his way back into my life, tried to control me again. Is still trying. So, I ran away to Paris, swearing I'd never be controlled by him or any man again."

"And you found me. I get the irony." He kisses the top of my head. "That's a hideous story. Today I'm hearing things you never shared with me. What else haven't you told me?"

"*Aaarrgghhh.*" My body shakes. I clamp my teeth to stop them chattering. "There was this terrorist bomb ... at the Boston Marathon."

He shouts his surprise, then pulls me tight against him, stroking my back until my shaking lessens. "*What*? I saw that on the news. You were there? You were hurt?"

I nod. How can I share this and stay calm? I haven't taken Xanax since arriving in Paris and meeting Raphael. *Breathe. Breathe. Breathe.* "A nail bomb got me. It still aches where I was hit." I tug up the leg of my training pants, trace the pale scar on my calf, show him the one along the side of my finger. "I had a badly-lacerated forehead." I lift my hair where a pale jagged scar runs along my hairline. "Another centimeter and I'd be dead."

Raphael makes a ragged sound in his throat. "No way." He traces the scar with a finger, then kisses it. "I should have noticed. I'm sorry." He's so close I feel his rapid breaths on my face. "So, this is why you're often jumpy?"

"Yes. Even worse than the physical scars are the mental scars. I was diagnosed with PTSD soon afterward. That's meant years of therapy. I leaned on Mom to get me through. We were making great progress. Now she's gone. I've got to be strong. Alone."

He puts his chin on top of my head. His jaw trembles. "You're not alone."

I swallow the lump in my throat, shake my head. "It's a lifetime thing, Raphael. There's no cure. I'd be a burden to you."

I hear the frown in his voice. "You could never be a burden. I'll help you through anything."

"You're so sweet, but you can't possibly understand what a big deal it is. My life is a constant struggle to maintain calm, to not give into anxiety triggers, my main one being stress. Chances are I'll need drugs and therapy for the rest of my life."

"I can Google, too, Sassy. I'll be an expert on PTSD before you know it. I can help you through this."

"Do you understand why I don't want us to live together? I mustn't lean on you, or anyone. But I want you in my life. I love you." A tear tracks down my cheek.

He brushes my tear away with his thumb. His lips curl into a smile. "It makes me so happy to hear you say those three words." He kisses my forehead. "Ssh. Ssh. Don't cry. To think ... I can't imagine ... what if—" He shakes his head, his eyes dark clouds. "Is that why you're so keen to run the Paris Marathon? You have something to prove?"

"Yes. I need to prove to myself I'm not afraid of terrorists." I say the words with more conviction than I feel. "I won't let what happened in Boston stop me doing what I love."

Raphael cups my face in his hands. "I'm proud of you. I'm always here for you. I'd even run a marathon or at least train with you."

"That's so sweet, but I've got this." I clear my throat, amused by the relief on his face. "Now you've heard more of my story, you must see I'm a complicated girl."

He hugs me close to his side, kisses the top of my head. "I love my complicated girl."

"I know you do." I rub a hand over his chest, feel his fast-beating heart. Beating with love and concern for me.

After a long hug, a silence where we were both lost in our own thoughts, Raphael raises his head. "Now ... don't be upset ... but ... to business, Sassy. While you were gone, I saw Madame Lavelle."

"Oh?" *Here we go again.*

His lips turn up into a smile. "I took her for an early lunch at Pain. Between the ham and brie baguette and two Paris Brests filled with coffee cream, I told her you'll be moving in as soon as 5A is ready. She'll let you know, but she's thinking two weeks before the remodel is finished. The plumber is the holdup."

"Thanks." I rub my cheek against his stubble. We sit, me cuddled into him, him stroking my hair with one hand while the other holds me tight.

He lays his head against mine and his curls brush my face. "We belong together, Sassy. When we're apart, I don't feel whole and I think you feel the same. I shouldn't have dropped the moving in thing on you when you were half asleep, but you know me, I'm spontaneous. To me, one of the dangerous things in life is to stand still. You've had a brush with death. You know how important every moment is. Be spontaneous. Seize the day."

"*Carpe diem.*"

"Exactly. Like running the Paris Marathon."

He puts his arms under my knees and lifts me into his lap. "You weigh nothing. Should I be concerned? You're not anorexic or something?"

"Ha. You've seen how I enjoy my food. I'm a runner. I'm skinny no matter what or how much I eat." I place my hand behind his neck, draw his face to mine, kiss him. "Now that I've made up my mind to move, I can't wait to see my sewing machine set up at a window downstairs."

He twirls his fingers through the ends of my hair which has grown halfway down my back. I haven't bothered finding a hairdresser in Paris. It's a relief after my weekly appointments in New York with the hours spent in the chair undergoing the torture of hair extensions, highlights and curling tongs to look the part at Romance is Born and for the soirees I attended with Xavier and Pa. "It's going to make all the difference."

"I'm counting on that."

"May I?" He undoes the brass buttons of my mustard-yellow puffa jacket I bought to salute autumn. "I want you so much."

"Please." I lean into him. "I want you too."

He slips my jacket over my shoulders; it whispers to the floor. Tugging at the bottom of my tank, he lifts it over my head, it follows the jacket. Putting his hands under my arms, he stands me up and rolls down my tight lycra running pants. I'm wearing nothing but my La Perla sports underwear. He crushes me against his body, runs his hands over my shoulders, down my arms, over my thighs like he's discovering my body for the first time.

"*Mon ange,* let me make love to you. I need to lose that desperate feeling I had when I came back here to find you gone."

"I need you too, Raphael, but I'm sweaty after my run." My voice is husky with the need to reconnect after our first fight. "I'll shower first."

"Why worry? I want you just as you are." He carries me to bed, lays me down gently. Eyes soft, he props himself on his elbows, kneels over me, straddling my legs. He unclips my bra, strokes my breasts, then trails his hands down my body, removes the rest of my underwear.

I reach up and roll his T-shirt over his head, throw it onto the floor. Brushing my lips over his chest, down his stomach, I trace each bone, each muscle. My heartbeat pounds in my ears like the roar of the ocean outside the summerhouse. The Hamptons are far away. I have entered another world where only Raphael and I exist.

He stills my hands. "Let me show you how deep my feelings are for you." He's all ripped abs from his daily gym sessions, his black jeans unbuttoned to his black Calvin Kleins.

Oh My God. I slip my fingers inside his jeans, work them over his hips.

He shakes off his jeans and his underwear, then drives me crazy when he lifts my hips and pushes my thighs apart.

Hmmm. I take slow, deep breaths as his hand sweeps over my thigh and his lips tease my breasts, sending hot blood shooting through my veins. I feel the strength of him inside me, then the weight of him moving against me. My entire body quivers.

"My darling angel," he whispers in English over and over again. "Never leave me."

I bring his face to mine, hold him close, my lips brush his neck. I don't want to ever let him go. He's mine. He's hungry. Sexy as hell. My hands roll restlessly, clutching his hair, his back, raking down his arms. It's like the first time we slept together, only more intense. We take our time. Nice and slow. I give myself to him, never more vulnerable in my life, but he's vulnerable too. My body has never felt quite like this before. We move together – kissing, touching, stroking. It scares me more than a little, the way I forget myself in Raphael's caresses. Making love with him, I feel in every way his equal, overloaded with pleasure. I want to recreate the intimacy and closeness we had before our fight. I need to hold nothing back. But some part of me knows my reservations and fears will return when I crash back to earth. But at this moment, I am free of doubt. How could I have misgivings about his love for me when he treats me like this? I rock my head from side to side, waves of pleasure wash over me. "Raphael! Raphael!" I grip his shoulders as his body shudders, and he cries out my name. I toss my head from side to side. This man is made to drive women crazy. To drive me crazy. How will I bear it when he moves on to make some other woman crazy?

"Sassy, this is where I belong," he murmurs when it's over, "in your arms. Loving you. Always. Only you."

My body craves him, but I'm afraid of his power over me. It would be too easy to become completely lost in him.

But being lost in him feels so spectacularly good.

CHAPTER THIRTEEN

Moving day is here.

Two weeks after our tense conversation, Raphael arrives early on Friday morning to help me move one floor down from the attic into Apartment 5A. After the extensive remodel, it passed the building inspection a few days' ago, and Raphael has been mysteriously going in and out. I've been too busy with coursework at the Institut and my bar shifts to give much thought to moving day, but I did catch something about furniture and a surprise. I sorted and packed my things before my bar shift yesterday, amazed at how much I've accumulated. I've no idea how it all fitted into the attic. After my initial reluctance to move, I'm craving the extra space.

Raphael passes me a takeout coffee and we toast each other. "Are you okay, Sassy?" He checks out my boxes stacked near the door. "You've been hard at work. I could have helped you with this." He puts a hand on my shoulder and watches me, no doubt afraid I'm going to have a meltdown leaving my beloved attic.

I walk around the empty space, remembering fondly the evening I moved in and the good times I've shared here with Raphael. "Don't worry.

It's all good. I'm excited and nostalgic at the same time. Rearing to go. Marco from 5B left a note on my door last night and offered to help. He's probably still sober. What do you say? Need his muscle?"

"That was thoughtful of Marco, but I'll be fine with the heavy lifting." He watches me out of the corner of his eye, no doubt still uneasy that he's done the wrong thing in hastening the move. He takes both empty cups and puts them onto the windowsill, rubs his hands together. "Let's get into it then. It's a cardio and weight session combined. No gym for us today. Let's move." He heaves my industrial sewing machine from the worktable, grunts while he adjusts it in his arms and heads for the door.

I grab the first box of fabric samples I've created and lead Raphael downstairs. I race ahead and put my box down beside the door, stepping aside to let Raphael stagger past and set my sewing machine onto the dining table. I pick up my box, enter 5A for the first time. Walking slowly across the shiny retro black and white diagonal tiles I spy a classic marble fireplace with baroque trims. I put down my box. "*Phew*. This apartment is beyond gorgeous, Raphael."

"That's the reaction I wanted." He takes my hand. "Let's do the tour."

Everywhere I look there's something amazing. "Wow, Raphael," I keep repeating. I'm staggered at how the rooms sparkle with early morning light shining through the large floor to ceiling windows, how the French doors climb up to pick out the adorable plaster cupids and the bunches of grapes dripping from the corners of the molding. "I love it. The ceiling is so high compared to the attic roof. Oh, and those black wooden beams are fabulous against the white ceiling." I can't resist rubbing my palm over the walls. With the suede effect, the walls are white and soft as cheese. "They're a masterpiece."

"I knew you'd love them. Let's go onto the balcony." He walks me past the opulent chaise he's already installed near the windows, opens the French doors, ushers me outside.

Paris is spread at our feet. The sun turns the terracotta rooftops golden and there's an even better view of the Eiffel Tower than from my attic.

"*Woo*. I can imagine sharing an evening drink watching the lights." I rub my hand over the scrolled steel tabletop and chairs with plump black and white cushions. "How much furniture did you buy? I owe you."

"It's a house-warming present. I set you up with a few things. If you don't like them, they can be exchanged."

I grip the balcony rails, try not to resent him for buying furniture without checking with me first, but I haven't had a moment to think about decorating. His choices are flawless. Of course. He's an artist. Why am I being bitchy? "It feels like home. Thanks." I hug him, think how much I love Raphael and Paris. I must accept his generosity not as an act of control, rather as an act of love. Back in New York, I told myself I wanted love, acceptance, happiness. Raphael has given me love and happiness. Now I must come to acceptance. Still, I would have liked black and pink checked cushion covers. Just saying.

Raphael wraps me in his arms. "I love doing things for you," he whispers. "Now let me show you the rest."

"You've outdone yourself." I marvel at the all-white marble bathroom with eighteenth-century gold fittings and the *pièce de resistance*, the opulent Louis XIV inspired bedroom with its marble fireplace and luxuriant burgundy cover fringed with gold which wouldn't be out of place at Versailles. Secretly, I can't wait to return the covers and replace them with my Monet set. "Raphael, it's heaven." I turn and embrace him. "Hey, we'll watch the Eiffel Tower twinkle through those French doors."

He gives me a wicked smile, takes a curl of my hair, twists it around his finger. "I want to watch more than the Eiffel Tower twinkle." He winks.

I clap my hands over my face. "As much as I love my attic, this apartment is brilliant." I want to run wild and whoop around this new space, but I restrain myself. "But the thought of cleaning it terrifies me."

"I've arranged with Madame Lavelle for her cleaner to come every week. I'm paying." He flicks me a sideways glance. "Don't pull that face. You hate cleaning. And you have better things to do. Concentrate on creating fashion."

A refusal bounces on the tip of my tongue, then I press my lips together. How long would it take to keep these floors clean? And those high ceilings? Raphael hates mess, so it's something he'd want to do, and I guess he hopes he'll be spending a lot of time here. "That's so thoughtful. I'm the luckiest girl in Paris. Because I have you."

He throws me a relieved look. "I love you, Sassy." He spreads his arms, encompassing the kitchen, dining and lounge room. "You still need more furniture. I'll take you to the second-hand markets at Vanves tomorrow."

"That'd be great. I'd like a French painted boudoir chair for my dressing table in the bedroom to match the antique bed. Some antique bookshelves would look great between the windows and doors here in the salon."

The side of Raphael's mouth quirks upward. "They would. And some elaborate antique mirrors. If we can't find them in Vanves, we'll go south to a few brocantes. In no time you'll be set up and able to focus on fashion design."

"I will."

I don't miss the sparkle in his eyes. "Now, to practicalities," he said. "Let's finish bringing down your things. I need to hang some artwork."

I never got around to finding art for the attic walls. But I needn't have worried. Raphael has it in hand. In the middle of the expansive living room wall, he hangs a huge oil painting in an intricate gold frame.

"*The Four Seasons of Paris*", he says, "a Raphael Valentine original."

"Hmmm. It's stunning. Like you." I stand on tiptoe and kiss his cheek, study the masterpiece. It's a polyptych, four gorgeous gold-edged panels. Pink flowered trees line the Champs-Elysées in spring with us sitting on a bench, champagne glasses in hand, facing the Eiffel Tower; the Hotel de Ville beach with our easily recognizable figures embracing after playing volleyball represents summer; autumn leaves fall near the Pont des Arts where we're picnicking on a golden rug; winter sees me wearing a long red coat walking through the snow beside the Seine towards Raphael. I've yet to experience a Paris spring or winter. Winter is coming. I hope it's as beautiful as his painting promises. I'd better buy a red coat.

"Like it? You don't mind my choosing art for you?" Raphael squeezes my shoulder.

"Not at all. Especially when it's a Raphael Valentine original. This," I hold out my hand to indicate his *Four Seasons*, "is truly amazing against the creamy wall." I stand beside him in front of the painting, put my arm around his waist. "I'm impressed how the brush work is more Monet than Dali, but I see a glimpse of Klimt's "Woman in Gold" in your metallic rendition of summer. It could be worth millions one day."

"That would be a fine thing." He grins. "Maybe I'm entering my 'Golden Phase'." I love the way Klimt used gold, which is how I see you, pure gold. You'll be my Adele Bloch-Bauer 1." He spins me around, leads me in a little waltz, kisses me on the lips. "I know how much you love the Museé de l'Orangerie and Monet's *Water Lilies* series."

"I visited with the Grande Dame again the other day. She told me Monet created those 250 paintings when he was going blind. His refusal to give up his artistic dream against all odds inspires me more than I can say."

Raphael nods. Putting down the soft cloth he used to dust the painting, he says, "It's great to have so much wall to cover."

"There's more?"

"I've got a surprise to hang in your bedroom, but it must wait. But I can't wait to give you a ride home after your bar shift and stay awhile so you don't get lonely in your big new bed." He winks and quirks his lip.

Raphael likes his surprises, so I don't ask. My heart flips at the thought of Raphael staying the night.

He takes my hand and leads me to the chaise longue covered in red velvet with gold trims. It looks like it was created for the Sun King, yet it's right at home in my living room.

"It's my favorite piece of furniture." He rubs his hand over the back. "I've used it in the past to pose my muses. Just kidding, Sassy. Don't look so shocked." Holding both my hands, he lowers me onto the chaise, then lifts me under my arms until I'm lying back against the padded end. "It looks like it was made to be here."

"It does." I have fun reclining like a glamorous muse against the padded end, fluffing out my long blonde hair, one arm behind my head like Klimt's muse, Emilie Flöge.

"You're my muse, Sassy. I want you to be my life companion as Emilie was to Klimt. Did you know she, too, was a fashion designer? So, history repeats. The fashion designer and the artist. With you in my life, I'm inspired to paint like never before. I want to paint you, my own woman, in gold. Now," he kneels before me, "let me show you what artists do to their muses."

Despite my earlier misgivings, how well we're getting along. I have both Raphael and a new apartment. I'm his muse. He's my muse. Inspired by him, I'll create designs which will bring Paris to its knees.

How many women are lucky enough to have a lover like Raphael before them on their knees?

CHAPTER FOURTEEN

I'm now four weeks into my course at the Paris Fashion Institut. It's more difficult than I expected. Instead of being a spontaneous meeting of creative minds from around the world intent on honing their design chops at a prestigious Parisian fashion institution, the Institut values traditional methods of design and follows a rigid structure, not to mention intense competition between students. But my teachers are excellent, especially Monsieur Etienne from design class. I'm confident with his guidance I can find my pathway into the Paris fashion world.

"Saskia, first you must be confident in your designs," Monsieur Etienne said in our one-on-one conference in his cluttered office during my first week at the Institut. He probed my current ideas, past influences, and future plans. "The sketches you submitted on application are cutting edge but show a lack of confidence. You must overcome this, or you will not reach the top of the fashion world." He leaned forward, tapped his finger on my drawings. "You do want to reach the top, *n'est-ce pas?*"

"Of course." At his words, a shock of fear zipped through me. I would never have expected that my lack of confidence instilled by my father would show in my designs. It made me question whether when I'm sketching, I reverted to my eight-year-old self, seeking Pa's approval. I swallowed and looked Monsieur Etienne in the eye. "I'll definitely work on it," I said, reassuring myself as much as him.

"Do not be upset by my critique, Saskia. You will receive more criticism than praise from me. That is how you grow." He adjusted his oversized black Dior glasses and flipped through my samples while I sat opposite him, chewing my lip, wondering if my Paris dream was over before it really began. He took off his glasses, lay them on top of a pile of papers. "I see your major design thrust takes the frock coat so beloved of French men of the past and giving it contemporary flair. Would you like my critique on this? Yes. Good. It needs shortening," he'd said, "and I suggest you add more flare from a seamed waist." He stands, uses his hands to demonstrate his point. "Also," he sits down, "add more flourishes in the form of braiding, over-size metal buttons or appliqué. With those additions, I believe you will have developed something unique which will entrance the modern Parisian man."

My heart thumps wildly, delighted that he likes my idea of the frock coat. "Thank you, Monsieur. That is most helpful. I was afraid to add too many flourishes. But your ideas make a lot of sense."

"Saskia, if you design a style such as a frock coat, it is expected to be a little fussy, a little complicated with both fabric and trims. Show your confidence."

"Thank you, Monsieur. I will follow through on your suggestions." Already in my mind I was raiding my boxes of braids and beads. Ideas were taking shape in my head. He wants fussy; he'll get fussy.

Monsieur Etienne continued. "You show complete mastery of fabric design and auxiliaries like embroidery and appliqué, but design must be your focus and those extra notions seen as enhancement. Your future is in the complete design with added embellishments which will create your unique style. You must display your own signature. Stretch your mind. Find inspiration everywhere you look."

I'd laughed to ease the tension that tied my stomach into uncomfortable knots. The need to let go and choose the more flamboyant path was what Monsieur Etienne was saying and what I had been denying myself. "That isn't too difficult with most Parisians dressing for maximum sartorial effect even to go to the market."

Monsieur Etienne laughed politely, then coughed, covering his mouth with beringed fingers.

Uh-oh. Sitting there in his retro St Laurent silky orange and purple paisley cravat, his natty green pinstriped suit with oversized lapels over an orange satin shirt with peaked collar, an insane amount of wardrobe pressure sat right in front of me.

Six weeks into the course, Monsieur Etienne announces our major end-of-course assignment, the New Fashion competition. He props himself against his desk, folds his arms displaying his solid gold "YSL" cufflinks, studies the eighteen of us. "Your brief is to create a range of clothing representing a particular historical period, then reimagine it in a contemporary setting as if you were a proper *atelier*."

He waits while the class buzzes with excitement, then continues. "Everything you learn in your course will assist you in producing your chosen range, from planning your collections, improving your pattern making skills, garment assembly and the finishing process. One other thing." He strokes his goatee, waits until he has our rapt attention. "You each need to create a website from which to sell your range of clothing. Online shopping is exploding. People eschew brick and mortar stores. Explore your creativity in every aspect of this task. Your esteemed judges will be seeking nothing less than excellence."

"Do we actually sell clothes from our website?" Reneé, one of the few French students, tosses her dark ringlets over her shoulder and frowns.

"*Oui*, but not before your assignment is judged." Monsieur wags his finger at us. "It is this assignment which will determine whether you graduate or return next year for further study. Give it your all. This is your chance to shine."

I decline invitations for coffee from my closest friends at the Institut, Zack, Samu and Jemi, who are keen to swap ideas on historical periods. I already know mine, so I am a step ahead. Texting Raphael, who's working in the attic, I ask him to meet me at my apartment.

"I'm so excited about this assignment, Raphael," I say when I burst through the door and find him sitting at my desk checking out drawings I've been toying with, "but I'm scared, too. I see it as make or break."

He puts down my sketches and smiles. "Calm down, Sassy. You look fit to burst."

"I'll start at the Palais Galliera. I'm sure to find inspiration in the museum. What do you think?" I babble like an overly excited teenager on her first date.

He stands, puts his hands onto my shoulders. "It's a wonderful space. My tailor Manu and I trawled its collections for ideas for my Parisian artist's look."

"I didn't know that. I love your look. It's a great combination of old and new. Which is exactly what my assignment calls for."

He takes hold of my arms above my elbows, gives me a little tug. "Earth to Sassy. You're trembling. Do you need a Xanax?"

"No. It's good trembling. It's excited trembling." Raphael's not yet used to my fluctuating moods. He's taking this looking-after-your-mental-health gig very seriously.

He smiles, nods. "In that case I'd be happy to go with you to Galliera and show you around. You'll be inspired by the classic clothing collections with their intricate embroidery." He heads for the kitchen. "How about we discuss your collection over a glass of wine?"

"You're my man." I chase him across the room, grab him around the waist, give him a quick kiss before plating up cheese, a fresh baguette he's just picked up at Pain no doubt, some duck paté and red grapes.

He plants a kiss on my cheek as he passes on his way to the balcony. "I'll always be your man, Sassy." He holds a tray above his head like he's a waiter at a swanky restaurant. "Follow me." He struts outside laden with champagne, glasses, and ice bucket.

As I carry the goodies, I think about how my Paris plan is progressing. I didn't have to give up the man I love. Instead, my love for Raphael inspires me to work harder, to press for success like he does. If there's anyone who exudes the supreme self-confidence Monsieur Etienne espoused, it's Raphael.

I am eight weeks into the Institut course. It's early Sunday morning. I'm free until my afternoon bar shift. Now that I've settled into my new space, I get down to serious work early each morning. Everything I need is at my fingertips. I found the ideal model pose on a vintage pattern in one of those green metal bouquiniste stalls along the Seine. After some preliminary planning, I'm ready to start. First, I create my croquis, the basic drawing I'll use while I hone my ideas for sketching complete outfits of trousers, coats and shirts to test on the mannequin staring at me from her corner. *You're going to love 'em*, I tell her.

Sitting at my desk, I struggle to refine my sketches from the photos I took of the historical collections at Galleria. I am intrigued by the late seventeenth and early eighteenth-century men's clothing on display with their classic cut with gold and silver embroidery that'd be at home in a Klimt painting. A perfect era for my collection. My sketches are rubbish, so I down tools, make two cups of coffee and head to the attic.

Raphael has taken it over in the early morning and afternoon to create a new masterpiece, while I go up to sketch sunrises and sunsets and to lie on my bed, look through the skylight, and dream. I have ideas for my collection based on the clothes Raphael wears when he's playing to the tourists on the Pont des Arts, but I'm not confident I can handle the enormity of such a unique idea. Maybe I'll get some inspiration watching him work.

He's sitting at his easel under the attic window, his hands moving a nub of charcoal in a slow, deliberate rhythm across a huge piece of paper.

"Sorry for interrupting," I say as I always do when I walk through the open door.

He doesn't hear me. His head's bobbing to whatever music comes from his earphones.

I walk over, stand in front of him, wave my hands. "Sorry for interrupting, Raphael."

He clicks a button, hangs his earphones around his neck. "*Pas de problem,*" he says as he always does. "Ah, coffee. You angel."

As he sips his brew, he glances my way and smiles as I poke about his things, lifting up a painting for a closer look or studying his range of colors lined up on a shelf. "I'm sketching the outline for that painting I told you about. It's going to be fresh and new and very, very big. I'll experiment with drip painting where I'll pour paint onto the canvas and let it tell a story. My magnum opus."

"Sounds good, if a bit messy," I say absentmindedly, not even sure what a magnum opus is. I thought it was a musical term, like in that Richard Dreyfuss tearjerker of a film. I sip my brew, then place it onto the windowsill while I check out the abstracts tilted against the walls ready for his stall on the bridge. There are so many. If anyone is dedicated to his art, it's Raphael.

"Raphael, how do you get ideas for your paintings? You're so prolific, while I'm struggling to get even one usable drawing."

He stops what he's doing, tosses his charcoal from hand to hand. "My best ideas come at night when I'm sleeping. When I wake, I set to work and paint my dreams. Van Gogh said he took reality and the things he saw in his dreams, then twisted them, distorted them, like Dali did with his melting clocks, or *Persistence of Memory* to give it its proper title. Coming up with the best visual representation of dreams is one of the main goals of Surrealists. I'm inspired by them, but don't really fit into any one category." He taps his headphones. "I also find inspiration in music, especially chosen for the subject. For this one, *Beethoven's Piano Sonata No 29* is just the thing. It has blistering speed which helps me paint fast."

"Hmmm. I could do with some blistering speed." I pick up a random painting propped against a wall and my stomach churns. "This looks like a nightmare, not a dream."

He nods, his face somber. "Like you, I have nightmares. Yours are about your Maman's accident and the Boston bomb. Mine are about my Papa. If you ever have the misfortune to meet that man, you'll understand."

"That's a scary thought." My mind flashes to my father. He's not totally a nightmare, but he made Mom's and my life a nightmare.

"He is a scary thought." Raphael walks to the window and studies the steel-gray sky. He takes a gulp from his drink before turning back to me, his lips forcing a smile which is more a grimace. "After I paint the vision I've seen, I add it to my collection. If you think these paintings are nightmares, I'd be interested in what you think of those." He points to a corner of the attic. "Even I can't look at them."

I lift a large white sheet from a stack of paintings, stand back, run my eyes over the collection. Shock crawls over my body. I'm watching a horror movie montage. Long shadows. Liquid flowing figures. Black angels. Terrifying demons. Screaming zombies. I cringe, my eyes riveted by the raw emotion in the faces. I draw closer. Each face has similar features. They bear a resemblance to Raphael, but they're not him.

Raphael stands beside me, looking at me, not the paintings.

I take his hand, which he flexes over and over. "They're amazing, but terrifying." I kiss his twitchy hand, horrified to know he has this ugliness inside his head. "Who does that face belong to? It turns up in every painting."

"Never mind." He wraps an arm around my waist, leans over, picks up a random oil. "I call these my Nightmare Art. I don't know what to do with them, but they're part of me. I can't throw them away."

Despite myself, I'm fascinated. "How could you possibly destroy them? They are stunning. You'll find a market." At that moment, a breeze blows through the window. It streams through his long curls, turning him into a tortured Gothic-hero, like Heathcliff on the moors, tormented by losing Cathy. A frisson of fear shoots through me. What am I doing here? Why did I let Raphael paint in my attic? The thought of all this ugliness above where I live turns my stomach. My breath is ragged gasps I can't control.

"Sassy." He puts down the painting, holds my head with both hands. Looking into my eyes, he says, "Calm down. It's all right."

I place my hand over his heart and breathe in unison with him. My breathing slows. I feel foolish for overreacting. "Raphael, I'm not sure what came over me. Sometimes I feel like I'm going a bit mad."

"I doubt it." He frowns and his eyes are deep and dark. "Do you think these paintings mean *I'm* going mad? Is that why you looked so afraid? Am I insane like some say van Gogh was? Painting screws with your mind."

"No, Raphael, no." I put my arms around him, although the thought had crossed my mind. "You're not mad. You're a genius. Like van Gogh."

He exhales a long breath. "Van Gogh didn't have a Sassy to keep him sane. That did for him in the end."

In the early afternoon, Raphael emerges from the attic on his way to Pont des Arts just as I aim another scrunched-up paper ball at the trash basket.

He kisses the top of my head. "Don't be dejected, *mon ange*. Sometimes creativity takes more time than we'd like. The muse won't be hurried. Once your idea is completely formed, your fingers will magically move across the paper, I promise you."

My jaw feels like a wound spring. "I need to conference with my mentor, Amandine, in two weeks to discuss my preliminary ideas. I've no sketches, not one drawing to show her. I'm fascinated by French dandies, but to turn that look into a whole range – coats, trousers, shirts, waistcoats, cravats—" I scratch my head. "Who has ever created a contemporary collection based on French kings' clothing? Am I too ambitious?"

He places a hand onto my shoulder. "You're overthinking it. Your idea sounds great, more than great. Don't follow anyone else. It's your fashion. Make your own rules."

I stand, wrap my arms around Raphael's waist, thinking about those horrifying paintings in the attic. "That's good advice. How are *you* doing?"

He pulls me close. "I'm feeling better now that I've told you one of my dark secrets."

"I'm here for you, Raphael. Secrets are best shared." *There's more?* "So, you're off to work at the bridge?"

"Yes. Today I'm taking a risk. Before today, I've never told anyone but a church father and Marcel about my Nightmare Art. Both said to destroy the paintings. But I've decided to display my first ever piece on the bridge today, the eyeless stone angel I drew at Père Lachaise cemetery after I dreamed she was chasing me around, trying to bury me in an empty hole. Maybe if I sell these paintings, the nightmares will stop. Perhaps that's what I'm supposed to do." He shakes his head, obviously confused.

After he leaves, I sit at my desk, try to work. But I can't, not after seeing those paintings and knowing Raphael has a past he hasn't shared with me. I've been selfish, thinking of my own needs. I should have encouraged him to open up like he did me. Like me, he has a troubled relationship with his father. We're two tortured souls entwined as one.

I must get out of the apartment. Inhale some soft Paris autumn air. Clear my mind. Study the street fashion. Be open to inspiration like Monsieur Etienne advised.

My Paris dream has taken a troubling turn. I hope Raphael's nightmares don't foreshadow a nightmare of my own making. If I can't produce a winning range of men's clothing for this assignment, what is there for me except further study? I don't want that. I'm too impatient. I must surge ahead. This four-month course must kick start my Paris fashion career. I'm on a fast track to prove myself. If I fail, it won't be from lack of trying.

I grab my coat, make a vow.

I won't fail. I can't fail. I will produce a winning range of clothing to impress Parisians, those arbiters of style. Just watch me.

CHAPTER FIFTEEN

I leave for my walk, hoping to clear my head. Taking deep drafts of autumn air, I shrug off the anxiety that's been plaguing me since I saw Raphael's Nightmare Art. Strolling along the walkways beside the Seine, I slowly unwind, admire Parisians in their classic clothing. Parisians are often labeled unfashionable because they favor a style that suits them, rather than follow trends imposed by fashion houses. If being unfashionable looks this stylish, good luck to them. It's the men I'm interested in for my collection. I'm running out of time. I must make a decision today on how to represent my historical period in a modern way.

In the men who walk by, I see a lingering influence going back to Louis XIV, the Sun King. Modern Frenchmen are so dapper the way they turn up their collars to expose the rich silk linings and how they wear their cravats and leave the top buttons of their jackets unfastened, showing off their on-trend shirts. The Sun King would not be out of place on these streets, well, maybe just a little with his long curly wig, forest green tights and buckled shoes.

My walk takes me to the elegant Île Saint-Louis, a peaceful oasis of calm in Paris's busy center. It's one of the most romantic addresses in Paris with stately residences dating back to the seventeenth century, their windows looking out onto the water, not looking inward to courtyards which is often the case in Paris. Walking its cute winding streets, I imagine seventeenth century gentlemen and ladies promenading arm in arm, swishing their luscious silks. Raphael's brought me here many times to eat my favorite wild strawberry cone from the fabulous ice cream shop, Berthillon, the best in Paris, maybe the world. We've visited art galleries, partied in his artist friends' stylish apartments, drunk wine on squeezy little balconies overlooking the Seine. Raphael longs for the day his success will be marked by his ability to buy into the real estate on this prestigious island. I have no doubt he will.

Outside a stationery shop where I've splurged on a padded silk appliquéd sketch pad, I nearly trip over an elegantly clipped black poodle taking its elegantly clipped owner for a walk. The owner bends down, lets her dog lick her ice-cream. Watching them eat makes me hungry, so I slip into Café St Regis and order a *tarte aux quetsches* to savor with my coffee, anticipating the flavor-burst of rich plums on my tongue. Just right for a chilly autumn day. When it arrives, I snap a picture. The burned orange is the picture-perfect shade for a frock coat.

After a twenty-minute stroll to work off the rich pastry, I arrive at Pont des Arts, Raphael's workplace, which connects the Louvre on the right bank with the Institut de France on the left. It once nearly famously collapsed under the weight of 45 tons of love locks.

Raphael's hard at work beside the glass panels which replaced sections of the love locks now removed by council workers. I feel sad that the City of Love has removed this outward symbol of love, but I'm thrilled that close by, Pont Neuf, the oldest bridge in Paris, leads to corridors of love locks down to the river. Love is not lost after all; it's simply found a new home.

Love on my mind, I watch Raphael creating his artistic best on the bridge. He deliberately plays to the tourist stereotype of an old-fashioned Parisian artist. Along with a jaunty black beret, he's all high black studded boots tucked into tight black stretch velvet pants à la Louis XIV. Today, he wears a knee-length burgundy coat over a white ruffled shirt. His white lace cravat is a stunning foil for his long black hair. I see no reason why his flamboyant clothes couldn't be combined with his bike leathers and fringed waistcoat. Now that would be a fresh take on a classic look.

I need something unique to set me apart from the hopeful students who dream of cracking the market. I've always preferred elaborate styles in silk and velvet, my two favorite fabrics. Raphael's dandy-ish look suits Paris, where males are every bit as fashion obsessed as females.

I sit on a timber bench, flip open my new sketchbook, draw his outfit, adding bike leathers instead of velvet pants.

Whipping out my cell phone, I walk over to where he's saying goodbye to a group of Japanese tourists who stagger away with a bunch of oils under their arms.

His eyes light up when he notices me. Taking my hand, he lightly kisses my forehead. "Hello, *mon ange*. I love seeing you here."

"I love seeing you too. Good crowd today." I check out his paintings, shivering when I see his Père Lachaise stone angel staring sightlessly at me. I hold up my camera phone. "Would you mind posing for me?"

"*Pas de problem*." He bows low in front of me like he's in Louis XIV's court. Passers-by work their cameras, capturing my gorgeous man as he acts out their French fantasies. My pic-of-the-day is Raphael, hands on hips, smiling beside one of the art deco lights while his coat flaps in the breeze and a *bateau mouche* tourist boat chugs along in the background. I add the hashtags #parisfashion, #parisart, #RaphaelValentine, #Pret-a-porter, #ArtonthePontdesArts on the back of my shiny new business cards and hand them around to the photographers and ask them to add the tags and include me if they upload to Instagram and/or other social media.

"Will you take a photo of me with my angel?" Raphael asks a tall redhead who's just finished snapping him with her fancy-schmanchy camera.

"My pleasure." She speaks in a thick British accent, posing us in front of the latest art exhibition from the sculptor, Danielle Parris, a gold and white fantasy in metal called *Enchantment on the Bridge.* "I'll email them straight to you."

"That's marvelous," I say when she's finished. "I'm Saskia Bell. Fashion designer." I hand her my business card.

"I'm Kate McInnes, freelance fashion photographer." She hands me hers.

"Monsieur! *Attends, s'il vous plaît.*"

"*Juste un moment*," Raphael hails the waiting tourists, then turns to Kate. "Thanks. I'll look forward to seeing the photos."

Kate scrolls through her pictures. "Outstanding," she says, "You're a stunning couple." She holds out the camera and, yes, I agree, we certainly do look good.

"Thank you, Kate. Let's keep in touch. I could use your services when I put together my website."

"I'd be happy to help. I'll upload the best photos on Instagram and share them on Facebook and Twitter and the rest. I just arrived in Paris on a six-month visa to work on my art."

"Excellent." I make a note. "Paris is full of inspiration. Follow me on Insta and I'll follow you back."

"Brilliant." She scrolls through her pictures, studying them thoughtfully. "You know," she says, "your boyfriend reminds me of Louis XIV in his getup."

"He does." There's my answer.

After Kate leaves, I sit on the bridge enjoying the sunshine, scrolling through my Raphael Fashion album and upload the stand outs to my Instagram account, @Paris_Fashion_Arbiter_of_Style. One of the pictures @British_Girl_Kate sent me is a winner. She's caught Raphael looking at me with such love in his eyes I tear up. I upload it for my updated profile pic.

I already have over ten K Insta followers who're 'liking' my snaps of random street fashion in Paris. I upload a couple each day to keep eyes on my page. Raphael at work on the bridge always gets most 'likes'. In the comments, people ask where they can get his look. When my online shop opens, they can get it from me.

The brand name pops into my head, partly because of what Kate has said, partly because it's been staring me in the face. I'll call my clothing line, 'The Sun King Range'. I Google to make sure the name is available. It is. I snap it up.

After I upload the pictures to social media, I spread a blanket onto the wooden boards. Place the baguettes, ham, cheese and tomatoes from the bistro near the Louvre onto a big plastic plate in the middle. I call Raphael over between customers.

"*Ma chérie.*" He sits down, kisses me lightly on the lips, spreads his coat, fluffs his cravat like a fussy king. "What have we here?"

"Baguettes. Chilled Sancerre. Seeing alcohol is forbidden on the bridge, I've brought paper cups," I say while I imagine his coat with a full-size regal appliqué on the back.

He taps his cup against mine. "Ah, you're becoming more French every day. *Salut.*"

"*Salut,*" I say in my I-can't-believe-I'm-in-Paris-picnicking-on-the-Pont-des-Arts voice. Holding hands, we lean against the bridge rail with sun on our faces, sipping wine, nibbling bread and cheese, watching boats on the water, crowds seething in and out of the Louvre, and lovers strolling arm in arm beside the Seine.

A trio of young men, guitars in hand, walk from the direction of the Louvre. They're wearing black velvet trousers, frilly white shirts and black waistcoats like Raphael's. I snap their photo while they serenade us, strumming their acoustic guitars. I video the second song, then upload it to Insta. My recent pics of Raphael already have over a hundred 'likes'. In fifteen minutes. *Holy crap.*

As soon as Raphael returns to his spot, a distinguished hatted gentleman walks up to him. They chat for a long time, much to the annoyance of a bevy of teenage girls twittering around him, working their phones, taking selfies with Raphael in the background. When the gentleman leaves, he has Raphael's Nightmare Art painting under his arm. I puff out a breath. One less creepy picture in the attic.

The girls descend on Raphael, begging him to sketch them. Raphael takes out his art folder and a nub of charcoal. His hand flies over the page while they preen, pout and prance. When they walk away, they skip and dance and keep turning back, watching him. They walk past me, kissing his signature, smiling through the black marks on their mouths.

I understand, girls. But hold back. He's mine.

After Raphael sells all his paintings, we ride his motorcycle back to Montmartre to meet Marcel at Caratello, down the hill from Sacré-Cœur. Sitting opposite each other, we hold up our faces to the warm sun at an outdoor table. I sip an almond cappuccino, Raphael, an espresso. We share a flaky strawberry *mille feuille.* I delight in the burst of fresh fruit and cream on my tongue. Sacré-Cœur glints pearly white above us, reminding me of a luscious ice cream with swirly peaks. I visualize candles flickering inside the church and send up a little prayer for Mom. How she'd love to be sitting here with us. She'd adore Raphael and his art and the way he adores me.

Raphael finishes his espresso, checks his watch, frowns. "Marcel's late. Again."

I am chill. I don't want anything to disturb our peace. "Relax, Raphael. It's Sunday. He doesn't open until evening. He's probably enjoying a lie in."

Raphael checks the street, folds his arms, leans back in his chair. "I worry, Sassy. He's often late for our meetings these days. I don't know what's gotten into him," he slides me a look, "but I have my suspicions."

I do too, but I don't want to give them voice. "He's good at work. I'm sure there's nothing to worry about." I reach for his hand. "You said you have something to tell me."

"*Oui, chérie.*" His hand trembles. "Today is the first day I sold absolutely every painting. I had to resort to selling practically every oil I had in storage in the lock box down by the river, along with the canvasses I brought with me today. But that's just the beginning. Did you see a man with a huge moustache talking to me after lunch?"

"Yes." I scoot forward on my chair. "Inspector Poiroit?"

"That's him. Monsieur Marion. I took you to his gallery in Le Marais one evening last week for an exhibition and left my card. Today he bought my entire *Homeless in Paris* series of four paintings along with my Père Lachaise angel."

"That's wonderful." I lift his hand and kiss it.

He cups my face in his hands and kisses me back. "That's not all. He asked for more paintings of the homeless. He especially liked the one of your friend Paul and his little dog Claude that you're always talking to on the bridge in front of Notre Dame. He loved the silver rain and the moody blackened Notre Dame with the toppling orange spire in the background."

"The burning of Notre Dame will be recorded in so many ways. Monsieur Marion knows the tourist market."

"He does. There's more." He taps his boot under the table. "He wants to exhibit two of my oils in his window. He asked for the story behind my Père Lachaise angel which he's going to display on a little plaque. I told him an exciting, purely fictional story and said there were plenty more paintings in a similar vein. He's mad for the idea. Says they'll appeal to his edgy hipster clientele. If they sell, and if he likes more of my work, he offered me my first show."

"Wow. That's stupendous." I stand and hug him, kiss his neck. "Your experiment paid off." I sit down. "Everything's coming together for you. I can practically see stars in your eyes."

"And for you, too, Sassy. You looked excited today taking photos. What was that about?" Raphael orders another round of coffees from a passing waiter, who happens to be Joaquin, Marcel's current boyfriend. Neither Raphael nor I like him very much. Joaquin has that pasty, gaunt look usually associated with addicts.

"I found my inspiration for my fashion line today." I watch Raphael narrow his eyes as Joaquin weaves back through the tables before returning his full attention to me. "Watching how people love your outfits, I decided to create a range of clothing based on yours for my assignment. It was my original idea, but I kept thinking I'd bodge something, to use one of your Brit-isms."

Raphael laughs. He loves his Brit-isms. "I'm chuffed to bits."

"I'm chuffed to bits too. Hey, do you think Manu would sew for me? I'll need samples and I won't have time to sew them all myself."

"*Mais oui*. He's always looking for business. And I have a friend who works in PR. She'll kickstart your line when you go public."

Uh-oh. Here we go. Raphael takes charge. "Oh. Really? Who?"

"No one you know. She's the best in the business."

"Are you talking about Inés de la Fressange, Raphael?" Marcel looks incredible as always in his open-necked red and white checked shirt tucked into his tight red trousers which he's rolled up to his ankles to show off his tan tasseled loafers *sans* socks. He clasps Raphael's shoulder, kisses me on the cheek before taking his seat.

Two guys at nearby tables check him out, he's that beautiful. But today Marcel has eyes only for Joaquin who's heading our way with a huge smile on his face and a round of espressos for the guys and another cappuccino for *moi*.

"*Oui*. I want Sassy to have every opportunity to succeed."

Marcel frowns at Raphael, frowns at me.

"What's going on here?" The tension between my two favorite guys makes me uncomfortable. "Do you know Inés, Marcel?"

"*Oui*, Saskie. I wish I did not."

"Marcel." Raphael's voice has an edge. "I don't want Saskia biased before she meets Inés."

I knit my eyebrows. "That sounds ominous, Raphael." Another job for Mister Google.

"Keep an open mind." He takes my hands, squeezes them. "Promise me, Saskia. Don't miss an opportunity when it's handed to you."

I'm saved from answering when Joaquin brings our coffees. His hands shake, the cups rattle. I slide a glance at Marcel, notice how sunken his eyes are when he pushes his shades onto his forehead. A pain stabs my heart.

Just when things are going gangbusters for Raphael and me, is Marcel, our best friend, descending into darkness?

CHAPTER SIXTEEN

Next morning, I stand outside the attic door chewing my knuckles, listening to Raphael whistle the *X-File's* theme. There's been re-runs on Netflix and Raphael's right into Scully and Mulder. He was so dead set about introducing me to Inés de la Fressange, he's not going to like my decision. Raphael never likes his choices questioned. He'll have to get used to it.

Yesterday was such a beautiful day for us. We were in sync. Raphael might have his first exhibition looming and I have finally settled on the theme of my collection. But is our relationship about to be derailed because of his need to be in control and my refusal to be controlled?

I have a nine o'clock at the Institut, which means a long metro ride, then a jog to the university. This conversation can't wait.

I blow out a breath, then give the door a couple of quick slaps.

The whistling stops, so today he's not listening to Beethoven. "Come in, *mon ange*."

I push open the door, step inside, am met with the familiar whiff of oil paint and cleaning fluid.

He doesn't look at me, just calls from where he stands at his easel on wheels which he moves to follow the light. "Hey, Darling. *Bonjour.*"

I swallow, partly from the fumes, but mostly from nerves. "Hey, Darling yourself. *Bonjour aussi.*"

I shut the door, lean against it, study Raphael while he works. He looks like a medieval monk in his floor-length red woolly jacket and paint-smeared hessian apron. The toes of his paint-splattered sheepskin boots jut out from underneath his coat. He's wearing a huge wool scarf, an 'Amsterdam' knitted beanie with ear flaps, and fingerless gloves. A chilly wind blows through the open window which dilutes the turpentine and chemicals. Combined with the mineral smell, there are bergamot and geranium aromatherapy oils chugging a wispy steam from a diffuser near the window. He says the smell calms him after his nightmares.

He lays down the brush, turns, smiles. "Your lips are a fetching shade of blue, Sassy." His cheery voice tells me his day has started well.

Let's hope what I have to say won't spoil his mood. "Brr." I rub my hands together. "A freezing autumn day will do that." I've thrown on his cashmere overcoat which he'd left slung over the chaise longue when he brought me home last night. The coat is so long it pools on the floor at my feet, but it's deliciously warm. I lift it off the floor like a Regency heroine dancing the cotillion, jumping this way and that to avoid the paintings propped against chairs and boxes. Judging by the way his oils are growing, I wonder if he spends all night in the attic.

He stops studying his work in progress, turns his face for a kiss, picks up his brush. The kiss is light and breezy, just like he is today. "This is stunning, Raphael." I wave my hand toward his painting. "You get better and better."

Laying his brush on the table next to his color palette, he reaches out and hugs me. "I'm nearly done, Sassy, except for a few finishing touches."

"Raphael, I need to—"

He frowns. "Can it wait just a minute?" He holds up a grubby finger. "I need your opinion." He makes a few brushstrokes, removes his gloves, washes his hands in the bowl of spirits on the side table beside his painting paraphernalia. He stabs a finger at his canvas.

It's one of his best. A haze of red, the details stark. I pick out the Evian, empty snack packets, the psychedelic coat. "Wow. You've painted Enzo sleeping in the doorway of Le Chat Noir." I step back and flex my fingers. "For Monsieur Marion?"

"*Oui.*" He taps his brush on the timber edging the painting. "I think it works. Do you?"

"I do." I check my watch. Bite my lip.

"What's up?" He puts his hands on my shoulders, kisses my forehead. "Are you okay? You're acting a bit loco. I haven't seen you this jumpy in a while."

I take several shallow breaths which hitch in my throat. "I'm fine, a little anxious. But I need ... to talk to you, um, about a couple of things." I take a step backward, perch on an empty stool, sit on my hands. "I have an early class, otherwise I wouldn't have disturbed you. I meant to tell you last night before you left."

"We were rather preoccupied." He puts his hands onto my knees where the coat gapes open. He traces the shape of my thighs, lifts me off the stool until my legs are wrapped around his waist.

"No, Raphael." I push against his chest. "Not now."

"*D'accord.*" He slips his hands under my arms, sets me onto the floor. He points to the oversized art deco railway clock he's set above the window. It would be more at home in Musée d'Orsay which was once a railway station. "Is there a problem with your assignment?"

I chew the inside of my cheek. "Not at all. It's going great. I'm churning out sketch after sketch now that I have my inspiration, just like you said I would."

"That's brilliant. So, what's up?" He picks up a fine brush and hunches over the bundled figure of Enzo in the lower corner of his painting, raising his eyebrows in a get-on-with-it way. "Your website?"

I curl and uncurl my toes inside my woolly slippers. "No. Isaak helped me with that. He's that computer whiz at the Institut I told you about."

Raphael burns me with his dark stare. "You need to talk to me about Isaak?" He lays down his brush, picks up a deadly-looking serrated knife. "Why?"

"Raphael, stop scaring me. There's no need for that tone. Or that knife." I grab his wrist and he drops the knife. I give him a shake. "Six of my work colleagues are meeting tonight at Oubliettes. We're on the clock at the Institut." I hold my throat with my hand, my pulse races. What's got into him? I was expecting a reaction, but not jealousy.

Raphael picks up his knife, layers rivers of light gray, black and silver onto the canvas. "As cozy as it would be for you to listen to live jazz in that dungeon in the Latin Quarter with a group of bohos, you can't, not tonight."

My jaw drops, then clenches. "*Pardonnez-moi*, Raphael? I *can't* meet with my friends. You've crossed a line here."

He flicks the knife blade. Tiny drops of black paint splatter the canvas. "Don't make this bigger than it is, Sassy. Any time but tonight you could meet your friends anywhere you want with no argument from me. But tonight I've arranged for us to meet with Inés de la Fressange. Le Kremlin at seven. We'll discuss marketing while she drinks her way through forty-five types of imported vodkas."

I grind my teeth. "Is she Russian or something?"

"Or something." He lays down the knife and picks up a clean brush with tiny bristles, dips it into black paint. "Her real name is Agnessa, but she prefers Inés. She prefers to be Spanish, at least this year where she embraces everything Spanish. She reinvents herself constantly. First she found a name she liked on the internet and changed hers legally."

I sigh. Do I really need Inés's backstory? "Raphael don't ever make plans for me without asking me first. I'm not a child." *And you're not my father*.

He narrows his eyes, glares at me. "You were happy with my recommendation for Manu." He strokes the bristles of his brush between thumb and forefinger, so he has stripes of black paint on the tips.

"Manu's different." I place my hand on his arm. "Manu knows your style. Hiring him made sense. He's happy for my business."

He places his hand over mine. "Inés, too, will be happy for your business. She can ensure your fashion line is a hit." He stabs the air with the end of his brush. "Talent is not enough. You can create the best product in the world, but if no one knows about it, what's the point?" He bends down so we're eye to eye. "With Inés, your name will be on everyone's lips. Paris is a very small town. To succeed, you must know the right people. Inés moves amongst the *demimonde*, as you like to call them."

"I know people too." I turn away, but he cups my cheek, turns my face, looks at me, eyebrows raised. I fold my arms. Jut out my chin. "My course covers marketing. Social media is the modern way to promote."

He laughs in my face. "Oh, Sassy. Social media." He clicks his fingers. "A flash in the pan."

"I beg to differ. My career is important to me, but Inés de la Fressange is not." I cram my freezing fingers back into my pockets. This conversation reminds me of talking to my father. Raphael thinks if he berates me long enough, I'll give in. No chance. "I Googled her."

"Googled her?" He swings his head my way, alarm in his expression. "Why did you do that?"

"To find out everything Inés has ever done." I slam my fist into my open palm to emphasize each point. "Every social event she has ever attended, every lover she has ever had, is splashed across the internet."

Raphael shrugs his shoulders, his eyes slide away from mine. "Oh," he says, "*You're* jealous now?"

"Raphael. Seriously." I pace up and down the room, trying to work off adrenaline. "You expect me to hire your lover of three years?"

"Three years? Hmmm." He smacks his forehead with the heel of his hand. "It was business as much as pleasure. She got me my gig on the Pont des Arts." He leans his face close to mine. "Do you know how impossible that is? Why me over all the artists in Paris who'd kill for the opportunity? Because Inés knows people. She said it was key to my success. And she was right. I've gained a following and several gallery owners are now regulars, come to talk business and buy my work. It's great marketing."

"So, Inés was a steppingstone for you. You used her."

He laughs like I have just made the funniest joke. "No one uses Inés. It's the other way around, *ma petite*. But, yes, I do use people sometimes, we all use people." He taps me on the shoulder with his brush. "Enter the real world. Welcome to the real Paris. The Dark Side of Paris." He starts whistling the *X-Files'* theme. So that's what he has been doing all morning instead of listening to Beethoven.

I stand up, stuff my hands into my pockets, shake my head, ignore his put down. I never expected him to say something so condescending but looks like he'd say anything to get what he wants. As if I don't know what the real world looks like. I know a bit too much. "What did Inés use you for?"

He throws his head back and snorts. "It didn't hurt her reputation to be squired around Paris by the man-about-town son of a leading French politician. We made a spectacular couple, according to the media. You read the stories. What do you think?"

"What happened to the spectacular couple? It didn't say." I press my lips together. "Did she find someone better to squire her about town?"

"I've no idea, dearest Saskia." He turns his back on me and picks up his knife. "I was the one who found someone else."

"Oh." Like Mulder from the *X-Files*, Raphael believes the supernatural world that visits him in his dreams is real. I'm more Scully, the skeptic. That doubting voice inside me never lets up. Did Raphael recommend Inés, not to help me, but to keep her close?

I have got to leave before I hate him. The Raphael I have spoken to this morning is not the Raphael I know and love. "I'll leave you to it then." I run downstairs to my apartment, rip off Raphael's coat and hit the shower. I'm so keyed up I could run to the top of the Eiffel Tower, but I'll save that for another day.

I choose clothes dressy enough for Oubliettes – Levi denim-wash jacket over an Ae'lkemi black and silver wide-legged pant dress, teamed with black and white checkered Converse sneakers. Throwing my golden puffa coat over it all, I grab my black leather tote and jog all the way to Abbesses's metro.

I keep my distance as people push and bump into each other, desperate to get onto the next train, even though one leaves every three minutes.

Hurrying along the tunnel to catch the train, I drop a couple of euros into the battered guitar case of the gaunt and gray quintet in the walkway who serenade commuters with melancholy songs. I feel bad they are so far from home and desperate. I turn back and drop another €5 into their case. I am rewarded by "*Blagodarya*, Mademoiselle." *Russian?* I scowl.

I step onto the platform as a train pulls in. The carriage is so crowded I squeeze in backwards, clutching my tote against my stomach so no one steals my last €10. The closing doors swoosh and brush my bag.

The train rumbles along in the semi-dark. I zone out, enclosed by black womb-like curved walls, watching the weak white lights zip past. I have a half hour to think, which isn't easy when you're sucking in your stomach, so it won't get stuck in the door every time it opens and shuts.

The carriage starts to empty. I pull down a tiny seat, sit, try to make sense of the morning. My head's full of Raphael's words, his arrogant attitude, his dismissal of what I want, his belief that he knows better when it comes to my career. How dare he push his old girlfriend onto me? Can't he imagine how uncomfortable that makes me feel? He can be an egotistical shit, but this is a new low, even for him.

I take calming breaths. Won't let him stress me out. Those condescending words were aimed to hurt me because I refused to fall into line with his suggestion. He's not used to my saying no. I need my dreams, just as he does. I'll do it my way. My followers on Instagram have skyrocketed since I upped my posts with Raphael's images. Plenty of businesses find their niche on social media and then transfer their success to more traditional markets. If I win the New Fashion competition, I'm on my way. That's my marketing plan.

I'll never be one of the Paris élite even while squired by my man-about-town, Raphael, but I'm going to make it in this city. My way. The only way for me.

The train screeches to a halt at Porte d'Orléans. I check my watch. I'm late. Taking the stairs up to street level two at a time, I hit the pavement running.

Now that I've made up my mind not to be manipulated by Raphael, a weight lifts. I'm meeting my friends at Oubliettes tonight. I'm not meeting Inés. Go me.

I run down the street so fast I am out of breath when I burst into Monsieur Etienne's design class ten minutes late, ignore his black look, throw off my jacket and take my seat next to Zack.

After class, I spend a cruisey afternoon at the bar. It's chilly outside, so our customers throw back espressos at the counter. Tourists flock in after the matinee at Moulin Rouge and order mulled wine while they check their bruises from being packed into theatre seats like sardines.

Marcel sends me to Monoprix to buy extra oranges, lemons, and clementines. My job is to warm red wine on the little gas burner at the back of the bar, stir in fruit juice, sugar, and bayleaves. The aroma is heavenly, reminding me of Christmas drinks at The Spotted Pig in West Village. I've hardly given New York a thought lately. I don't want to start thinking about it now, or I'll start finding more parallels between Raphael and Pa.

Marcel calls from the bar. "Four more, Saskie."

"Coming up, boss." I love making mulled wine because it gives me time to think. Straining the brew, I fill serving glasses and pop in citrus slices. Grabbing the gin bottle, I glug a generous dash, then stir each glass with a cinnamon stick.

Marcel nods when I carry the tray to the counter. "There will be a big crowd before midnight," he says. "There ees another gallery opening at the Centaquatre, so I 'ope Raph ees coming to 'elp me later. I'm not feeling well."

Uh-oh. I hand two mulled wines to tourists wearing Liverpool Football Club tracksuits, then slip the docket under a glass. "Marcel, I'm sorry you're not well." He's breathing fast and scratching his arms through his long-sleeved shirt. "I've no idea if Raphael will come." I fold my arms, roll my eyes. "I hate to leave you in the lurch, but I really do have to be out of here by seven. The meeting I told you about."

Marcel tugs his quiff and frowns. "*Oui*. I remember. Of course, you must go. But do I sense trouble in paradise?"

"Definitely." I bite my lip. "And trouble has a name. Inés de la Fressange."

He strokes his goatee, trimmed to match Joaquin's. "I was afraid of that." He takes an order for an espresso. "It was a bad idea for Raph to suggest 'er to you."

The anger swirls around my gut. "Raphael does what Raphael does." I take orders for six mulled wines from a group of tourists from Prague who tell me mulled wine is sold from every little hole-in-the-wall in their city.

"You found out they were an item?" Marcel yells over the hiss and clunk of the ancient wheezy espresso machine. When he places the coffee onto the counter, his hand trembles and the china rattles.

"Three years, according to Google." I head for the burner with fresh orders of mulled wine.

Marcel walks over and watches me add the fruit slices and cinnamon stick to each glass before I go to the counter and serve more tourists. "Inés was bad for Raph, Saskie."

"Oh?" I feel an uneasy twinge as I accept a credit card, run it through the machine, hand it back. "How so?"

There's a lull in orders, so Marcel takes my hand. His feels damp. Standing away from the bar, we continue our conversation. "She was into drugs. Raph 'ad never taken drugs before 'e met 'er. She convinced 'im LSD will 'elp 'is nightmares."

"LSD? That's old school."

"Inés was into it, no, ees into it. It's still big in Russia where it's practically legal."

I imagine Raphael grabbing onto anything to make his terrifying dreams go away. How dare she. But then, maybe I'm being too harsh ... "Did it help?"

"*Non.* The drugs made 'is nightmares more grotesque. Every time 'e closes 'is eyes, 'e sees skinned skulls. It all came to an 'ead when one night 'e tried to step out the window." Marcel points upstairs to the apartment. "You know how far eet ees from the ground?"

"*What?*" I clasp both hands over my hammering heart. "He tried to suicide?"

"*Non,* 'e wanted to step into one of his nightmares 'e said. If I 'adn't been 'ere, he would 'ave been dead. Any'ow, 'e learned 'is lesson. After that, no more drugs. No one's stronger than Raph when 'e makes up 'is mind. Then another nightmare 'appens, very bad. Inés taunts 'im. She ees a bitch, but Raph, 'e doesn't waver. 'E's never taken drugs since. I was glad when 'e met you and ditched Inés. You are good for 'im."

"He's good for me, too, Marcel. It's just that I can't stand it when he tries to boss me around."

Marcel shrugs. "'e wants you to succeed with your fas'ion, to 'ave the best chance. 'e's very excited for you. So, what 'ave you decided to do about Inés?"

"Nothing. Now that I know about the drugs, I'm even more determined not to hire her. And I'm even more surprised Raphael would suggest her to me."

Marcel comes closer. For the first time I notice his eye tic. "Everyone's into something in this town," he whispers. "At times, we like a bit of t'is or a bit of t'at. Do not judge us too 'ars'ly. But you're good for Raph. I just really 'ope 'e can 'ang onto you."

Oh? What's this? I thought it was the other way around.

CHAPTER SEVENTEEN

I jostle my way through the underground passages and the Tuesday night crowd at Oubliettes who have crowded in for cheap drinks and Jazz Night. I'm startled to see medieval instruments of torture lurking in dark corners. Then the relaxing sounds of pre-recorded jazz bounce off the curved walls, diffusing thoughts of Raphael's control-freak act this morning. I'm here for work. I'm here for fun. I'm here because I'm in control of my life.

I find my friends—Canadian Isaak, my best friend at the Institut, Samoan Samu, Rupert and Elspeth from the UK and Australian Jemi—gathered around a long low table in the basement.

"Hi, Sask." Zack stands, kisses my cheek, scoots sideways to make room. "Rupert got the first round." He hands me a glass. "He ordered your champagne."

"Thanks, Rupert." I accept the glass and take a sip of warm flat bubbles. "Sorry I'm a bit late. What're y'all drinking? Absinthe? Like in the wall posters? Or is it still banned?"

Zack punches my arm. "Nah. It's no longer banned, but I wouldn't recommend it. Tried it once. Nearly fell off the bar stool. We're drinking just beer, Sask, except for Samu with his soda and you with your champagne. We're here to work, not pass out."

Yes. Work. Why couldn't Raphael accept that?

I study the vaulted ceiling, the Che posters, the purple haze. "Why are we down in the dungeon?"

"So we'll have front row seats for the band," Zack says. "The BatCats are playing. One of my favorites. They remind me of a band in Montreal who played every Friday night. I'm hoping we're done before they come on stage."

Samu puts down his soda. "Let's break into pairs so we can work faster. How about it, Jemi?" He ruffles her surfer-white long straight hair. "And guys, I've got some good news to share with you later."

"Hey, tell us, mate," Jemi says.

Samu looks at each of us in turn and his eyes gleam. "Let's finish work," he says, "then I'll tell you."

"Okay then." Zack opens his laptop. "Sask, let's work together. I'm pretty much done, so we can concentrate on you."

I nod while I wonder about Samu's news. I'm so glad he said *good* news. "Okay. Let's go Zack." I open my laptop to my web page, tilt the screen his way as my home page loads. "I made the changes you suggested. Pretty cool so far, huh?"

Elspeth pushes her spectacles onto the bridge of her nose. "That leaves me and Rupert." Underneath her wild red hair and oversized black glasses, she's a stunner. I know Rupert is attracted to her razor-sharp mind. They're both in love with Marcel Proust so that's a good start.

Zack and I prop our laptops side by side, lean back against the brick wall, study our pages.

"Yours is stunning with its blue fabric theme and those silver highlights add some sparkle, Zack."

"Yes, now, let's finish yours, Sask. It still needs work. You need a better image to give your header more zap."

"Yep." I shrug off my coat and denim jacket, pick up my laptop, open my Pictures file. "I agree. I'll look for one."

As I scroll through my images, Zack looks over my shoulder. "That's a great photo of you on that bridge," he says. "Is that your boyfriend? Great gear. Like he's a throwback to the seventeenth century." He leans closer, studies Raphael's artist's garb.

"He does." I wrap my arms around my waist, study the two of us, so happy together that magical day. "He's my inspiration for my clothing range. Should I use it?" Raphael was so supportive that day, fun to be with. Nothing like the moody ogre in the attic this morning.

Zack leans forward, elbows on his knees. "That'll be great branding. Do it."

I import the image to my photo editing program. A few clicks sharpen it.

"Awesome," Zack says. "Now try a font from the era for your name and tagline." He pushes his knee against mine. I pull away. Zack's a little too fresh at times.

Soon my landing page is done. I'm ready to upload photographs of individual items and pricings for my online shop, but that will have to wait on Manu for samples and Kate McInnes for professional photography.

A buzz ripples through the space. Four band members stroll past us and onto the stage, bulky instrument cases bumping their legs.

Zack slams his laptop shut. "You guys finished?"

I shut my lid. "I need another drink. I'll get this round. Samu, don't start your news without me." I head to the bar while the band warms up.

When I place the fresh tray of drinks down, Samu raps the table with his palms.

"Make it quick." Zack's eyes stray to the band.

Samu leans forward, rubbing his palms together. "I talked to Monsieur Etienne today."

"Speak up Samu," I say. It's not easy to concentrate on what he's saying with the band tuning their instruments and the excited crowd pressing into the room, bumping our table as they pass.

"According to Monsieur Etienne and his advisors, at the last checkpoint the standard of our class assignment is so high, there's a possibility three of us will present our designs at the New Fashion show at the end of our course, not one. They're trialing a new format for the presentation this year, too, going completely techno, so that'll look good on our resumes."

"What does that even mean?" My chest tightens at the possibility of being one of the lucky three.

"So," Samu continues, 'the whole shebang is going completely digital. To have our chance at this tech presentation, we must make the shortlist, then go on to make the final three. Monsieur Etienne said it's likely the winners, especially the outright winner, will be picked up by a major fashion house and boom." He waves his arms in the air and gives an almighty clap.

"When will we find out if we're a finalist?" I press my hands against my burning cheeks, oblivious to everything but making the finals.

"Sometime before Christmas. This will give time for the finalists to add to their collections for mid-January graduation."

Holy crap. A couple months. I have so much to do. The Paris Marathon is looming. My training is intensifying. But I can't slacken off with my fashion. I'll burn the midnight oil every night. Whatever it takes.

Jemi leans forward, her face dreamy, glancing at each of us. "I wonder if any of us makes the cut."

"Yeah." Samu rubs his hands up and down his soda bottle. "Fast track to fame. The top three could be sitting right here." Samu swishes drink around his mouth, swallows. "May the best man win."

Elspeth nudges his side. "The best person."

I tune out. I'm already listening to the riotous applause as my name is called when I win first prize. The crowd claps wildly. A standing ovation. I step forward, clasp the winner's trophy—

"Look at Sask. She thinks she's won already." Zack waves his hands in front of my eyes, and I crash back to reality and the lilting sounds of jazz. I close my eyes and continue my delicious dream. Is that Bouchra Jarrar? Wow, The Kooples. And they all want me to work for them ...

The tenor sax soothes me. I lean against Zack's shoulder, vaguely aware when he puts his arm around my waist. My dreams float on the air like soft notes. I'll work on my designs until my fingers bleed.

"As awesome as this news is, gang, wait till you hear Elena sing." Zack picks up his drink and plays with the beads on the shoulder cut-outs of my top.

"Stop it, Zack." I push away his hand, sit up straight. Imagine if Raphael came in and saw us this close. He'd think I lied this morning.

Elena moves to the mic, playing to the crowd in her slinky black dress that loves every curve of her body. Her black hair's so glossy, it's nearly blue under the lights. Her red-lipsticked smile completely lights up her dusky features.

Zack leans forward, a goofy smile on his face. "Isn't she amazing?"

"I haven't heard her sing yet, Zack, but she looks amazing."

Elena begins her melancholy song. I'm instantly transported to another place, another time. Mom and my trip to the Kimberly has ended. We're both considering Kumpaya's prophecy. I'm in complete denial. We're sitting on a Darwin beach, watching the sunset the night before we fly home. The colors are brilliant slashes of orange, green and purple swirls. Brush strokes shimmer on top of the restless water, firing it into a boiling cauldron. The sounds of jazz from the band high up on the sand dunes drift on the darkening air, mesmerizing the hundreds who make up the multi-cultural crowd.

I'll remember this night forever, I recall thinking as Mom brought my hand to her lips and kissed it, wetting my fingers with her tears.

The sound of clapping jolts me out of my dream. I open my eyes to see Elena bow, smile, turn and chat to her band.

While I've been transported to my past, Zack has put his arm over my shoulder and pulled me close. "You all right, Sask? You look sad. And you're crying."

I brush away my tears, gulp my champagne, shake off his arm. "I'm fine. Memories came to haunt me, is all."

A stunning woman sweeps past us. Her blonde hair falls below her waist in curls much like mine when I work the tongs. It brings attention to her swaying hips and clingy red satin dress. Flouncing up to the stage, she whispers to Elena who hands her the mic.

I screw up my eyes, straining to place her.

She begins to sing, her sultry voice clings to me like humid air. The mournful wail of the trumpet and the chord progressions merge seamlessly with the melody. No one talks. No one moves. We sit, transfixed.

It's over. The audience slow claps and whistles. Some stand, raise their glasses, call, "Bravo."

Lifting her blonde hair over her shoulder, the singer bows to us, then strokes her hair, her smile as wide as Julia Roberts's, but not as sweet.

Uh-oh.

I slap my forehead.

Grit my teeth.

Let me crawl into a hole and die.

You sneaky bastard!

A choking sound emerges from my throat. I half stand, spilling what's left of my drink onto Zack's leg.

Inés de la Fressange.

I recognize her from Google images.

I'm still recovering from the shock, when Raphael strides past our table without a sideways glance and struts onstage. Inés runs her knuckles down his cheek. I want to rush onstage and rip her eyes out. He kisses her hand and escorts her from the stage like she's precious porcelain.

Bastard. Bastard. Bastard. I hate you. Hate you. Hate you. Traitor. Traitor. Traitor. My heart lurches in my chest. *Has he been watching me all night?* But what the freak? Look at the two of them. All over each other. Broke up with Inés, did you? Lying shit.

"Isn't that—?" Zack stabs a finger at my laptop. "Your guy?"

"Yes." I choke, brush a hot tear from my eye. "He *was*."

Raphael and Inés move onto the floor where the beat has drawn dancers from all over the club.

I swallow. Hard. Grab my glass. Crap, it's empty.

"I'll get you another." Zack zips to the bar and pushes his way through the thirsty crowd.

I'm only a few feet from Raphael, but he holds Inés close and dances with her to a slow jazz tune. They move with the familiarity of a couple who know each other intimately. Raphael's black hair, tight black leather pants, slim-line pearly white shirt and black leather waistcoat are an ideal foil for Inés's red dress and blonde hair. A lump clogs my throat. No wonder they were media darlings. People snap pictures of the hot couple, no doubt thinking they're celebrities they can't quite place.

Zack puts a drink into my twitchy hand. I gulp a mouthful like I'm parched after crawling across a desert on my belly for days. Bubbles burst in the back of my throat. Spluttering, I spray drink all over my long skirt.

When I finish mopping my face and legs, I hold my hand out to Zack and tug him to his feet. "Let's dance." If Raphael can make a spectacle of himself, so can I.

Samu pushes our table closer to the wall, so there's more room. He holds out his hand to Jemi, and they join us on the dance floor. That leaves Rupert and Elspeth. They're deep in conversation about Proust. I push past them, just as Elspeth says, "I get so caught up in his waterfall of words, the elegant evocation of longing ..."

Before we can begin our dance, one of the saxophonists puts down his instrument and picks up his guitar, belting out a flamenco riff.

"What the—?" Zack whispers in my ear. "Flamenco on jazz night?"

There's no mistaking the 12-beat rhythm reverberating around the cavern. I know it well from my Saturday evenings with Mira at the Nai

Tapas Bar in East Village. We'd sip sangria and watch the show, mesmerized by the dancing, the costumes, the energy, the hot Spanish guys, promising ourselves we'd learn flamenco, but never did.

Zack and I stand against the wall, watching Raphael and Inés make an almighty racket as they stamp their heels onto the floor, raise their arms in an arc, then dance around each other like they're two birds in a mating ritual.

Inés may not be wearing a frilly dress like the flamenco dancers I've seen, but her skin-tight red number flares around her knees, showing off flawless long legs in red dancing pumps.

Each beat of their shoes on the cement floor is like nails hammered into my heart.

Everything Raphael told me about Inés being in his past is so much crap.

I clap along so no one will hear my heart breaking. I want to run, but my shoes are nailed to the floor. How dare he put on this performance, embarrass me in front of my friends. How could he hurt me so much when he knows stress is the worst thing for me? I suck a ragged breath, feel the sweat on my top lip, my heart squeeze. I detach myself from what's before my eyes and imagine winning the fashion competition. *Breathe. Breathe. Breathe.* I've got this. He won't humiliate me ever again.

On the final beat, they throw their heads back, smile at each other, startle me by winking at me.

Inés tosses her head back against Raphael's shoulder. Her smile says look-at-me-I've-got-him-back.

Raphael stands behind her, his chin on her shoulder, his clasped hands at her waist. Looking me in the eye, his smile says this-is-what-messing-with-me-looks-like.

The band starts another round of upbeat tunes. "Wanna dance?" Zack starts to drag me to the center of the floor.

"No, Zack." I pull back. "I can't be here one more second."

"Don't go, Sask." He jerks his thumb at Raphael. "He's a douche bag. Don't give him the satisfaction."

"I don't care. I've gotta go." I grit my teeth, shrug into my jacket and coat, grab my things, all the while conscious of my burning face. "I'm off, guys," I stutter to my friends. "See you tomorrow. Enjoy the show. Uh, er, sorry." I flip my fingers in an embarrassed wave.

They're not looking at me; they're staring at Raphael who's in the middle of the floor talking to Inés. All my friends have seen my Sun King sketches for my collection. Now they're staring wide eyed at the Sun King himself.

I didn't think my choice for my historical collection through. How can I present a Sun King range of clothing, when the sun has gone from my life?

CHAPTER EIGHTEEN

"Where do you think you're going?" Raphael catches up with me outside the nightclub, his furious face inches from mine. He grabs my elbow.

I rip my arm away, surprised by my violence. "Home." My voice sounds strange, even to me, like some *doppelgänger* has taken over and is speaking from a dark room. The dark room is my heart, blackened with the shock of what Raphael just did. I settle my laptop bag on my shoulder. *How dare he!*

He grabs my hands, spins me around to face him in front of the flickering lights behind us. The veins in his neck throb, his chin juts out, his face flushes ugly red. "Had enough of your teenage friends? No doubt that was Isaak who had his hands all over you. It took all my self-control not to come over and prize you apart."

"You're ridiculous. You had hands all over Inés." I try to pull away, but his grip is a vice. "Let me go, Raphael. You're hurting me."

He drops his hands. "Sorry." He says it quietly, but there's steel in his voice.

I can't take this argy-bargy on top of my humiliation. "Go away, Raphael. I don't want to be alone with you."

His head snaps back like I've hit him. "You don't feel safe with me? Now who's being ridiculous?"

"Am I? Where's Inés?" I fling a look down the stairs. You went to such trouble to bring her here, surely she's dying to meet me."

He shuffles his feet, has the grace to look embarrassed. "I told her you weren't interested."

I turn away, start moving in the direction of Saint-Germain metro. Raphael follows close behind. "Why did you bring her, Raphael?" I toss the question over my shoulder along with a hard stare.

He shrugs. "You know why. Come on, Sassy. Stop. You're not going home. We need to talk."

I shoot a sideways glance at him. "Yes. We do." I speak in a robotic tone.

"Give me your stuff. You're loaded like a pack horse."

I think about arguing the point, but keeping my tote, I hand him my laptop. "Okay. Thanks. I came here to work, remember."

Walking awkwardly beside each other, we negotiate the narrow streets of the Latin Quarter eateries, pushing our way through slow-moving crowds who've stopped in the middle of the street to read *prix fixe* menus, three courses for €25. I love the atmosphere in the *quartier*. Love the lively music, the touters wiping their palms on their aprons like they have just left the kitchen where they have prepared a home-cooked meal just for me. But tonight, I don't want my favorite garlic mussels followed by boeuf bourguignon and crème brûlée. I want to be at Oubliettes, relaxing, dancing, listening to jazz with my friends instead of being dragged through the streets by Raphael like we're filming a modern version of *Taming of the Shrew*.

"Raphael—"

"Soon, Sassy." He turns a corner to the right, then hand on the small of my back, guides me through a black doorway. We walk into a cavernous space of what looks to be a high-class club full of long black chesterfield sofas with relaxed couples sipping drinks and nibbling *hors d'œuvres*.

"*Bonsoir*, Monsieur Valentine," a bartender calls from behind a shiny black counter which curves along the length of the room. "*Ça va bien?*"

I tug Raphael's arm, my heart hammering. "What is this place? A place where the *demimonde* meet far from the maddening crowd?"

Raphael tosses his head but doesn't answer. He calls "*Ça va?*" to the bartender, takes my hand and practically drags me down a dark corridor to a room with a low curved table and plush red velvet banquette set against dark timber walls. A black chandelier with dull candles hangs above the table, the flickering lights cast an eerie glow.

We've been followed inside by a topknot-wearing waiter in black bow tie, coattails and white apron that sweeps the floor. "*Bonsoir*, Monsieurdames."

"The usual, Jacques, and ...?" Raphael looks at me, eyebrows raised. "Veuve Clicquot?"

"Evian, thanks." This is not a champagne moment. I extricate myself from Raphael's grip, sag into the wide plush padded seat, pressing my hand against my chest. I keep my coat on for a quick exit.

Jacques leaves the room. I toss my tote onto the table, take a breath, don't hold back. Raphael's not going to intimidate me. "I can't believe you." Fury overcomes me and I stutter. "What the—*what?*"

"Sassy." Raphael drops into the seat next to me, curves his body to face me. "You're angry."

"Your degree is in rocket science?" I slam my palm onto the tabletop. "Too right I'm angry. You acted like a spoiled brat, throwing a tantrum because you didn't get your way." I shake my head, deny the tears forming behind my eyes. "Humiliating me in front of my friends—." I press my knuckles against my eyes. "I don't know you at all."

Shaking his head, he leans forward, runs a finger over a knot in the timber. "How could I stay cool when I saw you with that guy?"

I nearly choke. "You and your double standards. You were furious with me for refusing to meet with Inés is all. Nothing to do with Isaak."

He throws me a wide-eyed innocent look. "I felt like dancing the flamenco and no one dances it like Inés. I've missed that one thing about her."

I scowl. "That's BS and you know it."

He reaches for my hand. "I mean it."

I rip my hand out of his reach. "If you've missed dancing the flamenco so much, why didn't you teach me? You know I love to dance. We used to dance everywhere, even that night along the Seine where we got our feet wet. Flamenco is something we could have shared."

"I'd rather take you to Spain to learn from the experts like I did. But getting back to Isaak, you can't deny he had his hands all over you."

I'm outraged at his possessiveness, especially after his demonstration with Inés. "Stop it. Isaak's a friend and colleague."

"*Mon ange*, the way he looked at you—touched you—made me furious. He's in love with you."

I wipe my top lip where beads of sweat have formed. "He's affectionate is all. Nowhere near as affectionate as you were with Inés."

He slides his arm along the back of the banquette, so it lightly touches my shoulders. "It's not the same. Inés means nothing to me in the romantic sense. But Isaak. You're spending a lot of time together. Every day in class. Technology sessions. Meeting in clubs. He wants you. It's in his eyes. And why not? Who wouldn't want you? You shouldn't be hanging around in dingy bars with a bunch of teenagers. You're my girlfriend."

I'm fed up with the way he's skirting the real issue. A headache jabs above my eyes. "Raphael, it's not about Isaak. You're angry that I refused to drop everything to meet Inés, so you set out to deliberately hurt me." I massage my forehead, trying to ease the pain. "You succeeded, but you made yourself look small. And that bunch of teenagers are all older than I am. They're my network. They encourage me in my career. They mean everything to me."

"More than I do?" His mouth is a tight line, his eyes two slits.

Jacques knocks, enters, polishes the table, fusses with coasters, then places our drinks and a crystal bowl of deep-fried olives in front of us.

I'm ready to scream when he finally inclines his head and walks out the door after Raphael slips him a fistful of euros.

I run my hands through my hair, flip it off my face. "Raphael," I draw circles on the table with my finger, "teamwork is crucial for both of us. You're gathering your team around you – Monsieur Marion, Lamar, Bernelle and your artist friends. You won't like all my colleagues, and I won't like all yours. Take Bernelle." I snort. "Or Inés."

With pressure from his hand, he forces me to face him. "You're always going on about Bernelle, but she's harmless. And Inés should be a valued member of your team."

"Bernelle's far from harmless." I speak through clenched teeth. "And Inés will *never* be on my team."

"You say your career means everything to you, Sassy. Why not give it every chance?" He lifts my hair and runs his fingers down the back of my neck, sending shivers prickling down my spine.

I scoot away from him, but not before my breath hitches in my throat. "Sex is not the answer, Raphael. We're here to talk." I ignore my crazy beating heart and I can see the knowledge in his eyes. He knows I find him irresistible, but that has to change if I'm to be true to myself.

He checks his watch, frowns. "Let's talk then. Forgive me. I did the wrong thing turning up with Inés, especially knowing how bad stress is for you. I didn't think it through. I was a proper bastard." He shoves the table aside and drops to one knee in front of me.

I'm sure my eyes pop open like saucers. "Raphael, what—? Get off the floor. Now." I cover my mouth with my hands to stop laughing at his melodrama.

He sits back on his haunches, takes my hands in his, kisses my fingers. "I won't get up until you forgive me."

"Why did you do such a terrible thing?" I level my eyes at him, hold his gaze, search for the truth in his eyes.

He releases my hands, runs his fingers through his hair. "When you wouldn't listen to me this morning, I reacted badly because it was like you didn't care about what I want."

I toss my head. "Why can't you accept that I'm moving forward my way, Raphael? I explained why that's important to me. You don't understand, do you?"

"I don't always understand myself. I spent my childhood being pushed around by my father. When I grew up, I vowed I'd never feel powerless again. When someone crosses me, something inside me snaps and I lash out. I've been having anger therapy practically all my life."

"But you tried to make *me* powerless. You shoved Inés in my face. How do you think that made *me* feel?"

He lowers his eyes, takes my hand and absentmindedly rubs his thumb over Mom's opal ring. Didn't do her any good. It's not going to bring Raphael and I luck. "I hate what I did, Sassy, but it felt like a good idea when I planned it."

My jaw trembles with rage. "Raphael, you're a devious shit. Such a cold, calculated act. How could you treat someone you claim to love like that? You'll be on the floor until your knees are calloused. I'm not about to forgive you."

He frowns, leans his elbows on the banquette either side of my knees. "I'm sorry. I was acting out my jealousy. That Isaak—" He drops his head onto my knee, but I don't buy his act of contrition. And now he brings Isaak back into it.

The warning signs were there from the start. Why did I fall for a control freak when all too often he reminds me of what I ran from in New York? Even though my heart screams the opposite, my head tells me what I have always known – Raphael is wrong for me. I couldn't stop myself falling in love with him, but I can stop myself from becoming the person *he* wants me to be, rather than the person *I* want to be. I can't let this situation play over and over in our relationship. I must be true to myself. Unscrewing my Evian, I pour some down my throat. "Raphael, get off the floor." I screw the cap. "I can't forgive what you've done. It's over. We're over."

Ignoring the stricken look on his face which I'm not sure is genuine remorse or whether it's because he didn't get his way, I push his hands away, stand, grab my gear and rush through the door into the dark corridor.

I hear a scuffle as Raphael jumps to his feet, calling, "Sassy, come back."

Paying him no mind, I retrace my steps along the corridor, walk the gauntlet of high-class drinkers, no doubt members of the Paris elite like Raphael who obviously has enough clout to walk straight into a private room served by a private waiter and receive personal service. Like my father, doors open for Raphael. I want no part of that privileged life. I need to earn my own privileges.

I hold my head in the air. Ignore the men's lascivious looks. Ignore my thumping heart. Ignore the voices in my head which scream with every step I take, "Don't go! Don't go! Don't go!"

I go.

CHAPTER NINETEEN

One week without Raphael.

I've been keeping a diary since I began therapy. How it hurt to make today's entry. I'm no longer numb with shock. Today, my nerves are raw.

October. The Paris Marathon. Less than three weeks' away. I have my medical certificate, my race bib, my bracelet. I can't wait to get in line at the Arc de Triomphe on the Champs and run the spectacular route through the City of Light, the most beautiful marathon track in the world. In these challenging times, I don't expect the usual 40,000 will be running, but that's okay. At least it's happening.

Every chance I get, I up my training sessions. I run the steps at Sacré-Cœur's forecourt, backward, forward, backward, forward, dodging the crowd, until sweat oozes and my calves beg for mercy. To cool down, I tackle the hills of Montmartre behind Sacré-Cœur which I once found challenging, now I run up and down with ease. When I can't put it off any longer, I jog home to my lonely apartment. It's so empty without Raphael constantly popping in and out.

It's still autumn, but it feels like winter has come early. Gray skies. Trees open and exposed, like me. Each day is a day without oxygen. I constantly flash back to the breakup with Raphael, how I walked away, confused at how a relationship so beautiful quickly turned into one so ugly.

I struggle in design class despite Monsieur Etienne's coaxing to do better, and Zack nagging me to focus on the fast-approaching New Fashion competition. I nod half-heartedly to Monsieur and Zack, tell them I understand what they're saying. If they only knew what effort it took just to pick up a sketch pad, they might go easier on me.

I spend more and more time at the gym, exercising robotically, stumbling over my feet on the treadmill. Sleep eludes me. I toss and turn for hours, still not over the shock of no longer having Raphael in my life. Sometimes I go up to the attic just to smell him and his paints. I find some charcoal close-up sketches he's done of me. My fingers itch to grab a nub of charcoal and draw a big teardrop under one eye. While I check his art, I walk around in circles watching the attic door, expecting him to hunch over, take the three steps, stride across the room to me with his arms outstretched, asking, *how was your day, Sassy?*

Each day sucks. All the progress I've made since I left New York has come to nothing. Anxiety plagues me, threatens to overwhelm no matter how many times I visualize my happy place. I resist taking Xanax. Deep depression threatens to tip me over the edge. If I fall into the abyss, I won't have Mom to coax me out this time.

Two weeks without Raphael.

I'm in a dark, lonely place. Every day is torture. I can't make it on my own. Admitting to myself that I need professional help, I pick up the phone.

Doctor Sheila Benaseraff, the New York therapist I've been seeing since the Boston bombing, recommends Pascale Abreo, a Parisian therapist specializing in PTSD. "'Abreo' means 'wise counselor', Saskia, and that's exactly how I'd describe her. I'm sorry you're low and your strategies aren't working any longer, but I feel confident Pascale will help you."

In my first session, Pascale advises me to reclaim my focus. "Forget Raphael," she says.

I try, but in the back of my mind, he's always there.

It's like I've locked him away, hiding his unseen dimensions, his unopened rooms, the chapters of him written in languages I haven't been able to decipher. Now I never will. He will remain closed, his secrets hidden.

I throw myself into my work, struggling to come up with winning ideas for my collection for the Institut competition, to displace my misery over Raphael. Now that I'm in therapy once again, my creativity unlocks enough for me to come up with new concepts which pass Amandine's scrutiny. Encouraged, I work into the night, create appliqué for my frock coats and blazers; source lace for my cravats; return to Galleria for further inspiration, ask whether I can view the gentlemen's frock coats stored in the basement, to study their embellishments. It helps take my mind off Raphael.

Pascale helped me see that I was starved for affection when I arrived in Paris after all the negatives that went down in New York. Raphael dished out affection in generous bucketloads. Who could blame me for being dazzled by him? In my relatively sheltered life in New York, I had never met anyone like him. He was a bright star who drew me into his orbit.

Now we've broken up, my heart feels like it has shredded into tiny pieces. Many times I question my decision to break up with him. No, don't go there, I tell myself, I was right to do it. Raphael shouldn't have done that terrible thing at Oubliettes. Why did he hurt me deliberately? I had good reason to end it. I'll never give him the chance to hurt me like that again.

So ... why does it feel wrong? Why does it feel that the part of me which gives me life is missing?

During this morning's session, Pascale tells me that coming to terms with these situations takes time. "Take it day by day, Saskia. You need to go through all the stages of grief. You've been through shock and denial, pain, anger – now you're in depression."

"What's next?"

"Good news. You'll take an upward turn. Soon you'll reach acceptance."

"How long will that take?"

"Everyone works through grief their own way. You passed through the early stages and jumped straight to depression. Who knows how you'll negotiate these troubled waters? Eventually, to move on, you must come to accept the end of your relationship. It's over."

Your relationship is over. Over. Over. Accept. Accept. Accept. My days are spent riding a rollercoaster of indecision. I'm wracked by pain and guilt, constantly asking myself why did I do it. Then I swing to anger for thinking that way. I had to do it to save myself from a controlling relationship. But … *I miss you. Miss you. Miss you.*

"Saskia. Stop feeling guilty." Pascale says in the next session when I explain how I've gone back to guilt and how it feels like knives stabbing my gut. "It wasn't you who did that terrible thing; it was Raphael. Accept it. He wasn't the gentleman you thought he was. You feel betrayed."

Betrayed. That just about covers it.

Three weeks without Raphael.

The Paris Marathon is here. Nothing Pascale has said or I've done has snapped me out of my fugue. But it's this run I've been dreaming of, and training for, for months. Hope rises in me. I feel in control of this one thing.

The night before the marathon, my finger hovers over my cell phone *Favorites*. I'd like Raphael to come see me run, he was always so supportive, but Pascale advises against calling him until I'm stronger. *Why doesn't* he *call?* We've talked about it so often. He knows the marathon is huge for me. It's where I thumb my nose at fate. Where I prove to myself I can be a success. I'm not going into it to win; just running the course makes me a winner.

CHAPTER TWENTY

I've yearned for this day. Eight years since the Boston Marathon. The day is bright and beautiful, the blue sky brilliant with scarcely a cloud in sight, the air crisp, cool and clean. I shake with nerves, but I'm ready. Before eight o'clock in the morning, I march up to my fenced-in corral near the Arc. Show my bib and bracelet to the official, join the runners. Excited chatter and determined faces hover around, enclosing me in their excitement which matches mine. I start my warm-ups with a slow ten-minute shuffle, do some light stretches, then lunges, finish with leg swings to lessen my chances of injury.

Warm-ups complete, on a whim, I send Raphael an invitation to join my race on the Paris Marathon tracking app. My heart hammers when I imagine him downloading the app and watching my race. But then my heart plummets when I remember that he rarely checks his phone. I wish I could unsend the invitation. Why would he be interested in my run now that we're broken up?

I stop focusing on Raphael; concentrate on pushing away my pre-race jitters. Deep breathe. Jog on the spot. As the runners surge forward, so do I. I fall into line, my heart fit to burst at the anticipation.

We're off! Over forty-two kilometers to go. My heart threatens to jump out of my chest. I find the green line and follow it.

Hundreds of spectators and musical acts dressed in crazy costumes line the Champs to Concorde section where the pack circles, then sweeps down a blissfully car-free rue de Rivoli which is usually clogged with traffic. One of my favorite gardens, the Tuileries, zips by in my peripheral vision, then I'm running past the spectacular Louvre where, over the crowds, I can just make out the pyramid. Soon I cross Le Marais where the spectators thin as I make my way to Bastille. These are all places I love, especially the Hotel de Ville forecourt where Raphael and I spent so much time getting to know each other, but right now I just want to get past quickly. Checking my Fitbit, I'm doing well. Without too much effort, I'm not far behind the lead runners. My training is paying off.

I'm in a dream state as I run through Paris neighborhoods, but I pay attention when I glimpse the Bois de Vincennes ahead; the creamy château winks at me in the morning sunlight. We loop back to Bastille and some of the runners I've been following fall away, so my path is less crowded. I feel great. My confidence surges. Except for the tunnels and a slight rise in elevation (nothing as bad as Montmartre's hills), it's a very easy scenic stretch alongside the Seine. There's Musee d'Orsay, Notre Dame, and I don't miss my wow moment when the Eiffel Tower comes into view.

I've never been to the Bois de Bologne in the west of the city, but I've embroidered pictures of many of the French kings who used it as a hunting ground. I grab water at a station near the entrance. The road curves up and into the Boulogne Forest which is still heavily treed with few buildings even though I know kings once lived here and have left many beautiful chateaux. The park is much larger than Central Park in New York where I ran the Park Drives, sharing the tracks with other runners, walkers, skaters, horse carriages, and unbelievable congestion. Running my own race through the forest, I feel exhilarated. Then my thighs begin to burn. My heart is fit to burst with the effort to push my way to the front. More runners drop behind me, some bending over with exhaustion. I join the lead pack and together we attack the most difficult part of the course where we're really pushing our boundaries. There are not many spectators in the Bois, not many arms reaching out in encouragement, offering water, egging us on. They'll be waiting at the finish line.

The finish line!

A muffled roar fills my ears. A chill snakes down my spine. My legs grow weak. The more I try to push forward, the more sluggish my pace. My heart becomes a thick thrum of panic in the center of my chest. My body shakes. My pack leaves the woods and draws me with them as we emerge onto Avenue Foch.

Closer. Closer. Closer.

This is where it happened in Boston. My eyes strain to the finish line. Is there a bomber waiting? I scan my running companions. They appear unfazed, their determination written on their faces.

No. No. No.

I won't give in to my fear. I can do this.

Two hundred meters to go. I fight my fear. Increase my pace. The Arc rises in my vision, a fitting metaphor for my triumph. I check my watch. Just a few more paces. Flicking my eyes this side and that, I see no one who looks dangerous. Yes! I hold up my arms and cross the finish line in the middle of the lead runners. Just over two hours twenty minutes. Better than expected. The spectators go wild, cheer and clap. There are media, friends of competitors taking photos. I hunch over, hands on knees, regain my equilibrium. I don't care about photos. I've done it. I ran the Paris Marathon. I finished the Paris Marathon. Did you see me, Mom? You must be so proud of me. Did you see me, Raphael? I have done it like I said I would. I'm strong. I can do anything.

"Sassy?"

I straighten and he stands in front of me.

"You came?" My voice is hoarse and strange. I clutch my throat. Nearly topple to the ground.

He hands me a water bottle and I drink. "You doubted I would? I'd always planned to. I'm so proud of you." He holds up the app. "Thanks for this. I'd already downloaded it. I was with you all the way."

My earlier heart palpitations were nowhere near as severe as they are now. What was I expecting? Of course, Raphael would be with me. He's always been my Encourager in Chief. I jumped over many hurdles today – I have proved I can make it alone. But will Raphael be one hurdle too far?

He holds out his hand. "Come, Sassy. I'll take you home."

I'm shivering with exhaustion and cold by the time Raphael gives me a lift home on his motorcycle.

"Can I come up?" He stands at my door holding my ger, his brow knitted while I key in the code.

"Sure." I can't think beyond how I'm going to stand under the shower for the longest time to rid myself of the sticky sweat which clings to me.

We slog up the five flights of stairs to my apartment. I usually run, but my legs ache from the lactic acid which I haven't worked off yet.

I fumble in my purse for my key, wishing I could find the key to my life. My fingers tremble. Raphael takes it from me, pushes the door open.

What! I squeal, jump backward and land against Raphael. Instead of the cold mausoleum of an apartment I left this morning, there's a roaring fire spurting red and black flames up the chimney and holy crap, there are twinkle lights strung across the ceiling and cherry blossoms on top of the mantlepiece. I've entered the *Twilight Zone*.

Standing in the open doorway, I gawp at the fairyland, my shower forgotten.

"Like it?" Raphael helps me inside in his usual gentlemanly manner, his arm around my waist, practically lifting me down the stairs.

My throat's too dry to speak, but he breaks the silence. "Sassy, I hope you don't mind. This is a huge day for you. I wanted to cheer you up when you got home." He's wearing jeans and a red blazer which matches the red deep piled rug he's placed in front of the fire. I imagine lying naked on the soft wool beside him and smelling the fragrant firewood, breathing his heady fragrance—

I hurry to the fire, hold my fingers to the flames, reach up and cover my burning face.

Stop it. Stop it. Stop it.

I wait while my heartbeat slows, then clear my throat. I unwind my scarf and hold out my hands to the flames. I'd run out of firewood and didn't have the motivation to call for more but I see there's a stack on each side of the hearth. "You've run a marathon of your own to get this ready." My poor excuse for a joke.

"Nowhere near as difficult as yours. Did I tell you how proud I am?" He walks to where I'm shivering near the fire, helps me remove my long white shaggy shearling coat I'd stored in a locker before the race. It's the color of fresh snow, a mixture of silky fur and sumptuously soft suede. It's like a lover's embrace. I've been wearing it every time I leave the apartment.

I tug off my pink woolen cloche, shake my hair free. Tossing my hat over one of the new red velvet chairs in front of the fire, I watch Raphael hang my coat on a brass hook near the door.

He spies my shopping bags in the kitchen where I left them last night. "May I?" As he passes, I see shadows in his eyes, fresh furrows around them. He looks the same, but older. Do I look as changed as he does? Why not? I've lived a lifetime while apart from him.

We start unpacking like we're a cozy married couple who've been doing tedious tasks together for years.

He holds up a box. "What's this?" He's always been as inquisitive as a kid at Christmas.

"Some china and cutlery for my Thanksgiving dinner party next month." Pascale suggested gathering my friends around me would help me find joy. "Americans never miss it no matter where in the world we are. It's also my birthday, so I'm used to the fuss, only this time I'm the one making the fuss. My first celebration in Paris."

Raphael glances sideways at me while he unpacks. "I'd love to join you. I'd love to celebrate your birthday with you."

I let his words hang in the air.

When I ignore him, he says, "I didn't know you cooked."

"I've been watching YouTube videos. I'm going to roast the biggest chicken I can fit into my oven." I hold out a huge platter from under the counter. "I bought lavender-infused mustard to baste it." I hold up a pretty vintage bottle.

"My mother uses that too." He smiles his wonderfully warm smile. "What is it about the French and purple chicken, eh?" Using a sharp knife, he rips open a cardboard box, lifts out a plate. "You bought a retro dinner set." He examines a pink, cream and gold vintage butter dish. "Nice pattern. And what's this?" He reads the side of a smaller box. "Cutlery."

"Galeries Layfette had them on display. They look like rose gold, but they're copper. They'll add some glitz."

His eyes slide over the set. "Hmmm. Settings for eight people." He stacks shelves and studies the dining table. "You're inviting friends from the Institut?"

"Yes. Zack and Jemi. Also, Madame Lavelle and the Grande Dame. Oh, and Lamar." I was pleased Bernelle had a prior commitment. No way I want her around my celebratory table.

"I'm glad the Grande Dame's coming. I'd love to see her." Raphael is fascinated by my friendship with the French aristocrat fallen on hard times who waved to me from her balcony on my first day. He leans back against the kitchen counter and folds his arms. "How's she doing?"

"Taking one day at a time." *Like me.* "She's undergoing chemo for throat cancer and has lost her hair which is why she wears a long blonde wig." I'm fascinated by her foot-long electronic cigarette and blood-red lips which shoot satirical quips like machine gun fire when I go out for a drink with her. Which I've been doing. A lot. "She insisted I join her on her evening visit to Café de Flore the night we broke up."

Raphael squeezes my shoulder. "I'm glad."

"She's a good friend." I remember the night at Flore like it was yesterday, not weeks ago. The Grande Dame screwed up her eyes when she met me in the foyer, studied my face through her bulbous red Givenchy glasses and said, *Ca va, ma petite? You look like you could use a drink.*

Thinking of her brings a tear to my eye. "She needed cheering up after her latest doctor's report, but she was more concerned about me. A truly beautiful soul."

Raphael places his hand over mine which clutches the counter. "I'm glad she was there for you."

"The waiters love her. They brought us rum and lemon to toast Hemingway and his drinking pals. All the time I've gone with her they never let us pay."

Raphael nods as if that's how it should be, strokes my hand. "What did you talk about?"

"You." The rum loosened my tongue that night. *I broke up with Raphael,* I'd announced to the Dame as soon as we settled on our red velvet banquette looking onto the street, watching the well-heeled make their way up Boulevard Saint-Germain.

Do you really want to cut a man as handsome and talented as your Raphael out of your future just because he played a trick on you? she'd asked. *He adores you.*

A trick? It still annoys me that she took Raphael's side.

"What did she say about me?" He pushes himself off the counter, stands straight like he's a prisoner about to be sentenced. "Did she hate me for what I did?"

I shrug. "She said, *carpe diem.*"

Raphael nods. "*Carpe diem.* Seize the day. That sounds like her."

"Yes. She told me the full meaning of *carpe diem* was to *seize the day, trusting as little as possible in the future.*"

"So true, Sassy. We only have today." He clicks his fingers. "We write our own futures. That's what we need to talk about. Our future together."

I nibble the inside of my cheek. "What future?" I slam my hand onto the counter. "Oh well, let's get on with it. As far as I'm concerned, we have no future."

Raphael's eyes dart around the kitchen. "Before we discuss that, will you invite me to your first dinner party? At least as a friend. I couldn't bear to miss it."

"Let's wait till we talk." When I decided to host my first Thanksgiving/birthday dinner, Raphael didn't figure in my plans. We were over. Uh. We're still over. Kitchen sorted, I head back to the fire.

"Of course." He joins me, runs his fingers through his hair, musses it the way he knows I love. Layers of uncertainty slide over his face. "Sassy." He clears his throat. "I'm sorry for what I did. I can't believe I was such a *connard*. I understand why you couldn't forgive me."

My heart thumps over the crackle of the wood. "Go on, you *connard*," I tell the fire.

He touches my arm so lightly I might have imagined it. "We said some harsh words, but to me, nothing we can't come back from."

"You think?" *Boom-diddy-boom* goes my heart, homesick for him. "I'm not sure—"

"Ssh." He moves closer. "Lovers disagree. All the time. They forgive each other."

Thoughts swirl through my mind. Every word and action from that night are seared into my brain. "It was more than a disagreement. You tried to control me and turned nasty when I refused to let you. I gave up that nonsense when I left the States. I won't live my life that way ever again."

His face is so close to mine I see the plea in his eyes. "You won't have to. I've been seeing Philippe, my therapist, taking anger-management counselling again. I gave up the sessions when I met you and was no longer angry all the time. Even my nightmares are rare now, thanks to you. But when we hit that rocky patch, I regressed. I wanted to smash things. My paintings were pure anger. I spent too much time at Marcel's, drinking, imagining you behind the counter even though you were never there when

I was. I missed you so much. I want to fix us, Sassy." He mops moisture from his forehead with a large white handkerchief.

He's caught me by surprise again. "I found a therapist, too," I tell him. "But even with therapy, I doubt we can make it work. Neither of us called or texted in a month."

He rubs the back of his neck. "Philippe said to wait. I was afraid I'd triggered some dark mental state in you, but Marcel assured me you were coping." He holds out his arms, but I ignore them, he drops them to his side. "I was a mess over what I did. I hoped you'd call. When you didn't, I hoped you'd still be here when I came back and not dating another Frenchman ... or Canadian." He shoots me a look, one eyebrow raised. "You're not, are you?"

I roll my shoulders, easing the tension. "What do you think?"

He frowns, then his face clears. "How would you have time, eh, with work, class and training?" He puffs out a breath. "I brought you a present." He goes to the bathroom and returns with a large bouquet of red roses tied with a perfectly matched ribbon. "Please forgive me, *mon ange*." He hands them to me. "I treated you badly." He holds me by the upper arms and kisses my forehead. "I was such a fool."

"Right." I bury my face in the soft petals, inhale the fragrance, avoid his eyes. He has the knack of reading my mind. "Thanks. I'll put them in water."

I take the Murano glass vase from the second-hand markets from my cupboard, place the arrangement in the middle of the dining table. "They're so beautiful."

"So are you, Sassy." He takes my hand, walks me back to the fire. "I ruined everything. But I'll make it up to you." He holds out his arms and I let him embrace me this time. His hands skim my body, tracing the shape of my arms, my waist, my hips. "Is this okay?" He stills his hands; his eyes search mine.

Yes. Yes. Yes. "Yes," I manage between gaspy breaths.

"Do you want me to stop?" His dark eyes look uncertain.

No. No. No. "No."

"You've lost weight."

"Every pound I carry is another pound I've got to lift with every step I run. It paid off. I surprised myself with my time."

He lets that sink in. "Sassy, are you happy without me?"

"Happy?" I fall into one of the armchairs, clutch my knees with my hands. "Honestly?" I wrap my arms around myself and rock forward. *Everyone I've ever loved leaves me.* First my mother. I shake, seeing again the accident. Then my father disowned me. How abandoned I've felt these past weeks, even though I was the one who abandoned Raphael. I stare into the flames, think how sad it is that no matter how bright a fire burns, it's in its nature to die eventually. *Is that how it is with Raphael and me?* I ask the fire. *Did we burn too bright too soon and now only embers remain?* But there're no answers in the fire.

Raphael takes my trembling hands, gently lifts me to my feet. Wrapping his arms around me, he pulls me close. I lean against his chest and it's like all the unhappiness of the past weeks melts away. He says nothing. Just holds me for the longest time while our hearts beat as one. Finally, he talks, his breath warm on my neck, "I don't ever want to live without you, *ma chérie.* You're my life. Without you, nothing has meaning. I love you. Do you still love me?" He kisses my eyelids, runs his fingers down the length of my hair as if measuring the length of time we've been apart. "You don't have to say anything. Perhaps I've hurt you too much."

I keep silent, thinking, then shake my head. *If I take him back, how long before he tries to control me again?*

He holds my shoulders until we're looking into each other's eyes. "*Mon ange.* Talk to me. Give me another chance." His eyes flicker with what looks like fear.

What other man could make my heart race like Raphael? We might have burned down to embers, but they're red-hot embers. "Hmmm. Maybe."

He leans down and kisses me. An I'll-take-it-slow kind of kiss. "It makes me happy that you'll even think about it after what I did. You'll see I've changed." He presses me into the chair. "Champagne? I brought your favorite."

While Raphael pours the bubbly, I lose myself in the comforting sounds of my neighborhood. Mario the Italian's tread on the stairs. No doubt nursing the bottle of cheap shiraz he buys each evening. He greets Sergio, the Russian from the third floor who'll have a bottle of cheap vodka. They'll have a drinking competition, then when properly drunk, they'll belt out folk songs from Mario's balcony. Their voices sound pretty good together; no one complains. They compete with the bass drum-roll of cars thumping over the wet cobblestones. A motorbike roars around the corner and I'm on the back of Raphael's bike again, remembering our first ride through Paris in the rain.

He sits in the chair close to mine, we clink glasses. "*Salut*, Sassy."

"*Salut*, Raphael." I sip my Verve Clicquot. There's nothing quite like fancy champagne. "How's the painting going?"

His eyes light up. "I sold my complete Left Bank series recently." The buyer—an interior designer—has ordered as many as I create. No more am I the struggling artist. Monsieur Marion sold another of my oils today for a stupendous sum for an unknown."

"Oh? Which was it?"

"That one with bold block colors that blend every shade I've seen out of your attic window at sunrise. I haven't painted in your attic since we broke up, so it's the last in the series."

"You're doing well, but I've never considered you a struggling artist, certainly not the holes-in-your-trousers type." I put my flute onto the drinks table between our chairs. I shouldn't drink. I need a clear head.

"I did struggle to focus before I met you, *ma chérie*. Now." He puts his flute next to mine and presses his fingertips against his eyes. "Can we try again?"

I rest my head against the back of the chair. Am I mad? "Hmmm. I was coming to terms with life without you." I push back into the corner of the chair, fold my arms, study him.

He leans forward, brushes his fingers over my arm. "Together we'll work this out, Sassy. Let me show you my love."

Despite myself, my fingers twitch and I don't miss his slight smile.

He's so certain of my reaction to him. He squeezes my hand then releases it. "Let me show you how much I've missed you." He stands in front of me holding out his hands.

I don't move. I sit there, asking the universe what would be the smart move.

Raphael hesitates, then bends down, one hand on the arm of the chair, one hand on my shoulder. "I want to spoil you. How about I take you to dinner, give you some time?" His voice is deep and uneven.

"Perhaps." I hold out my hand and allow him to pull me to my feet.

He glances at me to gauge my willingness, I guess. "How about—?"

I fall into his arms. Hold him so close I can't breathe. I cling to him, my nails digging into his shoulders. My passion erupts like an uncontrollable wildfire. "Raphael. Raphael. Raphael," I cry. "I've missed you so."

"Sassy." He groans, picks me up and brands me with hot kisses to my lips, my forehead, my throat, then pulls me to his chest so I feel his heart throb, his hair tickle my face, his warm skin sear mine. He stands me on the rug, then with shaky fingers lifts my tank top over my head, kisses my breasts, hooks his fingers in the waistband of my running pants, rolls them down my hips. He crouches and kisses my naked thighs, asking, "Is this okay?"

"Yes," I whisper, loving the warmth of his lips on me.

He stands, runs his knuckles down my cheek, murmuring, "*Tu es très belle ce soir, chérie.*" His fingers lightly run up and down my spine until I'm a trembling mess.

I can't resist this man when he sets his mind to seduction.

He knows. He picks me up and carries me to the bedroom. "We're going to make love like we've never loved before."

That fire is a roaring flame inside me. He knows how to play my body with those sensitive artist's fingers of his, where to kiss me with his sensuous mouth, how to fill all my senses until I arch towards him, craving more.

I shouldn't be doing this, but ... *Oh My God.* "Raphael, oh Raphael."

I block my mind to everything except the way it feels to be in his arms again.

CHAPTER TWENTY-ONE

Twilight. My favorite time of day. The rain's stopped. The sky's pink-purple. Someone plays a moody saxophone from an upstairs balcony opposite the restaurant where Raphael and I share an apéritif. We sit side by side on a plush sofa before the fire, holding hands, listening to music, tapping our toes in time. I sip champagne. He sips Dubonnet. The delicious smells from the kitchen make me ravenous. I'm looking forward to my first proper meal since our breakup. It seems all's well in our world. But is it? Am I making a huge mistake letting him back into my life?

We're at Le Coupe-Chou-Chou in the Latin Quarter. I've checked my coat and now I'm baring one shoulder in my little red pre-loved Dior dress I picked up at an outlet months ago. Raphael's changed into a forest-green sports coat, a white silk shirt and tan trousers. Not his usual style, but he's hot, as always. I cover my mouth to suppress a grin. I imagine Raphael hunting in the royal forest, his charger in hot pursuit of a fox or whatever he's chasing.

Tonight he chased me.

And caught me.

I push thoughts of being coerced aside, close my eyes and relive the moment when Raphael's touch set every inch of my body on fire, transported me to a fantasy world where we enjoyed perfect sync.

Réne, our waiter, interrupts my daydream. "*Votre table est prête.*" He escorts us to a line of tables set against a brick wall. He adjusts the heat lamp above us although there's a blazing fire nearby. He must think I'm cold in my barely-there dress, but the fire inside me keeps me warm. He lights a small white church candle for our table and expertly drapes a soft red napkin over our laps. Before he leaves, he pours us both a Dom Perignon from the bottle on ice beside Raphael who nods his thanks.

"*Merci*," I say. Overhead, twinkle lights wink at me from a ceiling draped in red net. My gaze flicks over the Dom Perignon. The single rose Raphael brought from the bouquet he gave me is in a tiny crystal vase. He's gone to so much trouble. Negative thoughts pop into my head. Why did he wait so long to come back if that's what he always planned to do? I mentally slap myself. Our personalities are complicated. Why can't I relax and enjoy the night instead of overthinking everything?

He reaches across the table, covers my hand with his. "Is something wrong, *ma chérie*? Not in the mood for Dom Perignon? Shall I order Verve Clicquot?"

I sip my delicious bubbles, a smile wobbles on my face. "Oh no. The Dom's wonderful. Just getting used to seeing you again."

He tenderly strokes my fingers. "You're so beautiful tonight, *chérie*. But why is your face so sad?"

"Bernelle." I catch my breath and point. "She's across the room with Lamar."

Raphael acts surprised, but doesn't fool me. He has the knack of walking into a room and knowing instantly who's there. "She's always with Lamar." He waves a dismissive hand in front of his face.

I shoot a glance at Bernelle, who scowls at me, no doubt devasted to see me with Raphael.

She shrugs, raises her glass in our direction. forms her lips into a smile for Raphael, not me, before turning her attention to Lamar.

"Did you know they'd be here tonight?" I tug the curls I painstakingly created earlier while Raphael sat on the bed watching, telling me how pleased he was that he'd never have to go through the torture.

"Of course I didn't." He sounds a tad snappy.

"Hmmm."

Raphael leans forward, nails me with his eyes. "Believe me, *mon ange*. I had no idea they'd be here. How many times do I have to tell you she's nothing to me?"

Bernelle's the epitome of French beauty with her perfect surgically enhanced features. Her presentation is always flawless and her clothes' budget must be astronomical. Maybe one day I'll crack the code of French sophistication. I missed that gene even though I was born in the land of Coco Chanel, Yves St Laurent, and Christian Dior. But still. Raphael chose me. Why can't I get over her?

Raphael reaches across the table, holds both my hands. "I know things have happened to you in the past to make you doubt yourself—your Maman's death, your father's bullying, the bomb—but don't doubt my love for you." Kissing my knuckles, he says, "You're enchanting. There are many Bernelles in the world, but only one you."

I rub my forehead, annoyed at my insecurity. I should believe him. I shrug a shoulder and remember every session with every therapist over the years, even before the bomb changed my life forever. *Your self-esteem has taken a beating from your being treated as worthless by your father,* they'd say. I know it, but it's not easy overcoming lifetime habits. "Raphael, why did you choose me?"

Raphael laughs, shakes his head. "Sassy, can't you see yourself when you look in the mirror? You're spectacular. See how men look at you. I want you. No one else."

I hold his hands across the table. He's right. I must stop seeing myself as lesser because my father made me feel lesser. I slide a glance Bernelle's way. She's tapping her red claws on the table, watching Raphael with predatory eyes. *You're not getting him, bitch.*

Raphael presses his lips together, frowns. "Don't be upset, but I need a word with Lamar later."

"Sure." Raphael having a word with Lamar is nothing to snark about. Lamar's awesome. But Bernelle's a threat, no matter how oblivious Raphael is to her charms. I suck in a deep breath. Know I must always be on guard around her. "Why should I mind?"

"Sassy. It's business." He picks up the menu. "Would you like to share the Moules Mariniere?"

"Sounds perfect." My hunger deserted me when I saw Bernelle eating Raphael with her eyes.

In record time, a rustic black pot is delivered to our table. As Réne serves us, the shells click against each other, releasing the heavenly aroma of wine and garlic. "*Bon appetit.*" Réne bows his head, tops up my flute, then leaves us.

He returns before we've made headway on the shellfish. "Monsieur Valentine, the lady across the room," he nods subtly toward Bernelle, "asked me to gift you this bottle of Chateau Lafite 1865." He displays the bottle along his arm, draped in a white napkin like it's a precious swaddled baby. "There's a note."

Raphael nods, accepts the bottle and note. "*Merci*, Réne."

Réne fills two enormous red wine glasses from Bernelle's gift, then places the bottle beside Raphael before gliding to the next table to serve an elderly gentleman.

Raphael's eyes flit over the note. He folds it, slips it into his pocket, smiling like the proverbial cat. "Now, let's get into these mussels."

"What did Bernelle say?" I dip a tiny hunk of spongy bread into the sauce, stuff it into my mouth and wonder why the smooth combination of wine and cream tastes so foul.

"The note was from Lamar, not Bernelle, so no need for that pout, *ma chérie.* He's my agent now. I've been meeting with him about my first show. It's all arranged. I'm having my first exhibition at the Centaquatre."

Aha. Of course. Courtesy of Bernelle. What happened to Monsieur Marion? "Wow. Fast work. When?"

"Christmas Eve." When we're finished the mussels, he stands and flicks imaginary crumbs from his trousers. "If you'll excuse me, I'll pop over to Lamar, set up a meeting." Then he turns back, holds out his hand. "Come with me."

I ball my napkin and toss it onto the table. "No. Knock yourself out."

Raphael needs no second bidding.

I watch them, grit my teeth when the three of them laugh and chat like the old friends they are.

"All done." Raphael returns after a few minutes, five, to be precise. "Sorry for my bad manners in leaving the table, but I wanted to stitch up a meeting in case they leave. I'm having a business lunch with Lamar tomorrow."

"Great." I watch Bernelle watching us, her mouth a straight line. I sip my champagne. I thought this night was going to be all about us and where we go from here, instead I've been sucked into Raphael's whirlwind.

He points to my untouched glass of red wine. "I know you drink champagne only, Sassy, but you should try this. It's spectacular."

That word slips so easily from his tongue. "Red wine gives me a headache." Especially when Bernelle is the source.

"Not when it costs over €4,000 a bottle."

I grab my throat. "Especially when it costs that much. That's obscene." I dab my lips with my napkin thinking how Bernelle's gesture is like the way my father throws ridiculous amounts of money about, buying people with his 'sweeteners'. How many homeless could have been taken from the streets for that amount of money?

Raphael sips the gold-infused brew like there's nothing unusual about such an extravagant gift. "Do you want another dish of moules, Sassy? You didn't eat much."

"No, I'm done." I lay down my napkin, take a deep breath. "I hate sitting here under the watchful eye of Bernelle when we've just spent a month apart."

Raphael leans back in his chair and folds his arms. "Bernelle sees me as a business proposition. She's going to make a shitload of money off me, and money is her modus operandi. This bottle of Chateau Lafite will be a tax deduction."

The business proposition slinks across the room in her skintight little black cocktail dress slit almost to her waist. She stops beside Raphael's chair. Placing her hand on his shoulder, she looks at me and says, "*Bonsoir*, Saskia. A pleasure to see you again. It's been so long." She tosses her head so masses of her glossy black mane dance around her bare shoulders, but there's no pleasure in her eyes. "I thought I would come say hello and warn you that Raphael and I will be spending a lot of time together between now and his exhibition." Her eyes slide between us. Raphael contentedly sips his red wine. I angrily gulp my champagne. "I do hope you don't mind," she purrs with as much insincerity as she can muster.

I clench my teeth. "Why should I mind? He's all yours, Bernelle. Why don't you sit with him and drink your wine?" I struggle from behind the table, nearly spilling Raphael's wine into his lap.

Raphael jumps to his feet, knocking over his chair. "Sassy." His voice follows me across the room.

I flick a withering glance over my shoulder in time to see Réne execute a last-minute maneuver around Raphael's chair, holding his drinks' tray in the air, not spilling a drop.

Sorry Réne. It isn't the thing to make a fuss in a Paris restaurant. Restaurants are for eating, drinking and smooching.

Not arguing.

Clasping my face in my hands, I stagger in the direction of the ladies', hating that I created a scene. That's Raphael's forté. But I couldn't breathe with Bernelle fussing over Raphael. Leaning against the nearest pillar, hidden from view, I pop a Xanax, my first in a while. I don't like what it does to my body, but it's what I need at the moment. Stealing a glance at the table, I see Bernelle leaning over Raphael's chair, her face in his. Am I paranoid? He loves me, not Bernelle. *He does, he does*, I tell myself, but I'm not convinced.

A light touch on my arm. "Saskia, do not be so upset." Lamar's eyes search my face. "Bernelle and Raphael have known each other all their lives. She's always wanted him, but Raphael is immune to her charms. Growing up, he had eyes only for his childhood sweetheart. Oh, pardon, I spoke out of turn."

I clutch my throat. "Childhood sweetheart?" My voice is hoarse. "I haven't heard of any childhood sweetheart."

"I am so sorry. I should not have said that. Forgive me."

"Of course. You weren't to know."

"Raphael has suffered some dreadful blows. I want to see him happy. He has been one of my closest friends all my life."

"How is that so?"

"We all grew up in the same village. Bernelle. Marcel also. Went to the same schools. Raphael is loyal to his friends. There is a goodness in him. When he fell for you, he fell hard. Trust that his heart is yours and yours alone. He has been absolutely heartbroken this past month without you."

"Thank you, Lamar. You're a very good friend to Raphael."

"My pleasure, Saskia." He lightly touches my shoulder. "My wish is for you and Raphael to be happy. There will be complications, but it is so in every relationship. Oh, it seems Bernelle is looking for me. I must go. Shall I escort you back to Raphael?"

"No." Giving the Xanax time to kick in, I return to the table where Raphael's sitting alone, tossing back Bernelle's wine.

Lurching to his feet, he grabs my arm as I walk past. He pulls me close to his side. "I thought you'd left." He sounds both angry and afraid. "Don't walk out on me like that ever again. I brought you here tonight for a very important reason."

"What would that be?" I press my heart as Raphael helps me into my chair. "To see Bernelle?" The words fly from my mouth before I can stop them.

His face flushes a shade that matches the tablecloth. "You're completely obsessive over Bernelle." He sits. "Let it go. It's unhealthy."

My cheeks burn. He's right. "Ssh. Lower your voice. Everyone's staring."

He crosses his arms, glares around the room. "They can stare all they like. It's not like we're the first lovers to fight."

My stomach clenches. "We're fighting? Over Bernelle? Hmmm. I hate being a spectacle. If you don't tone it down, I'll walk out. And not just to the ladies."

"Okay." He drums his fingers on the table. "Sorry. No, I brought you here tonight to ask you a question that should put to rest your fears about Bernelle."

"What question?" My throat thickens. I grab my throat. Uh-oh. Surely, he isn't—

CHAPTER TWENTY-TWO

He is.

"Marry me." Raphael thumps his open palms onto the table. He pushes our glasses aside and water slops onto the tablecloth. "You're the one I want." He jumps to his feet. "Fuck," he says. "I've ruined our big moment. I should have been on one knee." He arranges himself in front of my chair. "Sassy?"

Reeling, I scrunch my napkin into a ball. All night, while we've been talking and eating and drinking, and I've been watching Bernelle, I never remotely considered Raphael would propose. "Sit ... down ... right ... now."

Raphael takes his seat, leans forward, quirks an eyebrow. "Will you?"

He's just offered me everything I could ever want, but— "Raphael. After a month apart with zero contact, you propose?"

He smacks a palm against his forehead. "Surely you always knew I'd come back."

I pick up my glass. Glug my champagne. Put the glass down. "How would I know that?" My voice is higher than I like. "*I* left *you*, remember. But *marry* you, Raphael? We've only known each other a short while. We've too much to sort out."

He knits his brow. Looks confused. "But we love each other. Why wait?"

"It's far too soon. I'm not a girl who's been dreaming of floating down the aisle of some gorgeous church wearing Vera Wang, a diamond tiara in my hair, my ethereal face misty under a white veil studded with Swarovski crystals. I want other things in life. Marriage is way down my list of 'Things to do before I'm Thirty.'"

"What. Is. Wrong. With. You?" His fingers rap the table in time with his words. He's obviously forgotten Philippe's anger management strategies.

People stop mid-chew. "Keep your voice down, Raphael." The restaurant is small and intimate, too intimate for personal conversation.

He takes my hand and squeezes it. "I want to spend the rest of my life with you. We're a perfect team. Say yes." When I don't reply, he lets go of my hand, folds his arms, gives me a narrow-eyed stare. "Why isn't now a good time?"

"Marriage is a huge commitment. I'm not ready. And I doubt you are either."

His lips form a grim, straight line. "I don't see marriage as a ball and chain. I'd never hold you back. Be as independent as you like. Just be with me. We could live together in your building for awhile if that's what you want." He grips the edge of the table, his knuckles white, a sign he's having trouble being challenged. He curses under his breath, then uses a more conciliatory tone. "Sorry. Philippe would be ashamed of me. I must learn to deal without anger. It's so hard."

"Hard or not, try, Raphael. Aggressiveness isn't the way to get what you want. Not with me. I'm done with aggression." I pat my hands in a downward motion. "And lower your voice. We don't want everyone knowing our business." Parisians don't share my love of personal space. They adore salacious drama and we're on the menu tonight.

"They shouldn't be listening." He scans the room. Everyone studies their plates. "Please, Sassy, I'm trying my hardest. I can't lose you again."

I want to hide under the table when diners turn their heads, eyebrows raised and listen with rapt attention, especially the elderly gentleman in a Savile Row suit who's been bumping elbows with me all night. I hand him my untouched glass of red. He smiles, accepts, obviously having heard how expensive it is.

I hold Raphael's hand. "If we take it slow, respect each other's boundaries, there's no chance of losing each other."

He twirls the stem of his wine glass. "I'd never risk our relationship again." He folds his arms and leans forward. "You're good for me. I'm good for you." His voice is soothing, like a jazz singer mesmerizing an audience. "You've helped me through my nightmares. You inspire my art. You're my forever girl. But how do I know you won't run off again if I put a foot wrong because you're so jealous?"

I cup my chin in my hand and stare at this gorgeous guy sitting opposite me. "Really?" But he's right. I'm jealous of Inés because she's known him intimately like I do. Then there's Bernelle, who's got the hots for him and doesn't try to hide it. I won't commit until I know for sure I'm the only one in his life.

He reaches across the table, brushes his fingers down my face. "Look at me."

I look. See the tenderness in his eyes.

He leans forward, his hands linked in mine. "You're everything to me. I'd like to offer you the moon tied with a red satin ribbon, but I only have myself to offer. I don't even have a ring yet. Don't worry, I shall design a spectacular one just for you."

I'm beginning to think I'm not as spectacular as he claims. Yet a newly hatched butterfly soars happily through my gut. I quickly pull a cloak of indifference around me. Every part of my being craves Raphael. But I crave independence. Despite Raphael's promises to the contrary, he has trouble with control. No wonder I have trust issues. My parents were married for twenty-eight years and Mom never had security. Father was a serial cheater, the man about town squiring the socialite-of-the-week. How do I know Raphael isn't cut from the same cloth? They say women are often attracted to someone who reminds them of their fathers. In many ways, Raphael reminds me of Pa. Did I make some subconscious choice?

"Come on, Sassy." Raphael's voice rises, crashing into my thoughts. The eavesdroppers unashamedly lean toward us. "I asked you a question." He flexes his arm muscles in a Mister Universe pose, points to his pecs. "I'm not such a bad catch."

A grin plays around my mouth at his goofy pose. If it were just about his perfect body, Raphael is a great catch. Mister Elderly Gentleman smiles at me as if to say, *what's not to like?* I sip my warm champagne and wrinkle my nose. *Gross.*

Ever-attentive Réne is at my side. Whisking away my tepid drink, he replaces my glass with an iced one, freshens my drink from the chilled bottle. He has bought into the import of this moment.

"I have given you an answer." My head says *no* to Raphael's proposal, but my heart screams *yes*. Marriage to Raphael could be so good, and my heart rate soars like I've just done a hard training sprint when I think about how great we were together for that brief time after we first met. I cross my fingers under the tablecloth. Touch the wooden table legs. Resist throwing salt over my shoulder. I hold out my hand to him and squeeze it when he places it in mine, hope in his eyes. A pang of regret shoots through me. I've scarcely made a start on my Paris dream. Getting married would complicate things. "No ... I can't marry you. Not now." My voice is hollow. My heart pushes against my rib cage, stealing my breath.

The diners gasp, denied their free champagne.

"*Whaaat?*" Raphael snatches his hand away, leans back in his chair, hands linked behind his head.

Mister Elderly Gentleman looks crestfallen. He's been rooting for Raphael all night.

"I'm sorry. It's a no. For now."

"Are you playing games with me?"

"This is not a game, Raphael," I whisper. "How can I marry you when I don't understand you? The way you danced with Inés at Oubliettes. And Bernelle. She never took her eyes off you tonight except to scowl at me. And this ridiculously expensive bottle of red?"

"Why are you so cynical? Oh, don't raise your eyebrows at me." He tilts his head to the side. "Why can you never let anything go? Can't you see we'll have a great life together?"

I sigh, cross my arms, lean my elbows onto the table. "Raphael, this is *my* life. You're trying to control me again. I told you I'm not ready for marriage. I want to be a strong, independent woman before I commit."

He frowns. "You proved how strong you've become at the marathon today. Oh," he hits the side of his head, "Maybe that's it. You're exhausted. I shouldn't have brought you out tonight. I'm so selfish."

"I feel fine. I'll sleep tomorrow." I tug one of my fast-drooping curls.

He tilts his head back, then smiles at the people around us. He leans forward and whispers. "But I wish you'd marry me. You don't have anyone else in the world."

I gulp a mouthful of champagne, take a deep breath, push away my anxiety. I think of the one and only photograph of my father stuffed into my wallet which I never look at. I destroyed my cell phone so he couldn't contact me. He's a schmuck, and I can't see a clear path to reconciliation. Raphael's right.

Raphael takes my hand and rubs his thumbs over my vampire-red nail polish. "Everyone needs someone. I'll never abandon you. I'll give you anything you want."

I sigh. "I want simple things, Raphael. Trust. Loyalty. Independence. You say you accept my independence, which is a good first step, although I'm not sure how sustainable it is. And trust? I've seen first-hand at Marcel's Bar how casual French relationships are. Some guys chat up a new girl each week." I want our love to be like a spool of the most high-quality thread, strong enough to last no matter what it endures.

Raphael reddens. "I might have done that once, but not anymore. I've changed. For you. I agree, we can't move on without trust."

Mister Elderly Gentleman nods. I'll bet his generation had no reason to distrust their partners.

"How can I trust you?" My eyelids twitch. I'm afraid he'll convince me. The sounds of the busy restaurant fade. I hear nothing while I wait on Raphael's answer. I see nothing but his set jaw and gorgeous dark eyes.

He lays his hand on top of mine where it's lying on the table, trembling. "You can count on me. Trust me. Always."

I take a sip of water while I digest his words. *Can I?* "There's another problem."

He blows out a breath. "You are good at finding problems. Tell me. Let's see if I can fix it."

"Take me to meet your parents. I'm an old-fashioned girl. I'd like to get to know your family."

"Words fail me." A grim smile plays on his lips. "As painful as that will be, you shall meet the parents. But be warned, I've kept you away from my family for a reason. Nevertheless, we'll drive down tomorrow."

I hold out my arms, palms up. "So soon? What about your bridge stall? Your oils for the gallery? Marcel? The bar? We can't just run off like a couple of irresponsible teenagers. And I was going to sleep the day away."

He laughs. "Ah, Serious Saskia. Don't worry. Paris will survive a day or two without us. You can sleep on the way. Off to Les Salles we shall go. My mother will think Christmas has come early."

I'm taken aback by his sudden cheeriness, but I detect a false note. "Don't think that meeting your parents and seeing you in your home environment will change my mind about marrying you."

He puffs out a breath. "You may walk away altogether after you meet them. My mind is already working hard, thinking of ways to charm you. Hmmm. Perhaps a picnic by the river on the way? A dozen cases of Verve Clicquot? A diamond necklace? What works for you?"

"None of the above, although the Verve Clicquot is tempting. Where is your village?"

He leans back in his chair, points to my clutch. "What happened to Mister Google?"

Using your cell phone in a Paris restaurant isn't the thing, judging by the dirty looks when I take it from my purse. I give a one-shouldered shrug, google 'Les Salles'. "Whoa, it's nearly five hours south of Paris. I'll freeze on the back of your bike. Oh," I scan a few lines, "it says its most famous resident is the politician François Valentine." I frown at Raphael. "Your *father*? It says he's Lord of the Manor. What a quaint medieval concept."

"That entry needs an update. It's *ex*-most famous resident now. But he *is* Lord of the Manor in his own mind." Raphael pulls a face. "We'll take Marcel's Citroen. It's old, but it's a sweet ride. My wheels are stored in a shed at the manor. I don't need a car in Paris. Marcel lends me his when I need to transport paintings."

"Will Marcel mind?"

"Are you kidding? He'll do cartwheels, especially when I tell him I've asked you to marry me."

"I'll be grateful for anything that has four windows and a heater. But why are you so dismissive about your famous father?"

"You're dismissive about yours."

"You're right." I'm ready to criticize Raphael for his attitude to his father, but when I read online news from the States, I always avoid the social pages so I don't see pictures of my father and his latest eye candy. I flip over his articles in the business section which show him steamrolling everyone in his path. "I hate his life."

"I hate my father's life too. Hmmm. How about dessert to sweeten you up? You deserve one after that marathon effort today."

After Raphael, dessert is my weakness. "Why not? Let's share a crème brûlée."

"Done."

"*Qu'est-ce que vous desirez, Monsieur Valentine?*" Réne hovers, flicks his crisp white napkin over his arm.

"*La crème brûlée et un Sauternes, s'il vous plaît.*"

"Sassy." Raphael leans forward, plays with my fingers. "I know exactly the type of ring I'll design for you."

"Hmmm."

Réne brings our crème brûlée. Anticipating its delicious sweetness, I drop my cell phone back into my clutch, much to the relief of Grumpy Diner two tables up who's paying his bill. I tap the brûlée's toffee top, wondering if I'll ever tap into Raphael's code. While the mixture of toffee and silky custard tantalizes my taste buds, I watch Raphael, that smooth operator, wondering what his next move will be.

Not being the dessert freak I am, he absentmindedly takes a scoop of crème brûlée then puts his spoon aside. Reaching across the table, he holds out his hand. "May I borrow your phone? I'll call the parents. I want to hear Maman's voice when I tell her I'm bringing home a girl."

"Really? Will she be pleased?"

"You've no idea."

When Raphael keys in the number, Grumpy Diner huffs, jerks his tie, stands up and strides to the door.

While he chats to his parents, Raphael holds the hand that's not shoveling crème brûlée into my mouth. By the time Réne pours our Sauternes, Raphael's made plans for an overnight stay. Tomorrow.

I've so many questions I need answered. First, his childhood sweetheart. Is she still down country? Will I meet her tomorrow? What's the story about that famous father of his?

While he's on the phone, I scrape the last of the crème brûlée from the edges of the dish, then wash it down with bubbly and Sauternes. I'm fascinated by the idea of Raphael in his family home. I can't imagine him under his parents' roof. He's an individual who dances to his own tune. I, too, need to dance to my own tune. Question is, will we learn to dance together?

CHAPTER TWENTY-THREE

Les Salles sparkles with twinkling lights and rooftops dusted with an icy sheen. The beauty eases my anxiety about what lies ahead. As we drive through Raphael's parents' village at twilight, I'm diving into the unknown. What will I learn about Raphael in his home environment? How will this visit end? Not for the first time, I wonder why I asked to meet Raphael's parents.

Raphael reaches across the seat and plays some music. "This is Beethoven's Pastoral Symphony," he says. "I play it on repeat each time I approach the country pile. Gets me in the mood. Can you hear the flowing brooks? The birds? The storm? ... then comes the sunshine. Get it?"

The music flows over me. I've never been much of a classical music fan, but I do get what Raphael's saying. "It's very dramatic, but I confess I'm too nervous thinking about meeting your parents to fully appreciate it."

He flicks off the music, although his head keeps bobbing like he's continuing the symphony in his head. "We're nearly there, Sassy. Down here it's an icebox in more ways than one." Pressing his lips into a straight line, he makes a sharp left, floors the accelerator, and the Citroen purrs up a steep hill.

I look over my shoulder at the disappearing village. "How utterly beautiful it is, Raphael. A fairytale."

He hunches over the steering wheel, his knuckles white. "You think? Growing up here was no fairytale. By the way, Mother returned from Tibet via China a couple of days ago. She's jet lagged."

I turn to him, concerned. "Why didn't you tell me? We should have waited."

"She couldn't wait to meet you. I told you she'd be mightily chuffed."

The house comes into view. I forget everything except how amazing it is. I press my face against the window. *Wow. Wow. Double wow.* "Raphael, you grew up in a château?"

He rubs his fingers through his hair. "The gothic splendor is something when you see if for the first time, but at the end of the day, it's just a house. A very big, cold, unfriendly house."

Surprised at the bitterness in his tone, I lose myself in the gothic splendor. Raphael's childhood home is straight out of 'Sleeping Beauty' with turrets at each corner, tiny windows with diamond-shaped lead lights, pretty Juliet balconies and towers, all topped with sloping gray slate roofs dusted with ice. "It's much more than a house," I whisper. As we drive closer, there's a medieval sundial, brick walls draped with vines, and a huge Italian-looking fountain in the circular driveway. "Look at that." In the weak setting sun, the honey-colored stone shines like molten gold and the windowpanes sparkle like glittering diamonds. I've lived in palatial homes all my life, but nothing comes close to this. "I'm blown away."

Raphael glances at me as if I've gone mad. Shaking his head, he drives around the turning circle and parks at the bottom of an ornate double-entry brick staircase straight out of an episode of *Game of Thrones*, the one where Queen Cersei does her walk of shame. "Prepare to be blown away all over again." He takes a deep breath, gets out of the car and comes around to my door. "Put on your coat." His breath is a puffy cloud.

He's only wearing jeans, shirt and sports coat so why the fuss? "Why don't you put on *your* coat?"

"The cold keeps me sharp." He pulls a red cashmere scarf from his pocket, slings it around his throat. "It's you I'm worried about." He reaches into the car, fixes the top button of my coat. "I'm dreading the meeting between you and my famous father. You'll see why soon enough. But after him you get to meet my sainted mother. You two will love each other."

"Why?" I chew the inside of my cheek, distracted by the meeting with his father. Is he anything like mine?

Raphael hesitates a beat. "Because I never bring girlfriends home. She'll go loco over you like I have. Papa might too, for all the wrong reasons."

"Really? Is this a riddle?"

"You'll soon figure it out." He helps me out of the car, then wraps me in the woolly blanket he brought along for our picnic by the river at the halfway mark. Lifting his hand, he waves half-heartedly to his father who I hadn't noticed standing ramrod stiff on the landing, watching.

"About time, son." His father's voice reverberates like a weapon shot from a great height. With his severely cut gray wavy hair and his gray suit and scarf, he reminds me of Frank Underwood from *House of Cards* before they shafted him.

Raphael turns me around so I'm facing him. "Remember, it's only one night."

"Promise?" I lean back against him, suddenly uneasy, then plaster a smile on my face.

His father's feet crunch across the snow, then stop in front of us. "So, son, you've come back."

Raphael says nothing. He and his father shake hands. No hug. No kiss. A reunion as frosty as the falling snow.

Raphael turns to me. "Papa, let me introduce my girlfriend, Saskia Bell. Saskia, François Valentine."

His father looks down on me, baring his large teeth in a caricature of a smile which reminds me of a savage dog. Two arrogant eyes bore into mine.

He's definitely scarier than Pa.

"*Enchanté*, Mademoiselle," he says after his scrutiny ends. He doesn't sound enchanted. He inclines his head over my gloved hand and drops it in the French manner that irks me. Intimate, yet dismissive. "Welcome to our home, Saskia." His English is flawless.

The blanket Raphael has wrapped around me slips down my arms, showing off my red woolly coat. Frank's eyes on me weirds me out. "Nice to meet you, Fr—sir." My voice wavers and hits a high note. "You have a stunning home."

"*Vraiment*." His tone conveys that he deserves every precious twelfth century stone. He gestures at the adjoining vine-covered wall. "I was hoping to show you my hothouse gardens where I grow roses and strawberries, but you're later than expected. Perhaps tomorrow."

I clear my throat. I think of the roses Raphael gave me last night. They'll be wilting by now, like I'm wilting here. "That would have been nice, sir." *Liar*. The idea of pottering around a hothouse with this man? No.

Raphael moves me aside and pops the trunk. "I'm sorry we're late, Papa, but the construction on the A20, you know ..."

His father nods, obviously doubting it was construction that slowed us down. And he's right. Raphael surprised me with a picnic by a river. After enjoying champagne, baguettes and paté, lulled by the gurgling water, we fell asleep wrapped in the blanket.

"Come now, both of you." Frank snatches my suitcase from my stiff fingers and leads the way to the stairs. "We must get you inside." He looks over his shoulder to check we're following. While we walk, he prattles on. "As always, Raphael, you're not dressed for the cold, but Saskia had the sense to cover up. And, son, don't you think it's time you got a grown-up haircut? Thirty is a bit old for shoulder-length girly curls, don't you think?"

Raphael's voice is ice when he says, "At thirty, I think my hair is my business, Papa, like everything else."

François turns around and opens his mouth, then thankfully shuts it again. "Your mother is waiting. I haven't seen her so excited for an age."

Arm in arm, we follow François up the stairs. I watch him swing my suitcase like it's full of feathers. His comment on Raphael's hair was out of line. Raphael's hardly a short-back-and-sides kind of guy like his father. Raphael's unruly curls suit his artist's persona. Or perhaps Raphael simply wants to be the opposite of his father.

Once the massive, studded entry doors creak shut behind us, like pulling up a drawbridge at the end of the day after a wearisome battle, I smother a gasp. The portico leads into a grand hall where a huge, gilded mirror takes up half the space. I know why Raphael dresses like the Sun King. I picture him running around, a little boy dressed in velvet pantaloons, frilly shirt and patent leather boots with golden buckles. I chuckle to myself to cover my nerves, but Raphael's so caught up in his own thoughts, he doesn't notice.

Our footsteps echo across the marble floor. The fabulous portraiture would do a museum proud. I love the huge fireplace with flames licking up the chimney, doing their best to warm the cavernous space.

François marches to the fire, then squats in front of it. "I'll stoke the fire, son. You go." He pokes around in the flames with what looks like a medieval lance. There's a loud *whoosh* and he jumps to his feet. "Take Saskia to meet your mother. She's in the kitchen. Leave that blanket with me, Saskia. I'll take it to your room with your suitcase."

Raphael bursts through the kitchen door, dragging me behind him, catching me by surprise when he calls out, "Mummy Dearest! How was Tibet?"

The room is deliciously toasty after the frigid outside. I thaw as we walk hand in hand to where his mother, who looks much younger than her husband, turns from stirring a pot on the stove.

"Raphie." With a happy squeal, she holds out her arms. Raphael drops my hand and steps toward her. "Tibet was a revelation," she says into his shoulder, "but suffers so much from the earthquake. I got held up at Guangzhou airport because of fog. The joys of travel." She moves out of Raphael's embrace but doesn't let go of his hand. "I'll tell you more later, but come, introduce me."

Raphael holds out a hand and pulls me forward. "Maman, this is my Saskia," he says. "Saskia Bell, meet Alexandra Valentine." He smiles at each of us. "My two favorite women in the world."

Alexandra leans down, holds me by the shoulders, kisses my cheeks, *bisou, bisou, bisou.* "Saskia. What a beautiful name. Welcome. It's wonderful to meet you. Raphael's been keeping you a secret." She claps her hands. "Please do call me Alex." She speaks with a plummy English accent, with scarcely a suggestion of French. So, Raphael's mother is English. Another secret he never thought to share.

"Thank you for having me, Alexandra, er, Alex. I'd love to hear about Tibet. I've never been, but I read that it's changing fast." I relax a little, loving how carefree Raphael appears with his mother. How different to the way he greeted his father.

"It is, my dear, and not for the better." Alex has black circles under her eyes, but she's a stunning woman from her gray chignon to her highly polished tan boots. Raphael has inherited her beautiful dark eyes, long lashes and mouth with lips that turn up at the corners. She could do much better than her dull tweed skirt and cream silk blouse with its old-fashioned neck bow. Typical English aristocrat. Not at all the elegant French dame I'd imagined. "What a beautiful coat." She brushes my arm. "I love a red coat in winter. So cheery." She turns to her son. "Raphie, hang Saskia's coat."

Raphael frowns when he helps me off with my coat and eyes my low-cut white shirt. Does he worry that his mother will think I'm risqué? I forgot to ask the dress code, but I think I should have gone with demure. He adjusts my woolen scarf, wrapping it twice around my neck.

While Raphael and his mother catch up, I move around the room, loving its olde-worlde feeling compared to the modern glitz of the homes I've lived in. Every item in the kitchen would have a long history, from the battered silver teapot on the mantelpiece, to the pewter drinking mugs, to the faded red toile de Jouy wallpaper which would make a great pattern on a blazer. I imagine the meals prepared here in the past, with people seated in elegant carved chairs at the timber dining table. "What a beautiful room, Alex," I say when there's a lull in conversation. "Cozy. Like a warm hug."

"Thank you, Saskia. I spend a lot of time reading in front of the fire." She tilts her head towards a small bookshelf. "Do you read the French classics, my dear?"

Crap. "I must admit, no. I'm still working through the, er, American classics. You know, Fitzgerald, Hemingway, Steinbeck. When my French improves, I'll tackle the French luminaries in their own language."

Raphael caresses my arm. "Saskia's fashion business absorbs her. She's going to introduce Paris to a new look."

François walks in and catches Raphael's words. He raises his eyebrows. "What new look could an American possibly introduce to Paris?"

I'm speechless. I hadn't expected such lack of diplomacy from a politician. Raphael takes my arm, pulls me away.

"Ignore him. He likes to shock so he can grab the attention." Raphael continues talking to his mother. "Saskia spends all her time designing," he tells her, "but she's working her way through all the novels Hemingway and the literati wrote while they lived in Paris. Often we take a walk together and follow in their footsteps."

I silently thank Raphael for the cue. "Yes, you know, *A Moveable Feast* and such. It's wonderful to read about Americans in Paris during the golden age. The amazing thing to me is most places are still pretty much exactly as they described."

François snorts and moves towards what looks like a drinks' cupboard.

Alex moves closer, smiles. "When you're ready for Proust, I'll help you, although Raphael is an expert. Has he told you?" Two red spots appear on her cheeks. "I don't mean to sound patronizing. Please don't take offense."

"None taken. And no, Raphael never told me he studied Proust. Some of my friends are big fans and discuss his work constantly." I see I must power through the literary world to impress Alex. I dare not confess I'm primarily a Regency romance fan and that my Kindle is full of Georgette

Heyer and Jane Austen along with the Victorian Brontës. I must check out Proust on Amazon.

Raphael kisses the top of my head. "Mummy and I both wrote our dissertations on the old boy." He picks up a well-worn copy. "You'll love it, Sassy. Proust was a dreamer like you."

Alex's eyes are soft when she gazes at her son. "We all have our dreams, Raphie." She turns to me. "I'm glad you're a dreamer, Saskia. Proust said in this book, 'If a little dreaming is dangerous, the cure for it is not to dream less, but to dream more ...' What do you think?" She takes the book from Raphael and offers it to me.

"The story of my life. Thank you." I brush my hand over what looks like a first edition of *Remembrance of Things Past.* During breaks between classes, Elspeth often reads passages out loud. I carefully flick through the tissue thin paper with gold edging. My father keeps fancy books like this in his office to appear intelligent, but it seems Alex actually reads hers according to the margin notes in spidery script.

François sidles over to me. He stands close to my shoulder and talks to my cleavage. "Tell me about your fashion business, Saskia."

I tug my scarf, making sure it hides my flesh. I love to talk about fashion, but not to Raphael's father. I wrap my arms around myself. "It's not a business yet. I had to start over in Paris."

"Of course. Paris maintains strict standards. Tell me what you've done so far," he enquires of my breasts.

I want to slap him, but instead take a deep breath before I answer. "I'm currently at design school." Judging by the look in his eye, I see it's old news. So, he's one of those aristocrats who research their children's love interests to see if they're good enough for their darlings. I walk away, looking out the window at the sun sinking below the horizon. I'd love to be sitting drinking champagne with Raphael and watching the colors change, rather than being bothered by François.

He's magicked to my side again. "Who did you work for in the U.S?"

As if you don't know. I consider wrapping myself in the floor-length curtain. "A brand called Romance is Born in New York. They show during Paris Fashion Week. Perhaps you know them?"

"*Mais oui.* I met Cate Blanchett during Fashion Week one year. She wore a striking gown by them. There were lots of beads and feathers. Were you there? I don't recall—"

"No." I fiddle with the curtain, drawing it across my shirt, ostensibly studying the pattern. "I stayed in the States exploring ideas for the upcoming season." I smile at the exhilarating memory of being drowned in silk, beads and lace, giving my creativity free reign while Roberto and Isabella were out of the country. "But I designed the beads and feather work on Cate's gown. I dream of one day showcasing my own designs in Paris."

He sidles closer. "I can help you with that. I've left the ministry, but I still have the ear of several government officials."

Raphael saunters over and wedges himself between his father and me. "Saskia is fiercely independent, Papa. She refuses every offer of help, even from me. She insists on making it alone."

"That's not how business works, Saskia." François's voice borders on a sneer. "In Paris, success is more likely if you're part of the inner circle."

My eyelids twitch on hearing that line again. There is a bit of like-Father-like-son going on. François is the last person I'd ask for help. "I'll consider my options. Thank you, sir."

I turn my back on François, walk toward the stove where Alex is checking dinner. "Something smells good." Maybe it's worth putting up with François to eat a homely meal.

"Are you cold, my dear?" Alex asks, eyeing my scarf. "We can add more logs if you wish. It's much colder than Paris."

"I've noticed that. It's a bit of a shock. The fire's fine." I walk close to the stove and hold my hands out to the warmth. "What are you cooking?" Even after our picnic, the divine smells make me so ravenous I could tear apart a wild boar with my bare hands.

"I've cooked beef burgundy. I hope you're not vegetarian or vegan. I forgot to ask Raphie."

"I've thought about it, but no. Paris restaurants are into meat. Beef burgundy is one of my favorites. I'm looking forward to a home-cooked meal. I haven't eaten one in so long." Mom was the best cook. A pity I never learned from her, but now I'm learning from YouTube. One thing about Paris, though, you don't have to cook. Their traditional food is like eating at home.

"I'm so glad. People have become so particular about what they eat." She slips her hands into a pair of giant potholders and removes a Stone Age casserole dish from the oven. She lifts the lid and I salivate over the rich, winey gravy and the little spring onions and squares of cubed meat bobbing on top. "Now my dear, would you like to freshen up after your journey?" She turns to her son who's gazing out the window, studiously ignoring his father. "Raphie darling, show Saskia to the restroom." She smiles at me. "Then we will get further acquainted over an apéritif."

François springs to life, opens the drinks' cupboard, an imposing affair in red timber with stained glass windows and built-in refrigerator. "What do you drink, Saskia? Wine, red or white? Gin and Tonic? Scotch? A Kir? I brought in everything, not knowing your taste."

"Hmmm," I say, "they all sound good."

Alex smiles. "Let's start with a Kir Royale, Francis, to toast Raphie and Saskia. Would you like that, Saskia?"

"Saskia loves champagne," Raphael says, "but if there's enough champagne in the Kir Royale, she'll go for it."

"I have Veuve Clicquot," François says.

"That'd be great," I say. A drink will soften the hard edges. Help me make it through the night here in this haunted house.

CHAPTER TWENTY-FOUR

We clink glasses, toast '*salut*', settle into stuffed chairs around the fire in the kitchen to drink Kir Royales. I'm sitting between François and Alex, with Raphael opposite me. I edge my knee away from his father's. I'm sick to my stomach after what Raphael hinted at in the bathroom. Something awful happened in the past that Raphael isn't ready to share. But he warned me to be super careful around his father.

Out of the corner of my eye, I study Alex's serene face, wonder how she abides François when she saw the way he ogled me in the kitchen.

"That was superb." I put my glass down. *Crap.* The parents are still sipping. Raphael hasn't touched his drink since the toast. He's leaning back in his chair, arms behind his head, staring at the ceiling like he's counting silver stars in the shiny blue panels between the oak beams.

François taps me on the knee. I jerk like I've been scalded. "Ah, a girl who likes her drink." He half stands, hands on his thighs, his face in my face. "Ready for another?"

"Oh, no." I clap my hands over my burning cheeks. "Sorry. I drank too fast. I was thirsty." Beside a dish of olives, a huge bottle of Evian glares at me. *Crap.* When there's a champagne cocktail to be had, who drinks mineral water?

Raphael drags his eyes away from the ceiling. "Nonsense, Sassy." He stands. "If you want another drink, you shall have one." He pours me an Evian, then walks to the drinks' cabinet. He measures the cassis, tops it with champagne, then adds ice and a fat red hothouse strawberry. "Anyone?"

François and Alex place their barely touched glasses onto the table. "We'll have our usual Vermouth and Campari, son." His father strides over, stands beside Raphael. "I brought in Dubonnet for you."

Raphael steps away from his father. "Thoughtful."

When Raphael hands me my second Kir, my mouth is dry despite the Evian. I sip and mull on this situation with Raphael's father. Alex's mate Proust said a little dreaming is dangerous and it's proving so in my case. My dreams have dumped me into the midst of this aristocratic French family with its undercurrents. I'm not one of them. I don't want to be one of them. If I marry Raphael sometime down the track that would make me one of them.

Alex sips her fresh drink, smiles at me, frowns at her husband and son who've retaken their seats. Her body language tells me she's uncomfortable at the simmering tension between her two men.

François watches me through half-closed eyes, deliberately shifting his position so our thighs touch.

I move my leg, flick him a look to communicate my discomfort, but he just smirks. I wanted Raphael to introduce me to his parents. I wanted to know his secrets. Now I just want to run back to Paris. Secrets be damned.

Raphael flicks a glance my way, takes a deep breath, then astounds me with his words. "Maman. Papa. I proposed to Saskia last night."

I open and shut my mouth, too shocked to form a sound. I never expected Raphael to play dirty, but he obviously thinks dropping a bombshell in front of his parents will force my hand. Wrong. It just exploded into a whole lot of shrapnel which will wound us both.

Alex has two bright spots on her cheeks, her mouth trembles. François's face is drawn with a sneer. They place their glasses down, stare at us, eyebrows raised.

Raphael stands, grabs my hand. Squeezes it. Tugs me to my feet then walks me toward the windows. "Maman. Papa." He flings over his shoulder. "Saskia wasn't expecting me to tell you. She's shocked. Give us some time."

"Of course, darling." Alex's voice is bright. "Use the sitting room."

Raphael tugs me away from the window, walks me out of the room, slamming the kitchen door behind us.

He pulls me into a sitting room, which thankfully is a football field length from the kitchen. "We'll have all the privacy we want."

I'm vaguely aware of ornate gold-framed vintage prints of early English agricultural scenes covering the burnt orange and sage striped wallpaper. The high, domed ceiling is painted pale cream, the exact shade of the thick carpet. All this perfection leaves me cold. "How dare you. We discussed it last night, Raphael. I said wait. Why couldn't you respect my decision?" My teeth chatter. The room is freezing and so am I.

There's a throw draped over the sofa. Raphael wraps it around my shoulders. "I'm sorry. I should have grabbed your coat." He starts a fire already set in the grate. "You'll warm up in a jiffy."

I slump into the wing chair closest to the fire, tugging the throw around myself, curling my knees under me. I tap my fingers on my leg, shiver, wait for the room to warm.

Once the fire's roaring, Raphael sinks into the couch opposite. Leaning forward, elbows on thighs, chin in his hands, he looks at me, and I'm shocked to see his face drawn with fear. He's gone too far and he knows it.

That dam behind my eyes breaks. I don't want to show weakness by crying, but that's my first response when stressed. And since we arrived, I've been stressed to the max.

He reaches a hand over the space between us, offers me his large white handkerchief, monogrammed with the family crest. It's soon sopping wet.

He rubs his hands over his face. "Sassy. I'm sorry. Don't cry. You're killing me."

Good.

He rakes his fingers through his hair. "Sassy."

I struggle to hear him over the blood pounding in my ears.

"I'm sorry." He hangs his head. "It just popped out."

I fast blink tears. "Popped out?" My voice shakes with anger. "Spare me. You gave this a lot of thought."

"No. The words were out before I could stop them."

I shake my head, snatch a handful of tissues from a box on the side table, press my eyes.

"I wanted to show my father you're off limits. You're going to be my wife, if not right away, then somewhere down the track."

I'm outraged. "I'm not a damsel in distress. I can take care of myself. After that stunt, I doubt I'll ever be your wife."

Pain flicks across his face. "You don't understand. He's a monster." He scrubs his forehead with another handkerchief.

I dab my eyes. "A monster? Surely you exaggerate."

"No way. Monster is the best description."

Wiping my face, I scrunch the tissues into a ball, throw them into the fire. "Keep going. Speak."

"Here's a secret for you, an ugly secret I'd rather hide, but, well, you asked. Anyway, you can find the sordid story on the internet. It's a wonder you haven't already."

My heart pounds. I hiccough and hold my throat, watch him struggle for words. "We're getting somewhere at last." I lean back and wait. I could have Googled, but I didn't think there'd be much of a story. Who knew?

Raphael mops his face then stuffs his handkerchief into his pocket. "My father seduces young women. He's been a player in Paris for years, using his power in all the wrong ways."

"Oh My God, Raphael."

"He was forced to resign his ministry only months ago, or his dirty secrets would have been splashed all over the tabloids. Well, they might still be. No telling with papers these days."

Thinking how Alex must have suffered makes me wonder again why my mother didn't divorce my father. She told me she accepted travel assignments to far-flung corners of the globe so the papers didn't reach her. After the accident, I found the tabloid in her study opened to the page splashed with the salacious story of my father and Hayley Attaschulle doing the social rounds. I killed Mom by being careless with the keys, but my father was just as responsible with his endless betrayals in their sham of a marriage he wouldn't release her from. I thought she didn't care about his infidelities, but I was mistaken. "How does your mother bear it?" I ask Raphael, the words dust in my mouth.

"With that English upper-class attitude that accepts men having affairs as their right. Whatever. She has him on a tight leash now he's living at home, but the way he was all over you tonight shows me he hasn't changed. I saw the desperation on Mother's face when he looked at you. This is why I'll never cheat on you, Sassy." His eyes are dark and hooded. "My father's cheating has haunted me all my life. I'd never do to you what my father did to my mother. And to me. And to—" He says no more, leaving me wondering who else his father hurt.

I doubt my virtue is Raphael's sole motivation for spilling our secret. "Your poor mother. Raphael, it still wasn't right to tell your parents about something private, something unresolved, between us. They don't know me. I don't know them. You have to work up to these things slowly."

He gives a lopsided grin. "Sassy, I don't do things slowly. I've gone about this the wrong way. I screwed up."

I slap my hand onto the arm of the chair. "Too right."

He leans toward me. "But if we don't commit to each other, you might return to New York. What about that guy your father wanted you to marry? You might go back to him after you see how ugly my life has been." He rubs his hands over his face. "I couldn't bear that. I love you, Sassy."

I grab a sofa cushion, hold it against my roiling stomach. I wish he hadn't brought up Xavier. "There's no chance I'll ever marry Xavier. I love you, Raphael, but I'm not ready for marriage. I explained I want to concentrate on fashion first."

"I want that for you too." He takes my hand, plays with my fingers while he talks. "I've rushed into this marriage proposal like I rush into everything, but I support your career one hundred percent. I'd never stand in your way."

"You think so?" I lean back, hug the cushion tight, think about how he hated me meeting with my friends at Oubliette's. If that's not standing in my way, what is? "There're so many undercurrents in this family. I hate drama. It stifles my creativity."

"You'd be marrying me, not my family."

"So ... what? You'd exclude them from our future? We'd never have to see them again?"

He shifts in his chair. "I haven't thought that far ahead. But shutting them out has worked for me. Although it's been tough not seeing Maman, I've found I deal well by forgetting the past and focusing on the future."

"You haven't forgotten the past. It's obvious when you're talking to your father. He's hurt you. Badly. You haven't forgiven him for whatever he did to you."

Raphael stands, walks to the fireplace, studies the family photos on the mantelpiece. He absentmindedly tosses another log onto the already fierce blaze and watches sparks fly. "That bastard doesn't deserve forgiveness." He turns to me, his eyes blaze like the fire. Then the fire in his eyes fades and he retreats into a dark place.

I go to him. I know what it's like to detach yourself from extreme pain.

He gazes into the flames, one arm grabs the mantelpiece, the other hangs by his side, his fingers clench and unclench. I take that hand and he looks at me with pleading eyes. He's the one suffering, not his father. I know the feeling. I haven't forgiven my father for hurting Mom and me time after time or trying to marry me off like I was a commodity. One day,

I'll make peace with Father. Until then, I have no right to lecture Raphael. But I still do. "You'll be a better man, a happier man, if you forgave him."

He faces me full on. I don't like the way he screws up his face so every pane is a dark shadow. "Is that why you won't marry me? I'm not good enough?"

Uh-oh. How did we jump to this? "I meant you'd be a stronger man if you forgave him. Your father's not hurting, you are."

He looks so vulnerable standing there. He frowns. "I'll do whatever it takes to convince you to marry me, Sassy, but forgiving my father is a deal breaker."

Uncertainty niggles at my throat. I reach behind his neck, tug his head down, kiss him. I mean it to be a quick kiss to take away that stricken look, but he responds. His stubble tingles my cheek, and I taste his whiskey-tinged lips and feel his body crush mine. Desire breathes through my mouth, seeps from my skin everywhere he touches me. My body presses against his, never wants to let go, but then my heart pulls me back.

I step away, swallow, take a deep breath, but my lungs struggle for air. I'm afraid of saying what I have to say, but I must. "Raphael, I love you. Perhaps I'll say yes down the track, but it doesn't feel right, not yet."

"What's going to make it right, Sassy? Tell me what to do." He places his hands onto my shoulders. We look into each other's eyes like we're shipwreck survivors wondering where we go from here.

"I can't marry you without being absolutely sure what I'm getting into. I came to France to make a better life than I had in the States. My choices must be right for me." I see my words piercing him, his face flinching. I look into the flames to avoid seeing his pain, but I hear the hopelessness in his voice when he finally speaks.

"To be sure of what you'd be getting into, you have to know all my secrets. Well, if you do uncover all my secrets, *mon ange*, there's no chance in hell you'll ever marry me. Walk away now."

What does that mean? Is he the one ending it this time?

CHAPTER TWENTY-FIVE

At the dinner table, I feel like I'm in someone else's dream. Raphael's words swirl around my head. I try to grab them and pin them down. He said he'd rather I walk away than tell me his secrets. My heartbeat races like I've upped the speed to the max on the treadmill. I pick up my napkin, dab beads of moisture from my upper lip. I popped a Xanax earlier and yearn for another.

Raphael leans close, whispers in my ear. "Are you okay, *mon ange*?"

"I'm fine." I'm not fine at all. I take deep breaths, control my breathing. How can Raphael and I move forward? My stomach clenches at the thought of life without him. Being apart this past month has proven that without him, my life loses its luster. But I must continue moving forward, with or without Raphael.

I calm myself by re-imagining the patterns on the Sèvres porcelain serving dishes on the table. How awesome they'd look appliquéd onto the back of a black velvet dinner jacket or the front of a T-shirt. I sip my champagne, block out the buzz around me by creating in my head a blue formal frock coat teamed with a pair of maroon trousers.

The sound of François pushing one of the serving dishes toward

Raphael intrudes into my headspace. "So, how are you two after your tiff?" he asks with his usual lack of tact.

Raphael picks up a large silver spoon, serves me some beef casserole, then loads his plate before pushing it towards his father. "We're fine." His tone says *back off.*

I hate being at this table. I'd rather be eating a simple meal of crusty bread and melted goat's cheese with Raphael in one of those little side alleys in Montmartre hidden from tourists than eating food of the gods off heirloom plates with these oh-so-polite-people with daggers drawn.

"Food okay, Sassy?" Raphael's voice shows his worry. He knows I'm having trouble coping and fears I'm going to fall to pieces.

I pick up my cutlery, throw him a wobbly smile. As much as I love Raphael, I can't see myself as a member of this family. Imagine Alex visiting my apartment. *Oh, my dear*, she'd puff after climbing five flights of stairs and getting a whiff of Raphael's stinky paints wafting down from the attic while she checks out my designs and tuts at threads and embroidery strewn on every surface. *Oh, my dear,* she'd say when she spies a pristine copy of *War and Peace* propping up my mood board. Alex would be at home in the exquisitely chic Place Vendome, shopping for jewelery at Boucheron, rubbing shoulders with European royalty, Middle Eastern sheikhs and Indian Maharajas. She'd be a lady who lunches at the Paris Ritz, sleeping overnight in a sumptuous suite with pure gold faucets in the shape of swans, which would blow my current annual budget in one night.

Alex's voice drags me back. "Raphie, if you don't mind my asking, how did you meet Saskia?"

Raphael scrapes his plate clean with a slice of baguette, dabs his mouth with a napkin. "I don't mind your asking. I love talking about Saskia. I want you to get to know her." He clasps the hand I'm not eating with. "Where do people meet in Paris, Mummy Dearest? In a bar."

"In *your* bar?" Alex leans forward, looks from Raphael to me, anxious to know more about this miracle.

Raphael nods, covers my hand with his. "It was." I see mischief in his eyes, but I don't care. "Saskia served me a beer or five on her first bartender shift."

I cover my mouth with my napkin to hide my giggle at his parents' sharp intakes of breath. Raphael's being provocative, but their reaction doesn't bother me. I was snobbish about working in a bar at first, but a girl's gotta eat. Even though I don't need the salary anymore, I enjoy it. I'm interested to know what they think of their precious upper-class son and heir proposing to an American bartender and wannabe fashion designer.

François raises his eyebrows, nods sagely, like his preconception of me is spot on. "Does your father know, Saskia? I cannot imagine a successful man like him would countenance such a thing. Doesn't he send you money?"

"He does, but I don't use it. He definitely would not approve of my work choice, but I enjoy the freedom it gives while I'm studying design. The customers treat me well; help my French speaking, too. I've learned all the bar words. And I get to hang with Raphael. Bonus."

Alex looks a little lightheaded. She wipes her forehead with the back of her hand, shrugs and smiles. "How perfectly sweet for you two. Dessert, Saskia? I bought Rum Baba at Luc's today. Luc's our local pâtisserie. His Rum Baba is Raphael's favorite. Have you tried one?"

My mouth waters at the thought of trying a new pastry. "No, but I'm up for it. I'm working my way through every pâtisserie in Paris. Strawberry *mille-feuille* is my current favorite."

François leans back in his chair, stares at my chest. "Wouldn't know it by looking at you."

Eeww. Worms crawl over my body. I splay my hand on my neck to make sure my top shirt button hasn't popped and my scarf is in place.

Raphael kicks my foot. He catches me by surprise and our boots bang together making a dull thud.

I lean over and give him a quick kiss and whisper, "Spot on."

We share a smile.

François twirls his wine glass, watching us over the rim.

"You will adore the Rum Baba." Alex prattles on, apparently oblivious to her husband perving on his son's girlfriend. "I'm serving it at Christmas along with Bûche de Noël. Raphael, please come down for Christmas and bring Saskia." Turning to me, she says, "We'd love to get to know you better. You could meet our friends and neighbors, people who have known Raphael all his life. It's such a long time since Raphael has spent Christmas with us. Would you like that, Saskia?" She sounds so desperate I'd like to say yes and put her out of her misery.

But it's too terrifying a thought. I open my mouth, but Raphael squeezes my shoulder and helps me out. "Not possible, Mummy Dearest. Christmas is so hectic for both of us. Saskia is more of a Thanksgiving girl."

Alex's face is drawn with disappointment. "Oh? Maybe next year?"

I feel sorry for her. If things were better between Raphael and his father, I'm sure we'd have tried to come. Although Christmas this year is out of the question with my fashion competition and Raphael's exhibition on Christmas Eve.

"Maybe," Raphael says, but the set look on his face tells me there's no chance of his ever spending the holiday with his parents.

I adore New York at Christmas. Mom and I had our ritual. We'd attend the New York City Ballet's iconic holiday classic, *The Nutcracker*, then head to Macy's, Saks Fifth Avenue, Bloomingdales and Tiffany & Co for the best store windows. Afterwards, we'd step inside a deli, café or store and be greeted with the jolly strains of Christmas carols. With all its drop-dead-gorgeous beauty, I'm yet to find out if Paris can hold a candle to a New York Christmas. But Christmas will never be the same without Mom. I'm going to create new rituals. With Raphael?

Alex refuses my offer of help in the kitchen, so I'm stuck with two men and tension between them so thick it's choking me.

François drums his fingers onto the table, drags his eyes from my chest and focuses on Raphael. "How's the artist's life, son?"

Raphael's fingers flex and bite into my shoulder in an involuntary spasm. "I refuse to answer questions about my art on grounds it will incriminate you."

François shrugs a shoulder. "Be civil." He refills his wine glass, offers the bottle to Raphael who shakes his head. "That is no way to talk to your Papa."

Raphael refills my glass. He's got his dark and dangerous face on. No hope of his remembering his anger-management strategies. When my glass overflows onto the coaster and floods the starched tablecloth, he mops it with a napkin, then slams his palm onto the table. "You ask me about my art after all these years?" Raphael's voice is clipped. "Why the sudden interest? The only thing that ever interested you was forcing your choices onto me."

François arranges his face into a saintly look and twiddles his fingers. "Politics is a much surer bet than dabbling in art. And so much more lucrative."

Raphael snorts. "I've never dabbled in anything."

"Except sculpture."

Raphael cups his head in one hand and for a moment looks absolutely devastated.

Sculpture? *What's this?* Why does Raphael look so wounded?

Raphael stares at his father with absolute loathing. No matter how much I hate the way Pa's treated me, I've never loathed him like Raphael loathes his father.

François smirks like he's won some competition. He twirls the stem of his wine glass. "Who makes a living from art while they're alive? Look at that poor bastard, oh, excuse me Saskia, van Gogh. Lived in poverty. Went mad. Died young. Hardly selling a painting, just one I think, while he was alive. Now his paintings sell for millions. How does that benefit him? You could be an exception, I grant. I've seen some of your work at a little gallery in Le Marais, but there are no guarantees. Monsieur Marion tells me you're planning an exhibition soon. I'd like to help make it the best debut exhibition Paris has ever seen, one befitting the son of a minister."

Raphael rakes his fingers through his hair. He clasps my hand, I squeeze it to communicate my support. "*Ex*-minister. I've made it this far without you, Papa, and I'll keep on making it without you. Grandmother's trust fund enabled me to support my dream. It's been a great journey."

"Following dreams is pricey, son. Take my money now I offer it. Don't be like Saskia who refuses her father's money then has to work behind a bar and put up with drunks pawing her. How can you stand it, eh?"

As opposed to you pawing me?

"Saskia, if Raphael will not be reasonable, convince him. There is a big jump from pulling beer for the dregs of society to designing clothes for the upper echelons. I could jumpstart both your careers. I am at a loose end. Let me help you both."

Raphael drums his fingers on the table. "Neither of us wants or needs your money. We'll never accept a cent from you."

"Let Saskia speak for herself. There's a rumor going round that women are our equals these days."

I'd like to wipe that prim look off his face, but can't think of a retort fast enough. I take Raphael's drumming hand in mine. "I'm with Raphael every step of the way on this."

Balancing a large tray, Alex pushes open the door and sings in her happy voice, "Dessert is served." When she places the Rum Baba before me, despite the tension, my taste buds go crazy and I'm just short of dribbling saliva down my chin. It's a work of art – layers of cake, cream and artfully-arranged pears and cherries. It seems a shame to eat it.

I roll my shoulders to ease the tension. Listening to Raphael and his father talk has helped me understand why Raphael tries to control everything and everyone around him. It's been his mechanism to survive. I glance at his shadowed face as he studies the beautifully prepared pastry. What memories are forcing themselves to the surface?

I overcome my reluctance to spoil a work of art and attack my dessert with a tiny spoon, savoring every delicious mouthful. Pushing my empty plate aside, I say, "That was too beautiful, Alex. Thank you." I sip the brewed coffee she's served, and it enhances the flavor of rum and cream on my tongue.

"You're most welcome." I notice she's hardly touched hers. Neither have Raphael nor François.

"Would you like a Sauternes, Saskia?" François holds a full bottle in the air.

"No thank you, sir. Coffee's fine."

"Doesn't it keep you awake?"

"Not at all." *Only Raphael keeps me awake.* I cover my mouth, hiccoup, sip my coffee, watch the candlelight catch the diamond shapes on the windowpanes. I love the way it flickers down the center of the table, highlighting the lacework in the white tablecloth and shimmering along the edges of the porcelain dishes. There's so much beauty in this house. What a shame it's spoiled.

When she finishes her coffee, Alex stands, and the men follow her lead. "Please excuse me, but jet lag, you know. I feel quite faint." She turns to me. "Would you like me to show you your room, my dear? You look pale."

I glance at the grandfather clock by the door. It's late, but I'm too wired for sleep. I stand, slip my arm through Raphael's, reluctant to leave him alone with his father. "Should I go?" I whisper.

Raphael puts his arm around my waist, leans into my ear. "*Oui.* Let Maman see you upstairs. Papa and I will clear the dishes."

So that's what they call it.

"Goodnight, Saskia." François stands behind his chair like a regular gent, then winks. "Sleep well."

I nod in François's direction, avoid his eyes. "Goodnight, sir."

"*Bon nuit, mon ange, je t'adore,*" Raphael whispers, hugs me tight. "You okay? Not too stressed? Should you take a pill?"

"I have it under control, thanks for asking. Goodnight."

Kissing the top of my head, he says so only I can hear, "Don't wait up. I'm going to have it out with him once and for all. If my girlfriend won't abide secrets, I must face them head on." The glint in his eyes tells me he and his father will have a blow-the-walls-apart-with-a-medieval-war-hammer-argument.

As I follow Alex up the curved timber staircase, I'm filled with trepidation. Will Raphael and François put the past behind them? The creamy walls are covered in life-sized portraits. Imperious-looking men stand proudly in gorgeous claret cutaway coats, frilly shirts and tight breeches. They look down on me, while women in lacy gowns and demurely clasped hands disturb me with their downcast eyes. Is that how it is in Raphael's family? The men rule and the women submit? Not for me. I'm a child of the 21st century even if my father's head is still firmly in the 19th as far as his daughter is concerned.

A fire crackles. I toss and turn in my sumptuous four-poster bed, surrounded by priceless antique vases and furniture. By the time the weak winter sun glints through a gap in the curtains, I'm fully awake. The fire's out. I'm cold and alone and headachy, my stomach twisted in knots. I check the time on my cell phone. Six o'clock. I huddle under the covers, uneasy about the day ahead. Today is the day I'm going to learn all Raphael's secrets. That is, if he accomplished what he set out to do last night.

There's a light tap on the door. As he walks in, Raphael looks exhausted. It's-been-one-hell-of-a-long-night exhausted. He walks across the lush carpet and leans over, gives me a quick kiss. "Good morning, my darling. I missed you last night." Misery is drawn on his face, defeat in the slump of his shoulders.

"I missed you, too." I stroke his face with the back of my hand. Under his black cashmere overcoat, I glimpse a light blue turtleneck. "I like your sweater. Blue suits you."

"Mother brought it home from the Shetland Islands years ago. I wear it to make her happy." Walking to the windows, he rips the curtains open.

Outside, in the distance, the trees shiver against a pewter sky. Keeping his back to me, he asks, "Did you eavesdrop last night?"

Surprised, I wrap my arms around my knees and talk to his back. "That's a strange question."

He turns and faces me, his brows knitted. "Why? I did it all the time when I was a kid. I'd sit on the stairs listening to my parents rage after my father's latest affair. It was the only way I ever knew what was going on."

My heart goes out to that little boy, alone, devastated as two people he loved tossed harsh words back and forth. "I heard raised voices but couldn't hear what you and your father were yelling. But I heard something shatter."

Raphael knuckles his eyes, says nothing.

"You look like you haven't slept."

"I never sleep when I'm down here." He tugs at his hair. "I'm so fucking over my father. I want to go back to Paris and never darken his door again."

I'm not unhappy with the idea of leaving, but then again ... "If it's not selfish of me, I'd like to see the village. In case we don't come back."

He folds his arms, rests his head against the windowsill, sighs. "Okay. We can do that."

I get out of bed, wrap myself in the puffy comforter. Walk over to where he's staring at the desolate landscape. Covering him with the comforter, I wrap my arms around his waist and lean into his back. Breathing in his freshly-showered scent, I whisper, "Darling Raphael, I'm concerned for you. You're exhausted."

"We didn't quit tossing insults at each other till around five o'clock."

"Any progress?"

He turns in my arms, a smile flickers across his face when he sees my Love + Grace flannel knit pajamas.

I grin. "No time to source a medieval nightdress online. Sleeping naked didn't seem right in your parents' house."

"Nothing is right in this house." He wraps the comforter around both of us, rests his head on my shoulder. "Papa's still laying the politician shit on me. He wants me installed as the local member, control me behind the scenes, in other words, influence peddling. Over my dead body."

"Don't say that." I hold him close. "At dinner, he said he supported your choices."

"I'm no farmer, but I do know pigs don't fly." He absentmindedly twirls his finger through my hair. "I hate being under this roof. I become a surly teenager the minute I walk up those stairs. You deserve much better."

"True, Raphael, but so do you. We can't build a life together unless we're open with each other. I know it's super painful for you, but for me to understand you, you need to keep sharing like you're doing now. You have so much hurt inside you." I brush the lapels of his coat, loving the feel of the soft wool. I put on a cheery face. "Let's go for breakfast."

"*Mais oui*. The parents have already left to source a mirror to replace the one I broke last night when Papa shoved me against it."

I cover my mouth. His words bring back bad memories of my father's violence when I was a kid, but my father would never break furniture, he'd break Mom and me. "Are you hurt? Did you hit him too?"

"As tempting as it was, I thought of you and kept my fists to myself. You can imagine the self-control that took."

I exhale a breath. "I'm happy you did."

"Now, Sassy, get dressed and I'll show you my village." He flops down onto the bed, legs crossed, hands clasped behind his head.

"Raphael?"

"Mmmmm?"

"Today you must tell me everything that happened here in the past. Then we can move on."

No reply. His face is wiped clean of worry. He's fast asleep.

CHAPTER TWENTY-SIX

The air is crisp and cold when Raphael and I set out for the village. The fountain in the middle of the driveway is frozen, which looks oddly beautiful with pointed stalactites suspended above the frozen water. Raphael is groggy after his short nap, I've still got a headache. Arm in arm, we stumble down the long driveway between skeleton trees dusted with fresh snow. How many skeletons are in Raphael's cupboard? Do I really want to know?

Raphael points to distant fields rising to meet hills shrouded in mist. "Do you like the view? Every time I see it, I want to be a landscape painter."

I throw my arm around his waist; we gaze at the view together. "I love it. It's like a picture postcard. You should paint it."

"I should. One day. And I love you." He raises my hand, kisses it. "Thank you for being here with me. I never would have come alone."

"You're welcome." The view is unique. Today is unique. Today is the day I hope the mist surrounding Raphael will be swept away.

Walking the narrow cobblestone streets arm in arm with my man, I'm warm and toasty in my overcoat, gloves, jaunty scarf and woolen cloche.

"*Bonjour*!" the locals chime as we pass.

"*Bonjour*!" we sing back, emphasizing the first syllable and raising the second. I love how the French language is sung like open-air opera.

Raphael flips up his collar, smiles and nods at people like he's Mister Darcy promenading arm in arm with Elizabeth Bennet.

The aroma of coffee and fresh pastries lures us into a little red shop on the corner of the main street. Under regal red and gold awnings, red tables and chairs are sprinkled with fresh snow. In the window, there's an artistic arrangement of hundreds of cakes and slices iced in jewel colors, as gorgeous as any cake shop in Paris.

Raphael holds his hands behind his back, rocks on his heels. "This is the pâtisserie my mother was talking about. Luc's of the Ali Baba." Seeing my frown, he says, "That's what I've always called last night's dessert." He grabs my hand. "Now, *entrer*, breakfast awaits."

Bells tinkle as we walk into the crowded pâtisserie, where it seems the entire population of Les Salles is hunting for their morning baguette.

The door bangs shut behind us. "*Bonjour* Monsieurdames," Raphael sings. The customers turn to see who's joined the queue, singing a chorus of, "*Bonjour,* Monsieur Valentine" and nodding at me.

A woman with a long dark braid turns from the counter and swings her head in our direction. Her hair has slipped out of its tortoiseshell barrette and tendrils trace the lines of her slender neck. Raising eyebrows in her pixie face, she nods coolly at Raphael, he nods solemnly at her. Baguette tucked under her arm, eyes straight ahead, she attempts to slip past us.

Raphael steps in front of her so she has to stop. "*Bonjour*, Cosette. *Ça va?*"

She hangs her head, brushes Raphael's arm, darts a look at me from under her long eyelashes, then rushes out the door, chased by a chorus of tinkling bells.

Another of his women? She's no Inés or Bernelle, but still ... I chew my lip. "Cosette? Who's she, Raphael?" *The childhood sweetheart?*

Raphael doesn't answer. His face is red, and he's got that moody look in his eyes, that darkness he had yesterday during our conversation in the sitting room. He ignores the stares of those in the queue who watched the exchange with interest. But he's in his own world, ignoring everything but his pain.

After an uncomfortable wait in line where I entertain several scenarios in my head, we're finally served and head outside, each carrying a freshly baked croissant and sipping takeout coffees. My hands shake with cold and anger at Raphael's mood. Is Cosette part of a bigger story, or is she a complete episode?

We walk in silence sipping our coffee, nibbling a croissant. "Cosette," he says, 'she is a long painful story, *ma cherie*. I will tell you about her, but not in the street."

I'll have to content myself with that. I toss my croissant packet into a bin and wonder whether I'm up for another of his stories. I'm already pretty sure of the short version of this one. She's probably the childhood sweetheart referred to by Lamar. How many more girlfriends am I yet to meet? I try to ignore my inner critic. Why shouldn't his past be littered with girlfriends? He's thirty years old, gorgeous, but seeing his past girlfriends increases my insecurity. I know it's my anxiety, but the old question nags: Why did Raphael choose me over all those stupendous-looking French women? Inés and Bernelle are sophisticated and glamorous while Cosette is a French ingénue, Audrey Tautou in 'Amélie'. Compared to these women, I'm a gawky child tottering in her mother's high heels.

We stroll along the main road until we come to the village church. It's made of stone with five high arches along the façade, one soaring over an imposing entrance.

Raphael throws his arm over my shoulder, hugs me close. "This is Eglise Saint Eutrope, the church where I'd like us to be married ... one day."

"Hmmm." Hand in hand we climb the cement steps that sit on top of each other like an Egyptian ziggurat. Not my ideal wedding venue. Too dark and imposing the way French churches are apt to be. "It's, uh, charming, but why is it so important to you?"

Raphael hesitates on the well-worn stone that dips in front of the entrance. "The priest, Father Mandon, saved my life when I was a small child. Helped me with my nightmares when they first began."

I swallow, my throat suddenly dry. I wish I had more coffee. I remember the faces in his Nightmare Art. "Were the nightmares about your father?"

His eyebrows knit together, his eyes two deep black pools. "*Oui.* I was about six, yearning for his love, but he chose to make me hate him instead."

"What did he do?"

Raphael escorts me inside and walks me to a panel of frescoes. We stand side by side. He studies the Holy Family. "Papa liked to toughen me up. I was a mummy's boy, he said. He wanted a real man for his son."

I squeeze his hand.

"At night, he'd come to my room after my mother left and tell me dreadful stories about what happened to weak boys who couldn't defend themselves. When I finally fell asleep and dreamed, I saw ugly figures superimposed with my father's face." He points to the Holy Mother. "I'd scream and scream, tasting hellfire's flames licking my toes. Outside my door, he'd say to my mother, *I'm not having a sissy for a son. My son will be a player. He won't be played.*

I clasp my throat. "That's hideous."

Raphael nods, a bleak look on his face. "I dreaded the nighttime. When he came down from Paris, I dreaded my father's footsteps outside my door. I dreaded the ugly visions when I closed my eyes. When I realized it wasn't normal for a father to act like that, I began to hate him. From then on, nothing he did surprised me."

My heart breaks. I clasp his hand. "I'm so sorry, Raphael. How did you bear it?"

He points to an ornately carved confessional at the side of the church. "I would run down here and confess all to Father Mandon. He prayed with me and as I was already interested in art, he suggested I try painting the terrifying visions." His eyes mist. "It did help. It set me on a path of art as healer. He must have found a way to get through to my father without breaking my confidence. Papa's nightly visits stopped. He sent me to Eton to get rid of me. To continue the toughening up process."

I wrap my arms around him. "Oh, Raphael," is all I can say. We both survived our fathers. Now we must find our way out of our dark mazes to discover real happiness together.

We walk around inside the church, surrounded by frescoes of Adam and Eve and the Nativity. Raphael steadies me when I slip on a crooked tile. "Watch your step. The church is built close to a natural spring, has a serious case of damp."

Eglise Saint Eutrope might be imposing with its faded frescoes, but unless you're Morticia Addams, you wouldn't choose to marry here. I point to a rather unpleasant-looking growth climbing the walls. "Do prospective brides and grooms turn up with buckets of bleach and scrubbing brushes before the ceremony."

Raphael grins for the first time today. "Hey, don't knock it. These days at least we don't have to wear galoshes to church."

Back at the castle, I follow Raphael inside to the kitchen where he helps me with my coat. He hangs it behind the door next to his.

He throws more logs onto the fire, we collapse before it, thawing out after our frosty walk.

"Okay. Let's talk, Raphael," I say as soon as I have my breathing under control.

"We will, Sassy." He links his fingers in mine. "Let's warm up first."

I lean forward, hold stiff fingers to the flames. "Raphael. Don't hedge. Let's do it."

"Not here. Maman and Papa might return early." He stands, opens the drinks' refrigerator. "Let me grab supplies." He holds a bottle by the neck in one hand, an ice bucket in the other. "The glasses are on that shelf, Sassy. I'm sorry there's no champagne left, but you'll like this Sancerre."

"But it's not even midday."

"Who made you the drinks' police? The French often have alcohol in the morning. You'll be glad of it, I promise. Follow me. Put on your coat."

"My coat?"

"It's cold where we're going."

I follow him through a secret door to the right of the entrance hall. Inside, a narrow concrete staircase wends its way upward in circles. "I thought the stairs in my building were bad, Raphael. Has anyone ever broken their neck here?"

"*Non.* I'm the only one who uses them. I could run up and down blindfolded."

When we finally reach the top, I lean against the door to his room, pushing away a feeling of dread.

I brace myself.

Suck in a deep shuddering breath.

I'm ready.

CHAPTER TWENTY-SEVEN

"Welcome to my lair." Raphael pushes open a heavy steel-studded timber door and stands aside for me to enter. He follows, holding the wine under his arm while he switches on an ancient heater near the one and only window. "Before last night, I hadn't been in here for years. Nothing's changed, except the dust got thicker. The cleaners refuse to climb those stairs."

"I don't blame them." I stand inside the doorway, sniffing ancient dust and mildew. "This was your room?" I'd expected a palatial suite like my bedrooms growing up, but Raphael's walls have peeling paint and are covered in old college certificates with curled edges.

"You're wondering why I slept here? It was the best way to keep distance between myself and Papa."

"Uh-huh." I put the glasses onto the nightstand. I've no idea how to start the awkward conversation, so I say the first thing that pops into my head. "Why do you call your mother, 'Mummy Dearest'?"

He places the ice bucket onto a chest of drawers, crunches the bottle into the ice. He turns to me, smiles. "It's a Brit thing. Maman and I once watched a documentary on the British royal family where Prince Charles addressed the queen that way. We later found out that it was their private joke. Now it's our private joke. It annoys my father no end."

"Hmmm." Scanning the room, my eyes are drawn to sculptures on a makeshift shelf at windowsill height. Some of men, some of a girl. "Wow. You made these? Why were you so disturbed when your father mentioned sculpture last night?"

He taps his bottom lip with his forefinger. "Other than drawing, which I started as soon as I could hold a crayon, sculpture was my first foray into art. I studied technique at Eton." He stands back, eyeing each figure, pointing to the largest of the men who take up a portion of shelf to the left of the window. "This is Dali, my earliest inspiration."

I recognize the bulging eyes and curled moustache. "It's good. Lifelike. Why haven't I seen any of your sculptures before?"

He shakes his head. "Each time I finished a sculpture, I wanted to smash it. It was never good enough. These are all I have left of the hundreds I created."

"Why would you smash something you worked so hard to create?"

He clenches his fists. "My father. Whenever he came home, he'd tell me to grow up, stop dabbling in mud. He taunted me about a caricature I did of him, which I'd created in a rage when I was fourteen. I took a hammer to it afterwards. He just laughed, called me self-destructive. But we both knew that as I hammered that sculpture to smithereens, it was his head I was smashing."

"Oh, Raphael." I hug him, hating that violence which simmers just below the surface. "Tell me about sculpture. How did you get started?"

He kisses my forehead, walks along the line of busts, touching a head here, a shoulder there, like he's reacquainting with old friends. "When I first felt the clay in my hands, it was every little boy's dream. I squelched sticky mud between my fingers and all these little worms scrambled around. My hands took a hunk of mud and I was in control. I forced that mud to become anything I wanted. Once I discovered I could study sculpture at Eton, I didn't want to learn anything else. I spent every moment I could in the art room."

I narrow my eyes when I see a young girl with a braid over her shoulder. I wave my hand to indicate the girl. "Cosette."

He puts his hands into his pockets, rocks on his heels. "It's a remarkable likeness."

Likeness be damned. Dali's no threat, but this girl is. She's a living and breathing threat. My heartbeat quickens. I scan the shelves. "Are there sculptures of Inés too?"

He shakes his head, sucks in a breath. "No. You wanted to know all my secrets." He rubs his hands over his eyes. "Inés is no secret. Cosette is my biggest secret."

I pinch the bridge of my nose. Feel faint. "What does that mean?" I stare at the many renditions of the girl. The first is a bust in clay, small and rough, yet it's a tender interpretation of a young girl with a bright smile. In the next, her carefree laugh becomes the sultry lips of a young woman. The most recent is a much larger sculpture of the young girl holding outstretched hands, to Raphael, no doubt. The final, a stunning bronze of a full-grown Cosette, could take its place proudly in any art gallery in Paris. "You grew up together."

Placing his hands on the pixie face, his fingers move over the contours in an intimate gesture. Then he takes my hand and steps away so we're both gazing at her. "Yes, these represent Cosette when she was young and innocent."

I shouldn't be jealous of his childhood friend, but I am. "She was very important to you, judging by how these sculptures preserve milestones in her life."

"*Oui*. Very important. We were neighbors." He leads me to the window, points to a large estate, just visible beyond a treed wood. "Each school break she sat for me. This line of sculptures represents the happiest years of my childhood before ..."

"Before?" I lean on the windowsill, arms folded, looking at the tranquil country scene, seeing a young girl running through the trees to Raphael, pigtails flying. "Judging by this morning's encounter, you're no longer friends."

"I'm not sure what to tell you." He gazes over my head into the mid-distance, his face drawn.

"The truth."

"Short story? I was sent overseas to boarding school, then afterwards I moved to Paris to study art. Cosette stayed in Les Salles to complete her education. One day I found out she came to Paris often, but not to see me."

I pick at flaking paint on the windowsill, like I could pick away the feeling of dread at what Raphael is about to share. "Why not?" My voice shakes.

Raphael rubs his brow with the back of his hand. "She wanted things ... I'd never have believed, except I saw—"

"What did she want?" I place a hand on his trembling forearm.

"A lover." He grips the windowsill.

It's coming. "Someone you ... knew?"

He gazes out the window, lips clamped together, refuses to look at me.

Dang-dang-dang-dong. The church bells mark the hour. Raphael stands as still and lifeless as one of his sculptures. I move away from the window, sink into the armchair, not wanting to look upon the agony drawn on his face. I suck in a deep breath. This is it. This is the secret Raphael says will make me walk away.

He paces back and forth, looks at me, looks out the window, flicks dust off a sculpture of Cosette. He finally stops pacing and props himself on the arm of my chair. Taking my hand in his, he sighs. "My father stole Cosette from me." His voice cracks. "She was only seventeen."

Hearing him say what I suspected doesn't make it any easier to hear. Pent up tears burst from my eyes. "No."

He nods. "Yes. I saw them. At a restaurant near the Palais de l'Élysée, the one where the politicians hang out. As I walked past, there they were."

He pats his pocket like he's searching for cigarettes, but he's quit. For me. I feel so sorry for him I wish I had a cigarette to give him.

"What happened?" I whisper. But do I really want to know?

His jaw clenches. "I walked to their table and confronted them. My father's friends smirked at me as I stood, open mouthed, frozen." He shakes his head. "I couldn't get the picture of her out of my mind for years – designer clothes, hair in a chignon, smoking. My country-girl Cosette. My father winked at me, his hands all over her. Cosette had the grace to look a little embarrassed." Raphael's face is red, his blood no doubt boiling with remembered rage.

"Did he end it when you found out? Or did she?"

"He ended it like the bastard he is. Once I found out, there was no fun in it. He said he only did it to get a rise out of me. He always claimed he could have any woman he wanted and Cosette was proof."

I swallow the lump in my throat. "How long?"

"Four years. The whole time I was in England." He slams his fist into his palm. "The conniving bastard sent me away to suit his evil ends." He grinds his teeth.

"Did you and your father argue about Cosette last night?"

He turns away so I can't see his face. "Of course." His tone is bitter. "He claims Mother has forgiven him. Why can't I?"

"You should forgive him." But I'm no longer sure.

His face pales. He looks at me, his eyes hard. "Why should I? He hurt my mother. He hurt Cosette. He hurt me. Hurting people is what he enjoys." He stands and paces, then stops. He has an odd look in his eyes. "I idolized him. I wanted to be like him. But I was never good enough."

"How so?"

"Everything between us was a competition. Anything I chose to do, he ruined it. He ruined my love of sculpture, he denigrated my choice of art as a career, he stole my first girlfriend ... he continually cheated on the mother I adored." He walks to the window where he stands looking out, covers his face with his hands. "He's a monster, like I said."

I push out of my chair, go to him, wrap my arms around his waist. My heart breaks for young Raphael growing up. But I can't help wondering: Where do I fit in? Am I the love of his life? Or is the love of his life here in his home village?

He wipes his face with a handkerchief, turns around, takes me in his arms. He pushes my hair from my forehead, kisses my scar. "You know the worst. Can you deal with it?"

I cling to him, feeling our hearts beat in time like we're one person, but we're like two sets of clumsy fingers fumbling over piano keys, not making the beautiful music I'd imagined when I fell in love with him. But it'll get better now that he's opened his wounds. "I think so," I whisper.

"I need a drink." He breaks our embrace, picks up the bottle of Sancerre, fills our glasses. With a shaky hand, spilling wine onto the floor, he passes me a glass, we clink, "*Salut.*"

I sip absentmindedly, thinking about what he's shared. How can I compete with a ghost? "Raphael." I clutch the stem of my glass and rub the coolness over my hot cheek. "Do you still love Cosette?"

He raises his glass to her sculptures. "I can't pretend Cosette didn't exist, *mon ange*, or that I didn't love her, but you're the most important person in my life now." He turns to face me. "I don't love you in the same way I loved Cosette."

I put my glass onto the windowsill before it drops from my shaky fingers. Is this what dying feels like? My ears no longer hear, my nose no longer smells, when I press my fist against my heart, I can't feel a beat.

He's at my side in one step. "Sassy." He places a finger under my chin and tilts my face. "That didn't come out right."

I pull away, clenching my hands into fists. "I think you made yourself quite clear."

He sets his glass beside mine. "No, I didn't. Words don't always mean what we want them to mean. Let me try again."

"Don't bother," I say through clenched teeth. I fold my arms. Shake my head. Disbelief washes over me. I ran away from New York and marriage to

Xavier, only to fall in love with a man who says he wants to marry me while all the time he loves someone else.

"Sassy, I'm sorry I've upset you, but you misunderstand. I've loved Cosette since I was a boy. But I don't love her the way I love you. Looking back, I never did."

I grit my teeth. "What does that mean?"

He shakes my shoulders. "Stop judging me and listen."

I fold my arms, tap my boot. "Get on with it."

He brushes his hands over his face. "When I met you, I'd given up the idea of ever finding the love I craved."

I clear my paper-dry throat. "What kind of love was that?"

"A grand passion." He takes a deep breath, reaches for my hand. "Such as I have for art. No. More than. I wanted a woman who would knock the breath out of me. We French call it *un coup de foudre*. Then there was you. In my bar. Lightning struck."

I clasp my heart, scarcely able to breathe. "That's beautiful."

"When I saw you at Marcel's that day, my heart was yours from the first moment. My eyes followed you everywhere. Watching you work, I sketched the many faces I saw in you, then went up to my studio and applied finishing touches before I met you in the street after your shift. I was the happiest man on earth when you decided to go all French on me and sleep with me that night. It was amazing to be with you. From that night on, I worked hard to keep you by my side."

My eyes prick with tears as I recall the stunning charcoal drawings he created that night in the bar and gifted to me when I moved into the bigger apartment, beautifully framed, now hanging above my bed. The Andy Warhol Marilyn Monroe type rendition captured so many facets of my personality like he saw into my soul. "*Un coup de foudre,*" I murmur. "I like that phrase." I swallow. "What if I told you I also had *un coup de foudre*."

His eyes soften. "I would be even more amazed. You were my dream, the one, my lightning strike. No question. I've always been afraid I'd lose you, you'd walk away, and then I did something stupid and you did just that. I wouldn't blame you now if you walked away for good. How can I expect you to become part of my fucked-up family?"

I've questioned my relationship with Raphael many times. His shadowed soul. His power over me. But if I left him, I'd be walking away from my life. "I'm not walking away, Raphael," I finally say. "That story must have been hard to tell, but you did so because you love me." I embrace him.

He whispers, "Thank you, God." He ends the embrace and crosses to his nightstand. Opening the top drawer, he turns to me, a hopeful look in his eye. "I have something for you. I've kept it stored here in my room where no one would ever find it." He takes a red velvet drawstring bag from an old cardboard box, blows dust from the fabric.

My eyes are riveted on the bag. "What is it?" I have a dreadful premonition.

"Grandmother and I were *sympathique*. She left everything to me when she died. Everything. A villa here in Les Salles, a pied-à-terre in Paris near Le Jardin du Luxembourg, a trust fund, her priceless jewelry. But this is something very special of hers." He unties the drawstring and takes out a small red velvet box.

Oh no.

"Don't look at me like that, *mon ange*." He flips open the box. "What do you think?" His voice is hardly above a whisper. This gift is precious to him but my mind flashes to Xavier on his knee, egged on by my father, holding out a truly hideous ring. Despite myself, my heart plummets. I'm being unfair to Raphael. He's no Xavier. With an effort, I bring myself back to the present. Lying on a bed of black velvet is the sweetest ring I've ever seen, nothing like the rock Xavier offered. This ring is a heart-shaped red stone surrounded by two smaller heart-shaped red stones, all framed by tiny diamonds. "It's exquisite."

"The gems are rubies, Grandmother's favorite. I didn't have a ring when I proposed, and I'll design one for you when we're properly engaged. Down the track. Meanwhile, I'd like you to wear this."

"But, Raphael, we're not engaged."

"It's not an engagement ring. It's a promise ring. I know you're not promised to me yet, but I'm promised to you. Wear it on your right hand if you wish."

Raphael believes absolutely I'm going to marry him or he wouldn't have offered me this precious ring. I look at him. He's staring at me, hope and love in his eyes. I look at the ring again, distracted. I don't want to hurt him with another rejection so soon after he shared that horrid story, but—

"Please, *mon ange*. You already wear your mother's ring, the lucky rare black opal. I'd love it if this ring brings us luck, too." He lifts up my right hand and kisses my finger. "I'd be honored if you'd wear it, either for a short time or forever. Either way, it's yours, as am I."

"Raphael, it's so sweet." But does he think by giving me this ring it'll be harder for me to say no to marriage?

"I see your head going round and round. I don't have ulterior motives." He brushes my hand with gentle fingers. "You have slender fingers like Grandmother, so I think it'll fit. She'd have loved you and would have been overjoyed to see you wearing her ring. May I?"

"*D'accord*, Raphael," I whisper. The ring fits perfectly. We watch it sparkle in the light, my red manicure a perfect match for the rubies.

Raphael holds my hands in his, kisses my fingers. "I want you with me forever, my love ... but, no pressure."

"Thanks, darling Raphael." I stand on tiptoe, wrap my arms around his neck and kiss him. "I love you. I'll wear your grandmother's ring with pride. But we're not engaged."

My phone chooses that moment to ring. I unwrap my arms from around his neck, fish around in my tote.

"Ignore it," Raphael says. "I'm not finished."

I check the screen. "Sorry. It's Monsieur Etienne from the Institut. Gotta take it. Maybe my Sun King range has made the cut."

Raphael squeezes my shoulder. "Of course. There's never been any doubt in my mind that you are one of the chosen, *chérie*."

"I hope you're right. Let's see what he has to say." I tap *Accept*. As I wait for Monsieur Etienne to speak, his most recent critique plays in my mind. *You have real talent and originality, Saskia, which is of course what we're looking for. And voilà, your confidence now shines through. Well done.*

My heart does its *thumpedy-thump-thump.*

I hold the phone close to my ear. "*Allo.*"

"*Allo*, Saskia," Monsieur Etienne says. "I 'av good news."

The blood pounds in my ears. I'm on my way.

CHAPTER TWENTY-EIGHT

There's muted excitement in meeting room 3B at the Paris Institut, where three jittery fashion students hope and pray for their big break. Like me, Zack and Samu are trying not to jump out of their skins at the prospect of their clothes being worn by top global models, scrutinized by the biggest names in Paris fashion. The offer of a six-month contract with a major fashion house is not too shabby either.

Zack's eyes blink uncontrollably, while Samu stands so still he looks like he's meditating. Despite dosing on Xanax, I'm so anxious, I only stop myself from collapsing by clutching the edge of the table I've been allocated.

I rearrange my sketches yet again, then rub my hands over my arms, warming up my goosebumps. The hard work is done. Now whatever happens, happens. I take deep calming breaths, telling myself it's an opportunity, not a threat. My heart does a little dance when I imagine strangers studying my sketches. Will the judges love my flared velvet trousers, fitted shirts, cravats, nipped-waist leather jackets and formal frock coats in lush cotton velvet I sourced from Tissura? Will I win this competition, or will I be left to scramble through the jungle of the fashion world still waiting for my big break in years to come?

The door opens. The meeting I've both feared and anticipated since Monsieur Etienne's phone call last weekend is about to begin. Raphael and I left for Paris straight after the call. We were back in town with time for me to practise my pitch with Raphael. He changed my language to high modality. *You must convince them you* are *the* best *new fashion designer in the world,* he said, *not that you* could *be the best.*

I'm buoyed by his encouragement, his assertions that my collection has outstanding merit. The right mix of modern and historical. Some of his suggestions helped improve the cut of the shirts, but otherwise I'm showcasing the styles I've workshopped with Amandine. *Knock 'em dead, girl,* I tell myself. I take my seat along with my friends, suck in a deep breath ... and wait ... and pray.

Monsieur Etienne indicates a gentleman who's followed him inside. "Students, this is Professeur Germain who represents Cité Universitaire, our controlling body. He oversees the New Fashion competition. He and his committee narrowed our shortlist to you three. Today, he will listen to your pitches, examine your sketches, check your samples. Afterward, he and I meet with the Institut's fashion advisors. The winner should be chosen before Christmas, allowing you time to prepare for the New Fashion Show mid-January. "*Bonne chance.*"

The professeur leans back in his chair beside the podium where I've been lectured by Stella McCartney, Azzadine Alaia and a Karl Lagerfeld, God rest his soul, representative, to name just three of the many top advisors to the Institut.

I'm wired, stretched tight like one of Raphael's canvasses. I tap my boot on the floor; watch the professeur dither. I clasp my chest, afraid my heart is going to jump out of my ribcage. Raphael acts so cool about his first exhibition. *Why am I a nervous wreck?* I know the answer. There's more at stake for me if I don't win. I could be winging my way back to the States, a failure.

Professeur Germain takes a small notebook from his briefcase, studies us. Thick black glasses disguise eyes which are sunken in his head. He startles me when he claps his hands together like he's a teenager who's just beaten a bad roll of the dice in *XCom 2: War of the Chosen.*

"Welcome, students," he says. "Congratulations on making the finals in our exciting competition. You have met the criteria with aplomb, but tradition dictates there can be but one winner." He scrutinizes each of us, nodding while we try to act nonchalant.

I scrutinize him back, fascinated by his flashy clothes which could be from my Sun King range – gold lame blazer with nipped-in waist, tight black leather trousers and red cravat tucked into a white frilled shirt. He sits with one leg over the other, swinging a silver studded black combat boot while he flicks through his notes. "So, who's first?"

I drop my head, focus on my French manicure, a skill I've learned over the years to avoid being chosen. Thick vines of fear take root in my mind. I breathe them away. This is not the time to be anxious. *I'm American. I'm competitive. I'm a winner.*

I look up. *Crap.* The professeur's staring straight at me.

I can do this..

He nails me with his gaze. "Ladies first. We will start with you, Mademoiselle ... er ..." The professeur swings his leg and consults his notes. "... Bell. Talk us through your credentials and your field of expertise, then I will examine your sketches. You hail from the States, *non*?"

"Ah, uh, *oui*." I flounder like a jumpy fish trying to free itself from a nasty hook. I take a sip from my water bottle. I've always been rubbish at interviews, forget the important things that impress people. Is that why Roberto and Isabella fired me? *Stop it.*

"Take your time, Mademoiselle Bell." Professeur Germain flips through his notes while I do my deep breathing. "You are amongst friends."

My mind flashes to the coping card from the box Pascale gave me at our first session. When I pulled out today's card, I read, *I'm the boss of my anxiety. Anxiety is not my boss.* I flick my hands to release the tension.

Zack lightly brushes my arm. "Come on, Sask. You're ready."

"Thanks Zack." I inhale, smile at the room, then focus on the professeur before launching into my spiel. "Thank you for the opportunity to tell you about myself, Professeur. I studied fashion at Syracuse University, New York City. The course included experimental textiles, accessory design, fashion drawing, pattern design, along with the history of art and the history of fashion. To complete my Honors, I prepared a portfolio-based component on fashion and the visual arts. I've worked for four years at the New York fashion house, Romance is Born, where I put those components into practice."

"That sounds most innovative and fresh." The professeur smooths his large lapels. "Tell me about your work in New York."

Breathe. Breathe. Breathe. I force away negative thoughts. "Um, they're a cutting-edge Top 10 New York fashion house whose clothes tell a unique story, fusing vision and design. They work in silk and velvet fabrics and hand-stitched appliqué using feathers, beads and silk stitching." The professeur's eyes light up. "I've included these same materials in my designs to demonstrate a modern perspective on the fashions worn by France's Sun King, Louis XIV."

"Interesting fusion of ideas. What was your role at Romance is Born?"

"I was specialist design assistant to the Head Designer where I worked closely with her to create our collections, five to six a year, which often incorporated my appliqué and shadow embroidery." I point to my sketches. "My frock coats are made in my fabric designs using silk and velvet, my favorites."

The professeur nods, scribbles in his notebook. Judging by his glitzy jacket, he'd probably adore some feathers and beads. He looks up, catches me unawares. "Why Paris, Mademoiselle?" He leans forward in his chair, pen poised. "I'm always interested in how our students find us."

"My mother is French, and I was born here, although I've lived in New York most of my life. I've often visited with my mother. Paris fashion inspires me like no other. I've never attended Paris Fashion Week, but my designs have. Last year, my appliqué in the Romance is Born evening wear collection was much remarked upon and chosen by celebrities for red-carpet nights. This helped my decision to study further at the Institut and launch my own fashion line here."

He scribbles something, then caps his pen. "How long will you be staying in France?"

I exhale a breath. When I left the States, I intended to stay in Paris for as long as it took to start a new life, as long as it took to make it in the Parisian fashion world, as long as it took to become strong and be independent of my father. Then I'd return to New York and start my own small fashion house. My love affair with Raphael has inspired my men's fashion line and my designs are just the beginning of my love affair with classic Parisian style. I never want to leave Paris because that would mean leaving Raphael and my fashion inspiration.

"As long as Paris will have me." I cross my fingers.

"If you win this competition," the Professeur continues, "you must remain in Paris. Your prize includes a six-month internship with a major fashion house, a commitment to the Institut's ongoing program, perhaps a guest lecturing position or taking on a specialist class such as your shadow embroidery and appliqué, skills which are fast disappearing. We would provide every assistance with launching your fashion line."

"There's no question of my long-term commitment to Paris." My only question is my long-term commitment to Raphael.

He nods, closes his notebook. "When you're ready, talk me through your collection." He turns to Zack. "Gather your thoughts, Monsieur. You're next."

As the professeur scans my sketches, I stand next to the table, wiping clammy hands on my silk wide-leg trousers I designed and sewed for this meeting. He picks up the drawing of my series of cravats in fabulous patterns, studies it, holds it at arm's length while stroking the cravat at his neck. "Mmmmm." He picks up my personal favorite, a sketch of a forest-green long velvet frock coat inspired by Raphael the night we dined at Le

Coupe-Chou-Chou. The huge appliqué in a mulberry and cream shade stitched onto the back was inspired by the plum tart I ate on the day I settled on my Sun King range.

"Your display in the center of the table is *exquise,* Mademoiselle Bell."

"*Merci,* Professeur." Manu tailored a complete outfit – white silk shirt with pearl buttons, gray satin cravat with shadow embroidery, green velvet coat flared from the waist in wide pleats, tight black leather trousers featuring side stitching—

The professeur studies the jacket for some minutes, looks at me, then studies it some more, runs his fingers through the lush velvet, strokes the appliqué, all the time mumbling what sounds like *exquise.* Finally, he flips through my Look Book of sketches and fabric samples, pausing occasionally to check something that catches his eye or rub a fabric sample through finger and thumb.

The room's quiet except for my heavy breathing. My world tilts. I feel weightless. I could fly out the window. I grip the edge of the table. I realize I've been holding my breath the whole time the professeur's been checking my designs. Forcing myself to breathe, I feel the air catch in my throat, the sweat prickle my top lip. No. No. No. *Don't panic.*

"Are you well, Mademoiselle?"

"Ah, *oui,* just extremely nervous." To calm myself, I close my eyes and visualize Raphael's arms holding me tight this morning, feel his hands stroking my hair, assuring me the judges will adore my designs.

You're the one, Sassy. Be calm. They'll choose you. These people know genius when they see it.

My tension lifts, my panic subsides. *I will do this.*

An hour later, sketches and samples surrendered to the professeur, Zack, Samu and I stumble from the room into the chilly corridor. As I shrug into my puffa jacket, I look at my friends, their faces red with excitement. Judging by the way it burns, I'm sure mine's the same.

Walking into the cafeteria, I see no one, hear nothing. I aim straight for the café bar to make a coffee. I've been dreaming of a restorative cappuccino all morning, but I couldn't stomach one before the meeting.

"Which one of us is going to win this thing?" Zack picks up a paper cup, nudges my shoulder. "The Professeur seemed especially taken with your designs."

"Was he?" I watch the coffee and milk dribble into my cup, then shake chocolate on top. As much as I love Zack and Samu, I want to win, end of story.

I fall into a chair at the nearest empty table, warming my hands around my cup. I inhale the rich aroma. Froth spills over the edge, burning my hands. "Crap." Cursing my stupidity, I reseal the cap, suck my fingers.

"Are you okay?" Zack pulls up a chair next to me. "You're pale."

I flick my fingers. "Erm ... yeeeass ... just ... the floor seems a little uneven, is all." I cling to the table, afraid I'll tip off my chair. "Oh, Zack. God. That interview ..."

Zack wraps his arm around my shoulder. "Sask, I was shaking throughout. It's over. Settle."

I hold my head in my trembling hands. I believe in dreams. I believe that my dreams will come true. *But not the way you expect*, Kumpaya said to me in the Australian desert. So many unknown factors. Yet my gut feeling says I'm going to win. I'm hanging onto that positive feeling.

I look up. Zack and Samu stare at me, brows knitted. I shake my head. My vision clears. "Sorry I lost it, guys," I say, voice shaking. I hold up my cup, we laugh and toast each other.

"It'll be a tough week or two." Samu takes a huge draft of his drink. "Seeing we have to all prepare like we're the winner, I've more silk screen prints to make."

"I have to think of yet another way to drag denim from the '60s to the 21st century. Any ideas?" Zack looks at us, eyebrows raised.

"I'll help both of you. Being busy is the best way to stay sane." My mind races ahead to the clothes I've yet to complete for the catwalk if I win. I need more outfits. Manu has tailored several garments already, but I'm leaving nothing to chance.

My mind flicks to the professeur and his gold lame jacket. A bit much Elvis Presley King and not so much Louis XIV King. But still ...

My focus is firmly on my Sun King.

CHAPTER TWENTY-NINE

Since the meeting at the Institut, I've been sleeping so lightly I could hear a mouse wearing bootees tiptoe across the floor. I'm waiting to hear if I've been placed first out of the three finalists in the fashion competition. Monsieur Etienne said there'd be no word until Christmas. But there's no room for anything else in my brain.

Raphael zips his boots, zips his coat, pats his pockets, checks his wallet, his keys, his phone.

He slept over last night after working late in the attic on his magnum opus. He has an early meeting with Lamar at the gallery, so he's moving around quietly so as not to wake me.

I flutter my eyes and he's looking at me, face tight. "Don't worry about me, Raphael." I try to smile, hating how I feel sticky with sweat. "I won't hear from the Institut for weeks, but I can't stop fretting. I'll start preparations for my Thanksgiving dinner to take my mind off it."

He sits on the side of the bed, takes my hand. "Great idea, *mon ange*. Look at you, stick thin. You weigh no more than a child." He picks up my hand and admires his grandmother's ring which I've moved to my middle finger as it was in danger of falling off. He turns over my hand, examining the fine bones sticking out of my wrists. "I know you're having a hard time coping with the stress, I understand that, but aren't you Monsieur Etienne's star student?"

"Thanks for reminding me." I watch Raphael, loving how he's so supportive, how his jacket stretches across his shoulders, how his leather trousers mold his legs. Why didn't I jump at his offer of marriage? I could busy myself with wedding plans. Flares of longing shoot through me, but there's no time to rip those clothes off his back and have my way with him.

But things are far from perfect between us. Look how much time he spends with Bernelle, more than he spends with me. I totally get that Bernelle's role is crucial to his success, but I hate how she snaps her fingers and he runs to her.

He drops a light kiss on my mouth and I smell my lavender toothpaste. "Promise me two things," he says. "One, you'll eat today. Your refrigerator is a disaster. Go to Farrin's. Order something healthy. Not just your usual coffee and croissant."

"Food is the last thing I crave." I roll over onto my back and look at him, craving him, wanting to eat him all up. "What's the second thing?"

"I'm worried about how you're handling this stress. Isn't it time to see Pascale again?" He kisses me. "You look like you've got no strength. Perhaps you should cut down on gym."

"Exercise helps my anxiety. But to put your mind at rest, I've made an appointment with Pascale for early next week."

"*Bien.* Now, don't forget to eat. Go a bit easier on exercise. Have a sleep in for a change." To take the bossiness out of his words, he drops another kiss onto my forehead. "Have the best day, my darling." Brow knitted, he runs his hand over my head and leaves.

After a fitful doze, I drag myself out of bed, wrap myself in a light woolen throw because Raphael has lit the fire and the apartment is warm. Lurching to the kitchen, I open the refrigerator. Raphael's right. There's a block of moldy cheese, a tub of out-of-date Greek yoghurt, a half empty jar of Nutella with mold on top. Ugh. I dump them into the bin. I'll go to the market before work and fill the refrigerator with delicious food and drink. Some ham, cheese, a baguette, paté, grapes, a pastry or two. A bottle of Verve Clicquot. I'm suddenly thirsty. I spy a half glass of Dubonnet Raphael left beside the sink last night. I take a sip, choking on a chunk of soggy lemon. As the whiskey sears my throat, I'm glad for the buzz.

I take my glass to the French doors, look out over the city, but Paris stares at me from a steely winter sky, in the same gray mood as I am. Sipping my disgusting drink, I listen to the familiar clump of feet on the stairs, the slamming of doors as tenants leave for their daily search for work. The smell of warm croissants from the street stirs a hunger in me. Farrin's it is.

The doorbell rings. I jerk, splash drink over my wrap. I dab at it with a tissue, my eyes flicking to my clock. Drinking at nine in the morning? *Am I turning into my father?*

Who'd come calling this early? Probably Madame Lavelle with a message. Maybe the Grande Dame. When I saw her last evening, she wasn't well. Perhaps she's come for another rant about her doctor.

Bunch of crumpled tissues in hand, I wrench open the door.

It takes my alcohol-fueled brain time to register that Raphael's father is standing there dressed in town clothes – suit, tie, biscuit-colored cashmere overcoat, cashmere scarf, holding a fancy walking cane and jaunty black hat. I jump back, dropping the tissues, clutching the throw tight around my body.

A gurgling noise escapes my throat. *What the hell?* I hate the way his eyes linger on my damp breasts. Fool. I should have dressed before I answered the door.

He thumps his cane. "Saskia. Invite me in. Smells like you're having a little party. May I join you?"

"No." My voice rasps. "I'm not dressed."

"Even better. Don't mind a drink for breakfast either served by my personal barmaid." His sly grin curdles my already-roiling stomach.

"What are you doing here?"

"In Paris or at your apartment?"

"At my apartment."

"Would that be *our* apartment? Raphael nearly rode over my foot in his Hells Angels gear just now, so keen was he to avoid me. It baffles me why he'd choose to live in a crumbling old ruin."

"Ask him."

He shrugs. "He won't talk to me. Not a word since you both came down for a visit and left without so much as goodbye, breaking his mother's tender heart. But never mind, it's you I came to see." He rests both hands on the mother-of-pearl handle of his cane. "His exhibition is Christmas Eve. That's why I'm in town. Alexandra has shopping to do." He tisks as if that's all women do.

Since when were you invited to Raphael's exhibition? "Sir. Please go. I've a busy day ahead."

"You young people. Always busy. But take the time. I think you'll like what I have. But I'm a civilized man." He pushes forward. "I don't talk on doorsteps."

I hold my ground. "Stay away from me."

"Don't be a child."

Isn't that what you like? Children? I slam the door in his face, but he's too quick. He shoves his tasseled shoe in the door like he's a gangster in a Hollywood mob movie.

"Be reasonable, Saskia." He thumps his cane on the floor. "I have legitimate business."

I hate the smug look on his face. "I have absolutely no business with you."

He smiles, but it doesn't reach his eyes. "I have something you want ... badly."

Surely ... no ... he can't mean—

He smirks, pats his coat. "Gotcha as they say. In my pocket."

I stare at him, wondering what he's on about.

Mario is struggling up the stairs to his apartment opposite mine, wheezing, cradling his paper bag like It's a baby. Sergio from level 3 is with him. Another marathon drinking session is about to begin.

'*Stai bene*? Are you okay, Shaaskiia?" Mario calls in Italian.

"*Sto bene grazie*. I'm fine, Mario." I give him the thumbs up. "This gentleman is just leaving." I take a step toward François and hiss. "Go. Or I'll ask my friends to help you leave."

He taps my shoulder with his cane. Ignoring my gasp, he says, "These drunks are your friends? Does everyone in this dump get drunk before breakfast? Look, if money's the problem, I could set you up in a little apartment on rue Faubourg Saint-Honoré near all those fabulous fashion houses."

"Not everyone is as lucky in life as you. And I love living here. With my people."

"Oh please, get off your soapbox and dress. I'll take you for coffee and some food. Looks like you're wasting away."

"No."

He leans forward, bares his teeth which still remind me of a vicious dog. "Does winning this fashion competition interest you?"

My face burns, my heart skitters, my hands tremble. I shake my head even though I'm nodding inside.

He raps his cane onto the floor, walks toward the stairs. "I give up. You're a fool. You deserve to fail."

I slam the door, throw the lock, lean against it, panting. I pace the sitting room. Collapse onto the sofa, clutch a cushion to my stomach. The alcohol has made me ill. I vow never to drink in the morning again.

I call Raphael. He doesn't answer. I clutch my cell phone. Shoot off a quick text to him:

`Your father visited. I'm off to Farrin's. Love you. S x`

I push open the café door, gasp. François sits at a table under the window watching me, toying with a tiny espresso. He checks me out from my favorite hot pink Valentino velvet overcoat to white knee-high boots.

I pause on the threshold, consider walking to the next café, then ask myself, why should I? Farrin is a good friend. Times are tough. He needs my support. I walk past François without acknowledging his presence. "*Bonjour! Ça va, Farrin?*"

Farrin grabs a large takeout cup from beside the coffee machine. "*Ça va* Saskia." He smiles and the machine hisses and gurgles. "Your usual? With *pain au chocolat?*"

"*Oui.*" It'll be satisfying ripping a pastry apart and chocolate will sweeten the sourness of the day.

When I turn from the counter, François calls out. "You dress high class for a barmaid. Or do you do a little lap dancing on the side?"

Glad there are no customers to hear the insult, I ignore him, head for my favorite little table in a private corner near the bar refrigerator. Shaking with rage, I sit, watch people pass the windows. I check my cell. *Why doesn't Raphael call?* He's busy. I shouldn't have bothered him. I can handle François.

"Well, if the mountain won't come to Muhammad—"

I jump. "*What?*"

François looms over me, smirks. "You can't hide from me."

My stomach lurches. I tug my scarf around my throat, pull my velvet cloche over my forehead. "Leave me alone."

Farrin serves my almond cappuccino and pastry. It smells divine. "*Merci beaucoup*, Farrin."

"Bring me another espresso." François drags a chair from another table and sits opposite me, blocking access to the refrigerator.

An icy dread creeps over me. I was a fool to stay here. If Raphael finds us together ... Oh My God, he'll go ballistic. I grab my coffee, glad it's to-go. I push the table toward him, ready myself to stand and run.

François pushes the table back, locks me against the wall. "You're not going anywhere, Saskia. I've several hours to kill while Alexandra shops for a gown for Raphael's exhibition. You're an entertaining way to pass the time."

I shudder. Upend my coffee cup, gulp a large mouthful. "Let me go." I stamp my boots on the floor. "I've a thousand things to do."

"Really?" He drums his fingers on the table. "Does that include helping Raphael prepare for his exhibition? Like a good girlfriend would? Or are you so caught up in your own life you ignore his needs?"

Enraged, I pick up my croissant, rip it in half. I know François's just winding me up, but it strikes a chord. "He doesn't need my help." Is that correct? Would Raphael appreciate my help or is Bernelle help enough?

Farrin sets an espresso in front of François. Slides me a glance. "Do you want another, Saskia?"

"Non, *merci*."

Farrin turns back to François.

"*Merci*." François hands Farrin a twenty euro note, shoos him away like he's a pesky fly. "Now, Saskia." He takes a sip of his drink. "You're in trouble." He puts down his doll-sized cup, plays with his cashmere scarf, tugging the fringe through his manicured fingers.

"Trouble? What trouble?" *Oh, God, why did I bite?*

He smirks, raises his eyebrows. "You have a mental illness. You unravel when stressed. Just look at you. You're jerking around like you're walking a tightrope over an active volcano." He taps his fingers on the side of his tiny cup.

I grab my throat. I can scarcely breathe, especially with the table pressing into my stomach. *How dare this creep spy on me.* "So not your business, sir." I roll my eyes, look past François onto the street hoping Raphael will materialize. What happened to handling this myself? I absentmindedly rip my pastry into ragged quarters, rub my stomach.

"Bad taste in your mouth, *n'est-ce pas?*"

"Hmmm." I check my watch. *Raphael, please come.*

"Saskia." François slaps the table, making me jump. "Pay attention."

"Huh?" I toss down another mouthful of brew. Should I call Farrin for help? No. He has a line out the door. I must handle François myself.

"I thought you'd be one of those people into that mindfulness crap. *Carpe diem* and all. You're not seizing this moment."

"I wonder why." I hold up my cup. "I've finished. And I'm finished with you." I give the table an almighty shove. "Some of us have to work."

"Oh, the bar." He grabs my hand as I push past. "How ashamed your father must be. His little girl, the only daughter of a New York property mogul, a barmaid. Children," he tisks, 'such disappointments." He tugs my arm so hard I nearly fall into his lap. "Now I have your attention, look what I have." He pushes me back into my chair, smirks, takes a large white envelope out of his pocket. He puts it into my hand and closes my palm over it.

I recoil at his touch. "What's this?" I step to the side, hold it by the corner like it's full of anthrax, throw it onto the table.

"You're such a fool. I fail to understand what Raphael sees in you. You must be hot in bed." He picks it up and holds it out. "Open it."

A woman in a short skirt stands in front of the refrigerator. "*Excuse-moi*, Monsieur?"

"Pardon." François stands to the side while she helps herself to a fruit juice, his eyes on her legs as she leans over.

What a perv.

When the woman leaves, François taps the table. "Open it." I should throw it away, unread, but instead I slide a shaky finger under the seal, pull out an embossed document, scrunch my eyes in disbelief. It's a full list of my fellow classmates at the Institut, followed by the details of the New Fashion competition, the judges, the shortlist of three, with a blank for the winner's name.

François looks at me from under his brows. "Saskia, do what I want, then just a word from me and I'll guarantee your name is in that place." He stabs his finger at the blank space. "I want to taste some of that hotness."

Influence peddling. Raphael was right. "You're so disgusting. A sorry excuse for a father. And a husband." A cold knot freezes my insides. I should never have opened the document. Now I can't unsee it. I drop it into my ruined pastry. Chocolate oozes through the paper.

François snatches it away, dabbing the stains with a napkin, his face wreathed in an unbearable smirk.

My heart hammers so hard the throb reaches my throat. What if the Institut traces this document to me? I could be disqualified. I could be thrown out of France. What has he done, the lascivious letch? I hurry toward the door. Try to control my breathing. Too late. The door opens, crashes against the wall. *Oh ... My ... God.*

Raphael's hands fist at his waist, his face burns a furious red. His eyes, dark and dangerous, wide with shock, shoot fire at his father.

He stands inside the door, looking at us. "What the fuck are you doing here with Saskia, you sneaky bastard?"

I'm such a fool.

Raphael's stricken expression tells me just how much of a fool.

CHAPTER THIRTY

No. No. No. This can't be happening. François set a trap. I fell right into it. *Fool.*

I push the table away. Hurry toward Raphael. Grabbing his hand, I plead. "Don't be angry." Could I have chosen dumber words? If anything's going to make Raphael angry, it's his girlfriend sharing a *tête-à-tête* with his father.

Raphael drops my hand like it's white hot, plants his legs wide apart. He slams his fist into his palm repeatedly. His mouth opens and shuts, but the only sound that comes out is a groan.

François folds his arms, watching like he's an interested bystander, not the instigator of the drama.

If I didn't already hate him, I do now. I take a deep breath, edge closer to Raphael. "Please, Raphael. Believe me. This is a mistake. Don't be angry."

He holds out a hand towards me, palm up in a stay-away-from-me gesture. "I'm angry at him, not you."

Philippe's counseling hasn't prepared him for this situation.

When he speaks again, it's to his father. His voice is hoarse like his throat's been raked with hot coals. "What are you playing at this time, you reprobate?"

François raises his eyebrows, speaks in a faux-innocent voice. "I invited your charming girlfriend to share coffee with me, son, or is she your fiancé? Saskia won't tell me anything even though she's wearing my mother's ring. Why choose a barmaid when you could have that saucy Bernelle I hooked you up with?"

My heart freezes. I inhale through clenched teeth. So Bernelle—it wasn't my imagination.

Raphael flicks a gaze my way, shakes his head, then stabs a finger at his father. "Shut your mouth."

I chew my thumb, hate that I've been so stupid. I knew François's habit of hitting on Raphael's girlfriends and now this situation has brought Raphael's wound to the surface again. Why didn't I run when I saw him here? I can't believe my stupidity. Cold balls of fury roll around my stomach. I won't let this man come between us. "Come, Raphael," I hold out my hand. The coffee line is out the door. Cell phones click. "We can't talk here. It's not fair on Farrin."

Raphael's veins throb in his neck like they're pumped full of fury. "Farrin can handle it."

I point to his father like he's a slug that's just crawled from under a rock. I take a deep breath, try to steady it. "Raphael, he was here when I arrived." My voice shakes. I turn to François. "Tell him."

François's eyes dart from Raphael to me. "He can work it out himself." He tisks, shakes his head.

Raphael's eyes flare. "Why did you go to Saskia's apartment?"

François's face lights up like a flashbulb. He chuckles, smooths his hair. "I knew she'd love a coffee with her father-in-law."

The air whooshes out of me like François punched me in the stomach. But like a good boxer, I recover quickly. Hands on hips, I snarl, "Shut your mouth."

I plead with Raphael. "I refused to come. He lay in wait."

François can't stop the sly grin lighting his face. "You should have seen her, son. The way she greeted me at the door. A wanton in her wrap, nothing underneath ... and she'd been drinking whiskey ... at nine in the morning. Impressive. But I hear her papa likes the bottle a little too much. The apple doesn't fall too far from the tree, as they say."

Raphael grabs François's arm, lifts him up and shoves him toward the door. "Arsehole."

A police officer in bike leathers walks in. He hesitates at the door when he sees Raphael and his father pushing and shoving.

"*Aidez moi.*" François holds his hand in the air like a drowning swimmer signaling a lifeguard.

The officer strides over and clamps Raphael's shoulder. "*Calme*, Monsieur, *calme. Composez vous.*"

"*Pardon.*" Raphael drops his hands. I can see by his twitching fingers what a massive effort it takes.

"*Ullo*! Monsieur," Farrin calls to the gendarme, holding a large takeout cup, "*Ton café est prêt.*"

After taking his coffee, the young officer looks from Raphael to his father. "Messieurs, *arrête tes combats immédiatement.*"

Raphael and François nod like obedient children. "*Oui*, Monsieur," they say in unison.

They don't fool me. I'm not sure they fooled the law, either.

As soon as the gendarme jumps onto his white motorbike and roars away, Raphael's hands are back on his father's shoulders.

François stabs a finger into Raphael's face. "You heard the man, son. You always were a hot head." François pushes Raphael backward in my direction. "But you must wonder who your girlfriend's meeting every time you leave her."

Red spots flash before my eyes. "How dare you." My voice is thick with fury. "Especially after your affair with Cosette. Have you no soul?"

"He told you about my little indiscretion?" François chuckles. "Then why didn't you run when you saw me?"

Raphael's face flushes an ugly red, his fingers twitch. He's wondering the same thing. So am I.

"Raphael. Let it go. He's not worth it. He's only here to hurt us."

François rubs his hands together. "Well, Saskia, aren't you ungrateful?" His tone is mock rage. "I bring you a gift, and you say I hurt you." He tut tuts, shakes his head, rolls his eyes. "Take care how you speak to me, Mademoiselle." His voice turns nasty. "A word in Professeur Germain's ear and you'll never win this competition. And I will ensure you never work in Paris, not even behind a bar. You'll be thrown out of France."

My feet feel frozen to the floor. I'm sure I'm as white as a ghost. Does he have that kind of power? Judging by his smirk, he believes he does.

Raphael lays his hands onto his father's shoulders, spins him around, throws him his hat and cane, pushes him out the door so hard François nearly falls flat on his face. "Get the hell out of here. Stay away from us."

I let out a long breath. Maybe Raphael will calm down now.

He walks to the table, picks up the chocolate-smeared document. "What the hell?" He scans the smudgy page, then collapses into my chair, head in his hands. "How did he get this?" He raises his head, looks at me.

I feel guilty even though I'm not. "I don't know, I never—"

"Fuck you didn't." He slams his fist onto the table so hard I jump. His eyes rove my face, searching for the truth. When I say nothing, he says, "He was the obvious choice, wasn't he? With his corrupt friends, he can move mountains. Unlike me."

I swallow hard. Pull François's chair beside him, sit. "Raphael," I hold his face in my hands, "look at me."

He turns slowly, rakes me with his eyes, eyes full of pain and regret. "He could ruin you, Sassy. He doesn't make empty threats. He fights dirty, the pathetic bastard."

I twist my fingers through his curls. "You know what he is, so believe me when I say I had nothing to do with this list. He brought it—"

He waves the document in my face. "Deep down I know that. But it brought back painful memories. Cosette asked for his help getting into a university course. My father doesn't give favors and expect nothing in return." His voice is ragged; there's an undertone of pleading.

I shake my head over and over. "No, Raphael, no. This is not like it was with Cosette. I've had no communication with him. I'd never ask him for anything. He turned up at my door ..." Tears prick my eyes. "But he knows everything. My PTSD. Everything."

Raphael closes his eyes. Shakes his head. "The fuck he does." He picks up the paper again, shakes his head. "He buys everyone. What did he ask for in return for winning?"

"What do you think?" I rip the document in half, crunch it into a ball, toss it onto the table.

"That's an empty gesture. He'll have copies." He sounds tired, I've-had-enough-I-can't-take-any-more tired. "He asked you to sleep with him, didn't he?"

I stoke his arm. Lean against his side.

He wraps his arm around me, pulls me close.

I only have one chance to get this right. *Please God.* "Raphael. I'd never do what he asked." I clasp my hands like I'm praying. "I tried to leave the café, but he manhandled me. This paper may be bogus anyway. His plan was to break us up. Or at the very least, cause a rift between us."

His phone pings. He takes it out of his pocket, checks the screen. "I know how he works. I trust you."

"Thank you, Raphael." But does he?

He looks up from his phone, an apologetic look on his face. "Bernelle just reminded me I have a dealer to meet. I raced down from the gallery as soon as I saw your text, so I'm behind." His voice is hollow and spent. He's waited so long for his career break, and when it finally arrives, so does his father, intent on spoiling it. Forever I'll regret that his father used me to do it.

I shake his arm, not wanting him to leave. "Don't let your father spoil this for you. For us. I love you. You're going to have the best opening night ever." Then I recall François's dig. "Is there anything I can do to help?"

"No. You have enough to do. I'm good."

"Are you sure?"

His shrugs his shoulders. "Perfectly sure. But I can't talk about what happened here until I get it straight in my head." His voice is distant, his eyes empty. "Today's made me question things. About us."

I put on my brave face, but my stomach clenches. I sit up. "Like what?"

"Meeting my father down country was the worst idea you've ever had. What if he pulls strings so you can no longer work in Paris? Paris knows how to close ranks against outsiders, especially that entitled crowd he runs with. He's dangerous." Raphael stands, his eyes flit around the café, looking at anyone and everyone except me. "I'm sorry, but I can't deal with this and my exhibition. I love you, Sassy, but I need us to take a break."

I'm left standing in the café surrounded by caffeine-starved humans, feeling my dreams and my heart crumple at my feet. But it's my fault. It's what I deserve.

I don't know how long I've been standing in the middle of the café, unaware of the activity around me, unaware that outside rain is falling in sideways sheets and Parisians are walking along the street clutching black umbrellas.

Farrin puts his arm around my shoulder. "Sit down, Saskia. I'll bring you another coffee."

I hang my head, mortified by the public scene. I clutch the back of my neck, thinking of the crowd watching the fight. When I raise my head, the café is as empty as I feel.

I really need a coffee by the time Farrin places it in front of me, along with a couple of my favorite Italian pistachio almond biscotti. "*Merci*. I'm sorry, Farrin."

He pats me on the shoulder. "Do not even think about it. Are you okay is all that concerns me."

I nod, absentmindedly dunk the hard biscuit into my drink, watch it fall into my coffee and imagine it's me falling into oblivion. I want to swallow a handful of Xanax, take to my bed, stay there till my world magically steadies itself on its axis. How could François do what he did? How could he know exactly where to throw a wrecking ball into Raphael's and my relationship?

François knew both of our weaknesses, that's how. He knew how much I want to win the fashion competition, and knew my being with him would enrage Raphael.

I sip my coffee. Try to put things into perspective. Paris is my dream. Paris is my home. I want no other. Now I'm in danger of losing everything. Raphael sees through what his father did this morning. So why is he taking a break from me just when I need him?

Outside, people look as cold and miserable as I feel. No. I can't take to my bed. That way François wins. People rely on me. I've appliqué to finish for Catherine. Calls to make. Marcel's for work. An uneasy feeling flickers through me. Raphael's and my relationship is so fragile. The thread that holds us together snaps every time there's a provocation. Maybe I'm not good for Raphael or he for me. Maybe François was right in throwing Bernelle at him. She's the one fighting for his exhibition, while I'm doing nothing but taking care of my own needs. She's the one who knows the right people to invite, while I know no one.

I sigh, flick through 'Notes' on my cell phone. I've got to:

- set up meeting with Manu for more trousers for my online shop

- call Zack and Samu to check their progress. (1) *Ask Samu if he's made screen prints from the fabric designs I sketched him and* (2) *tell Zack about my idea for a full-length denim coat with shadow embroidery and sparkles around the hem.*

- shop for fabric for my dress I'm making for Raphael's opening night.

I push my hair back from my face, check my list again. *Buy dress for Raphael's first night.* I delete that earlier entry. Raphael asked me to splurge on an haute couture gown for his big night. A designer evening dress in

Paris costs between €10,000 to €60,000. I refuse to spend that much. He wants me just this once to forget my rule of having no man provide for me. But I'm making my dress myself. It'll be even more fabulous than the €35,000 red silk dress I lusted after in the window at Madame Bellerose's on rue Faubourg Saint-Honoré. The neckline scoops to the waist, the bared back and thigh split will rock Raphael senseless. It'll be a dress to blind him to Bernelle's wiles. Should I bother? Should I give him up? Is that where this is going?

I give Farrin a quick hug, step outside, buoyed by his "*Bonne chance*". My boot lands into a pool of muddy water. It splashes the hem of my coat; brown spots spray the pink velvet. I should have paid more attention. By not walking away from his father before he showed me that document, I've really muddied the waters between Raphael and me. I look up at the gray clouds. Clouds are gathering, shadowing, threatening our love.

CHAPTER THIRTY-ONE

After yet another restless sleep, two days before my Thanksgiving dinner, I sit up in bed and text Raphael. I've had enough. How long is this break going to be? I'm over waiting for him to come see me and talk to me. Trust issues that surfaced during the fight with his father must be resolved. I can't eat or sleep. I've become increasingly anxious every day we've been apart. I chew my lip, plan my words. I'll get this sorted once and for all. We have to decide if we're together or apart.

I resent that he's left me alone to stew on his hurtful words. It's like he casually threw a grenade into the café with his *I need a break* statement and didn't care that it shattered me. I'm going to set him straight. Raphael must learn that it's not good enough to lash out at someone you love, then do nothing to heal their hurt. I text:

Raphael. We need to talk. Sxx.

Surely, he's calmed down. Surely, he knows he over reacted. Surely, he doesn't believe I invited the loathsome creature that is his father to the café. I hit *Send*, lay back on the pillows, close my eyes.

When he texts back right away, I nearly drop my phone.

Sorry haven't come around. Busy with exhibition.

`Can it wait till your party? I'll come early and talk. Rx.`

I sigh. My waiting game continues.

`Okay. See you then. Sxx.`

My heart beats fast, imagining Raphael arriving at my apartment with one thing on his mind, soothing our troubled waters. He'll apologize hand on heart for misjudging me, for taking a break from me, then stay behind after everyone leaves. My body aches for him. Does his ache for me? Or does Bernelle slake his ache?

Seeing Raphael at my door on the night of my Thanksgiving celebration stops my heart. Then I stop myself. His flushed face reminds me of his furious face that day at Farrin's when he lashed out at me.

I get tingles seeing him in his faux-casual jeans, button down shirt and sports coat. He always has that effect on me, but I'm going to push away my lustful thoughts until he apologizes.

"Come in, Raphael," I say, casual as you please. "I'm glad you're early."

"*Bon anniversaire*, Sassy." He kisses me lightly, hands me a huge bouquet of heavenly red roses. "I brought these to dress your table, but I see it's already dressed." He removes his scarf and coat and carefully places them on a hook near the door.

"Thank you, Raphael. Always room for roses." I head for the kitchen with my face buried in the blooms and my mind buried in that ugly scene at Farrin's, thinking again how Raphael made me feel powerless and has done nothing to fix it.

He follows me, lifts a saucepan lid and the room fills with the aroma of steamed vegetables. "The apartment smells amazing." He gives me a lopsided grin. "I've never tasted your cooking."

I appreciate his trying to keep the conversation light. I'm thankful for the time to pull myself together, to calm myself. "Neither have I." A nervous giggle erupts from my throat. I'm a little light-headed from the champagne I've been sipping for courage. "Tonight, will be a revelation for both of us."

"Come here." He takes my hands in his. "You look gorgeous in pink silk. You made it?"

"Hmmm. Yes. Years ago in New York. A sample." I remove my hands. "These roses need water."

With his artistic eye, he arranges the roses. He's brought Cinnamon Dolche, red with deep pink specks, one of Mom's favorites. I inhale the strong scent and Mom's in the room with me.

When we've placed them on the side table near the entrance, he covers my hand with his, raises it to his lips and kisses it. "I brought a little something for your birthday." He reaches into his pocket and hands me a tiny black box.

"Thanks." Flipping it open, I see an exquisite silk padded antique cameo edged in gold filigree. *A birthday gift or an I'm sorry gift?* It's so beautiful and such a thoughtful Raphael gift, but I'd rather he'd given me the gift of his time.

"Do you like it?" he asks. "Some say It's the Sun King's first wife, Maria Teresa; others say it's Athénaïs de Rochechouart de Mortemart, one of his favorite mistresses. Her corn-colored hair reminds me of yours." He pulls the necklet from the box, and with a "May I?" lifts my hair and clips it behind my neck. "See?" He walks me to the mirror beside the door. "What do you think?"

I inhale a deep breath, fiddle with the cameo. "It's beautiful, Raphael." I gaze at the face. Her blue eyes are wide open. Surprised. Like mine. When Raphael makes up his mind to woo, he's a pro. He'd rather do anything but face our trust issues. "The perfect gift. Thank you."

"The same shade as your dress. We're always in sync."

I turn around, look him in the eye. "Really?"

He holds me on either side of the neck, his touch sends shivers juddering through me which I do my best to hide. "Let's always be in sync,

Sassy. I'm sorry for those things I said at Farrin's. I'm a brute. I wasn't thinking straight. Seeing you with my father brought out the demon in me and—"

Thunk. Thunk. Thunk.

My medieval door knocker cuts short Raphael's apology. *Crap.* He was just getting started.

"*Merde.*" He removes his hands. "Who would turn up this early? We'll talk later, Sassy. Promise." He walks to the door, adjusts the rose centerpiece as he passes.

Uh-oh. Nothing's sorted. I'll be a nervous mess until the party's over. No. I need to be in control. To enjoy my special night. I gulp the rest of my champagne. I love this man. We'll sort it out.

"*Entrez.*" Raphael ushers in Zack and Jemi who're wearing matching denim from Zack's range which didn't make the cut.

Following close behind are my two favorite mother figures, Madame Lavelle and the Grande Dame, both wearing vintage evening gowns resplendent in beads and sequins with wraps around their shoulders that appear suspiciously like real fur. They look around in amazement. "Saskia," Madame Lavelle says. "You've done wonders with the decoration."

"*Merci. Merci.* Welcome." I put on a happy face, accept kisses and birthday wishes.

Raphael's on the job. After taking the ladies' wraps, he pours drinks from my makeshift bar near the balcony door. "More, Sassy?" He holds the champagne bottle over my flute.

I nod. I never say no to champagne. I chuck it back, a happy buzz fills my head.

Thunk. Thunk. Thunk.

Lamar and Bernelle enter, wreathed in designer black and friendly smiles.

Bernelle. What's she doing here? My throat's dry despite my champagne. I put down my glass, clench my hands into fists until my fingernails cut into my palms. Bernelle is a challenge I wasn't expecting. All the Xanax in the world won't be enough to deal with her. "Welcome," I murmur, signaling Zack to take their coats to the bedroom as Raphael's deep in conversation with Madame Lavelle.

Raphael comes over to see to the new arrivals' drinks. Bernelle kisses his cheek, then surprises me by kissing mine.

Judas. My hand itches to slap her.

"Happy Thanksgiving and birthday, Saskia." Bernelle raises her glass of bubbly. "I'm sorry for turning up so last minute. I don't eat much, but drinking is another matter." She points to where Lamar places two magnums of Verve Clicquot onto the drinks' table. "That should about cover it."

"Thanks," I say, the perfect hostess. Once she found out Raphael was coming, she couldn't stay away. I go to the kitchen for another place setting. When I'm out of sight, I slap my cheeks, grit my teeth, try to snap out of my snit.

Damn you Bernelle.

This is my *night.*

I won't let you ruin it.

I've broken the French dinner party tradition. Raphael and I sit side by side, surrounded by laughter, beautiful cookery smells and everyone digging into my Thanksgiving food.

With YouTube's' help, the stuffed purple chicken and vegetable casseroles are delicious. I've made Mom's pumpkin pecan pie from her little handwritten recipe book I found in a kitchen drawer at the Hamptons. Zack and Lamar help themselves to seconds, then thirds, until the dish is clean.

Raphael places his hand over mine where it fiddles with my glass stem. "Sassy. What a great meal. Let's make this a regular deal, celebrating Thanksgiving and your birthday with friends."

"You mean I have to cook once a year?" My eyes fly to Bernelle, and I wonder if we'll be together long enough to fall into a regular routine.

Raphael tastes pumpkin pie from my spoon and whispers, "Sweet. But I don't need dessert. I have you. You're all the sweetness I need." He lowers his head, lightly kisses the top of mine.

Am I? Brushing my fingers over the spot, I turn to him. "Speaking of sweet, Raphael, please pour the Sauternes."

After he's done, he and Madame Lavelle walk across to the coffee table before the fire. He lifts a large box I hadn't noticed tied with a huge orange and black bow, brings it to the table, pushes my empty plates aside, places it in front of me. "Surprise."

"Saskia, you said no gifts," the Grande Dame says, as Madame Lavelle and Raphael take their seats, "but dear Cadence and I could not resist. We all know your addiction to Verve Clicquot. This case should keep you happy for some time. Happy birthday to the sweetest girl."

"How wonderful of you both. *Merci.*" I move around the table; tears prick my eyes. I kiss them both, humbled that I have these two wonderful women in my life.

"Sask." Zack catches my hand as I pass him and Jemi on my way back to my seat. He reaches down between their chairs, stands, hands me a beautifully framed photograph. "Happy birthday from your class at the Institut."

I study the hopeful faces of the students who are yet to discover where their love of fashion takes them. The faces blur into one – François's face. His offer to buy me the winning position still looms like an elephant between Raphael and me.

"Thank you, Zack, Jemi." I place my hands on their shoulders, kiss their cheeks. "This will be the first photograph I display on my office wall when I'm Head Designer of some high-end Parisian fashion house." I say it in a jokey tone, but everyone knows I'm not joking.

"That's the spirit, Saskia." Jemi raises her glass. "Most likely you'll have your first trophy for your shelves come January."

"Amen to that." Raphael leads a round of applause. He raises his glass in a toast and everyone joins in. "To Saskia's success."

Lamar stands before I have time to process the confidence shown toward me. "*Bon anniversaire*, Saskia. Here's a little something from Bernelle and me." He comes around the table, kisses me, then presents me with a framed signed limited-edition invitation to Raphael's exhibition.

Holding Raphael's hand, I look at his striking image on the embossed paper and the paintings from his collections in a collage behind him, I have trouble swallowing. I've known him since this exhibition was but a dream. Now it becomes a reality in a few short weeks. "Thanks so much, Lamar, Bernelle. I'll treasure it always."

Raphael takes the gifts and places them onto the coffee table. As he returns, and starts clearing the dishes, the Grande Dame grabs his hand. "Raphael, not so fast. What did *you* bring Saskia?"

Raphael puts down the dishes, looks at me, face flushed. "I bought Saskia something personal. I gave it to her earlier."

"Of course you did." The Grande Dame winks at me, no doubt finding amusement in my burning face. "But is there something you can share with all of us?"

Raphael sits next to me, quirks his eyebrow. "Yes, Madame." He places his arm over my shoulder and tugs me closer. "It's around Saskia's neck."

The Grande Dame nods her head. "A beautiful antique cameo, Raphael. I adore it. I believe it's one of the Sun King's mistresses, Athénaïs de Rochechouart de Mortemart. But come on, I heard a whisper about a momentous surprise."

Taking my hand, he leans toward me and says quietly, "Forgive me. I wanted to give this to you after everyone leaves, but the Grande Dame has put me on the spot. I should never have mentioned it to her, but I was so excited." He stands, walks to the bedroom, returning with a large, padded envelope in his hands. After sitting down, he says, "Saskia, I bought you, well, I bought us, something very special that we can share, I hope, for many years."

"Come on, come on." The Grande Dame claps her hands, setting her bangles jangling. "Tell us. Tell us."

Butterflies ripple through my core, anticipating what this gift might be. I don't like public announcements, but Raphael finds it impossible to be quiet about anything. I hold my breath, my hand clammy in Raphael's, waiting, watching the emotions flit across Bernelle's face. She looks like she's dreading this announcement as much as I am.

Raphael exhales a breath, taps the envelope on the table, then says, "Saskia. I bought us an apartment on Île Saint-Louis."

I grab my throat, make a gurgling sound. "*What?*" Everyone around the table gasps. An apartment? A rather ostentatious birthday gift. Something my father would do.

Raphael shakes the contents from the envelope and holds them out to me. "These are photographs until you see the real thing." He flips through the booklet, and I see it's one of those gorgeous old apartments overlooking the Seine which we both adore. "You'll love it." He raises his glass, everyone follows his lead. Leaning down to kiss me, he whispers, "*Je t'dore,*" while the photographs are passed around the table.

My breath hitches in my throat. He's one of those exhibitionists who hire a skywriter to write *Will you marry me?* across the blue. That's Raphael. Spontaneous. If I'm to make a life with him, I must accept this about him. But can I? "That's a most generous gift, Raphael." He means well, but I can't help comparing his gift to my father's offer to buy me an apartment on Fifth Avenue if I married Xavier. I want to scream and run from the room, instead I organize my twitching lips into a smile.

The Grande Dame winks at me. "Come on Saskia. Doesn't this gorgeous man deserve a kiss? If you don't kiss him, I will."

"Go ahead," I snark. "Raphael won't mind."

He laughs good naturedly. "Hey, Saskia. Don't be giving Madame ideas."

Why can't he understand me? I don't want material things which is all Pa ever gave me. I want Raphael's love. I want his trust. I asked him to come early, give us time to sort things out before my party. Instead, he comes bearing expensive gifts, cutting short the time we needed. Am I making a huge mistake staying with a man who reminds me of my father in so many ways? But deep down I know Raphael's generosity is given freely, no strings, It's part of him. Everything Pa ever gave me came at a price. A price I refused to pay in the end.

I inhale a deep breath and think positive thoughts. I scoot closer. Wrap my arm around his neck. Pull him close. Kiss him. "You're wonderful. *Je t'dore*," I whisper.

The party's over. The Grande Dame and Madame Lavelle collect their wraps and leave. Zack is up to his elbows in suds in the kitchen and Jemi's been dancing around in her bell-bottom jeans flicking a dishrag at him. Lamar and Bernelle sit in the red chairs before the fire enjoying drinks with Marcel, who turned up after dinner, bearing another case of Veuve Clicquot. At least my champagne situation got sorted tonight.

Raphael and I put on our coats, step through the doors onto the balcony, close them behind us. Being outside with winter only a few days away is magical, with the sky bathed in a golden glow from the city lights. But I didn't drag Raphael out here to admire the view.

"You look nervous, Raphael. What's up?" Is he dreading our upcoming talk after the guests leave?

He takes my freezing hands and clasps them in his warm ones. "I'm sorry, Sassy. It's your birthday and I feel like an arse doing this, but I can't stay the night."

Shock jolts through me. "What?"

He holds my hands to his chest, I try to wrench them away. "Bernelle and I have work to do. There are some finer points to sort before we meet with sponsors early tomorrow."

With a mighty effort, I finally wrench my hands from his, jut my hip against the balcony rail, face him, try to control my rage. *Bernelle wins. Again.* The thread snaps. Hot blood surges through my veins. My voice shakes when I say, "You're kidding, right? No one works at midnight in France. I've been waiting all night to talk to you. It's been torture. We can't go on like nothing's happened."

"Sassy." He places his hands onto my shoulders, smiles when I shiver. He pulls my coat collar high around my neck. "We're good. What a beautiful party. We're going to be together forever in our new apartment. The rest will sort itself."

"No, it won't." My lips press into a straight line, I shrug off his hands. "You accused me of some terrible things at Farrin's, none of which were true. You showed you don't trust me. You took a break from me and I don't even know if we're together. That apartment on the Île looks wonderful, but I'm a long way from moving in with you."

Sighing, he leans his back against the balcony rails, draws me into his embrace. "That's why I came early. To talk about that day. To fix us. To tell you our break was over. To tell you about the new apartment. I've always dreamed of moving to the Île as you know. It's perfect for us. Why won't you give me a chance? I'm trying. But everyone turned up early tonight when I'd just begun my apology. The French are never supposed to arrive earlier than twenty minutes late."

"I'm not up for another French cultural lesson. That day at Farrin's, Raphael?" I grit my teeth. "Why did you lash out at me?"

He hugs me closer, brushes a hand over my hair. "Surely you understand my reaction after Cosette." His voice is awash with anger and pain.

"I do understand." I feel his heart beating against my ear. "But I don't understand how you could ever believe even for an instant I arranged the meeting with your father or asked him for the winners' list."

"My father's corruption knows no bounds. I shouldn't have doubted you, you're right. I should have talked to you after I calmed down, but Lamar and Bernelle demanded all my time. They're working around the clock for my exhibition, and I must do the same."

A sharp rap on the door. I remove myself from Raphael's embrace as Bernelle waltzes out in her enormous black fur coat, hat and scarf like she's an extra on *Game of Thrones*. She pushes between us, wraps her arms around his neck and embraces him like a lover. "Come, Raphael." She gives me a sly wink over her shoulder. "Sorry to drag him away, Saskia."

My mouth opens and shuts. I'm speechless at her brazenness. I grab the freezing rail for support.

Raphael turns from Bernelle, peels my hands from the rail, wraps his arms around me. "*Bonne nuit*, Sassy." He kisses my lips long and hard. "I'm so sorry to leave you. I'll see you in the next few days."

Whoosh.

They're gone.

Everyone's gone.

I shiver on the balcony. I'm never a priority with Raphael. I have a better understanding why after seeing him with Bernelle just now. I know Bernelle kissed him, not the other way around, but it seemed so natural the way they fitted in each other's arms. I'm right in thinking a French sophisticate like Bernelle suits Raphael more than I do. That's what she's been trying to prove ever since I came into the picture. Maybe she's right.

Raphael texts several times a day to say he's coming around, but some last-minute emergency eventuates courtesy of Bernelle who's doing her best to cut me out of his life.

Time for one last shot.

Alone in my apartment a week after my party, I text him:

`No face-to-face talk, it's over. S.`

"Sassy, sorry for messing you around." He steps over the threshold fifteen minutes after my text, wearing ripped jeans, unbuttoned shirt over a T-shirt, leather jacket over his shoulder, hair mussed from his bike helmet.

My heart longs for how it used to be. He'd turn up at my door and we'd fall into each other's arms, hungry after the separation, no matter how brief.

Those days are over. I tug my soft housecoat close around me for extra warmth even though I have a fire chugging away in the living room. "Bernelle's always your priority."

He reaches for me, holds my elbows. "Stop it, Sassy. That's your anxiety talking. You're imagining problems. Time is the problem."

I step backward out of his arms, consider his words. My PTSD does make me imagine the worst. But I'm justified imagining the worst in Bernelle's case. She's trying to convince him she's better for him than I am. She has his father's backing, whereas his father sees me as something he stepped on. Hosting Raphael's exhibition has strengthened her hold on him. "I'm calling it as I see it, Raphael. You're a strong person. Always in control. But Bernelle's controlling you. When she kissed you on my balcony, you didn't seem to mind. In fact, you looked quite comfortable in each other's arms."

He puts his hands on his hips and blows a breath. "You've got to get over Bernelle. It's not just Bernelle, *ma cherie*. It's my exhibition. I'm pleading with you. Understand. I've waited all my life for this opportunity and I'm not leaving anything to chance. You've no idea the work involved."

I feel him slipping away. His focus is on everything in his life but me. I hold his elbow and lead him to the sofa where I've set two glasses of chilled Sancerre, hoping it'll remind him of the day he gave me his grandmother's ring. I touch the ring for luck, inhale a deep breath. "I do have some idea. But to move forward, I need answers. Now," we clink, "let's talk about that fight with your father."

Raphael opens his mouth. His phone pings. "Sorry." He checks his screen with his free hand. Relief floods his face.

My blood boils. "Bernelle?" I put down my glass, grit my teeth.

He half stands. "Yes, she wants—"

"Sit." I dash the moisture from my top lip. This is it. I won't take any more. "If you run to her, there's nothing for us to talk about. We're through.

If you want our relationship to survive, I'm your priority right now, not her."

He drops his phone onto the table, covers his face with his hands. "You're right, Sassy. I've been an arse." He looks up. Tears in his eyes. "I've got so much to say to you. I've put it off because apologizing doesn't come easy for me." He massages his scalp with his fingertips. "I don't know where to start."

"Start at Farrin's." I'm being a hardass, but it's the only way to sort this.

I see the darkness in his eyes. "A nightmare. I'm overwhelmed by hatred for my father, but guilt gnaws at me for hating my own flesh and blood. Seeing you with him—" He shakes his head like he's trying to clear the memory— "I had a brain snap. My hatred just exploded."

I place my arm around his waist and squeeze. "That's a good start."

He places a hand over mine where it's resting at his waist, then lifts it to his mouth, kisses it. "That day threw me off course, on top of which are the demands of an art show. I never knew it would suck every molecule of energy from me. It's one giant PR exercise. So many egos to stroke."

I take his hand. "Keep going, Raphael. We're getting somewhere at last."

By the end of tonight, I'll have my Raphael back.

But disquiet bubbles through me. How long before we have to jump the next hurdle and that fragile thread snaps altogether?

CHAPTER THIRTY-TWO

As I slam the cab door and walk towards the Centaquatre gallery in Montmartre to attend Raphael's first exhibition, happy butterflies flutter in my stomach. Raphael and I are close to resolving our trust issues. Now I need to resolve the Bernelle issue which he continues to deny is an issue. When he sees me in my special dress tonight, he'll be all mine. He'll whisper, "*Tu es très belle ce soir, chérie*", like on the night he proposed. I hold my left hand up to the light, wink at his grandmother's sparkling ring.

Tonight's our night.

I won't let anything, or anyone spoil it.

I enter through the arched doorway and am instantly bathed in soft light from skylights two stories high. Glass side panels glimmer like rainbows, but the queuing crowd is dressed in two colors only – red and black as requested. After checking my coat, I rub my hands down my thighs, feel the softness, the sensuality of my silken dress, like velvety rose petals brush against my skin.

I'm not immune to admiring glances as I sashay through the main hall feeling as dazzling as the thousands of Christmas baubles dangling from the ceiling. I stop to watch a group in a side room wearing gelato-colored satin pajamas performing Tai Chi to ancient Chinese music. Looking at them calms me. I should add this gentle exercise routine to my growing arsenal of coping strategies.

Bernelle. She glides up to me on her sky-high heels, champagne glass raised in salute. "*Bonsoir*, Saskia. You finally show up." She stretches her mouth into a smile slick with shimmering red lipstick. Glossy. Confident. Sexy. She looks me up and down like a school principal checking her student's regulation uniform. No doubt she's checking whether my dress outshines hers. "I wasn't sure you'd come." She looks down her cleverly crafted nose.

"Why wouldn't I? I sleep with the artist." I enjoy her flinch. Nothing she can do tonight will burst my bubble. I've worked my look—hair, make up, dress—but Bernelle's low-cut fire-engine red satin Balenciaga with its huge shoulder bow screams for attention. With those flashing green eyes fringed by extra-long fake lashes and the best nose money can buy, her fight face is firmly in place.

A waiter in black and white pushes past in the direction of the exhibition hall holding a tray of champagne in crystal flutes.

I spin on my heels, nearly topple over, snatch one, gulp a generous mouthful, then remember Pascale's lecture on mixing drugs and alcohol. *Whoops.* But I need a few mouthfuls of bubbly for the extra shot of courage to stay one step ahead of Bernelle. At my appointment with Pascale last week, she injected me with ketamine to settle my pre-exhibition nerves. A niggling pain flares behind my eyes. I root around in my black Chanel clutch. *Crap.* I've forgotten Tylenol.

"Lost something?" Bernelle shoots up one perfectly arched eyebrow, her French sophistication set back into place.

I take a deep breath, chance it. "Do you have Tylenol, er, what do you call it, ah, Doliprane?"

She shakes her head, tisking. "What a pity you'll have a headache on Raphael's special night. You should have come prepared."

Bitch. I check the time on my Bvlgari Serpenti watch, jut my chin, stand my ground in my six-inch red satin Louboutins. "Raphael will be waiting for me. I'm a touch late after finalizing arrangements for his after party."

Touché. Bernelle purses her lips like she's tasted out-of-date paté. "Ah, *oui*. That thing at the apartment on Île Saint-Louis. You haven't even seen the apartment. You're a strange one. You show no appreciation for what Raphael buys you."

Oh, so the gloves are off. I sip my bubbly, watch her through half closed eyes. She's taking a rise out of me because she's desperate to win Raphael. The champagne loosens my tongue. "What would you know about how I show my appreciation, Bernelle? I'm his girlfriend, not you, as much as you'd like to be."

Her look says she'd like to spit in my eye, but instead she metaphorically grabs my throat. "I've been to his apartment several times ... uh, helping decorate."

Ouff. My stomach does an unwelcome lurch. Really? Since when does Raphael need help with aesthetics? *Pfft*. She's lying. I shrug. "Anything Raphael buys will be fabulous. He doesn't need any help."

Bernelle sips her champagne, rolls her eyes. "One would think you would at least have checked it out before moving in. But then again, anything would be an improvement on that crumbling heap of stones you call home."

I won't bother explaining how much I love my crumbling heap of stones. My building is a grand old Parisian dame, elegance in every line of her body, even if her exterior shows the degradation of a long and well-worn life. When I arrive home in the middle of the day, the sun shining on her makes her beautiful. And I don't plan on abandoning my two onsite 'mothers' just yet, no matter what Raphael hopes. "I like surprises." *Liar*. Guilt claws my stomach. Bernelle's right. I should have embraced Raphael's gift instead of mulling over how his generosity reminds me of my father's 'sweeteners'.

Bernelle dismisses me with a flick of a wrist. "Raphael should have asked me to organize the after party. What do you know about French food? Is McDonald's catering?"

She'd have been more comfortable ordering osetra caviar and sautéed escargots and Emmental cheese than I, but give me Mister Google and I'm no slouch. "Raphael loves burgers and fries. He likes the taste and touch of American influence. You know." I dispense innuendo as generously as McDonald's ketchup on fries.

"Pah." She purses her lips. "Uncultured American."

I deliberately smooth my chignon with my left hand, watch her scowl at Raphael's ring which I moved to my engagement finger tonight. *Strike two for me.* But I don't miss the challenge in her eyes. She organized this night for Raphael, tying him to her with her constant demands. She's the last dark shadow looming over my happiness. Tonight, she'll make her play. I know it. I chew my lip. I'm no fan of the chignon, but it's *de rigueur* at such events. I've this irrational fear that more than my chignon will tumble down before this night is through.

"Raphael's exhibition is that way." Bernelle points to the opposite end of the main hall as if I hadn't visited earlier today to bring Raphael a coffee and baguette and kisses for luck. *"Excuse-moi."* She pirouettes on her stilettos, her gold bracelets clanking. "I'm off to see to the *hors d'oeuvres*. The caviar should have been served by now. These waiters." She totters away shaking her head, leaving me feeling sorry for those waiters.

I carefully maneuver down the stairs to The Stables. Under the night lights, the exhibition space takes my breath away. For a moment I'm light-headed, detached, wonder if the night is a fantasy and I've dreamed the whole thing. But no, it's real. I'm in Raphael's dream.

The room is the perfect backdrop for his abstracts. Pinpoint lighting illuminates his ornately framed paintings. Soft evening light pours in from the arched windows, bounces off the red damask walls. Blood-red roses in ornate crystal vases are artfully arranged around the space. I stroll to a vase to inhale their fragrance, but I'm overpowered by Chanel No 5.

Guilt squeezes my heart. This is why Raphael spent so much time setting up the space with Lamar and Bernelle. They've achieved perfection while all I did was nag him to spend more time with me. I'm ashamed of my mean-spirited judgment clouded by jealousy. I must apologize.

I begin making my way toward the end of the hall where Raphael said to meet. I'm shoulder to shoulder with smiling women sparkling in diamonds wearing fabulous black or red dresses, and men in black tuxedos, red satin waistcoats and red silk bow ties. It reminds me of many a New York art exhibition first night, but for pure drama, Raphael's outshines them all. There's such a crush around his paintings, it's impossible not to get stabbed by an oversized Hermès clutch, but seeing the night come together brings a warm feeling to my heart. From a distance, I catch glimpses of paintings he created in the attic. I'm part of this night. I'm part of Raphael. I'm part of his dream.

I take a break from fighting the crowd, flip my silk scarf over my shoulder, step back, lean against a side wall, take tiny sips of the Armand de Brignac I snatched from a passing waiter. I flash to the Bollinger and Dom Perignon on ice for Raphael's after party. My heart throbs with excitement when I imagine us sharing a glass, toasting our future on the little balcony overlooking the Seine.

There he is. At the far end of the room. Looking staggeringly gorgeous in his red and black bespoke suit, Manu's gift. My fingers tingle, my heart flutters. My wonder turns to concern at his flushed face and how he's running a finger under his collar. Uh-oh.

My heart slams against my rib cage. François and Alex. What are they doing here? François was banned from the guest list after his stunt at Farrin's. Did someone stuff up or did François just barge in, in his usual entitled way?

Seeing François brings back the memory of his threat, *you'll never work in Paris.* Now I'm as stressed as Raphael. I press my fist against my heart. Try to forget his odious father. François and Bernelle won't ruin this perfect night.

I place my barely touched drink onto a passing waiter's tray, then start pushing through the crowd. It's like walking through a wall.

Bernelle brushes past and hits my arm. The extra wattage in her eyes tells me she's spied Raphael. "See François with Raphael? François wasn't supposed to get an invitation, but I thought it mean of Raphael to deny his father entrée to his first exhibition. Raphael doesn't yet know, but François gave a very generous donation to proceedings." She holds out her arm like a traffic cop. "But we can't have any scenes tonight, so I'd best intervene. Personally," she slides me a glance, "I think his papa is cool."

I exhale a breath. How dare she go against Raphael's wishes and invite François? Raphael will be in a rage when he discovers François has donated to his exhibition. A biting retort hovers on the tip of my tongue. "You would," I stutter, but Bernelle's making a beeline for Raphael who's much more interesting than his girlfriend.

I stagger after her, stumble in my heels. Champagne fizzes in the back of my throat. My headache screams for attention. I lurch and stumble into a black suit.

Strong arms wrap around me, hot breath scorches my neck. "Good evening, Saskia."

François. Ugh. I shove him away. *Oh My God.*

Alex pushes past her loathsome husband. She gives me the full *bisou* treatment. "And how are you, my dear?" Her eyes sparkle. "You're looking so beautiful. Raphie said you were wearing a haute couture gown tonight. What a lovely choice. You must give me the name of your designer. Raphie will be so proud." She knits her brows. "He said he hasn't yet seen you."

François's lascivious grin lights up his devil's face. "My son is one lucky man." He drops his eyes to my cleavage. "Whoever designed this dress knew everyman's fantasy."

I tug my scarf across my chest. *Oh My God. Checking me out in front of his wife. Douche bag.* I step backward, bump into a pillar and hit my head. *Ouch.* Doesn't help my headache.

Alex looks from François to me, her cheeks aflame. "My dear, please show me to the amenities."

I stagger down the 19th century staircase, Alex beside me. I rush to a stall, lose the champagne. I wipe my mouth, sit head in hands on the toilet seat, clutching my stomach, dreading having to talk to her.

Rap. Rap. Rap. "Saskia. Are you ill?"

I open the door, stagger to the sink, grab a towel, dab my mouth. "Er, yes." *Your husband makes me ill.*

"You look so pale. It is impossibly crowded in the gallery."

I rinse my mouth, turn, lean backward, grip the sink behind me. "The crowd is great for Raphael, but the noise and crush gets to me." That's the truth at least. "I have such a headache. Do you have a, er, Panadol or something?"

"Of course, my dear." She ruffles around in her bag, hands me a foil envelope. "Keep them."

"Thanks." I toss back a couple with some tap water and drop the rest into my clutch.

"Everyone who is anyone in Paris is here," Alex gushes. "There are so many people from our set I would like to introduce you to but for now you need to sit awhile." She leads me to a red silk-covered armchair just inside the door. I fall gratefully into the soft seat, lay my head back, praying she won't mention François, or I'll vomit again.

She takes the chair next to mine, leans toward me as a French dame in black Dior enters with a nod and a "*bonsoir*". "Why aren't you with Raphie? Have you had an argument? Oh, I hope not."

My headache threatens to burst my skull. "Oooh. No. Yes. Sort of. No."

She clasps my hand in her palm, rubs it. "Every time he rings, Raphie can't stop talking about you. He's a different man since he met you. So much calmer."

"Uh, that's lovely, Alex." *Wish I could say the same.*

"François said you suffer from nerves. Let me help. I could share several ways I've found to stay calm amid chaos."

You certainly must, to stay with François. "Thanks, Alex. I have it under control. I'm learning what works and what doesn't. You're very kind." Alex *is* kind. She could be a mother to me, except she's married to François.

The French lady walks to the basins, sanitizes her hands, smiles as she leaves in a swirl of silk.

Alex touches my knee. "Your fashion course must be close to finished. François tells me you're hoping to win the Institut competition."

François. François. François. If she says his name again, I'll scream. "The competition's tough."

"I'm sure you have it in the bag, as you Americans say. Raphie says your designs are uniquely wonderful."

"I hope the judges agree. My immediate future depends on winning."

"I'm sure you will. Is your headache a little better? Yes? Good. Come. Stand beside Raphie. Be a team."

Alex watches while I repair my face. She hands me eyeliner and mascara. "You are very beautiful." Her voice sounds hollow. "No wonder men are fascinated."

I apply eyeliner in an upward sweep. Try to steady my hand. I frown at her in the mirror, snap, "Raphael is the only man I want to fascinate."

Alex blanches, steps back.

"I'm sorry." I touch her arm, kick myself for sounding so cutting. Alex has done nothing to deserve my snark.

Alex gestures to a point near her nose and I'm afraid she's going to cry. "You missed a mascara spot here."

"Thank you, Alex." I give her a quick hug. "I'm sorry. You go ahead. I'll follow and join the team."

CHAPTER THIRTY-THREE

I give the Panadol time to kick in, push open the bathroom door, fired to mingle, to smile for the photographers, to support Raphael. To be a team, LOL. Every time I've imagined this night, I've imagined Raphael's stupendous success. I can't wait to see him, congratulate him on making his dream a reality. François won't ruin the night. Or Bernelle.

As I round the corner from the bathroom to access the stairs, Raphael and Bernelle are huddled under the staircase. *What*? My heart hammers. Raphael stage whispers to her, his eyes watching the stairs. While he's distracted, she reaches up, tugs his head to hers.

Raphael breaks away, but not before her lips land on his. Bernelle's making her move.

Whoa. I gasp, nearly lose my balance. I clutch my stomach, feel it clench. So, the stupendous success and fulfilment of dreams tonight are Bernelle's.

I stagger along the corridor like I'm having a bad attack of vertigo. *I knew it.* I push my heart back inside my chest. *Bitch. Hosting Raphael's exhibition. All you wanted was to steal him from me.*

Her bracelets clang as she tries to hold on to him, but he slips from her grasping hands.

Bitch! I take a deep, shuddering breath, make incoherent noises like an injured dog.

Bernelle sees me, winks, walks briskly to the stairs.

Red spots dance before my eyes.

She leans over the balustrade above where Raphael straightens his tie. "Listen to me, *chéri,*" she says loud enough for me to hear. "*I* made you. *I* worked so hard for you. Saskia has your ring, but you have my heart." Bernelle gives me the victory sign, strolls up the stairs, cheeks flushed, chignon perfect, while I have to restrain myself from tearing my hair out by the roots. "*Je t'aime tant.*" She shouts her final insult.

How dare she tell Raphael she loves him. I cry, "Noooo," but only incoherent sounds pop out.

Raphael groans. Did he finally get that Bernelle wants him?

"Ra-ph-ael!" I scream my heartbreak in every syllable.

Raphael swings around. Stares, face flushed, hands clenched, a where-did-you-come-from? expression on his face. "You were right about Bernelle." He runs a finger under his collar. Steps toward me. "I'm so sorry you saw that, Sassy."

Not as sorry as I am. I hold up my hand. "Don't come closer." Fury surges through me, a hot flood. My face burns, my heart races, my head hurts. I dab sweat from my brow with the back of my hand, catch the balustrade so I don't collapse. I shake so badly my teeth chatter. I force my legs to move. I've got to get away.

He catches up with me in a few long strides. He palms the air between us. "Be calm, *mon ange.*"

"Don't *mon ange* me." I stagger upward. These steps feel like Mt Everest in high wind.

He tries to take my hand, but I brush his away. He's so close I smell his scent which I now know is the hideously expensive Ambre Topkapi. No wonder he thought nothing of buying me an haute couture gown.

He reaches my side. "Sassy. I hate to see you so upset." He lowers his head, whispers, "She tried to kiss me. Not the other way around." He grips my shoulders, forces me to stop. "As I told you, I'd never risk our relationship. I love you."

"Is love enough, Raphael?" My earlier confidence has left me. Was that bright, shining girl who entered the Centaquatre tonight, determined to rekindle her relationship with this glorious man, even me? I don't recognize her. She's left the building. Despair overwhelms me.

He puffs a breath. "What you saw was nothing. Nothing."

"Nothing? Your tie's crooked, your hair's a mess, her lipstick's smeared on your cheek. Nothing?"

He frowns, scrubs his face with his handkerchief, adjusts his suitcoat, runs his hands through his hair. "I'm sorry. This doesn't look good."

"It doesn't." I flick my hand in his face. The sight of Bernelle's lipstick on him enrages me.

"Sassy, the night's going so well for me. I came to find you. I wanted you to be the first to know how many paintings I've sold."

"That's stupendous, Raphael. I'm so pleased for you. You know I am." I clutch my stomach, groan.

He steps closer; worry clouds his eyes. "You're ill. How much champagne have you drunk?"

I root around in my purse for tissues. "Not enough to cope with this."

We're nearly at the top of the stairs. He gives my arm a little shake. "It's only ever been you for me, my love." He rips a hand through his hair. "Every time I turned around tonight, Bernelle's been right in my face." He clenches his hands by his sides. "I'll break all ties with her after tonight. I'll find another gallery to show my paintings. Monsieur Marion's offer is still open." He holds my hands, pulls me to his chest, wraps his arms around my back. "I want only you. I need you by my side. Trust me."

"Trust you?"

"Yes." He walks with me the last few steps, his arm around my waist. "But there's no time to talk now. Are you well enough to greet people with me? Get photos taken with me? This show is what I've worked for. I have to work the room."

"What if someone saw you and Bernelle?" I grab the handrail, sway.

Raphael puts his hand over mine. "Steady on, Sassy. This is Paris. No one cares."

"*What*?" I fast-blink tears hovering at the edge of my eyes. "I care."

He frowns. "It really doesn't matter what people think."

"It does to me." I talk over my roiling stomach. I dab a tear. I can't deal with the stress of Bernelle any longer. She's been in my face since the night I met Raphael. I'm done. I'm over it. I twist his ring around my finger. I'll get through this night. I love him too much to humiliate him publicly.

"Hey lovebirds." A flash blinds me. "Look this way." Kate McInnes stands at the top of the stairs, snapping away as I totter toward her, Raphael beside me.

A frowning Lamar stands beside Kate, holding a bunch of red roses. I see it in their eyes. They've heard at least some, if not all, of our conversation. It would be Lamar's worst nightmare – a public display between his star client who's going to make him rich and his client's girlfriend having a meltdown.

"You're looking exceptionally beautiful, Saskia." Lamar kisses me on the cheek, *bisou, bisou, bisou*. "Love your dress," he says. "Did you make it?"

I hold my head high. Heat burns my cheeks. I wanted to tell Raphael, but not like this. "I did."

Raphael says nothing, just flicks his eyes from shoulder straps to plunging neckline to the side split, then smiles without humor.

"Great job. You are good." Lamar hands me the roses, kisses my cheek again. "Thanks for all the times Bernelle and I stole Raphael from you." He turns to Kate. "Let Saskia fix her lipstick, and Raphael, you have a red mark on your cheek, there. Kate, take shots of them together in front of Raphael's paintings."

"Not so fast." Raphael scrubs his cheek with his handkerchief. His jaw's clenched, his face flushed, his eyes slits. He stares stonily at me, his eyes colder than the Seine in winter, full of hurt at my choosing independence over his money.

I'm suffering a severe case of stoniness myself. I'm proud of saving him so much money, but he doesn't see it that way.

Raphael whispers in my ear. "You wouldn't break your rule? Not even for me? You wouldn't let me buy you one dress? Any other woman would have rushed out and found the most expensive dress in Paris. I wouldn't have minded. Anything for you."

I rub my hand over one of the gold knobs on the nearest post. "Raphael, I'm a dress designer. I'm proud to wear my creations. Do you buy art for your walls? No. You create your own. It's the same principle. I didn't need or want to go out and buy haute couture just because you can afford it. I couldn't spend that amount of money when I could make it for a fraction of the cost. Despite my upbringing, at heart I have simple tastes."

He takes his time to consider my words. "Fine, Sassy. You've made yourself clear. Is that why you haven't been to see the new apartment? Because you can't stand me buying you expensive things? Or is it just another way to keep your distance?"

That stings, but it's close to the truth. I've been wrong to treat him with suspicion because he buys things for me like my father did when he wanted something. My blood whooshes in my ears. What can I say? I'm saved from answering when Lamar beckons us.

"Over here, you two." Lamar calls from beneath the largest artwork in the room. "Talk later." His voice snaps with impatience. "Official photographs need to be done before everyone crowds us."

"*D'accord* Lamar." Raphael takes my elbow, gives me a crooked smile while the cameras whir and flash. "If you don't mind, Sassy," Raphael whispers, "a few shots in front of my special painting."

"Okay." As the flashbulbs explode, I work hard to keep my tears at bay.

Lamar arranges us in pose after pose—arms wrapped around each other, cheeks touching, Raphael standing behind me, his arms on mine around my waist—while I will my bottom lip to stop quivering. Photographers mill around, some kneeling, cameras at odd angles. Every moment preserved for posterity.

When the media move away to snap celebrities crushing around Raphael's Nightmare Art, he clasps my shoulder, draws me closer. "*Mon ange*. You shook the whole time photographs were being taken. I'm here for you." He rubs his hands up my arms like he's often done when I'm super stressed. "I adore you. I'm sorry for my reaction to your dress. No one could have created a better style for you. I love it."

Before I can respond, my nemesis walks up, face lit like she has her own secret stash of kryptonite. Lamar's by her side, his face apologetic. She elbows me aside, slips her arm around Raphael's waist, tries to drag him away. "Raphael, come. Now."

Raphael shrugs off her arm. "A moment, Bernelle." He leans down and whispers in my ear, "Sassy. I'm sorry you're hurting. I blame myself. But I can't do any more now to reassure you. A first night is crucial. Please understand. There's something in your eyes that frightens me. We'll talk this through. Don't do anything rash."

I'm too numb to give him more than an eye roll.

He shakes his head. "I have to go. If you won't stand with me, please wait here. I beg of you, my darling, don't leave." Sighing, he walks beside Bernelle back to the largest oil painting in the room.

A feeling of impending doom creeps over me. I knuckle my eyes. They feel like hollowed out sockets. Raphael and Bernelle. She suits him. A princess in her Balenciaga haute couture gown. She'd happily buy gowns with Raphael's money. She's uber sophisticated, like him. From the same Parisian inner circle.

"Stand here, Raphael." Bernelle grabs his hand and poses him in front of his magnum opus. The clique of photographers tussle for the best shot of Raphael standing alone and moody before his masterpiece.

I detach myself, ignore their voices, but I can't ignore my niggling chest pains. *Panic attack*. I dab my upper lip with tissues. Control my breathing.

Count to ten. I ignore the way my breath seesaws, study the painting at the center of the buzz, the painting Raphael's been working on in my attic since the first day he moved in. I've never understood it. Now the meaning hits me like someone smacked my head with a full roll of sketch and tracing paper.

The colors drip, fade into one another like they're soggy from rain. Abstract renditions of the twinkling Eiffel Tower and the Arc de Triomphe predominate with translucent water seeping from top to bottom, all but washing away a pale Sacré-Cœur and a shadowy crowd on the steps holding little French flags. How could I ever forget that night and how we connected, two souls becoming one? The most beautiful night of my life. Discovering Paris with the most beautiful man I've ever known.

There we are. Front and center.

Raphael has painted pinpoints of light focusing on two figures clad in black, riding a red and black Harley. His long hair escaping his helmet. My blonde hair flying behind me, my arms around him, my cheek against his back. The night we met. Our first bike ride together. Our first night in each other's arms. The magic is in the painting.

It meant as much to Raphael as it did to me.

Now it means nothing.

We're over.

Raphael flicks his eyes my way while Bernelle stands with him before the painting, introducing him to an old gentleman, immaculate in tux and black bow tie who whispers something in Raphael's ear. I recognize Mister Elderly Gentleman from the restaurant the night Raphael proposed. Raphael beckons me.

I've no desire to join the crowd who've cornered Raphael, but giving Bernelle a wide berth, I greet Mister Elderly Gentleman. I pose between them. Raphael throws me a grateful smile. The look on his face is so tender and yearning my legs threaten to collapse. "Stay Sassy. Please. Be with me."

"I can't." I move away before I lose my resolve. My feet propel me across the floor. No way I'm listening to him negotiate a price for his painting.

I nod to Monsieur Marion who arrives, shakes Raphael's hand, chews an unlit cigar.

Raphael gestures at the painting as if explaining the story of its creation to Mister Elderly Gentleman and Monsieur Marion who nod attentively, turning their heads occasionally to smile and nod at me. Lamar joins them. Bernelle drapes herself around Raphael, arm around his neck, leg around his knee. Flashbulbs pop. He pushes her away and I can tell he's angry by the way he mouths something to her.

I can't take this shit any longer. I toss the roses onto a recessed shelf. Spin on my heels. Fall against Marcel's chest.

"Saskie." Marcel wraps me in his arms, his chin on my shoulder, then he kisses the side of my neck. "I am sorry to be late. Big crowd at the bar." He moves away, grabs two glasses of champagne from a passing waiter and they check each other out.

What? Are he and Joaquin over? "That's fine, Marcel." I shake my head at the bubbly. "You haven't missed much."

He sips his drink, studies the crowd. "Huge turnout." His voice slurs. Has he been drinking ... or worse? He tosses back the second drink. "*Mère de Dieu,*" he shouts. "Raph's parents are 'ere?"

I give a one-shouldered shrug. I'd forgotten about them. Now I watch them twittering around Raphael. "Bernelle's idea to invite them."

"She always had a soft spot for François. I always wondered if they had something going on. Come, Saskie. Let us find out what is going down. Look. Bernelle is posing with Raph's papa. Where is Alexander?" He tugs me in Raphael's direction, giving his friend a cheery wave. "Raph ees selling 'is favorite painting? No way. 'e never would. 'e as saved a whole wall for it at zee new apartment."

I let go of Marcel's hand, hold back. Raphael can use his wall for something else. Maybe a life-size portrait of Bernelle. I want to run from the whole situation – Bernelle, François, all the challenges I've set myself.

Everything seems too complicated. Why did I ever dream Raphael and I could make it? I arrived in Paris ready for an adventure, but my adventurous spirit has deserted me. I feel daunted. I'm losing the gains I've made. I've arrived at a place where I'm fitting into someone else's dream again. Instead of Pa's, it's Raphael's. Enough. Time to move on. Alone.

Marcel puts down his empty glass. "Saskie, what 'as 'appened 'ere? Why are you so sad?"

The effort of holding back tears is too much. I'm dizzy. My heart's beating crazy fast like I've run another marathon. "The night is wrecked. I'm leaving."

Marcel tugs my arms. "*Non.* You must not. It ees Raph's night. A night the two of you will remember forever and tell your children and grandchildren. Raphael's girlfriend cannot walk out on 'is big night."

I snort. "With Bernelle all over Raphael, they'll deduce she's his girlfriend." Behind him, Bernelle is cozying up to François. This woman has no shame. She wants both father and son. Doesn't she know François's history? Doesn't she care? Or is she part of François's history?

Taking my hand, Marcel says, "You are ill. How much 'ave you drunk?"

My breath knots in my throat. "Not enough to make me numb. I'll catch a cab. You stay. Raphael needs his best friend."

Marcel hugs me. Thankfully, the media is too busy with Raphael to notice. "Tonight, you need a friend more than Raph." His eye twitches. "I must congratulate Raph."

Raphael draws apart from his admirers and hugs Marcel. I watch their earnest expressions, their frowns as they look my way. They're both worried about me. They needn't be. I'm putting this night and Raphael behind me, surging forward to follow my own dream. I'll put all my energy into creating my winning collection, energy I won't have if I continue this roller coaster life with Raphael.

Marcel returns, takes my arm. "Raph wants you to stay 'ere, to calm down. 'e thinks you are over-reacting to the stress of the night. 'e will talk to you soon."

"No. I can't stay any longer." What's there to talk about? It'll be a mammoth challenge living without Raphael, but a clean break is the only way for me to push forward. "Coming, Marcel?" Checking over my shoulder, I steal a last glance at Raphael. No matter how much I hurt, and will go on hurting, part of me wants to stay and support him. But I just can't. Returning his ring will have to wait.

Raphael's stony eyes light on me. How alone he looks. Then I shake my head. He has plenty of supporters; it's me who's alone.

He doesn't need me.

I clench my teeth, grip Marcel's hand, stare straight ahead. We move past groups clustered around Raphael's paintings, listen to their excited chatter as we pass, up the stairs we go and finally reach the front of the building.

I steal one last glance behind me, but Raphael's not following. Did I really expect him to?

He doesn't need me.

I don't need him. I don't need him. I don't need him.

CHAPTER THIRTY-FOUR

Marcel helps me out of the cab into the drizzling rain in front of my Montmartre apartment. I should be preparing to host Raphael's after party on Île Saint-Louis, not slip-sliding on the slick cobblestones of rue des Martyrs.

My damp dress and long coat cling to my knees, tripping me on the stairs. Only with Marcel's arm around my waist do I avoid falling.

After he opens the door to my apartment, I stand on the threshold, crushed. It hits me like a blow to the solar plexus.

Apartment 5A.

Raphael and I. So many happy times.

"Saskie, this place chills me. Have you moved all the furniture?" Marcel tosses my damp coat onto the kitchen counter, removes his overcoat, then his suitcoat. Wrapping his suitcoat over my dress, he tugs the lapels until my face is close to his. "You cannot stay 'ere alone."

I hug Marcel's coat around me. Even though it's damp, it's warm. "Thanks, Marcel, but I'll stay here. There are some bits and pieces here." *Alone. With memories of Raphael.*

Marcel nods. Searching the kitchen, he finds a half-empty bottle of

Dubonnet, pours two shots. Handing me one, he says, "Drink. I will turn on zee 'eat. I would make a fire, but you 'ave no kindling."

I hate whiskey, but I gulp a mouthful, stare blankly around me, not seeing or thinking anything coherent. Instead of numbing the pain, my headache worsens. I grab four painkillers from the kitchen cabinet, wash them down with a mouthful of water. "Hmmm, Marcel. Fire would be nice." No more fire for Raphael and me. I watch while Marcel crouches, fiddles with the knobs of the ancient heater like Raph has done countless times. I drink another mouthful of Dubonnet. Ugh. Then I remember being caught red handed by François drinking in the morning. I slide the glass onto the kitchen counter. "Thanks, Marcel, you can go now. I'm a misery guts." I slide to the floor, lay my head on my knees. "I'll be fine."

Marcel walks across to where I'm sitting, my back against the kitchen counter. "I cannot leave you alone, Saskie," he says tenderly, stroking my shoulder with gentle hands. "Raph asked me to stay with you. 'e meant at the gallery, but same thing." He hands me a box of tissues, then drinks his Dubonnet, his eyes puzzled. "Why are you so upset? Was eet François? That man ees trouble."

I wipe my face. Blow my nose. My thoughts skitter; tears prick my eyes. "No." My throat closes, not wanting to say the two words together, but Marcel isn't going to leave until I do. I may as well get it over with. "It's ... Raphael and," I clear my throat, "and ... Bernelle." As I say their names out loud, a pain stabs my heart, sharp and brutal. I bang my head against my knees, groan. "I can't take it anymore."

Marcel throws back the last of his drink and offers me mine. I shake my head. He knocks mine back then kneels before me. Holds my face in his hands. The concern in his eyes makes the tears fall. "What 'ave they done?" His words fire like staccato beats.

I tug my hair. "You really don't want to know."

He places his hands onto my shoulders. "I am beginning to think all relationships are shit." He grimaces. "Saskie, you and Raph are the perfect couple. What 'ope is there for the rest of us if you break up?"

My heart is a large rock that's been chipped into thousands of pieces. *Perfect couple?* "Relationships ruin you, Marcel. You become the person you don't want to be. You do things you don't want to do. You say things you shouldn't say. To stay together."

Marcel sits beside me, wraps an arm around me, pulls me close so my head is on his shoulder. "Saskie. Surely eet ees not that bad." He strokes my hair. "How shit Raphael must be feeling. If ever a man loves a woman, 'e loves you."

"I can't fight for him anymore." I sob on Marcel's chest, drenching his dress shirt. "Bernelle will fit his new life better than I will."

"*Pfft.* You are irrational. Bernelle ees just 'is friend who 'as worked so 'ard for 'im. Raph loves you. You love 'im. End of story."

Bernelle's worked hard for Raphael, it's true, just not the way Marcel means. "I do love him, but after tonight, I realize love isn't enough."

Marcel flinches. "Love ees always enough. Do not be so 'ard on Raph, Saskie. Many times 'e is a fool, but 'e loves you, of that I 'ave never been in doubt."

I raise my head and look into his eyes. "She tried to kiss him when she knew I was watching."

Marcel blows out a breath. "That ees heavy, but not Raph's fault. Why blame him? All kisses are not equal, Saskie. Even if Bernelle did kiss him, it would not 'ave been a lover's kiss. They are work colleagues and lifelong friends."

"You had to be there."

"Listen, Saskie, I kiss you nearly every day – Hello. Goodbye. Good luck. Thanks. Some kisses are friendly, some spiteful, some only shared with a lover, some one-sided where feelings are not returned." His breathing ups a notch. He's talking about himself now. His eyes fill with tears. "Joaquin sat at the bar and kissed a man while I watched. A betrayer's kiss. Do you think that ees zee same as zee way 'e kisses me? No. But it 'urt."

"Joaquin kissed someone in front of you. That sucks." I was right to judge Joaquin. But I'm not so wrapped up in my misery I don't notice Marcel's high color, the way he picks at his skin, his glazed eyes which can't focus. He's totally drunk and drugged. I push him away and struggle to my feet. "Marcel, you should go. Find Joaquin."

He stands, hangs his head, wrings his hands. "It ees too late, Saskie. Joaquin left me. Turns out zee man at zee bar means more to 'im than I do. I now know that kiss was a lover's kiss, one no longer for me."

"Go. Tell him how you feel. I'm sure the guy at the bar is only a fling."

"*Non.* I go to Raph's party. Get more drunk. Please come. Raph would be so 'appy."

"No, Marcel." I take off his suitcoat, hand it to him. "Before you go, would you unzip my dress?"

"Of course." The zip glides down my back. Marcel's hands trace the knobs of my spine, slowly, deliberately. "Saskie, you're so beautiful." He kisses me between my shoulder blades.

Stiff with shock, I spin around. Too fast. My dress falls from my shoulders, revealing my breasts. I quickly cover myself. "Marcel? What was that?"

He drags his eyes from where he'd glimpsed my nakedness. "I 'av always loved you."

"Not that way. Go, Marcel. You're drunk. You don't know what you're doing. You're upset over Joaquin. I'll forget this ever happened or we can no longer be friends."

"I know what I'm saying. I'm bi. You always belonged to Raphael. Now you don't, you say. Give me a chance."

"Go." I'll always belong to Raphael in my heart.

It's just that our bridge has burned to the ground one too many times.

I lock the door behind Marcel, stagger to the bathroom, throw up, then clutch the basin while my head spins. Emotions whirl around my head –

the anticipation when I dressed for Raphael's exhibition, the shock of seeing François, the devastation of hearing Bernelle seducing Raphael. Splintered hopes stab at me, shards of jagged glass. I throw up over and over until my stomach's sore. I take two painkillers and sit on the bathroom floor, my arms wrapped around my knees while my headache slowly lessens to a low throb.

What a night from hell. I made a dress Raphael would love. I wanted to wow him. But he couldn't see past another rejection of his generosity. Standing up, I let the ruined silk slip down my body. I'd imagined Raphael slipping it off tonight. I'd imagined a lustrous pool at my feet as we fell into each other's arms. I regret that I asked Marcel to help, toss the sorry bundle behind the door, wrench off my jewelry—the black opal earrings, my lucky opal ring and matching pendant—all inherited from Mom. Mom. Last, I rip off Raphael's ring. Devastation hits me again.

Mom's gone. Raphael's gone. He'll never be part of my world again. Never again will he pick me up from Marcel's, bring me home on the back of his bike and make love to me. Never again will I hear his baritone serenading me while he paints in the attic. Never again will he come down from the attic with the day's oils under his arm, look over my shoulder, comment on what I'm sketching, sewing or stitching.

Stumbling into the shower, I turn on the faucet. Scalding water flows over me, but when I'm done, I'm still freezing.

Wrapping myself in a large soft towel, I flash back to our shared shower the night he proposed. We took our time drying each other. I relished his familiar, spicy scent as he leaned over me, massaging away my stress. We'd broken up. But I took him back.

This time it's over. I won't take him back.

Buzz-buzz-ping.

I pick up my cell. Raphael's called several times while I showered. What's there to say? Walking around in senseless circles, I put my foot through a canvas he missed when he moved all his art to his new apartment. I yelp more with frustration than pain. Picking up the picture, I see it's a

Dali-styled rendition of a happy me at Caratello on the day I named my men's fashion range. He's captured all the light and hope in my eyes. I hurl the canvas across the room. The frame cracks against the buttery-soft wall Raphael painted. I look around for more things to throw, but the room is empty of missiles.

Buzz-buzz-ping.

Alex texts me: `My dear. Where are you? Raphael is frantic. Answer his calls. Please be safe. Alex X`

I text back:

`Pls don't worry. Not feeling well.`

While I stare at the phone, another text comes in:

`We need to talk. I LOVE YOU! R. X`

Talk? Love? Too late. Not happening.

Turning my phone to silent, I toss it onto the nightstand. Tugging my towel tight, I circle the living room. This isn't how my encounter with a sexy Frenchman was supposed to end.

"*Aaaaaargh.*" I stride to the balcony door, look over the rooftops glistened by rain. Car tires thud and whoosh over the cobblestones, while my head fills with Bernelle's whispering, "Rapheeelle. *Mon chéri.*" I collapse into a heap in the middle of the floor. Maybe if I sleep, I'll wake and the nightmare will be over. I crawl close to the heater, curl into a ball.

I toss. I turn. My body is utterly exhausted, but no sleep for me. My eyes ache in their sockets. I shiver. Have I done the right thing breaking up with him? I'm going to ask myself that question every day. Well, I didn't actually tell him I was breaking up with him, or return his ring, but he should have gotten the gist when I walked out. Did I break up with him because I panicked? Couldn't handle the stress of the night? I don't know, but I have to face my new reality. No more his mouth on mine. His hands on my body. Our hearts beating in sync.

I thump the floor tiles with closed fists, relishing the pain, imagining I'm thumping Bernelle's he's-all-mine-face.

I'll go to the attic. Maybe I'll sleep there.

Raphael has moved all his painting paraphernalia to his studio in his new apartment, but when I push open the door, I breathe in the lingering smell of paint, of turpentine, of Raphael. I stumble across the floor to the bed and collapse onto the mattress, wrap myself in the ratty old quilt, remember the first night when he carried me inside, tore off my wet clothes and made glorious love to me. How beautiful the way he comforted me through my nightmare of Mom, the first of many times we found comfort in each other's arms. He was so hot. Is so hot. We've had amazing moments, and challenging moments. We're better because of each other.

But there was always Bernelle.

Gathering the quilt tighter around me, I curl into a ball, try not to think about the fun they'll be having at the after party, eating, drinking, chatting, dancing. My trust for Raphael has always been tenuous and tonight proved I was wise to be wary. He didn't cheat on me, but I always felt it was just a matter of time. My mother put up with my father's cheating throughout her marriage until she jumped onto my motorbike and killed herself. The tears well up again when I finally admit the truth. She meant to kill herself. It was no accident. She felt her life was over.

He wants a divorce so he can remarry, Saskia, she'd said over the phone two weeks before her birthday. *After years of forcing me to stay in the marriage, threatening I'd never see you again if I divorced him.*

I've blamed myself for Mom's death. Anger replaces my tears. It wasn't me. My Father was the rock that broke her.

Slivers of light leak through the skylight and windows. The light Raphael loves so much. Not so bright this Christmas Day. My first Christmas without Mom. No eating her delicious roast turkey and sipping eggnog around the fire with friends while listening to the ocean crash to shore. Here in the attic it's just another shivery winter's day. Without Raphael, in my heart it'll always be winter. *But it was your choice*, I remind myself.

I scrub my face on a corner of the quilt. No more tears. We all must live with our choices.

I wrap myself like I'm an Egyptian mummy, lie back, watch the sunrise through the skylight. What would Mom say to me now? In my head I hear her voice: *Don't go backward. Forward, my darling.*

I clamber off the bed, head to the kitchen, boil the kettle. I rip open a sachet of instant coffee, drop it into a coffee mug. Sipping the disgusting brew, I sit back on the mattress.

I can't stay in Paris. Where he is. Where she is. He's right. Paris really is a small town.

I sip the coffee. It leaves a bad taste in my mouth. Was disobeying Father my first mistake? By now I'd be married to Xavier, living the pampered life of a socialite, appearing at a different soiree each night dressed in designer gowns made by someone else, heading up a charity or two in the Hamptons, being one of those Ladies Who Lunch while my husband counts his millions. Father would love it if I came crawling back. He'd squash me back into the box I escaped from. And there I'd stay, beaten and lost.

Stay in Paris? Go back to New York?

When I escaped to Paris it was a rational decision. If I run back to New York, it'll be pure cowardice.

But ... I've lost. Lost the man I love. Lost the fashion competition. I should have heard by now. Maybe I'm disqualified because of what François did. Who was he going to bribe to make me the winner if I slept with him? But my gut feeling is that the whole thing was a sham, like François.

I reach over and put my empty coffee cup onto an old chair. Think about what life would be like back in New York. "Ha!" I scream out loud. Like I don't already know.

Pa's triumphant face when I turn up on his doorstep, begging bowl in hand. He'll insist I throw away my fabrics, my threads, my dreams, my 'passing phase'. He'll be adamant I move into an apartment of his choice on Fifth Avenue. There I'll dance to his and Xavier's tune for the rest of my days. *Aargh!*

I thump my head onto my knees. Pa was right. I can't do anything on my own. I couldn't fight for the man I love. My fashion career has tanked. Tears pour down my face, a breached dam.

I check the blank screen on my cell. I'll call Pa. I hover my thumb over the *On* button. It's not right to be shivering alone in an empty attic. Don't I deserve better?

If I go back to New York, I'll have a gilded roof over my head. I'll have warmth. I'll have riches. The price of giving up my dreams.

Everything I love in Paris is gone.

CHAPTER THIRTY-FIVE

I'm not sure how long I sit on the bed wrapped in the old quilt. It smells of Raphael; I cling to the fragrance. Feelings of failure tear me apart. I'm overwhelmed by dread. Why did I think I could make an impression in the Paris fashion world when New York spat me out? Paris doesn't need me. I'll never succeed. I'll never see my fashion dream come to fruition.

Raphael always believed in me. He had utmost faith in my creative ability. Why don't I?

I consider my options. Move forward. Strong. Independent. Alone. But how? Where to start?

I need to talk. To someone. I always called Mom at decision time. But Mom's gone. Forever. But I have the best friend in the world. I reach for my phone. We're always at the other end of the line for each other despite the different time zones. I decide against FaceTime. Mira doesn't need to see my red face and swollen eyes.

"Merry Christmas, Sia." Mira sounds groggy when she answers. "Wassup? Did you get the care package I sent? I couldn't deny you your New York Christmas treats."

"Sorry for waking you." *Crap.* I'm the worst friend in the world. I haven't sent Mira her gift. I wanted to send her tickets to the Institut New Fashion show, but I've not heard if I'm in the lineup. "Merry Christmas back at you, girlfriend. Your gift is way cool. It wouldn't be Christmas without struffoli from Ferrara's. I can taste those little bliss balls bursting on my tongue already." My voice catches. "I needed to hear your voice."

"Anytime, Sia. You okay? Homesick at Christmas? You sound a bit strange."

"Uh ... no ... just missing you ... what's happening? You sound terrible. Too much partying? Did Roberto and Isabella throw a Christmas Eve bash?"

"Christmas Eve bash? Partying?" Mira's tone drips with sarcasm. "I wish. You've been gone, what, five months? So much has changed. No Christmas party. No bonus. No nothing." Mira's voice drawls with tiredness. "Isabella had a baby boy a month ago. She and Roberto exchanged partying for diapers and pacifiers. Now it's just work, work, work. For the staff, that is. You woke me. I was taking a snooze on that fancy sofa in the showroom like you used to. I have a gazillion things I should be doing, but I'm wrecked."

"Working on Christmas Eve? You're kidding, right?" I'm glad it's no longer me pulling all-nighters for Roberto and Isabella. Did I sound as exhausted as Mira?

"No kidding. I've been chained to the workroom ever since you left. Last minute, Isabella handed over the new collection to me. I'm in charge of production. And the designs are so not me. I don't know what pregnancy hormones were affecting her brain when she sketched her ideas. My team hate every item. There's no enthusiasm for the line. She chose ghastly colors, ghastly styles and ghastly fabrics to match her ghastly designs."

"But you're Head Designer. You have a say in the collection. At least the fabrics?"

"Nope. Now that you're gone, we no longer have your fabric designs, so they've outsourced to a firm that spits out generic patterns on generic materials. It infuriates me because I know you had all those stunning sketches you worked on in the Hamptons. They should have bought them from you when you left. Now there's little to make Romance is Born stand out from the chain stores." Mira's voice shudders and I'm not surprised. To say, 'Romance is Born' and 'chain stores' in the same sentence is truly unsettling. "Ugh. You heard me right, Sia. Our designs used to be so dreamy when we used your fabrics." She snorts. "Before I fell asleep tonight, I'd been sitting at my worktable sewing some passable appliqués onto the back pockets of a pair of ghastly geometric print pants. So wrong."

"Mira, what're you saying? That's never been Roberto and Isabella's style. They're a Top 10 New York design house."

"Their style seems to be the least of their worries at the moment." Mira's puffs out a breath, fatigue leaks through her voice. "I don't mean to sound whingy, but I haven't had a decent night's sleep for ages so may be exaggerating. You used to walk around like a zombie and fall asleep at your sewing machine. Now that's me. But, hey, I can't wait to come see you in Paris."

"We'll see each other soon." Maybe sooner than expected. And not in Paris. Maybe in New York. "I rang to hear all those exciting stories and the vibe in the New York fashion scene. I needed some cheering up."

"You and me both. But you're the one with the exciting stories, girlfriend. I was scrolling through my news feed before I fell asleep, saw that your gorgeous French boyfriend had his first art exhibition last night which sounded like a huge success. There was the best picture of the two of you underneath this fabulous huge painting which they said could fetch a king's ransom. That man's a keeper."

I suck in a breath, not wanting to remember, not wanting to experience the loss all over again, but thankfully Mira isn't finished, so I don't have to report the whole debacle of Raphael's exhibition while it's so raw.

"Have you heard about your fashion show?" Mira sounds like she's put her exhaustion to the side. "Paris is everything you dreamed of, right? I tell you, Sia, you had a lucky break getting out of here even if you were pushed. How I envy you."

"Envy? What could you possibly envy me for? You're a Head Designer. I'm a fashion student."

Mira sighs. "You took a huge step. You followed your dream. You scored a place at the Institut. The Paris Institut of Fashion. You're creating your own designs, using your own fabrics." She clicks her fingers. "Probably this close to putting a collection together, having your own atelier, doing it all just like I thought I'd be doing, but am so not."

Yeah – I've taken a leap of faith, but fallen flat on my face. I can't share that with Mira now, not after her tale of woe. But Mira's given me a lot to think about. I can't wait to replay our conversation in my mind, make some choices. "Thanks for chatting, Mira. You need your sleep. Take it easy, you hear? Good luck with the collection. I'm sure you'll find a way to make the outfits less ghastly. Hope to see you soon. I'll let you know about the show asap. I gotta go. Love you." I press *End.*

I knuckle my eyes, lean back on my bed, confused, not cheered.

I stare at the phone clutched in my hand. Then look out the window across the zinc-colored roofs now lit with a weak winter sun. *Oh Paris. What have you done to me?*

You changed me. Let me believe anything and everything was possible.

Wait. Hold that thought. Anything and everything *is* possible. What am I doing wallowing in misery? A wave of hope washes through me.

Mira's call has jolted me to my senses.

She's right. I do have it good. Just lost sight of it tonight. But I'll reclaim my joy of being in Paris. I'll move forward. Raphael helped guide me this far, but I don't need him or anyone now. I have me, my talent, my ambition. I'm not going to lie to myself. Despite my insecurities, I know I'm good at what I do.

How could I have considered returning to New York? When Roberto and Isabella fired me, failure overwhelmed me, but it was the best thing in the end. Paris has given me my dream of designing fashion for me, no one else. The whole experience has challenged me, changed me, and I'll improve over time.

How could I have thought for a moment I could live without fashion? Even though Mira's story was kinda sad, it still excites me to think about her creating a whole collection which will be strutted down a New York catwalk. No matter how ghastly she thinks it is, it's a unique creation. Who else gets to create on such a grand scale?

Fashion has always been, and always will be, my life. A life without fashion is no life at all. I've learned so much at the Institut. It's been a priceless experience to be mentored by some of the best people in the business.

I won't give it up. Not for anyone or anything.

I won't turn back.

Going back to New York was never an option. It was just my misery talking.

Paris is my dream.

I'll start again if I have to. I'll sign up for another term at the Paris Institut. My determination to succeed burns afresh in me.

I swing my legs off the bed. Before my feet hit the floor, my cell phone kicks into life.

Buzz-buzz-buzz. Buzz-buzz-buzz. Buzz-buzz-buzz.

I check the screen.

New York. Don't recognize the number.

Dread presses against my chest like a spreading machine.

Bad news? Is Pa ill? Has something gone wrong at the summerhouse? Is Mira calling back from an extension at work?

Before I drive myself crazy with possible scenarios, I press *Accept*. I've got to stop imagining the worst. It might be great news.

"Saskia."

Xavier. His voice booms down the line. "Come home."

Crap. Trust him to hunt down my new number. I inhale a deep breath. Get my fight mojo on. *Pfft.* He doesn't bother me. He's like an itchy rash I thought I'd never scratch again. "I'm fine, thank you. How are you?"

"You've made your point." He echoes my father's words. "Your father and I tolerated your little rebellion. Enough's enough. Come home."

Xavier is a twenty-nine-year-old guy, yet he sounds like a peeved parent. I don't hold back my snicker, not caring if he hears. "I *am* home. Paris is my home." And it is. I'm not going to run away again.

Xavier snorts. "You say the stupidest things."

A smile plays at the corner of my mouth. Power surges through me. "Then we do have one thing in common." I'll continue to live in my apartment and create fabrics for my designs in the attic. I'll use all four main methods of textile printing from my original sketches. I'll need to add block, roller and heat transfer to screen printing which I've majored in up till now. I *will* stay in Paris. Paris is not going to be a flash of sunlight before I step back into darkness.

"Saskia, you're a New Yorker." Xavier snaps. "Your father and I are now the biggest property developers on the East Coast. Come home. Be part of the rush."

My chest feels light, a surge of freedom passes through me. "Never. I want nothing to do with you or my father."

"The Real Estate Winter Ball." He pushes on as if I hadn't spoken. I hear the rustle of his old-school Rolodex. "Two weeks' time. You're my plus one."

"Take someone who doesn't mind five hours of protracted boredom. Take my father. You'd make a dashing couple."

"Your father has a date. With the woman he's marrying."

My throat clogs, the old familiar dread clenches my stomach. "Whaaat? Which woman?" But I already know.

"Not so full of sass now, are we? Hayley Attaschulle." The way Xavier says her name borders on reverence. He's always worshipped money, and Hayley is one of the richest women in New York.

It's a kick in the gut. "Nooooo," I say. How dare Pa marry the woman who caused Mom such grief.

"It's true." Xavier's voice sizzles with triumph.

If I didn't accept it before, I accept it now. Pa never cared for Mom or me. He hung onto us like possessions. During those painful years when he abused us, Mom kept her dignity, lived her private life, but couldn't hide the trapped look in her eyes. Yet she motivated me to be independent. To not fall into line with Pa's plans for me. He's always done exactly what he wants. Making money. Screwing over people. Fucking ... no ... marrying, his mistress.

Douche bag.

"Saskia. Our engagement stands. I won't confuse the tabloids by turning up with someone other than you. The word is that you're my fiancé." His words are beyond smug. He's becoming more like Pa every day.

"Fiancé? Wonder who put that word out there. Take along that boyfriend of yours, what's-his-name? Marko. Thoroughly confuse them. I'm not marrying you. There'd be three of us in the marriage."

"If that's the way you want to play it. Fine. Nevertheless, this union has to happen." He sounds like he's sucked a lemon. "Come home, live the life you were born to. Playing the struggling creative doesn't suit you."

"Doesn't suit you, you mean. What would you understand about creativity? Everything you do begins as a thought in my father's brain."

"Talking of brains, why don't you use yours? Sources tell us you're existing on the tenuous dream that you'll break into the Paris fashion industry. You're so naïve. You have to grease palms or you'll go nowhere."

My breath knots in my throat. Is this how the world works? "What sources?"

"Your father and I hired a private detective as soon as you left New York. Naturally."

"Whaaat? OH MY GOD. You two disgust me."

"You're an heiress. We needed to know you were safe, what with all the terrorism and demonstrations and things blowing up in Paris. You work behind a bar in the red-light district—"

My heartbeat zooms into overdrive. I feel like there's smoke shooting out of my ears. First François spies on me. Now these two. My face burns, my body turns rigid. I lurch to my feet, pace, try to work off the adrenaline, try to block the ugly picture of spies watching my every move. I peer out the window. Is that a P.I. down in the street having a coffee, his face hidden behind a newspaper? His hat pulled down, his collar up. Is he wearing gumshoes? Did he follow me when I jogged around Montmartre? Does he ride the metro with me? I shiver. My teeth chatter. All this time I've lived an exhilarating lie, believing for the first time in my life I was free. Living how I chose. Instead, I've been stalked. Every aspect of my life reported back to François, my father, Xavier.

"How dare you." My voice grates. My gut feels hollowed out. Empty. My life in Paris has been an open book. "I'm done." My thumb is about to press *End*.

"Hey. I'm not. What about that corrupt skirt-chasing politician who visited your apartment and brawled with you and your boyfriend at that café? Someone sold pictures to one of those trashy celebrity magazines and your father nearly had a coronary reading that bad publicity. Don't you give a thought to how your dissolute life affects his reputation, and mine as your future husband?"

"OH MY GOD." I scream on top of my voice. Every tiny hair on my body lifts. They know about Raphael. And my bar work. And my fashion debacle. Everything. "How ... dare ... you." I recall Farrin's customers snapping photos on their smart phones. Someone recognized me and sold the photos to U.S. gossip magazines. I grit my teeth. My freedom has been an illusion.

Xavier's voice takes a particularly nasty tone. "That brings me to that Hell's Angel of yours. He's a hottie all right. I get the attraction, wouldn't mind a bit myself, but he's into some deep shit. Does he deal drugs as well as take them? Did he get you hooked? And that bar manager of yours, Marcel what's-his-name? Saskia, it's not like you to hang with guys like that. What's happened to you? That sweet girl I'm going to marry?"

My head spins. How dare this cocaine-sniffing pariah criticize my friends and me. "I grew up," is all I manage.

"Come, Saskia. Put that life behind you. Your father is going to cut you off completely if you don't come home and marry me."

"I'll not participate in your charade." I smack the wall. It gives a satisfying thud. "I'm not coming back to New York. I'm safer in Paris where I don't have to swim with sharks like you and Father."

"But you *must* come home." I hear his shoe stamp the floor and imagine him bending over to brush a speck of dust off the toe.

I laugh out loud. "I *must*? Are you kidding me? Get lost, Xavier. Don't call again."

I fix another cup of coffee, tug the quilt tight around my neck, walk to the window. I gulp mouthfuls of the tepid brew while gazing at the zinc rooftops, the Eiffel Tower and down at the crowds, laughing and jolly, waving bottles of champagne, toasting each other this frosty Christmas morning. This is the view I've loved since Day One. It's mine. I'm never giving it up. My dream. To live an independent life. Even though I was sidetracked by Raphael, I'm close to achieving every goal I set myself before I left New York.

The day stretches before me – empty, open, free. Downstairs in my apartment, I dress for the day in skinny jeans and a super warm yellow cashmere sweater.

While I untangle my hair from its rat's nest, I think about how far I've come since I arrived in Paris. It's going to be tough without Raphael, but I can do tough. This must be what Kumpaya meant when she said my dreams will come true, but not in the way I imagined. I always saw Raphael as part of my dream, not anymore, but my fashion dream is very much alive.

I release a deep breath, blood rushes to my brain. Something breaks in me. Something good. My melancholy crawls out the door. Hope seeps in. I'm in control. Thoughts flood my head like a riptide at a Long Island beach.

I actually hum a few bars of *We are the Champions* while I open 'Notes' on my cell and create a new list.

- *Leave Marcel's. Time to move on.*
- *Renew my contract on Apartment 5A and the attic.*
- *Ring Monsieur Etienne.*

I don't care if it's Christmas Day. Hope turns into happiness. I don't need Pa. I don't need Xavier. I don't need Raphael.

Raphael.

Who am I kidding? His loss hits with surprising ferocity. The giddy freedom of our daily lives was something I never expected to share with anyone. We were a perfect couple in so many ways. We worked towards our dreams, applauded each other's efforts, our highs, our lows. Raphael's dream has arrived. I'm tottering on the brink of mine. I don't begrudge him his success, but if I don't make it this time, I'll feel slightly jealous. It seems like my dreams have taken a more circuitous route than his, but I can't fault his determination to push forward.

I've always dreamed of becoming a Head Designer. At Romance is Born I came close to achieving that dream. That dream was like a cluster of balloons, pretty on the outside but full of empty air. Roberto and Isabella burst my balloon with a pin handed to them by Pa. It brought me to the brink of emotional collapse, but I brushed myself off and ran away to Paris. Life in Paris has taught me how to fight for my goals. To reach for the stars. To believe I'm worth it.

I'll always be surrounded by talented people. People with better connections. Better looks. More experience. But I'll never compare my success with other's. My journey is my own.

My phone vibrates in a happy dance along the floor.

Buzz-buzz-buzz, buzz-buzz-buzz.

I check the screen. Several missed calls from Raphael, and a text from him:

Urgent. Call me Sassy. Something's happened. Marcel wants—

...but ...

My heart pumps. My throat's dry. My hands shake with excitement. I'll check Raphael's message later. Marcel probably wants me to take more shifts at the bar seeing it's Christmas and super busy. Well, why didn't he call himself? But ... well ... I've more important things on my mind.

A phone call.

Monsieur Etienne.

I'm dizzy as I swipe the screen. Hope surges through me. It's happening.

I clamp my teeth to stop them chattering. I know it's good news. I feel it.

I've won the fashion competition for sure.

I clear my throat, speak in my most confident voice. "*Allo* Monsieur Etienne. Merry Christmas. I was about to call."

CHAPTER THIRTY-SIX

The third and final segment of the Paris Institut's holographic New Fashion show is about to begin. It's been a couple weeks of utter chaos since Monsieur Etienne rang on Christmas morning, told me they couldn't choose an outright winner, so not one, but all three finalists are up with a chance tonight. For the last two weeks I've practically lived at the Institut 24/7, planning every aspect of my show, putting final flourishes to my presentation, filming digital segments to rock the crowd. With my complete focus on my fashion, I've hardly had a moment to think about Raphael except to understand his need to be engrossed in his exhibition. I've learned that a first night leaves room for little else.

All other aspects of my life have faded to black. My fashion has been my food and drink as I planned this night of nights.

My debut. My moment. My dream taking flight.

Finally, it's happened. Mom's not here to share the moment when my designs hit the catwalk, but I'm delighted enough for both of us. Even though it was always about winning for me, since I've come to terms with myself and my dreams, I no longer feel I have to win to justify coming to Paris. In the past weeks, as I dreamed up my styles, stitched until my fingers hurt, I realized it's enough that in a brief amount of time I've been given a chance to shine, to show my fashions to Parisians. No matter what happens tonight, I'm a winner.

The battle for first place in the New Fashion segment is down to the wire. Zack, Samu and I are in the ring. I'll probably never know if the judges couldn't choose an outright winner because they found out their list had been compromised by François Valentine. Whatever. The audience is choosing the winner by acclamation tonight.

I lean forward in my front-row seat, twisting the gold chain of my Dior clutch. I've taken great care of my health in preparation for tonight. Pascale has supervised a series of ketamine injections and is monitoring my use of Xanax. I've stayed away from champagne. But I'm jittery. I need an 'off' switch.

"This is the scariest night of my life," I whisper to Zack who's sitting beside me.

"Suck it up bitch. Samu and I are done. We can sit back, chill, enjoy watching you suffer." Zack grins, slapping my arm with the back of his hand.

"Your presentations were amazing," I say. "You've set the bar high."

I'm guessing few in the auditorium have seen a holographic fashion show before tonight, but judging by the reaction, they're wild for it. I'm thrilled that the Institut trialed this format, giving us the chance to use technology to display our fashions digitally from every wall of the auditorium, adding another level of difficulty to our presentations.

Zack's denim range has out clapped Samu's Polynesian Dreams. What will the audience's reaction be to my Sun King range? Will they love it? Or will they give it the silent treatment? My chest contracts. I second guess my choices. Why didn't I choose something more relevant? Do modern Parisians even like the Sun King? Why oh why did I choose him?

The room darkens. The audience makes so much noise I can't hear my thumping heart, but I feel it crashing against my rib cage. I've put everything—my emotions, my talent, a great deal of money—into creating my designs. Winning would prove to my father I can make it on my own. But even if I don't win, I've proven to myself I'm strong.

The music is at first faint. The audience quietens. It builds to a crescendo until the room is an orchestra of perfectly synchronized acoustic guitar playing The Beatles' *Sun King*. Now everybody's laughing. Everybody's happy. I clap and stamp my feet to the slow marching tune, but my throat is too dry to whistle and hoot along with the audience.

The black room dazzles with dancing pinpricks of gold and red light. I grip my chair, watch my name and tagline appear on the four walls over a burnished golden sun – 'Saskia Bell's Sun King Range – True Style Never Dies.' An image of Louis XIV, France's Sun King, appears, his long dark curls reminding me of Raphael's.

The room fades to black.

This is the moment.

I press my fist against my chest. My heart vibrates as the holograph takes us inside Louis XIV's glittering extravagance of the Versailles Palace's Hall of Mirrors. The images flicker around the room, and I'm struck full of self-doubt. Is my storytelling too ambitious? The era I'm projecting is an era when aristocrats were loathed in France, while the outfits they wore were envied. Will my idea of reimagining this style in a modern Parisian setting work?

Versailles comes alive. All four walls of the Institut's auditorium flicker with holographic images of glittering chandeliers, curved painted ceilings, and gold statues, heralding the arrival of the Sun King. We hear his footsteps, then the virtual model saunters towards us along the mirrored hallway. He's dressed in a burgundy frock coat, tight black trousers, white lace cravat. He stands amidst a group of modern-day artists holding palettes and brushes. I'm transported to Raphael at work on the Pont des Arts – velvet blazers, velvet trousers, cravats, high boots. If I take nothing else from my relationship with Raphael, I'll always be grateful for the way his sartorial choices influenced my range.

"Aha, genius, Sask." Zack links his arm in mine. "Not hard to recognize your—"

Zack's words are cut short when an American behind me says, "Who's gonna wear gear like this? Give me that guy's denim any day."

I twitch at the sting, but I don't let it crush my confidence. Americans aren't my target audience. Whoever spoke is right about one thing, though. Zack's denim designs suit a broader demographic, while mine target a narrower demographic of those French men who long for the old classics and have the panache to strut the style.

"Ignore him, Saskia." Jemi whispers from behind me where she's sitting with my class from the Institut. She places her hand onto my shoulder and squeezes.

I turn my head. "Thanks, Jemi." I search the crowd behind her but it's too dark to see who the American might be. I shrug. I really don't care.

Zack clasps my hand. "Listen to that clapping. The crowd loves it. Don't let one guy piss you off."

My muscles relax slightly. "Thanks." I cross my fingers. "I hope you're right."

The audience claps even louder when the images of Versailles fade and dozens of Sun Kings strut up and down the walls and across the ceiling in a diagonal route. The segment was a nightmare to create, but the audience stamps and whistles. Thankfully, the American keeps his thoughts to himself.

Tears prick my eyes when my designs on the King—tight black leather pants, white fitted shirts with full sleeves and lace cravats—are set off by magnificent knee-length frock coats with nipped-in waists and peaked lapels made of a rich burgundy velvet embroidered with stitches of gold like I saw at Palais Galliera. They look exactly how I imagined them. *Will the fashion industry love them as much as I do?*

I wring my hands. I'm still thinking about that when the King exits.

The auditorium goes black. Around me, the crowd whispers.

Pulses of light shoot through the room, keeping time with the ever-increasing volume of musical beats. I lean forward. My breaths come short and fast. I know what's going to happen next. My photographer friend Kate McInnes and I worked on this choreography for days, using every gadget on her high-speed camera.

On all four walls, one white door opens against the black background. My heartbeat keeps time, *thump-thump-thump,* to the marching music. Four Sun Kings walk through the door, then eight, then sixteen, until all four walls of the auditorium are projected with the King in a full range of formal wear in rich fabrics and colors, most created from my copious sketches of muted sunrises and sunsets on Long Island.

"Sask" Zack brushes my twitching hands. "This is amazing. It's the first time I've seen it all the way through."

Another brash American voice ripples down the front row. "What poncy clothes. Even those Polynesian dresses beat this stuff hands down."

My body tenses. A sharp stone grinds in my stomach. I press my knuckles against my mouth, hoping few in the audience share this opinion.

"Calm down, Sask." Zack takes my hand away from my mouth. "Listen to the audience. They love it. Every Frenchman will be beating a path to your door begging you to dress him."

"Right on, bro'." Samu stage whispers to Zack, then says to me, "My dresses are way cool, Saskia, but your presentation is miles better. People love it. They want some magic in their lives and you're giving them theatre. They're imagining Sun King gloss rubbing off on them by wearing these styles."

"Ssh," someone nearby scolds.

The holograph morphs to a single Sun King walking towards the audience in loose black trousers and an intricately embroidered forest-green frock coat over a black waistcoat. This was the most complex segment of the presentation. I've tried to show how perfect my range looks in contemporary Paris, in the places I've visited with Raphael. Life with him has been a whirl. I see it now. The parties, the art galleries, the picnics. Even though Raphael's out of my life, it was too late to cut him out of my presentation.

Telling the story this way works. The audience claps and stamps their feet when in fast forward, the holograph images show a sumptuous contemporary Parisian soiree and a champagne-sipping crowd. I've been to multiple parties with Raphael in exclusive apartments just like this, but now the ladies in black evening dress are outshone by men in black trousers, white full shirts and colorful jackets with black lapels trimmed with intricate stitch work. Not a black tuxedo in sight.

"I love this, Sask," Zack says. "The art on the walls is reflected in their jackets."

Flutters of joy tickle my belly. I hope everyone is as observant as Zack. "I'm glad you noticed."

The scene changes to a large group picnicking on the lawn of the Champ de Mars, overseen by the Eiffel Tower. How beautiful it looks. My face warms as I remember lying on Raphael's lap on a perfect summer's day soon after we met, him feeding me bites of baguette and paté and sipping champagne while we shared our dreams of success. Now the ladies change to summer dresses, while the men wear autumn-toned trousers and colorful jackets over slim fitted white shirts, much like Raphael wore on our picnics.

The scene fades. The audience stands, claps, whistles, then sits again when they realize there's more to come.

I take a deep breath, hoping the audience will love the finale as much or more than they loved the picnic segment. Heralded by the strumming of loud guitars, the Sun King marches in, a larger-than-life figure visible from all four corners of the auditorium. He wears tight black leather trousers, a leather beret and a gold lame coat over a white shirt. The coat would have been over the top, except for its black leather lapels and pocket trims which would make it a stunner at any Parisian party. As the music fades, the Sun King pirouettes, opens his coat to reveal a nipped-waist black leather waistcoat not unlike the one Raphael wears when he rides his motorcycle. The Sun King winks at the audience and shouts, "*Longue vie le roi soleil!*"

"*Longue vie le roi soleil.* Long live the Sun King." The audience shouts, rising to its feet, carried away by the moment. The King nods, bows and waves his way out the door.

The applause doesn't stop when the King exits. "Encore." the audience shouts. My tech team have prepared for this. My 'gold coat with leather' segment can be played on repeat. The room rings with shouts of "Long live the Sun King!" as the King repeats his entrance and exit several times.

I'm delighted by the audience's response. I'll never forget this beautiful feeling when people were transported by something I've dreamed in my mind and created with my hands.

I try to stand to acknowledge the applauding crowd, but my legs wobble, so I suck in a deep breath, look around, amazed by the audience's reaction.

"You okay, Sask?" Zack rubs my back. "It's all over bar the clapping which seems like it's never going to end."

"I'm fine." I raise my head. "It's just so ... so ..." I can't find the words to describe such a once-in-a-lifetime experience. If I had any remaining self-doubt, it vanishes under a deafening thunder of applause. Whatever happens, my fashion choices are validated. My story tonight was that true style never dies. I've nailed it.

"That was superb, Saskia." Samu brushes my hand. "You've got this."

"Thanks, Samu."

Zack laughs. "You're the winner, unless the clap-o-meter is broken."

Zack and Samu draw me to my feet, hold me steady. My friends and colleagues from the Institut crowd us and pat our backs. My eyes focus on Monsieur Etienne and Professeur Germain standing behind the podium, clapping along with Directors of the Institut and the advisors, representatives from Karl Lagerfeld, Stella McCartney and Givenchy. They're looking our way, smiling and nodding. They fist pump in my direction. Wow.

The luminaries wait for the audience to stop clapping, but it seems it never will. Finally, the professeur holds up his hands, speaks into the microphone. The audience sits. A pulse beats wildly in my throat. I lean forward, waiting for the results of the clap-o-meters hooked up to the techies' laptops.

"In third place," Professeur Germain says at last, "we have Samu Ioane with his Polynesian Power presentation." The audience claps and whistles and Zack and I hug him before he walks to the podium to accept his trophy. Holding his heavily tattooed arms in the air, Samu doesn't look disappointed. Grinning broadly, he steps aside, checking out his statuette while he waits for Zack and me to join him.

Now it's Zack's and my turn. My throat's dry. Did I win? Euphoria pulses through me.

Professeur Germain leans close to the microphone and speaks. His lips move, but I hear nothing but the throbbing in my head, the thumping of my heart. The clapping, whistling and cheering has deafened me. All I hear is a gurgle, like I'm swimming underwater.

The spotlight sweeps past my face, blinding me. Zack grabs my hand. "Sask Congratulations. You won."

Butterflies flap against my stomach wall. The noise sounds distant, like it's across the street in another apartment and I'm wearing earmuffs. I shake my head, try to clear it. Words start making sense. I feel elated. I feel ... like a winner. "OH MY GOD!" I jump up and down, screaming. I push Zack towards the podium to collect his runner up prize. He hesitates, smiles, throws his arms around me, kisses me before marching up to Monsieur Etienne.

Samu and Zack stand side by side on the podium, watching me.

It's my turn.

I stand rooted to the spot, listening to Professeur Germain make the announcement. "Clearly judged the winner by your acclamation, we have Saskia Bell's Sun King Range."

The hooting audience explodes. I'm blinded by flash bulbs. The shock leaves me grinning like a loon. I whisper, "Mom, I did it. I did it."

"Go, Saskia, go. Get up there." Jemi pushes me from behind and sets me in motion toward the podium.

I walk up the steps on jelly legs, hoping I don't stumble and fall flat onto my face. I manage to stand in front of Professeur Germain who reaches out to me, gives me the full *bisou* treatment. Then it's Monsieur Etienne's turn to kiss me and hand me the winner's trophy. The media rushes forward, kneels and surrounds the podium, snapping picture after picture. I barely glance at the trophy before I hear "Speech! Speech! Speech!" *OH MY GOD*. Each of us were told to prepare a winning speech, but I've been so excited, I forgot my notes. But I've left nothing to chance. Every moment I took a break from the preparations, I ran through the words I'd say tonight if I won.

"Thank you," I begin, my voice wobbly. I hold my trophy in the air with both hands waiting for the audience to calm down. I take a deep breath and manage to get through the words I've memorized, despite the media and the camera phones flashing. I congratulate Zack and Samu; I thank the Institut for the honor of having my designs shown in such an amazing format; I thank the directors for their valued input throughout the course and their help in finessing my designs. I salute the Sun King to wild applause, making much of the fact that many consider him to be the originator of haute couture. I thank Raphael, not by name, but by calling him someone who gave me the modern-day inspiration for my collection. Finally, it's over and again the audience rises to its feet, yells and whistles. A few more, "*Longue vie le roi soleil!*" ring out.

I stand on the stage between Zack and Samu. Monsieur Etienne relieves us of our trophies. The guys each take one of my hands and raise my arms in the air like I'm a boxer who's just won the Heavyweight Championship of the World. My heart thumps so loudly It's a wonder it doesn't drown out Queen's *We are the Champions*. We bow to the audience, fingers entwined, arms behind us, over and over again while the clapping and snap fest persists.

"Once I saw the Sun King, I never stood a chance, did I, Sask?" Zack leans across and whispers in my ear.

I know he's not referring to Louis XIV. "You've been the best friend I could ever hope for." I kiss his cheek.

We reclaim our trophies, leave the podium. Zack and Samu each hold my elbows and help me down.

Milling at the bottom are Monsieur Etienne, Professeur Germain and members of the Fashion Advisory Board who shake hands and congratulate us.

"Quality design such as you demonstrated here tonight is what keeps the fashion industry fresh and innovative." Professeur Germain smiles while he adjusts his forest green silk cravat.

Monsieur Etienne nods to each one of us like a proud parent. "To find not one, but three, superb designers in one class at the Institut is extraordinary." He tweaks the outsize lapels on his mustard blazer. "I will text you details of the board meeting next week where we will discuss your immediate futures in the industry. Members of the board are compiling offers from their houses to present to you."

One of the board members, Ella Max, one of my favorite designers of sustainable fashion, steps forward in a gorgeous black silk evening gown that flares around her feet. She kisses my cheek, draws me aside. "Saskia, congratulations. I've been closely watching your designs at the Institut. Your classic style suits my range. I'd love to meet with you regarding having you design for my Paris fashion house. I'll have my assistant schedule a time. Now go, enjoy your night."

My insides flip. *Holy. Freaking. Wow.* "Thank you, Ella." Being approached by one of my idols is overwhelming. Before I have time to take in the fact that she's considering offering me a design position, the three of us are surrounded by the media pack.

"Hold that pose. Guys, stand either side of Saskia. Trophies in the air."

My head whirs like their cameras. I kiss my trophy, the symbol of my first success in Paris's fashion world. My first trophy to display on my office shelf. It won't be the last.

Journalists separate us. They shove recorders in my face. A waiter thrusts a champagne flute into my hand. I take a sip, shutting my eyes for a moment to enjoy the bubbles dancing around my mouth. Magic. I try not to be overwhelmed by the crush that builds around me, the congratulations, the kisses, the handshakes, the questions.

"Saskia, how do you feel?" I'm asked so many times.

Fabulous. Especially now the champagne has kicked in. "I feel honored. I feel amazed. I feel humbled," I say, over and over. *I feel like a winner*, I don't say.

"Chevvy Artemas from *Marie Claire.*" A business card presses into my hand. "I'll call to arrange a fashion shoot and an interview."

"Awesome," I say, dropping the card into my clutch.

A man in a beret thrusts out his arm and waves a card at me. "Blinky Fornescue from *Kable News*. We'd like to put you on a fashion panel on Parisian classic style we have slotted for two weeks' time. Details on the card." Another flashy card slips into my clutch.

"Fantastic." My heart pumps with all the attention. This is the first time in my life I can remember being in the spotlight alone. Who knew it would feel so good?

"Madame Bellerose from Chez Bellerose in rue Faubourg Saint-Honoré, Mademoiselle Saskia." In her classic little black dress, blingy shoes and blonde chignon, this lady is the epitome of style.

"*Enchanté*, Madame." I've visited her shop so many times, immersing myself in the fabulous styles the pampered ladies of Paris choose to wear.

"I'd like to discuss selling your designs in my boutique on the Champs-Elysées," she says. "I so admired the amazing red dress you wore to Raphael Valentine's exhibition and I discovered you created it. It reminded me of a Dior I once had in stock. Simple, sexy lines. I'd love more like it." She looks me up and down. "And many like the dress you are wearing tonight. Your creation?"

Freaking. Wow. Wow. Wow. "Yes, Madame Bellerose." I stroke the pleats of my little black dress and hope she can't see my knees knocking.

Those butterflies flutter away. "But I need to see what commitments I have after meeting with the board next week."

She smiles. "I understand. Whenever you have time, please call on me at the boutique and we'll talk."

Light hands squeeze my shoulders from behind. I spin around to see— "Mira. You made it." A waiter takes my empty glass. Trophy under my arm, I give Mira a one-armed hug. "I'm so glad you're here." I can't say the same when over her shoulder, fake smiles on their faces, Roberto and Isabella approach.

I don't want anything to ruin my happiness tonight. I've been surprisingly calm since the winner's announcement, but at the sight of my old bosses who shafted me, my joy flies away. The old insecurities taunt me. *I'm not good enough. They fired me.* I know that's rubbish. It was because of my father, but I can't erase the lingering effect of their betrayal. "Mira, what are *they* doing here?" I hiss.

"L'Amour dans sa Vie was so thrilled Isabella recommended you, they sent tickets. Thanks for mine." Mira's glowing. "The best Christmas gift ever." She talks fast, looking over her shoulder at the crush of people pushing toward me. "What a fabulous night. Your presentation was unbelievable. Coming to Paris was the best choice you ever made. I want to hear all about it. I'm at George V for three days, compliments of Roberto and Isabella, can you believe? I know you'll be busy, but please call me."

"Of course. I'll try to come around tonight." I hug her tight. Perhaps in the future she'll join me in Paris and we'll work together again.

Roberto lunges forward, hauls me into an awkward hug as soon as Mira walks away. "Saskia, you look *fab*ulous. No doubt your dress is your design. Those psychedelic metallic pumps are to die for. Brand?" He holds up his iPad, ready.

"Trade secret." I'm not telling him they're H&M imitation leather, but knowing Roberto, he's already taken a sneaky snap and he'll Google them on his cell phone.

"Your hair is so long." Isabella looks cutting edge in a figure-hugging electric blue evening dress I remember, with my shadow embroidery in silver on the bodice. "I love how you've curled it. Paris suits you. My God. That show was *fab*ulous. I wish—" She looks uncomfortable, says no more.

Hurt at their dismissal stabs me again. What did I expect? An apology? I take a deep breath and smile. Thank God they fired me. I entered a whole new world thanks to them. When I say, "Thank you, Isabella," I mean it.

"Dresses like you're wearing tonight would fly off the shelves in New York," Roberto says. "We're at George V. We'd like to set up a meeting to discuss carrying a range of your daywear at our flagship boutique in the Hamptons. You'd have full control over your designs, but we were thinking of those *fab*ulous sunset prints you're so fond of. We haven't found anyone who can combine colors and patterns like you. Think about it." Taking Isabella's hand, he melts into the throng.

It's all coming together. My designs are in demand, but I have no intention of working with Roberto and Isabella. I'll not give them a second opportunity to betray me.

Pride floods through me. What else in the world equals having a whole room ecstatic over my designs. A magnitude of emotions course through me. I'll sift through them later. Make sense of it all.

Tonight, my Paris dream has come true.

CHAPTER THIRTY-SEVEN

"Sassy?"

I swing my head towards a voice that calls from the edge of the crowd. My legs wobble. I clutch for something to hang on to, but there's nothing.

This man's no holograph.

The *real* Sun King is here.

I clutch my trophy against my chest. Try to get my body to back off its overexcited response at the sound of his voice calling my name. When is my heart going to get the message that our boat has sailed?

He's a dark star crashing into my orbit. I'd wondered what I'd do if he turned up. I have my answer. My pulse races, my cheeks burn, my body trembles. No. No. No. Regardless of how much time we've spent apart, whether minutes, hours, days, weeks, my heart flutters when I see him. I can't hide the flush on my skin. Stony dread sets in every pore. Did he come to gloat about his perfect life with Bernelle? I look behind him but don't see the bitch of an art gallery hostess. Thank God.

I square my shoulders.

I won't let him get to me.

The journalists are silent for a heartbeat, watching him push through the crowd, his eyes on me. Then they erupt, sensing a breakout story. The whir and click of camera shutters deafen me. I'm faced with a flight or fight response. I can't run from my own first night. But I can fight.

"Sassy?" Raphael stands in front of me, eyebrows raised. His tight leather motorcycle pants and black studded boots are a devastating combination he knows I adore. The sample burgundy frock coat he wears that Manu made for my collection formalizes the look. He holds out his arms to me like he's just walked out the door an hour ago to take the Harley for a spin and is back to see if I've made any progress on that design I was fussing over when he left.

I shake my head. Shrug a shoulder. Take a step back. No way I'm falling into his arms tonight.

He startles when I offer my hand, not my cheek, but he takes what's offered.

"Isn't that Raphael Valentine, the famous painter?" The guy from Report Hollywood yells and the rest of the pack come running.

Report Hollywood shoves a mic in my face. "Hey, Saskia, didn't you break up with Monsieur Valentine on the night of his first exhibition?"

How do these guys know everything? "I'm not here to talk about relationships, or the Valentine exhibition. I'm here to talk about my fashion."

It's my turn to startle when Raphael puts a light hand on my bare back. I shiver at his touch, momentarily lose my power of speech, so Raphael explains to the thrusting mics, "We had a misunderstanding, that's all." He pulls me closer to his side, well knowing the effect he has on me, taking liberties, pretending we're still a couple.

"Raphael, get your hands off me." I stage whisper in case there're lipreaders in the room. I play nice for the cameras while my mind whirls. How dare he answer questions meant for me. How dare he still have such a devastating effect on me.

"Mademoiselle Bell. Brett from Fashion Futures. Are you and

Monsieur Valentine together again? You're called media darlings on Instagram. Are you?"

Raphael looks down, blocking Brett and his mic. "Don't say no, Sassy. I need to talk to you."

"There's nothing to talk about."

"You tell him, Sask." Zack shoves away mics that thrust into his face. He offers me a plate of hors d'oeuvres, little pork rillettes on toast. "You should eat. You look faint."

I shake my head. "I'm okay, thanks Zack." I suck in deep breaths. "I've got this."

Zack frowns. "Don't let him boss you around, Sask. Remember what he did."

I clutch my heart. "I'll never forget it, Zack."

Raphael's face turns puce. "Sassy—" He bunches his fists, treats Zack to a murderous look.

Zack ignores Raphael, winks at me. "Samu and I are going to Oubliettes with the class. The BatCats are playing. Join us later?"

I grab his arm, not wanting to be left alone with Raphael. "I'll see. We've got early morning television, don't forget."

Zack nods. "I know. If I don't see you at Oubliettes, I'll pick you up at five o'clock. Don't stay out too late." He glares distastefully at Raphael.

Raphael's brows move into a bemused arc. He offers his hand to Zack. "Congratulations, Isaak. You have a bright future."

"Thank you." Zack's voice drawls with reservation as he reluctantly shakes hands.

Raphael reaches for my hand, but I clutch my trophy, blocking him. Shaking his head, he says, "Sassy, those designs of yours— I'm so proud of you, but listen—"

My gut twists at his pride in me. I'm carried away by the excitement of the night, but not so carried away I forget we're no longer lovers. "Thank you, Raphael. As you know, you were my inspiration for tonight's show." I don't forget it was Raphael inspiring me, encouraging me, loving me.

He steps toward me. "I know everyone wants to interview you," he says, "but we need to talk. It's urgent. It's about—"

"Whatever you have to say to me is not urgent."

His face reddens. "Sassy, it's important."

I hold up my hand. "This is so not the time or place for this conversation. Please leave." I'm done. I spin away from him, give my full attention to the job at hand.

"Saskia. Here. That's great." *Click. Flash. Whir. Click. Flash. Whir. Flash. Click. Whir.* "Look this way. Hold up your trophy. Smile. Great. Superb."

Raphael watches my act from the sidelines. There's a mix of restraint, desperation and respect in his eyes. No matter what's happened between us, he's proud of my success, knowing more than anyone how hard I've worked. His dedication to his art was a spur that kept me moving forward with ever increasing self-belief.

"Adriana. 4WZ. Is your dress your own design, Saskia?"

"Yes. Like it?" I twirl to show off the intricate knife pleats, the halter neck, the open back. I hold the silver trophy in a victory salute.

Raphael's at my shoulder again. "Sassy." He touches my elbow. "I must talk to you. Something's happened."

"I know. You kissed Bernelle this time?"

"Not that. You're right to see me as an arse, but—"

"Too right." I cut a pose for Vogue Paris who've pre-arranged a cover story.

"Please, Sassy. I'm begging you. Five minutes. It's about Marcel."

"Marcel?" A pulse throbs at my throat. "Why didn't you say? Fine. Five minutes."

"Thank you." Raphael sounds truly humble.

"*Une minute.*" I hold up my finger to the media, then lead Raphael to a small, curtained area to the side of the podium.

The pack follows, but Raphael shouts, "*Reculer! Reculer*! Back! Back!" in rapid-fire French and English. They don't try to follow when we push through the curtain into the dim recess where stage equipment is stored.

I stand next to a sound box. Raphael stands two feet in front of me fiddling with his tie. My heart thuds in my chest. I'm hyperaware that journalists are close. And hyperaware that Raphael is closer.

Talking fast and low, I fire the first volley. "Why has it taken you so long to come see me if something urgent happened?" I taunt. "Why turn up tonight? At my show? You know how important tonight is."

Raphael comes closer, says nothing. For the first time ever, he chews his bottom lip.

"Talk," I say, fiddling with my clutch, feeling an unwelcome dread washing over me. "Time's wasting. The media's waiting. Marcel?" Did Marcel tell Raphael about the pass he made when he brought me back to my apartment? Surely not. Raphael would have a different reaction.

"Yes, Marcel." He talks quietly and deliberately. "I've tried to see you before tonight. I came to your apartment after the exhibition, but you weren't there. I returned every day, wracked with worry. Madame Lavelle hadn't seen you. The Grande Dame called me the worst *connard.* No one at the Institut would tell me anything. And Marcel, it's been a nightmare." He blows out a long breath.

"What?" I flick my hand in frustration, try to hold back the anxiety. "Tell me."

"Sassy, please stay calm. I don't know how to make this easier." He reaches out a hand to me. "Marcel OD'd the night of my exhibition."

"Holy fuck." I swear my heart stops. My knees weaken and I clutch the sound box. I would have fallen to the floor and taken the box with me except Raphael puts a hand either side of my waist. Shaking all over, I forget to lower my voice. "*Whaaat*? Is he—? Oh no, no, no." Tears spring to my eyes. "Don't tell me—"

"No." Raphael stands me straight and rubs my back in circles, strokes up and down my arms, to calm me. "Thankfully his new boyfriend Victor found him in time. I've been working the bar and nursing him back to health with Victor's help. Marcel's back at work now but has a long way to go before he's clean. He wanted to come tonight, but couldn't. He's desperate to see you."

I grab my throat. Oh, Marcel. Don't tell me you felt so guilty you did this? "Why? Why did he do it?"

"Who knows?" Raphael looks at me, I see guilt in his eyes.

"He must have said something."

Raphael's fingers clutch my side. "He tried to reconcile with Joaquin but that didn't work out. He took it hard. It may have had something to do with his overdose, but we can't know that. That dickhead got him addicted to ice. That's why Marcel changed. He was crushed about our breakup. He drank too much on top of the drugs." Raphael blew out a breath. "Ice pushed him over the edge. He had a heart attack."

"OH MY GOD!" I chew my knuckles, groan, remember the two glasses of champagne at Raphael's exhibition and the two shots of Dubonnet Marcel had before he left my apartment. "It's my fault. I should have stopped him drinking. I should have ... I shouldn't have ... Why didn't you call me?" I shouldn't have been so dismissive when he told me he loved me.

Raphael brushes his hands over my head. "I tried so many times," he whispers. "Marcel begged me to find you. He wanted to see you. To know you were all right. He said you were a mess when he left you that night. I couldn't reassure him because I knew nothing."

I try not to cry. "You should have found some way—"

"I tried every way I knew. I called. I texted. You blocked me. I know how important tonight is to you, and understand you resent my coming, but you could be anywhere in the world tomorrow. This is the only place I knew you'd be. I had to tell you face to face."

Crap. I'd deleted every message from him, not caring to read a word. I hadn't scrolled back to see what he wanted to tell me about Marcel in his last text before I blocked him. I felt I had to get on with my life. "Oh, God, Raphael, I was so focused on tonight, but I should have been helping

Marcel. I knew he wasn't in a good place when he left me that night." I grip the edge of the sound box, my heart racing. "I wasn't there for him. That will haunt me forever. I'm a selfish bitch."

Raphael places his hand over mine. "Don't blame yourself."

"I can't help it. I need to see him. Now. We have to go."

"No. He's okay. Later. He'll like that. He'll want to hear all about your show. He won't want to hear that you walked out on it."

I'm torn between the media frenzy waiting for me and rushing off to see Marcel. I cover my face with my hands. "I need to see him. To make sure—"

"He's not going anywhere." Raphael removes my hands from my face, compassion in his eyes. "See this night through, *ma petite*." His face is so close to mine, I see new lines etched around his eyes and mouth. Lines of worry. About Marcel. "I'm so proud of you, Sassy. Your show was amazing. It feels so right to be with you like this. I miss this. Please give me another chance. Take me back. I want to fix us."

I long to touch him, but I'm not going to be mesmerized by him like I've been in the past. I take a deep breath. "This is about Marcel, not us. I've missed you, Raphael. I won't lie. But there's no us to fix. I can't take our on again off again relationship any more. It's too draining."

He shakes his head, blows out a breath. "You turning your back on me made it clear my heart belongs with you." He places a hand on his chest. "I've been a fool. I should have dealt with Bernelle right from the start. I love *you*. You're part of my dream. Surely, I'm part of yours. We need each other."

Annoyed at the prick of tears behind my eyes, I say, "No we don't. There'll always be *her*." I remember watching her touch him every chance she had. Did she do it on purpose to upset me, or was she so attracted to Raphael, she couldn't keep her hands off him – a hand on his chest when she said hello, a kiss on both his cheeks every time she greeted him, leaning against his shoulder as they talked, even running her hands through his hair. Yet Raphael insisted it meant nothing. A tear escapes down my cheek. Even though the time apart has allowed me to see things more rationally, the image of Raphael and Bernelle together is burned into my mind.

Raphael thumbs my tear. "Not listening to you was a horrible mistake. When I saw how hurt you were, I hated myself." He tugs his hands through his hair. "You're my lightning strike, my *coup de foudre,* remember."

I grit my teeth. "Yet you let her kiss you under our painting. *Our* painting. The one Marcel told me you'd never sell."

"Sassy, I wanted you by my side that night and it all turned to shit. She kissed me when I was distracted by those two men and their bidding war on our picture. When they saw I didn't want to part with it, they offered me the world."

"That worked in your favor then. But everything has a price, doesn't it?" My stomach clenches. The idea of his selling something that he'd worked on so long in our attic, those carefully thought-out highlights of our relationship, just to let it decorate someone else's wall, is something I'll never forgive him for.

Raphael leans toward me. "I didn't care about the money. All I was thinking was how it broke my heart to see you walk away with Marcel and I couldn't follow. In retrospect I should have said 'fuck it' and raced after you. You're more important than any show. Not seeing you since has been the worst nightmare. I'll do whatever it takes to win you back." He's standing in front of me, clasping my hands, looking directly into my eyes. "I should have never let you escape. I got the call about Marcel just after I reached your apartment after my party wound up. I raced to the hospital and spent days and nights by his side." He takes out his handkerchief, mops his face, reliving the memory. "We nearly lost him."

My hands tremble. "I'm glad you were there for him. You're the best friend he could have. I'll be forever grateful to you for that. But ... how much did you get for the painting?" How much richer did ending us make him is what I really want to ask.

"Their bids didn't interest me. That painting is ours. It captures the moment I fell in love with you. The night I knew I wanted you by my side forever. I couldn't sell it. Selling would symbolize the end of us. I wasn't prepared to accept that."

He *what?* "All this time I thought that painting was history, just like us. Where is it then?"

"It's hanging in the living room in my ... our ... new apartment where it's meant to be." He astounds me further by saying, "About Bernelle. We aren't together. Never have been. Never will be. Her arrogance and snobbery were never for me. But they suit my father. They're together now. Have been since the night of my exhibition. Apparently, they've had a thing going for years." He shakes his head. "They left together."

"*Whaaat?*" No matter my low opinion of Bernelle and François, the news astounds me. "How's Alex taking it?"

He puts his hands onto my shoulders, and I warm to his touch. "She's relieved. Glad to finally divorce. She's planning to buy an apartment in Paris to use as a travel base. Meanwhile, she's staying with me." His voice tilts with an edge of hope. "I told her about a beautiful apartment in an old building in Montmartre that might be coming up for sale in the future. And it comes with an attic where she could dabble in her love of watercolors."

I suck in a breath. He really does believe we have a future together. The thought of Alex in my apartment is sweet. But I'm not planning on leaving any time soon. I place my palms over his heart and feel it pound under my fingertips. Our hearts always beat as one. A surge of longing passes through me, I feel our loss like a sharp pain.

He leans down so we're forehead to forehead, places his hands over mine, whispers. "I'm so sorry for all the pain I've caused you."

I took a risk when I came to Paris, but loving Raphael has been the greatest risk. I'm not sure I want to take the risk again. I've been devastated each time Raphael and I've lost each other. The first time I fell into an abyss of misery and depression. The second time I had my work to keep me afloat. But I can't turn off my heart, my love for him.

"Sassy." His voice seeps into my consciousness. "Do you love me despite everything? If you say you don't, I'll walk away. But God, it'll be hard without you in my life. My muse. My inspiration. The one who holds my heart."

Do I want him to walk away? It would be like finding the other half of myself, then losing it. I've proved I'm strong. I can win battles alone. He's offering me his whole self. He's always offered that, but I've thrown it back in his face, afraid to trust, afraid of being controlled, afraid I didn't shape up against the women he's known. But I'm better than those women. I can commit. I'm loyal. I'm me. The pulse in my neck throbs. Throbs for Raphael. I love him.

There's a scuffle at the curtain, a hand pushes through the gap, a body materializes, then another and another.

Raphael gives another barrage in staccato French. "Mesdames, *revenir, revenir, revenir*." They retreat. He pulls me close so only I hear the words. "Sassy." He shakes me gently by the shoulders. "Don't give up on us. We have so much together. I love you with all my being."

My heartbeat races, my stomach flutters with renewed hope. "We've achieved more together than alone, I'll give you that. We were going to set Paris on fire. We've each made a start." Is a future with him possible? He sets me on fire, He's my inspiration, He's always had my heart. But he broke it. Can he put the pieces back together? Of that I'm not certain.

"Sassy?" he whispers, "Give me another chance."

His sincerity envelops me. We did have it good. He helped me discover who I am. Become stronger. Confident. Without his support my journey would have been far more difficult. Maybe I'm willing to take a small step. To test the waters again. My heart drums, my pulse pounds in my ears. "I love you, Raphael. That's never been in question. Love wasn't our problem. Trust was." How many times has trust let us down? Right from the start, I never really trusted him. I realize now, in so many ways, I've misjudged him.

Hope lights up his face. "You'll never have reason not to trust me again. I'll make sure of that with every breath. Please forgive me. I'll never risk hurting you again. These past weeks have been torture. I'm not whole without you. Without you, nothing has meaning. I've never felt this way before and I'm sure I'll never feel this way again."

"Hmmm. Do you mean that?" I press my hand against my heart which is pumping with desire. I imagine life with Raphael by my side again. As much as I've lied to myself, it's the life I want.

"Yes, I do. We have issues, but nothing we can't sort out."

The curtain rips aside. Flashes bathe us in harsh light. Our *tête-à-tête* is over. There's so much more to talk about. Maybe the interruption is a good thing. I need time to think things through without pressure. This is not the time or place to make a momentous decision. Hah. I've grown in some ways, but I'm still not spontaneous.

Cameras shove into my face. I stumble backward, Raphael catches me.

Raphael maneuvers himself between me and the mics and the cameras. "Ladies and gentlemen, let's take this outside before someone gets hurt."

Raphael and I step into the bedlam of the auditorium.

The media aren't finished with me yet. They surround me. "Saskia, smile. Saskia, pose with Monsieur Valentine. Saskia, kiss Monsieur Valentine. Saskia, tell us more about how you found your place in the Paris fashion world."

I follow their directions in a trance-like state, but my mind is on what Raphael has asked of me. I kiss Raphael a time or two, teasing the cameras, each kiss a remembered taste of his lips, the sweet smell of his breath, the electric touch of his skin. Does he crave me like I crave him? Having him by my side lights that spark I'd missed so much.

He hands me a glass of champagne and, always concerned about my weight, feeds me small crackers smeared with delicious duck paté. He crosses arms with me and we toast my success in champagne. Vogue Paris captures that shot. I'm giddy with champagne. Giddy on Raphael, who's pressed against my side, his curls whispering against my neck, his Ambre Topkapi fragrance messing with my head.

Holy crap, pinch me, I've taken a momentous first step into the Parisian fashion scene. People want to talk to me, take my picture, write stories about me, interview me. This little success feels sweeter than I dreamed it would be when I left New York. I wonder how Pa will react when he reads about my show. Will he be proud of me or furious with me because my disobedience paid off and he gets no benefit from my success. But I don't care. This is *my* success.

Raphael leans over me and whispers, "I love you, Sassy."

I say nothing, but warmth spreads through me and bathes my heart.

"I'll do whatever it takes to prove my love."

"Hmmm." *Promises. Promises.*

"Come home with me to the Île Saint-Louis. To our apartment. Just be with me." He puts our empty champagne glasses onto a passing waiter's tray, takes two fresh drinks.

Accepting the flute, I say, "I'd love you to show me the apartment, and I'd love to see Alex and stay the night, but Montmartre is my home. It suits me for now. I'm not ready to move in with you. Ask me again in a year."

Raphael nods, tries to hide his disappointment. "Okay, Sassy. We go at your pace. Whatever you need."

"I'm taking it slow, Raphael," I whisper into his ear, ignoring the blinding flashes in our faces. There's nothing Paris loves more than lovers. "This may sound selfish, but there are things I must do which I hope you'll do with me. After we leave here, take me to see Marcel. Then let's have a drink at Oubliettes with my friends. Tomorrow, I'd like you to meet my best friend Mira from the States who I've told you about. Let's see what happens. We're not rushing it like we did in the past. Perhaps if we'd taken it slower—?"

"So?" He takes a ragged breath. "You're giving me a chance?"

I want this man by my side forever. My love for him is strong. So much of what he shared tonight shows my misjudgment. "Yes. I'm giving us a chance."

I'm still flushed with excitement when I clasp Raphael's hand, step out of the auditorium, lead him through the rabbit warren of Institut rooms. Fortified by champagne, I say, "Raphael, there's one more person I need to speak to." I pull him into one of the darkened meeting rooms. "I'm going to make a call. Stay with me?"

I dial the number I know by heart. Glancing at my watch, I wonder about the time difference, then think, who cares? This is more important than whether NYC is ahead or behind Paris.

Someone mumbles at the end of the phone. I pray it isn't Hayley Attaschulle. As buoyed as I feel, I'm nowhere near buoyed enough to play nice with Hayley.

"Hello? Who's this?" Whoops. I woke him up.

"Pa?" That's all I manage over the lump in my throat. I squeeze Raphael's hand for courage.

Raphael kisses my cheek. "You've got this, Sassy."

"Sasky." Father's words are no more than a sigh across the miles, a mixture of joy, grief, shock. "I've just been watching your fashion show online and must have dropped off. I'm one proud father. You're a chip off the old block for sure. I'm sorry. I never knew you were a genius."

I try to control my sobs rising in my chest, shaking me to my core. "I love you, Pa."

"I love you, my Sasky."

Ten minutes later, I end the call after Pa amazes me by promising to board a plane and visit. He wanted to come right away, but I convinced him to wait until my feet are on the ground again. Honestly, I need time to prepare myself for the reunion, to make sure I'm strong enough, that Raphael and I are in a good place.

As Raphael and I step outside, a light rain sprinkles magic dust on us, reminding me of our first night together zooming through the streets of Paris on his motorcycle in the pouring rain.

His gleaming red and black Harley waits, illegally parked on the curb as always. He wraps his arm around me, making sure my coat is buttoned tight and my scarf is wrapped securely around my neck. He kisses me on the forehead, then lightly on the lips.

"I never thought we'd do this again, Raphael," I whisper over the lump in my throat.

He brushes my cheeks with gentle hands. "I always dreamed it would happen again. Here. I'm more prepared than the first time." He hands me bike gloves, helmet, snaps the clasp under my chin.

"Thank you."

"Now ... ready? Let's ride."

My arms around his waist, my cheek resting between his shoulder blades, the old excitement throbs through my veins, even more exhilarating than crossing the finish line at the Paris Marathon. This is what I love. This is who I love.

Raphael. Paris. Fashion. Art. Harley motorbikes. I need them all.

"I'm ready."

He revs the engine. Loud and throaty. Just how I like it. He accelerates and we're away. Paris is at our feet.

Kumpaya was right. My dreams have come true, just not in the way I planned.

Fini

KEEP READING the companion novel to Paris Dreams - *Le Petit Paris Cookery School* – a generous blend of food and love. Coming soon.

LE PETIT PARIS COOKERY SCHOOL

CHAPTER ONE

ANGÉLIQUE

Who wouldn't love my life? I was thinking about that yesterday when lying on my therapist's couch on rue de Bourbon le Château. I have my dream job teaching cookery at my very own Le Petit Paris Cookery School. Students come from all over the world to learn to create traditional French food. The fifth-floor kitchen of my shabby chic apartment nestled in the backstreets of *Saint-Germain-des-Prés*, one of Paris's preeminent suburbs, is where they come to learn. But as good as that sounds, dreams come at a price. On the surface my life looks perfect, but inside I know different.

Yesterday, I had my monthly visit to my therapist Celeste who just doesn't get me after all the time I've spent on her couch. I wouldn't waste money on her sessions, but Papa insists I endure her. "She is your lifeline to reality, Angel. You have to keep talking. Something is just not right with you."

Papa's not the only one who thinks I need fixing.

Celeste is his partner in crime. They echo each other which makes me think they discuss me behind my back.

"You must move on with your life, Angélique." Celeste was already talking as I burst in the door of her consulting rooms, late again. Lingered too long over that second coffee. Ah, coffee. The answer to driving the blues away, momentarily at least. A few shots of espresso, a froth of steamed milk and suddenly life was supposed to fall into place again. Just like that. But coffee lied. Like Celeste.

Celeste turned from her picture window and her perusal of her collection of rare birds twittering amongst her topiary trees. Brushing the stiff lapels of her white suit, she ran her eyes over my running get up, frowned, wagged her finger at me. "Looking over my notes of our last session, it grieves me that you are still in denial over your mother's death. You should have moved on to acceptance by now."

"You think, Doctor?" I do have a little trouble convincing myself Mamie's gone and Celeste has picked up on that. That's because Mamie never leaves me. I hear her voice goading me onto bigger and better things like she did when she was alive. Any day, any time, I can conjure up her spirit – not the 'Eye of newt, toe of frog' conjuring like those witches in *Macbeth*. No, I see her in the kitchen we created together. I see her in every suite of amazing rooms we restored and decorated from ideas we gleaned from watching re-runs of *Escape to the Chateau D.I.Y.* on Mamie's big screen in her room.

When I didn't answer, Celeste ran her hands over her severe black bob and came at me with her peculiar brand of tough love. She didn't even wait for me to be seated. "Your mother's dead, Angélique. Accept it." It sounded like an order. Like she wanted to grab me by the ears and shake me.

Accept it. Accept it. Accept it. She's got it wrong. Supposedly the first stage of grief is denial, but in my experience, acceptance comes first. When Papa told me about the accident, I understood what he was saying, clear as a bell. I understood that my mother would never hold me in her arms again, never laugh with me, never share the future with me. She ... was ... gone. My life with her was over. I understood all that instantly and my heart broke into a gazillion pieces. That was the first step. But how can human beings withstand so much hurt? *That's* when denial begins. After acceptance, denial floods in like a tsunami, easing the wounds, covering them. But I'll never forget that first moment when I heard the news and hovered over an abyss.

I was still hovering over an abyss when my legs had collapsed from under me. I'd fallen onto Celeste's couch, folded my arms, clenched my teeth, glared at her. It's one thing to accept Mamie's death, but I haven't come to terms with the way she died. The coroner ruled out accidental death and concluded that she committed suicide. Maybe she was unhappy enough to kill herself, but that's not the Mamie I knew. Mamie and I had so many plans. She wouldn't choose to leave me. But the truth could be that Papa killed her and I helped him. If that's the truth, I'm going to have to live with that for the rest of my days. If Papa had given her what she wanted, if I'd returned to live in Baltimore with her like she begged me to, would she be alive today?

Celeste sighed, jiggled her head so her bob bounced jauntily on her shoulders. So irritating. I can't stand jaunty. "Speak to me, Angélique."

"Doctor Celeste." I blew out a breath, pushed myself up on the couch while I waited for her bob to stop jaunting. Why do people insist on a rigid time frame for grief? Surely everyone handles grief differently. I let my words leak from between clenched teeth. "I do actually accept Mamie is dead. Papa and I cope the best we can. But in different ways."

"How different?" Her dark eyebrows swirled under her hair. She toyed with the humungous pearl dangling from her neck, flicking it from side to side, mesmerizing me.

I clasped my hands together and pressed them tightly. "Unlike Papa, I'll never leave my apartment to live anywhere else, because that would mean leaving Mamie. Papa, bless his soul, can't stand the sight of the apartment because he feels so guilty. He can't stand the sight of me, either, because I look just like Mamie, he says." I'd turned my head away so Celeste wouldn't see my tears. I watched her birds flying from tree to tree in her courtyard covered with net. "Which totally sucks." I banged my fists together. "I've lost Mamie. Why should I lose Papa too?"

Celeste looked the teeniest bit sympathetic. Maybe she saw my tears after all. She walked around her desk and knelt beside me, lifted one of my hands in hers. "Accepting is growing, Angélique. Selling that apartment would be a good first step." She stroked my hand.

My face burned. My teeth clenched. My body stiffened. I wrenched my hand from hers. I was one of those birds trapped outside her window, but I don't want to escape the net that holds me prisoner. "My apartment has been home all my life and I never want to live anywhere else. Why should I?"

Celeste rose, looked heavenward for inspiration. "I've said it repeatedly. You can't keep living there. It's unhealthy. You're not dealing. Move out. Move on. Then we might see some progress."

How dare you. "I'll move on when I'm good and ready."

She stood, puffed out her cheeks. "And when will that be, Angélique? You do see that's the answer, don't you?" Celeste backed up to her shiny black desk, picked up a compact mirror, checked her lipstick.

"No, I don't." I jumped from the couch and stormed out.

"Time's up," she chirped to her birds.

On my jog home from Celeste's rooms, I told myself that I understood where she was coming from. Most people wouldn't choose to live in an apartment where a family member died tragically. But everyone copes in their own way. Some people do burn their bridges and make a new start. Not me. Living in the family apartment is my joy as well as my penance. I owe it to Mamie, I owe it to myself, I owe it to my cookery students to face each new day as it rolls around.

I'd never admit it to Celeste, but every day is a struggle to get out of bed.

Every morning starts the same. I open my eyes, pull the covers over my head, hide from the world that's busily doing its thing outside my windows. As I grapple with anxiety and exhaustion from yet another late night, Mamie's voice is in my head, kidding me like she always does. *Buck up, Angel. Today is the first day of the rest of your life. Get out of bed. Get on with it. There's a beautiful day a'waiting. Get cooking. That's what you were born to do.*

Bonjour, Mamie.

I throw back the covers. Open my eyes. Swing my legs onto the floor.

I get on with my day.

I have no choice.

I must be strong.

Or Mamie will give me no peace.

Snuggling into my fleecy robe and slippers, I patter across the thick carpet, unlock the French doors to my tiny balcony, lean against the iron railing which is as cold as my heart. A Paris dawn is breaking, gorgeous with its purples, pinks and blues spread across the sky like brushstrokes from a master's hand. I grip the rail, feast my eyes on the changing colors and say hello to a new Paris day, let the warmth flow through me. *Yes, Mamie, this is the first day of the rest of my life. And you're right, what a beautiful day.*

I tug my robe tight, watch the sun begin its journey over the horizon. The gorgeous blue-gray sky turns soft. It would be more ethereal without the noise, but Paris traffic is around the clock. Buses, taxis, cars, and bikes whizz in the distance with gay abandon along Quai Voltaire beside the Seine. I could stand here all day watching the crazy morning show as Paris gets down to business, but I have business of my own. Taking a deep draft of noxious fumes, I assemble my thoughts.

Today, I'm on the clock.

I've prepared so hard for this intake of my cookery school, I can't sleep,

I rarely eat, and if it wasn't for champagne, I wouldn't drink. My next course begins this evening and I have so much to do before my buzzer rings. I smile at a dove clucking under the eaves, and I swear it smiles back. A good omen. I have before me two weeks of fun, food, and new friends. The loneliness that gnaws at me will be swept away with my new influx of students.

Locking my balcony door, I quickly shower, don my running gear, fly down my circular staircase two steps at a time. I jog up the street, around the corner past the Fontaine *Saint-Michel*, take a right to *Shakespeare and Company Bookshop* and my café of choice. I'm not the only Parisian to discover Archie's smooth blend. There's always a line out the door. It's totally worth squeezing into the miniscule space for the brilliant Aussie brew. Sometimes if there's a spare chair and I have no pressing business, I linger in the tiny room over a healthy vegan pastry, enjoying the banter as a new day begins. But not today.

I take my coffee to go and stroll home along the Seine where the bouquinistes are setting up their green tin stalls, displaying vintage books, movie posters and all sorts of bric a brac. Beyond them, across the river, the glorious Notre Dame shines golden in the bright sunlight, at least what I can see above the protective fences. It's all too beautiful – the air, the rustling new leaves of the plane trees, the river, the sounds. Tears prick my eyes as I recall good times with Papa and Mamie when as a family, we browsed the stalls together.

"*Bonjour,* Georges." I wave to my favorite bouquiniste who sells me original artwork from time to time.

"*Bonjour,* Angélique. How is your papa? I haven't seen him for many weeks."

"Me either." I shrug. Wave. Hurry away. *Papa. I need you.* Whenever I look for clues as to why our family combusted it always comes back to this: my mother's loathing for the rickety staircase in our elevator free building. I can still see her white knuckles clutching the balustrade as she painstakingly climbed upstairs. *Bugger. Bugger. Bugger,* she'd curse. She. Was. Not. Happy.

Leaning against the concrete balustrade overlooking the river, I feel a little unbalanced, reminding me of how Mamie suffered from vertigo. Which is why I doubt the suicide finding. Her vertigo could have caused her to lurch into the weak railing and fall five floors to her death. I'm not a detective, but one day I hope to find a clue that will prove my theory.

If only Papa had listened to her. *This is how you maintain your petite figure, mon amie,* he'd say in his quaint Frenglish to accommodate my American mother who refused to speak French even though she'd majored in French Language at the Sorbonne. That's how she came to live in France. She'd managed to snavel a semester guest lecturing at the Sorbonne. Just when she was ready to return to Baltimore, she met Papa, and the rest, as they say, is history. But I have my mother to thank for my excellent unaccented English which I speak every chance I get.

Papa's refusal to listen to Mamie's complaints about living in a medieval, multi-storied apartment, *sans* elevator, was typical of their relationship – Mamie complained, Papa joked. Eventually Mamie realized she was never going to live the luxurious Parisian life, even though Papa could well afford to give her what she dreamed of. She wanted to take me and return to Baltimore, but I wasn't having it. Was the coroner right? In a fit of deep depression did she choose to leave this life via the rickety staircase she so hated? That's how it looks. But the police searched, and she didn't leave a note. Someday Mamie will find a way to tell me what really happened.

I ignore the gullible tourists eating their expensive *petit déjeuners* at the bustling cafes on the corner near Saint-Michel. I pause in the lively square at the fountain, a symbol of the reconstruction of Paris by Baron Haussmann. I love it because it reminds me of one of my favorite places in Paris, the Medici wall fountain in the Luxembourg Gardens where I often sit and meditate surrounded by romantic sculptures, beautiful trees, climbing ivy and silky water. Tourists in the square here are struggling to follow their guide who waves a bright red umbrella. I listen for a while as the guide gives her history lesson, then wend my way through the backstreets of Saint-Germain to home.

My fairytale building never fails to take my breath away. It might be shabby and old-fashioned compared to the gentrified buildings surrounding it, but I don't care.

I inhale a breath, clutch my heart with my free hand. It's mine. No one will take it away from me. I'm never leaving.

No matter what Celeste says.

ABOUT THE AUTHOR

Denise Covey is an Australian author who, pre-covid, always kept her bag packed ready to go. Immersing herself in the olde-worlde cultures of France, Italy and Spain, provided fertile ground for her imagination. Now she travels through the pages of her books, and invites you along the journey with her.

Sign up for her newsletter for her latest releases in both
Contemporary and Paranormal Romance
https://dencovey.blogspot.com

Reviews are solid gold for authors.
Please leave a review on Amazon or
wherever you hang out socially.

Thank you!

facebook.com/denise.covey
twitter.com/DeniseCCovey
instagram.com/deniseccovey

ALSO BY DENISE COVEY AND HER PEN NAME, SILVER TREE

FAST AND FURIOUS SHORT FICTION

Love Hurts

Paranormal

Halloween

THE FIRST BOOK IN THE RENAISSANCE PARANORMAL ROMANCE

Betrayed

IT HAPPENED IN PARIS

Paris Dreams

Le Petit Paris Cookery School - out soon!

CPSIA information can be obtained
at www.ICGtesting.com
Printed in the USA
LVHW041919131121
703259LV00006B/79

9 781922 486165